Cosmic Dancer

Other books by Lianne Downey

The Liberator:
A Psychic-Spiritual History of the Orion Empire

Speed Your Evolution:
Become the Star Being You Are Meant to Be

From readers touched by *Cosmic Dancer:*

"What really ruins the idea of reincarnation is when people think they've been someone famous. I love the way you turned things on their head. That's when I started to take this seriously, on a much deeper level."
—Linda Jo Hunter, author of *Lonesome for Bears*

"I had these vivid dreams while reading the book…I know they were past-life flashbacks, because they had a reoccurring theme from other dreams I have had in the past and evoked a deep emotional response of the reality of the situation."—Pamela S.

"I started seeing my Blue-Light friends again, and more often."—Tom

"Reading *Cosmic Dancer* ignited something within….I am going back to full-time dance and will go on to teach again as I have taught in previous years. However I now know, just like Amelia in *Cosmic Dancer,* that my dancing has its own purpose no matter what limitations I may have, as others will benefit from seeing my dancing, and my students' dancing, in a very healing way."—Jasmin K.

"I could not put it down."—Jo H.

"When I began 'Walking Lessons,' I experienced a dimensional shift into the love of the inner planes and teachers!!! The frequency of that chapter contains healing vortexes that surely will affect permanently anyone who has been inwardly directed to read it. I am going through a very deep and love-filled time."—Lorian H.

"It's one of those books I turn to when I need to calm down."—Bri C.

"The book brought me feelings of hope and suspense and in the end, you found that you wanted more of this positive love feeling. I will be looking for the sequel."—Michael L.

"As a librarian, I've recommended this book to three library systems for their collections."—Laura V.

"Wishing I could stay awake later nights to get further faster. "—P. C.

Cosmic Dancer

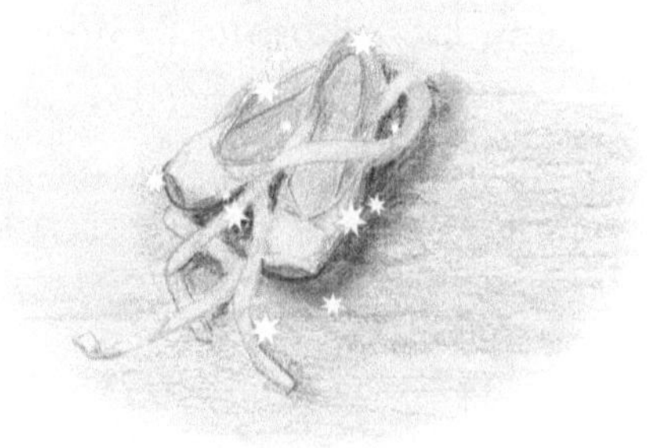

Lianne Downey

Jolibro Publishing
www.jolibro.com

This is a work of fiction. Names, characters, places, and incidents are the products of the author's imagination or are used fictitiously. Any resemblance to actual events, locales, or persons, living or dead, is entirely coincidental.

Visit the author at **liannedowney.com**

Cover ballerina & butterfly art by Roslynn E. Moore (mooreillustrated.com)

ISBN 978-0-9824691-1-8 (trade paperback)
ISBN 978-1-953474-06-3 (dust-jacketed hardcover)
ISBN 978-0-9824691-3-2 (ebook)

Library of Congress Control Number: 2010911664

Subject keywords:
National Indie Excellence Award Finalist; NIEA; past lives; reincarnation; afterlife; visionary fiction; historical fiction 1960s; dance fiction; ballet fiction; life between lives; panpsychism; psychic vision; Ernest L. Norman; *The Voice of Venus*; Shamballa; Light Beings; higher-dimensional worlds; multiverse; alcoholism; alcoholic mothers; alcoholic parent trauma; children of alcoholics; Michigan fiction

Jolibro Publishing
www.jolibro.com

To Joseph, for lifetimes of love.

What appeals to the caterpillar? Leaves.
  To the butterfly? Nectar.
So it is. The butterfly cannot eat leaves,
  will die if it's given only leaves, fresh and tender.
The butterfly needs a garden.

—*The Other Voice*

** Sketches herein were torn from Amy's diary and notebooks*

1

The Vision

*T*he first vision flashed into Amy's mind while she drowsed
through her freshman history class wishing she were somewhere else, not cooped up inside the old brick high school in
Deerhorn Creek.

This claustrophobic building sat on a hill above its precious
football field, not far from the dead center of Amy's hometown
in the southwestern Michigan hills, which was not far from Lake
Michigan but too far from the kind of culture that would have
supported her number one passion.

She had tuned out Mr. Michaels' droll lecture about pre-com-
munist Russia and focused instead on the tall windows that lined
one side of the room, where chilly March winds rattled the massive pine tree outside the glass. With a thousand needle points it
clattered against the panes, scratching and tapping, chattering
out a rhythm for her restlessness. She imagined a warm summer
day, soft grass, gazing up through bristling branches to watch
the boughs split sunlight as the wind rustled them from side to
side. It was one of her favorite places to be, lying beneath a tree,

looking up at flickering lights. Anything that sparkled, she loved.

Is it really God who makes the wind blow?

Surely some Intelligence, she decided, but definitely not some ancient wise man sitting on a throne, moving tree branches. Too simple for such an all-permeating Intelligence, which was so evident in results but so aggravatingly hidden from common view. Scientists couldn't pin It down, religionists couldn't prove It, but who could deny their sensation of It?

For Amy, God was a feeling.

For example when she danced, especially when her ballet teacher wasn't looking and she made up her own steps, she felt as if she moved in unison with something beyond herself, some Force that lifted her limbs effortlessly. A buoyancy filled her up and, like the tree branches, she had to move. The sensation didn't pass over her; it filled her up with joy and demanded that she dance its silent compulsions.

That must be God, she decided, *pushing from the inside.*

At that very instant, Mr. Michaels said the word *carriage* and the vision came blazing into her mind.

Like a tantalizing bauble, it lingered for a moment—more tangible than television, more real than a dream, more colorful than the ordinary world. With it came such *love* that her heart leapt as if she'd been swept into the arms of a beloved grandparent.

She stopped breathing for a few seconds.

In weeks to come, she would try to describe the vision in the safety of her diary. But her words fell too flat to capture the rainbow scintillations emanating from the wing tips of the crystal butterfly that so suddenly appeared in her mind.

No, not an insect. A *carriage,* shaped like a butterfly but made of transparent crystal. Although she could see nothing of them because the crystal flashed with such dazzling intensity, she instinctively knew that the hollow body carried passengers.

How she knew this preposterous thing, Amy had no clue. Nothing in Catherine the Great's legacy resembled anything like this; nothing on Earth, as far as Amy knew, came close to it. So why was this amazing creation causing her insides to tremble with recognition?

At the first inner glimpse, Amy's heart squeezed tight and she felt comforted, embraced, cared for, important, and above all, *loved* as if by the butterfly itself. Such feelings were so rare to her that they baffled her almost more than the vision itself, which lasted only a few seconds.

Filigreed crystal wings folded gracefully upward and then pulsed gently, like an ordinary butterfly resting on a flower. Yet the carriage was massive, with wings and body large enough to fill a jet runway, despite the delicate insect-feet that supported it. Was it weightless? Racing energies flickered in and out of the filigree, creating a rainbow aura that extended hundreds of yards in all directions. Definitely this was not an insect, yet the carriage seemed *alive.*

From within the blinding light, Amy could barely discern a pair of crystal doors set in the butterfly's body, just below the raised wings. But that was only because she instinctively knew where to look for them. Intricate, etched designs glittered from the matching oval doors. She imagined a ramp emerging so that passengers could alight, although the doors remained tightly closed and she saw no one. But again, she knew they were there.

Then the magnificent wings began to beat more rapidly, opening up to their full glory and closing again, stirring up vibrant swirls of light and color in the surrounding atmosphere. Into this glorious halo, the butterfly lifted, making one long, banking turn that sent streaks of light streaming into Amy's consciousness before it disappeared.

She gasped as if she'd seen the vision with physical eyes, it was that real to her.

A few of her classmates turned to stare as Mr. Michaels finished his sentence, "...in the Kremlin museum."

Blushing, Amy cleared her throat and coughed a few times

and her classmates, satisfied, turned blandly back toward the interminable lecture.

Her best friend, Pam, gave her a questioning look but Amy shook her head slightly as if to say, "Nothing, it's nothing; turn around."

Pam shrugged and turned back to listen to the lecture, or to pretend she was listening.

But Amy's brain scrambled to process what it had somehow taken in whole—and from where?

Certainly it was not a hallucination. Although the year was 1969, hallucinogenic drugs weren't much more than a rumor in Amy's small town. And even if she'd had access, she would never touch them. Mind-altering substances terrified her: alcohol, drugs, even medicines a doctor prescribed. Way too risky.

Which is why she knew immediately that she could never tell a soul what she'd just seen.

She shuddered as the familiar fear engulfed her: a mental hospital on some lonely spit of land where they'd shoot her up with drugs and throw away the key. In her drugged stupor, no one could tell if she were sane or not, so they'd sign her away for life and that would be the end of it.

She had no idea where this phobia originated but she'd always had it. Kids teased about the "loony bin" in Kalamazoo, but she'd never been anywhere near it. She didn't know anyone who had, but if she met one of the patients, they would have frightened her. "Crazy" people scared her almost as much as the chance of being wrongly diagnosed as one.

Amy's mother knew all about this fear. When she wanted to torment her daughter, she used it with excruciating psychological efficiency. She could win any argument by insisting they should send her off to a shrink, she was "such a problem child." Amy was never sure her mother wasn't crazy enough herself to carry out the threat. They'd take her to one of those places, her mother would sign the papers, her father would say nothing, they'd give her the drugs, and she'd never see daylight again.

So when it came to telling someone she had a vision, Amy's courage utterly failed.

Still, she couldn't forget it.

As a dancer her imagination was keen, but never before had it produced such living color and motion, so totally beyond any logic she'd experienced in her fifteen years. She couldn't shake the feeling that she had been in the presence of this butterfly carriage before.

She had seen it before.

But where? How?

A deep tremble shook her, rattling bones and veins and blood and flesh.

How crazy am I?

2

Angels, Angels, Everywhere

Despite *her fear and* vow of silence, Amy's mind blossomed under the influence of her vision, in ways she wouldn't realize for a long time. But it was a lonely awakening.

No matter how things turned out for Joan of Arc in the long run—sainthood and all that—Amy still wouldn't risk telling anyone what she'd seen. Not Pam, nor any of her other friends at school, none of her teachers, and certainly not her older brother, Tom, nor her little sister, Beth. She couldn't talk to her father and especially not to her mother! The very thought sent spears of panic into her stomach.

At least she hadn't heard voices…

"Amy!" her mother bellowed up from downstairs the next morning.

The rasp of it hit Amy's nervous system like electric shock and left a dull clench of dread in its wake.

"Get up! NOW!"

Every morning that horrible sound pierced Amy's gently sleeping consciousness and erased her dreams before she had a moment to remember them. In a few minutes, her mother would begin the litany of Amy's offenses from the day before. Then she'd start in on poor Beth.

Tom was already up and cranky.

"C'mon, it's my turn!" he yelled fifteen minutes later as he pounded on the door of the upstairs bathroom they shared.

Amy's parents owned a two-story house with pale green, clapboard siding in Deerhorn Creek, Michigan (population 3,335). The house sat on a side street in the newer northwestern quarter, but in truth *every* street in Deerhorn Creek was a side street except for one.

Until she was five, Amy's paternal grandparents lived across town in the white house her father grew up in, on tree-lined Free Street just up the hill from the Sinclair gas station. Gramps had a deep chuckle, smelled like beer when he kissed the top of her head in the summertime, and always called her Pumpkin. He played a beautiful, solid-backed violin made for him when he was growing up in Detroit, a rare thing for a man to do in Deerhorn Creek. But he also owned a curved-back mandolin that he strummed with a pick in a quick, back-and-forth motion that gave it a strange, tremulous sound. This music seemed to come from nowhere in Amy's family, and it inspired her own artistic longings. She loved her grandfather dearly.

And everyone loved Grandma Delphine, a French-Canadian beauty famous for her cooking.

When Amy stayed with them as a toddler, Grandma Delphine would take her out to buy mushrooms, Amy's favorite food. She'd fry them in her rich, buttery way and let Amy steal them from the pan. Then she'd put a scant spoonful of coffee and sugar into Amy's milk and let her drink this *café au lait* in one of the precious, Bohemian crystal goblets from the china cabinet.

Her mother complained that this was unnecessary spoiling, but Amy could never resist those sparkling, brightly-colored liqueur goblets twinkling on the shelf. She was drawn to them, staring at the light that played through the clear-etched facets in the green or cobalt or blood-red cups. Over and again, she traced with her eyes the hexagonal crystal stems whose sharp edges made the light dance. No one could pull her away, so despite her mother's protests, Grandma Delphine let her drink her "grown-up" drink from these priceless objects.

Amy's most cherished memories involved those fragile goblets, her grandmother's mushrooms, and the Christmas "bubbler" lights Gramps fought the snow to hang around the outside of his house. Warm and cozy in Grandma's kitchen, she remembered Gramps lifting her up to a window to watch the colored bubble lights glimmer and flicker in endless, hypnotic motion. Like her grandmother, Gramps seemed to understand Amy's fascination with things that sparkled. No one else did.

But when Amy was four, Grandma Delphine contracted what the town doctor called "a mild bout of the flu" as he sent her home. Amy was allowed to visit briefly, amid hushed adults, as her grandmother lay in a bed they set up for her in a downstairs room. Shortly afterword, her mother explained that her grandmother had died and she would never see her again.

Poor Beth! She never got to know her! And Amy's heartbroken father never forgave that doctor.

Amy couldn't remember doing it, but years later family members told her that at the funeral her four-year-old self sat on her grandfather's lap, patting him and assuring him everything would be all right. He'd clung to her fiercely and wouldn't let anyone take her from him. Soon after, Gramps sold the white house on Free Street and moved to Florida. She missed him terribly. There he remarried, a widow he met in Fort Lauderdale.

Despite her mother's harsh assessment, Amy always liked this step-grandmother she was told to call Simone. She wore heavy perfume and jangling bracelets of gold and gems gathered on her world travels. She loved to play bridge at the yacht club, and she treated Amy kindly.

When her family drove from Michigan to Fort Lauderdale to see the house Gramps built for Simone, Tom, Beth, and her parents fussed over the indoor pool, but once again Amy's heart was captured by the glitter of a giant chandelier hanging over the dining table. It was Gramps's pride and joy. He loved the sparkling crystals as much as his granddaughter did, although no one else understood their fascination. Somehow, gazing into those clear, gleaming prisms with their infinite rainbow reflections transported Amy into a feeling she couldn't explain, something holy or exalted that lifted her above every mundane thing in her mundane life. Words couldn't approach it.

Shortly after Amy's fourteenth birthday, Gramps died of lung cancer, making Simone a widow again. They shipped his body back to be buried in the Deerhorn Creek cemetery beside Grandma Delphine.

Amy refused to cry during the grave side ceremony but once she was home alone in her room, the sobs erupted, relentlessly knocking the breath out of her. She hoped Beth wouldn't come barging in but she couldn't stop. She felt so abandoned! Gramma Jean, her mother's widowed mother, poured out her love to Amy, Beth, and Tom whenever she visited, but she lived in New Hampshire so those visits were rare. As guilty as she felt about this, Amy knew her sorrow was as much about her own loss of an adult ally as it was about her grandfather's loss of life.

Then suddenly, swift as a pheasant scared up from the brush, she felt Grandma Delphine's presence in the room. A warm, loving sensation of *all is well* passed through her.   As abruptly as they'd come, her tears stopped and a powerful sense of *knowing* filled the empty places in her heart.

Gramps is with me now, and we will both always be with you.

It was as clear as if she'd heard her grandmother speak the words aloud!

She never told anyone, of course. It was too precious. They might laugh, or doubt and ruin it.

After that, she often felt Grandma Delphine's influence, especially in the kitchen. Not as a ghost—she simply dipped her thoughts into Amy's own, so naturally that Amy did indeed feel as if she weren't alone.

It's not that she didn't love her parents. Or appreciate her siblings. It was just that, well, her family life…she couldn't think about it really.

Especially not with Tom pounding on the bathroom door.

"Come ON! It's my turn!"

Outside the second story window, she could see the wide-spreading magnolia that would soon burst into bloom with big flappywhite blossoms. It was the only distinction between the Longwood's and the other middle-class houses on their wide, shady street. The special tree filled their ample front yard with dappled shade in summer and dropped flame-shaped seed pods all over the grass in the fall.

In their back yard a weeping willow and a Scotch pine, common as snow shovels in Deerhorn Creek, cast enough darkness to make the rear of their house seem gloomy even in midsummer. Only one corner of their yard caught sunlight year-round. That's where she and her dad planted a garden, right up against the fence, ignoring her mother's admonitions that it would all come to nothing.

Amy adored her father. With Beth tagging along, he taught her how to plant carrots (which grew big and sweet, as if to spite her mother). They also planted tomatoes and her least favorite, string beans. He put up a bird feeder and from the back windows in winter they counted black-capped chickadees, brilliant red cardinals, and blue jays that scattered dark seeds over the white snow.

When she was younger, in the summers he took them all canoeing on the Tompkins River—until her mother stopped wanting to go as she grew heavier. Gradually, their family camping and fishing trips came to an end as well.

Outdoors, especially in the woods, Amy's father seemed to glow. He found fascination in all sorts of living and growing things. If she loved trees and birds and natural beauty, it came from his influence. But indoors, where he spent more time now, he grew silent and aloof. Her mother said it was because he worked hard all day and had to talk to lots of people. Amy decided it was his way of dealing with the problem no one spoke of in the Longwood family. He favored a drink or two in the evenings but that only made him more silent, while Yvonne Longwood's alcohol consumption brought out a vicious streak that never entirely left when she was sober.

Once she poured her first martini, Amy, Beth, and Tom practically tiptoed from room to room to avoid her verbal attacks. She could explode without warning—and someone always got hit by the shrapnel. Not physically, but inside, where the damage lasted longer.

Meanwhile, like the carrots, her father's silence grew.

Tom's fist hammered so hard on the bathroom door that Amy jumped out of her reverie, smearing a streak of pink Bonne Bell into her ear.

"All right, all right," she sighed, slamming the gel tube into a makeup bag and grabbing some tissues.

She jerked open the door and glared at her brother Thomas—Tom to everyone but their father. He was seventeen and would graduate soon. Angry red blotches still peppered his face. Amy figured they got worse because he was scared now. Too many recent graduates wound up in Vietnam and Tom hated the idea of war. Yet he wasn't the type to burn his draft card and head for Canada, either.

Of course he never talked about this and she wasn't about to bring it up. She was his little sister and nothing she said or did would ever be taken seriously by him.

"It's all yours," she mumbled as she brushed past him and headed for her room. If she hurried, she could finish there in peace before Beth showed up.

She slipped into the comfort of her own private space and closed the door. It was the only room in the house with enough color and clutter to satisfy Amy, and the only place in the world besides Mrs. Q's dance studio that made her feel alive.

Downstairs the living room carpet was beige, the couch was tan, and the walls were painted olive green or paneled in dark wood. To Amy's sensibilities, the house always felt slightly unclean. Not that she wanted to clean it, mind you. But in the mornings the coffee table usually bore one or two ashtrays overflowing onto the blond wood, day-old coffee sitting in the bottom of an old cup, and at least one empty martini glass competing for space with dated copies of *Reader's Digest* and *Life Magazine*.

In the family room, the sticky, sickly-sweet residue of spilled drink mix spotted the plywood bar her mother had stained fake mahogany. One of Amy's hated jobs when they did clean the house was to scrub off this foul-smelling stuff that had cigarette ashes sticking to it. Across the room, unfinished projects draped her mother's sewing machine.

But Amy's bedroom gave her sanctuary. After her mother bought her a hideously flowered bedspread, Amy begged to paint the walls a pale blue-violet to bring out the only color she liked in the gaudy pattern. Now the walls glowed with the heliotrope of an evening sky after the sun has set and the oranges and pinks have faded, just before the onset of darkness.

The room held things Amy loved: the moth-eaten, stuffed white musical rabbit who had heard all her secrets since she was a kid, although the music box had long since stopped working. In a corner, an old straw trunk she rescued from Gramma Jean's attic in New Hampshire. It held treasures and trash she couldn't part with, especially anything sparkly or shiny: bits of pyrite, jars of glitter, old wrapping paper. These things were rare in her world so she rescued and saved them.

On her bookshelf lay a paperback of yoga poses she begged her mother to buy for her. Late at night on her bedroom rug she mimicked the stick-figure illustrations. The odd contortions seemed vaguely familiar and came naturally to her. None of her friends had ever heard of yoga, so she kept this ritual to herself.

Next on the shelf, a volume of poems by Baudelaire she liked because of the French-English translations on facing pages. She never read the poetry much but she loved French, although she couldn't speak a word of it yet. Pam, who knew this, bought her a used copy of *Le Petit Prince* entirely in French for her birthday.

Then the library books: Native American spiritual legends and a script of *Macbeth*. She liked the legends better than anything she heard when girlfriends invited her to their church services. And despite the dense footnotes and the downtown librarian's raised eyebrows, she was determined to wade through the Shakespeare. She could barely make out the meanings, but she knew Shakespeare was important, even if her teachers neglected him. The rest of the shelf held dictionaries and other things parents and grandparents thought she should own.

Everyone in her family found escape in reading, but for Amy, books let her explore dreams of a better life, a more poetic life. If she'd known a little more about herself, she might have realized it was also a more *familiar* life she sought. But she was "only fifteen." No one encouraged her to think about self-discovery. Her life seemed either decided for her and thrust upon her by adults, or she coasted into things as if by accident. Decisions didn't seem necessary. When she stumbled across things that made her heart sing a little, she was glad and liked them very much, sometimes passionately, like dancing. Otherwise, she accepted events, objects, and circumstances grimly as they arose, never realizing any hint of power to do otherwise.

Yet as if to contradict this unconscious limitation, the walls of her bedroom bore other ideas.

For instance, beside her bed hung a ripped-open, brown paper grocery bag on which she'd pasted anti-war headlines from underground newspapers she found in Wilton. Next to them she stuck magazine cutouts of Eric Burden, Donovan, Mick Jagger, the Beatles (especially Paul), Simon and Garfunkel. For all her apathy about the life handed to her at home, the idea of non-violent political activism stirred her deeply.

She'd seen an old photograph of Mahatma Gandhi in a magazine, leaning against a walking stick, wearing his homespun loincloth. It sent chills running all over her body. She cut it out and added him to her collage. She'd never heard of him before, and it took her a long time to find a teacher at her school willing to mumble something about a foreigner who led some kind of radical political movement—but "radical" in Deerhorn Creek was a dirty word in 1969.

To prove it, the school board fired Amy's English teacher because she got her students to read about racial prejudice in *Death at an Early Age,* and because she introduced them to a subject so new to Deerhorn Creek, she was accused of distributing "Marxist propaganda." The subject? Ecology, a new word in the school board's vocabulary.

So Amy looked up Gandhi in one of the *World Book Encyclopedias* that gathered dust in their family room and learned all about passive resistance.

Then she tried to get Pam interested in wearing an MIA bracelet with the name of a missing soldier stamped on it, but Pam said it gave her the creeps. What if the soldier was dead?

The other side of Amy's bedroom featured a ballerina poster Gramma Jean gave her. White pearls shone against the dancer's sleek dark hair, while soft layers of radiant white chiffon draped gracefully along the raised leg of her perfect arabesque, leaving a halo of blurred white against the dark background where she moved during the photo exposure. The dancer exemplified the simultaneous accomplishment of balance and movement, that hallmark of "impossibility" that makes ballet so compelling. Beneath her were words by William Henry Ward, *If you can imagine it, you can achieve it. If you can dream it, you can become it.* Amy loved the poised, dark-haired dancer, an ideal to strive for. But so far the words in the caption had failed to convince her.

She settled down to finish her makeup at the desk her mother built for her from a door and two narrow chests of drawers. Yvonne Longwood's bursts of creativity always surprised Amy. She displayed many talents during her sober hours, but those were increasingly rare.

On the wall above the desk gleamed yet another beacon that called to Amy's unconscious memories, although this one was far more subtle: a galactic spiral of broken mirror-tile fragments she had snagged from Pam's mother as she carried the glinting shards out to the trash one day while Amy was visiting. Pam thought Amy was nuts, but she insisted she could glue them to her wall as art.

Now the curved slivers of glass flickered out at Amy like the spiraling petals of a silvery-crystal flower.

Sometimes she just sat and stared at them, the swirling pattern calling to her from something she loved, deep and subtle, beneath the layers of daily mental prattle.

Unaware of the connection, she thought now of the butterfly vision as she rubbed more of the pink gel on her cheeks and smeared on the white lipstick her brother called "lard lips." Carefully, and with only mild disgust, she parted her long, straight, dark hair down the middle, looping it over her ears to keep it out of her face but making sure that she pulled a swath forward on each side to cover as much of her forehead as possible. She hated her high forehead, although she'd been told it made her look like Grandma Delphine. She didn't like much of anything else about her looks, either.

Right on cue, she heard nine-year-old Beth pattering down the hall.

Her little sister, always eager to know what Amy was doing and why, and could she come along? Like last Friday. "No, Beth, you can't go to the dance with me!" Amy needed to insist, ignoring the look of terrible dejection on her sister's face. A fourth-grader! Where did this girl get such notions? But she loved her little sister (and her brother, although it would be years before she'd admit it). Maybe because of their mother, the three had formed a special bond. They were like prisoners of war, sticking together to help each other avoid conflict with their unpredictable parent.

Their father? Solid and strong, kind and loving, but usually absent during these events. This morning he was already at work. As far as Amy knew, he went to work at the dress-pattern factory after he got home from World War II, some time after he gave up his career as a stunt pilot when his family started to grow. He stopped flying long before Amy was born but she didn't know why. She did know that he didn't like his white-collar job. If he were home now, her mother would lob subtle sarcasm instead of hollering at the angry pitch now rising from the kitchen, where Amy would soon try to swallow her breakfast.

Beth burst into Amy's bedroom without knocking. "Can I borrow your belt?"

"Which belt?" Amy asked suspiciously.

"You know…" Beth dug through the pile of clothes on Amy's floor and came up with Amy's favorite: a strip of soft, dark-brown suede with long fringe that reached all the way to the floor when she wore it with jeans. "This one!" Beth gleefully wrapped it around the waist of her salmon-plaid dress.

Amy laughed. The fringe landed in a pool at Beth's feet, about a foot too long. "You silly goose! How do you expect to walk with that on?"

Beth pouted a little as she looked at the pile of suede fringe by her shoes. "I can do it," she insisted, grabbing up the ends. "I'll just hold it like this when I walk."

Amy laughed again. This girl would do anything to be a part of her big sister's life. No matter how ridiculous she looked, she still wanted to wear Amy's clothes. Especially her favorite clothes.

"No, Beth, you can't wear my belt to school," Amy said as gently as possible.

Beth's normally sunny face wilted and her blond curls failed to brighten her disappointed eyes.

Amy took pity and added, "But only because that belt doesn't look right with your dress. And you can't wear pants to school, remember? The dress code doesn't allow it."

Beth looked at her blankly, not ready to accept this reality.

"But you said when you borrowed my perfume to see Jeremy at the dance that you'd let me borrow something of yours! Remember? Last Saturday? And this is what I choose!"

Jeremy. The last thing Amy wanted to think about. She'd worn the fruity cologne Gramma Jean had given Beth because she didn't want to overwhelm him with her mother's Taboo or Emeraude, which made her gag anyway. *What if Jeremy doesn't like perfume?* she'd worried at the time. Now she thought wryly that she should have sprayed herself with OFF! instead.

"Look," she interrupted her own thoughts, "if you promise to be good, I'll let you borrow it for a while this weekend, okay? Only you have to promise me that you'll wrap it around your waist twice. I don't want you tripping over it and getting hurt. I'd never hear the end of it."

"Oh boy!" Beth's face exploded in joy. "Can I wear it to Marcia's house on Saturday?"

"We'll see," Amy mumbled as she gathered the belt back from Beth's reluctant offering. "It depends on the weather. Now go finish getting ready!"

"But I *am* ready," Beth protested.

"Well, fine, but now you're finished here, too, so goodbye." She pushed her little sister firmly out the door. "And next time, knock before you barge in." Futile request, she thought, as she shut her door and leaned against it.

Jeremy...

No! I won't think about him, or that terrible night. Think of something else, she commanded herself. She straightened up and marched over to deposit the belt at the back of her closet. *Anything else. The butterfly...*

Instantly her mind filled with sparkling color. She stood for a transcended moment, recreating the vision. She longed to reach out and touch the cool crystal wings, to open the carved rainbow doors.

A wave of gloom crashed over her.

It's only a fantasy. No more real than Clara.

The thought of last year's *Nutcracker* deepened her despair and the carriage vanished from her mind.

Why had Mrs. Q picked her for the leading role, anyway?

Amy knew she wasn't a good dancer. Her mother's uncharacteristic silence after the performance at Wilton High School confirmed it. Yvonne must have been publicly humiliated by her daughter, Amy reasoned, since everyone from both Wilton and Deerhorn Creek was there. Except for her father, who avoided this embarrassment by working late that night.

When her mother, Tom, and Beth came backstage afterward with the other families, they just stood there and stared at her awkwardly. Then Tom broke the tension with a crack about her dancing around in her nightgown. Beth chimed in with gushing admiration for the other costumes and whined in envy at Amy's star status. But her mother, dressed in her best oversized sheath, never said a word. Amy cried silently all the way home, in the dark back seat of the Plymouth where no one could see her. She felt so ugly—and so alone.

Now she stared at her distorted reflection in the mirror fragments.

Maybe I was the only one taller than the dancing mice. I'm the tallest in Mrs. Q's class. I fit the costume, that's all. And I don't look like the other girls when I dance. I've tried and tried, but I just can't blend in.

Even in recitals Mrs. Q always singled her out.

"Amy, you stand there," she would command. Or, "Amy, I want you to break off and do these steps."

But Amy loved the feeling of movement so much—dance was everything to her! If she couldn't dance, she didn't know what she'd do. So she put up with these humiliations, hoping that Mrs. Q would let her stay in the class. She had to keep dancing. If she ever quit, she knew that she truly would go mad. Completely bonkers, insane, fruitcake, nuts. And they might as well cart her off to an asylum!

She frowned as she shoved back her straight dark hair, watching it fall behind her narrow shoulders in a mirror fragment. One last recrimination passed through her mind: *Everyone knows Clara is supposed to have curly blond hair—like Beth's.*

She colored with renewed humiliation and turned away abruptly, glancing at the clock. For a second she caught sight of a gold spark that flickered beside the mirror but dismissed it just as quickly. It was late; time to face breakfast.

Downstairs, she tried to swallow sugary cornflakes with cold raw goat's milk (cow's milk didn't agree with her) while her mother reminded her that she was not only clumsy, but rude and inconsiderate, having left yesterday's clothes lying in a heap on her bedroom floor so that her mother would have to look at them all day, and she was an ungrateful brat because she never appreciated the *hours* her mother spent driving her to and from ballet classes.

They'd had this argument so many times before. Wilton was actually only five miles away, but at the other end of a country road that passed over hills and through hay fields, orchards, and scattered houses, so the short drive seemed to take forever. Unless it was snowing, and then it truly did take longer and her mother's nerves couldn't handle the slippery roads very well. On those days, Amy felt sorry for her mother. But on other days, was it so difficult? She only went once a week. How else could she get there?

Her mother wagged a stern finger in Amy's face. "In fact, young lady, when you get home today, I want to talk to you about those classes."

Amy choked on a corn flake and coughed. When she finally got it down, her stomach rejected it and clamped into a sudden spasm.

She knew her mother's every vocal nuance better than any chick knows its nest. She sensed serious trouble. Once before she'd heard this tone and only her father's intervention stopped a major upheaval in her life.

She couldn't argue about the clothes on her floor. She wasn't sure what to say about the driving. Every trip to Wilton was a nightmare for her anyway, with her mother's constant criticism on the way over and her complaints on the way home. But fear shot through her when her mother mentioned the classes in that tone. Once before she had threatened...

But what good would it do to argue? The volume would only increase, the ensuing fight would give Amy stomach cramps that lasted all morning. So she kept eating in silence like her siblings and hurried out the door as soon as possible.

Her mother was an unstable volcano. These were only sputterings, she told herself. Better to be far away when she finally erupted. She'd cool down and the anger would be frozen into new lava rock, dark and forgotten by the time Amy got home.

3

Amy's Dream

After a long day avoiding Jeremy and sidestepping questions about him from Pam and Julie and the others, Amy locked herself in her bedroom after supper that night, before her mother had a chance to remember anything about ballet classes.

Downstairs now the second and third rounds of martinis were being poured but she felt safe. Beth was busy with homework and Tom was out with his friends. Amy reached into the straw trunk and pulled from the bottom a white, soft-leather diary with a golden lock. Another gift from Gramma Jean.

Her mother's mother was as sweet as her mother was sour. Just like her other grandparents did when she was young, Gramma Jean seemed to understand Amy's more sensitive nature. Though she lived far away, her presence reflected back from so many things in Amy's room: the dancer in the poster, of course, but also from the lavishly illustrated volume of *The Secret Garden*, and from the ballerina doll perched on a shelf in her stiff, gold-glittered tutu, and from the girl wearing pink in a meadow (Gramma Jean's first attempt at oil painting).

Amy's albums of classical music also came from Gramma Jean, tucked between Jefferson Airplane and the Moody Blues.

"Mozart for studying, Bach for deep thinking, and of course, Tchaikovsky for dancing," she instructed Amy with a wink.

Tchaikovsky suited her mood right now. She slipped the big black disk out of its case and onto the little turntable.

On the windowsill where it caught the afternoon sunlight gleamed a tiny tree made of twisted copper wire with green-glass leaves woven into each branch. More of Gramma Jean's handiwork, which Amy snagged for her own because her mother thought it tacky. To Amy, the little tree shone as beautifully as the woman who made it.

Now she stared at the clear green leaf-beads as a strange thought occurred to her. Did her grandmother ever see something like the butterfly carriage? Maybe a tree that sparkled with crystal clarity?

She opened the pages of her diary reverently and began to write. She often scribbled out her dreams and desires and doodles and problems on its quiet, uncomplaining pages. Sometimes she used words, sometimes crude drawings to express herself. This night, something unusual happened.

It was so subtle she almost missed it. The words came out in two voices—her own, and another. A wiser voice.

For example, when she wrote, "Why wouldn't Jeremy look at me in English class?" she got an immediate answer.

He feels guilty.

When she wrote, "I don't know how long I can avoid him," these words followed:

Then stop trying. Talk to him first and break the ice. You need to talk about what happened.

And then her pen dove into an issue she usually avoided.

The wiser voice suggested that her mother's drinking might have nothing to do with whether or not one of them didn't do their chores, or whether her dad forgot to buy steak sauce on his way home.

As Amy's hand passed rapidly across the page, her mother became less of a mother and more an ordinary human being, a very troubled one, with a damaging habit that was ruining her health and creating chaos at the center of Amy's family.

Could it be that she actually contrives that chaos, to give herself an excuse to take the first drink? the other voice suggested.

Amy knew these weren't dead grandparents speaking to her from beyond the grave. Not that such things weren't possible; she'd already experienced them. But this time the personality behind the voice felt familiar, yet not. She knew it, but she didn't.

Intrigued, she tried questions she didn't dare ask anyone else, scribbling, "What was that butterfly? Why did I see it?"

The other voice didn't respond. Amy tried to coax an answer but the words didn't flow quickly or effortlessly like before. They were few and weak, and distinctly unwise—her own ideas, she realized, and they clearly didn't go far.

Maybe its wisdom was how she knew that the voice—like the vision—came from beyond herself. It didn't have her limitations.

Thank goodness she wasn't hearing it audibly! She shivered as if a blast of cold blew through the closed window and with it came the image of orderlies holding her down, a nurse with a syringe…

With effort, she pushed the fear aside. I *am not* crazy, she reminded herself firmly.

The words simply fell from the tip of her pen naturally, full of love and comfort she could feel as tangibly as if a beloved grandparent were standing in the room with her, only *more*. That's the only way she could explain it, just *more*. More love, more feeling, more intelligence, more clarity. And nothing to fear.

She didn't know what else to call this phenomenon except the Other Voice, so that became its official name in her diary, though it wasn't a *spoken* voice. More like an infusion of thoughts distinct from her own. If only they hadn't gone away!

A wash of sadness and longing came over her. She laid the diary aside and flipped off the light. For a while she stared up into the darkness, her eyes refusing to close. Then she fell into a deep, deep sleep.

What Amy dreamed was not a dream at all. It was a memory, and a test. If she remembered, she'd be safe. If not, her worst fears could easily come to pass. Her waking self had no idea how real the threat was, or how close.

✳ ✳

By the time she lay dying, Marta Lauber was an elderly widow—and she wasn't afraid, she was frustrated.

She wanted to explain to Carl, her youngest, why this final journey did not frighten her. She needed him to understand that her only fear was the strength of the grief she could already sense welling up inside him. But she couldn't find breath enough to speak.

Of her three boys, now all grown and married, Carl was the one used to bring her yellow globeflowers and wood violets in the spring, when they spread their bright carpets across the high valleys of southern Switzerland, beneath the sharp, snowy peaks of the Eiger and Schreckhorn. As a little boy, he clung to her fiercely, followed her around the kitchen, tugged at her skirts in the alpine meadows. She should have scolded him for it but she never had the heart. She couldn't bear the sight of his eager little face crumpling in disappointment.

The real problem right now was that Marta's ideas about life and death didn't fit the usual traditions, so she'd always kept them to herself. Growing up on her father's farm with seven brothers and sisters, she knew they would laugh and call her crazy if she told them about lying on her back in the grass on the high meadows in summertime, feeling as if she were inside the earth and it was inside her and she were spinning along with the planet, joined in glorious, eternal oneness with the universe. Yes, they would laugh—and her parents would scold that they were too busy raising children and tending the brown, short-horned milk cows that provided their livelihood to listen to such "silly prattling."

Many an afternoon, when she should have had all her mind concentrated on her chores, Marta looked out across the valley and up at the towering mountains that surrounded the green, rolling acres and she knew, in her heart, that there must be some Design behind all the beauty her eyes took in. But she never talked about it. None among her siblings would understand, and she feared her father. Her mother was a quiet, fearful woman herself and Marta felt that any talk of such a thing might disturb her.

As it was, her mother died at an early age, half from the fear of life itself and half from pure exhaustion. Life in the Alps in those days was not easy for any woman, and her mother had eight children to feed and clothe and nurse and worry over, and a husband whose tenderness was limited to small, almost imperceptible nods of approval when she set his dinner before him, and an occasional pat or pinch when he thought the children would not notice.

Marta noticed. She noticed many things as she grew up. By the time she reached maturity, when most of the young women in her village were married off to nice young boys from neighboring farms, Marta had grown quiet and thoughtful and withdrawn from others.

But she loved to dance and sing with them on those few chilly nights when chores were set aside and some excuse arose for a little social relief. A neighbor's newborn child was cause enough for celebration, or a good year's milk output, and of course, the holidays in which Marta and her siblings were allowed to participate.

Her favorite came right in the middle of summer. She never understood why they celebrated, or what began this time of feasting and freedom from the daily load of work, but she liked it because the valley grew warm and the sun would sink slowly behind the peaks, casting blue-violet shadows across the still green fields. The food heaped on long wooden tables seemed more succulent to her, and the songs that lasted far into the night floated out into the wind and disappeared.

As a child, she believed that birds heard the people's songs and learned their new melodies, then celebrated their own special time of harmony and togetherness. She imagined they called it The Feast of the Summer Night of New Songs.

Marta was never very good with words. But her heart was full and her mind grasped a larger picture of life than she ever heard discussed. So she kept quiet.

As she grew older, her parents bemoaned the fact that she had grown into such a strange girl, surely no suitors would want her. But a young man finally appeared, gangly and awkward and more fearful of Marta than she of their first wedded night together. Partly because Marta's family was not wealthy and partly because they were a little ashamed that it took so long for their daughter to find a husband, they kept the wedding simple.

Hans Lauber's family wasn't wealthy, either, but together the newlyweds were able, with hard work that never seemed to end, to eke out their living on a small plot of land his father provided. They raised three children of their own before a cow went crazy with fear during a thunderstorm and knocked Hans down, smashing his head into the old bare wood of the lean-to that served them for many years as a barn.

The villagers wondered why Marta never cried, and her own children thought it strange that she showed no emotion when their father died. Many times they talked about it among themselves. Finally the boys decided that she must have cried late at night when no one could hear, because their mother always tried to shelter them from pain—physical or emotional.

None of them understood Marta then, and neither did they

understand now, when she lay dying of old age.

She had no fear of death. And Hans died in such a freak, sudden way that the pain never had time to set within her heart. By the time the reality of his absence seeped into her, it was too late for tears. She knew life was governed by a great Scheme. While she didn't envision a single God Being who pulled the strings, she knew order and harmony prevailed. When something happened that seemed wrong to her, a so-called "accident," she knew that merely meant that she could not see the full picture.

So it was with her husband's death; so it was when one of her babies died of the whooping cough; so it was with every single event in her long, long life that did not fit *her* notion of how things should unfold. When despair threatened, she reminded herself that every circumstance had reason and purpose, even if she couldn't detect what that might be.

She never told Hans her ideas because he never liked to talk much about anything. When one day she ventured to ask him what he believed, he replied tersely, "It all boils down to the Golden Rule." End of subject. He never asked what *she* believed. And she never brought it up again.

So by the time her boys were filling the shingled and shuttered farmhouse with their noise and squabbles, Marta had firmly decided not to hold herself out for ridicule by trying to explain to others what she understood about life eternal. They wouldn't care and wouldn't understand. She'd been very sure of her silence as she tended her flower boxes and scrubbed dishes, floors, and little boys.

Until now.

Her watery eyes moved to look at Carl's rumpled form, kneeling beside her bed in anguish, his face buried in the bedclothes, giving every indication that his heart would cease when hers did.

Yves and Thomas—and their wives and children, and Carl's wife Bettina and the baby—were scrounging in the kitchen for food to fuel the waiting hours. Marta was glad they'd left her alone with Carl. With all her heart, she wanted to explain to him why he shouldn't be sad. But her lungs were failing and her lips frozen with fatigue. She could not break through their silence.

Finally, desperately, she started to hum. Broken bits and pieces of sound, barely music at all.

Carl looked up at her, his teary eyes full of love. He smiled, touched her papery cheek.

She used to sing that tune to soothe her boys to sleep, rocking them in the old wooden crib. He tried to hum along—then she heard the sound catch in his throat.

She nodded and smiled weakly back at him.

He leaned close and kissed her. "To last me," he said, "until we meet again."

The water fell from Marta's eyes and she closed them, relieved at last. *He understands.* She nodded slowly, still smiling despite the liquid escaping from beneath her eyelids.

Carl shifted his bulky frame to lean against the bed and nestled his head in next to hers. They didn't need words.

A few moments later she heard his steady breath. She opened her eyes.

Poor thing. He's worn himself out! And now I am alone ...as always. It's fitting, I suppose.

For a time in her youth she longed for someone who would understand her even without words. But those were old dreams, dreams of a young foolish girl, long ago replaced by practical necessities.

She swallowed back a cough so she wouldn't wake Carl, dear Carl, who had understood all along! Her heart expanded with new love for him. But Life was ebbing slowly from her body. Soon she would have no choice but to let go.

That was when she first felt it, other old longings rekindled, like embers blown alive by a stream of breath. Her eyes closed again but opened inside her mind, where a dazzling pinpoint of Light expanded slowly into a large oval—oddly familiar.

She longed to reach a hand into the scintillating mass, maybe scoop some of that Light into herself—because just to gaze upon it filled her with deep desire.

Long moments passed, then gradually Marta stretched toward that Light. It receded. She reached for it. Without realizing, she pulled up away from her toes, pulled up through her body and slid out through the top of her head.

Following the oval Flame, she stretched up to the ceiling and then out through the high, shingled roof and into the cold night. But she couldn't feel the cold. She was basking in the Light that drenched her with the most wonderful feelings of vibrancy and promise! Her lungs no longer ached and she rose, faster now, high as the jagged peaks that ringed her valley with beauty...

And then she stopped.

Carl woke, had cried out in anguish. The others came running. They clustered around her bed, crying and clutching one another. Marta could feel their grief. High above in the starry night, she could hear their sobs echo through the valley and they tore at her heart.

I have to go back! This is wrong! It's too easy! I must comfort them...

A flicker beside her caught Marta's attention. She turned to look and gasped at the luminous figure that hovered near. The Flame was now a woman in a gossamer summer dress, beaming a radiant smile at Marta. She beckoned, as if to help Marta over an earthen berm dividing one pasture from another.

An angel? But I know her!

Soft words of encouragement filtered into her mind. With graceful gestures, the woman gently explained, then engulfed Marta in a mental Embrace.

A profound sensation of well-being overwhelmed her—infinite, unconditional, all-encompassing. She suddenly felt that Carl and the others would be fine without her—they would never be alone!

Relieved, she broke into a grin and grasped the woman's hand.

Marta's Earth family slipped away behind her, as if they had been nothing more than a dream.

❋ ❋

Amy stared at the potato on her fork. All day, familiar people and places looked strange and new to her. Expansive notions filled her mind.

This potato, for instance.

How many of them had she eaten in her life? So why, now, did it suddenly strike her as an act of extreme importance, as she bit the morsel she lifted toward her mouth, to consume it with an attitude of humble appreciation?

Too late now. The thought lodged itself and she could only stare at the baked potato, this living creation that shared the planet with her and was about to give its life for *her* nourishment—that's the kind of thought it was. Deep-down chills fluttered through her torso as some long-held memory of tribal ritual rekindled within her.

She stared in turn at the fried chicken with the grease hardening beneath it, and the cold canned string beans lying untouched. She thought of the chicken when it still bore feathers and of the bean vine reaching for the sun.

Then she thought of the people who had tended these growing, living creations and all the people who worked so hard to bring them to this moment in which she was going to consume them. A deep, resonating realization warmed its way through her, beginning in her solar plexus and spreading up to her heart, which overflowed with gratitude.

Silently, as if she'd been doing this ritual all her life, she thanked the potato, then the chicken, and the bean plant. *Thank you for giving your life to sustain mine,* she spoke mentally to each one in turn, and she extended her gratitude to every unknown person who helped them reach her fork. The immensity of her emotion over this caused tears to tremble and threaten at her lower lashes.

Quickly she brushed at her eyes and glanced around the table to see if her family had noticed.

They were engrossed in meaningless chatter, Tom trying to keep the mood light with one of his stories. No one was paying any attention to her. As usual.

She looked back at her plate. She'd never realized how connected she was to everything in the universe! Never felt it so keenly. She could never be alone here. Not a second of her life passed without some unseen interconnection with all other living creatures and creations, so many supporting her! Giving to her in ways she might never realize. Making sacrifices for her benefit—

"Amelia!"

The rawness of her mother's voice snapped her back to the present.

"Huh?"

Amy hated her full name. She figured that's why her mother used it so often.

"I asked you a question."

"You did? What was it?"

She saw that the rest of the family had cleared out. How long had she been staring at her plate? No doubt Tom went off to visit friends, and Beth ran upstairs to hide in her room. Her father was probably in the family room reading or watching television.

Her mother stood over her expectantly, wiping greasy fingers on the green stripes-and-floral housedress that tented her figure hopefully but didn't hide the bulk beneath. She shook her jowly head, "One day your mind is going to wander off in a daydream and you'll be hit by a car crossing a street," she pronounced as if it were a certainty.

Yvonne always uttered curses like that. If one of them stood behind a horse at the county fair, they'd certainly be kicked. If she didn't wear mittens, she'd die of pneumonia. If it started to rain, they'd better get into the basement quickly because a tornado was coming for sure. She'd think of the worst outcomes first—and not think beyond that. Whenever something good happened, she immediately named a terrible thing that could bring it all to a quick end.

"I said, when are you going to call Mrs. Quantos like I told you and tell her you're quitting? You know what we talked about—how you've been losing interest this year. I don't think you should continue wasting your time. It's costing us a lot of money."

Amy froze. Her mother hadn't forgotten.

She shifted into a tone that often caught Amy and her siblings off-guard, a gentle "I-really-love-you-and-know-what's-good-for-you" coo. "You don't want to spend all your time in ballet classes, do you, Honey? Don't you miss the things your girlfriends do? What about your friend Pam? She doesn't take dance classes, does she? She's such a nice girl; she seems so well-rounded and active. You're going to be a sophomore next fall and you'll have so many other things on your mind! Maybe you'll want to try out for cheerleading. You might be *good* at that," her mother intoned sweetly, letting the implication hang in the air.

Amy's stomach tightened. Her mother was stabbing at every uncertainty she'd ever had. *How does she do that?* she wondered angrily, but felt herself waver as Yvonne poked each doubt in turn. She was a master at it. *Okay, so maybe I'm not a very good dancer. But I love it! I always have!*

She wanted to shout, Forget after-school activities! What could I possibly miss that was more important than dancing?

But the words stayed in her mind and a memory from a recent class crowded in. She'd been having trouble with a pirouette. Try and try again, she kept falling out of it before she completed the turn. Hot, tired, frustrated...

"Didn't you tell me you wanted to join the school paper? Don't they have meetings after school? How will you do both? I'm only thinking of you, Honey. I want you to be happy," her mother smiled sweetly.

She'd hit another truth. Pam joined the newspaper staff in January and Amy had to listen to her describe how much fun she was having during the same hours Amy was sweating and toiling to please Mrs. Q—who never seemed satisfied.

But what about Mrs. Quantos? For eleven years she'd been Amy's teacher, ever since she played her first Bon-Bon in *The Nutcracker*. Mrs. Q wasn't the kind of woman you approached casually. She kept her students at arm's length with an aloof dignity that earned respect but could knot Amy's stomach with a sideways glance.

As if reading Amy's thoughts again, her mother added, "Don't you worry about Clareta Quantos. She can be pretty intimidating, I know. If you don't tell her tomorrow night that this will be your last class, I'll call her myself. We've already decided this, haven't we? But I think it would be better if you told her." She patted Amy's hand in a maternal gesture.

She knew this wasn't a question; it was an order. "Okay," she mumbled, as fear sent a sharp knife through her, along with another uneasy sensation she couldn't identify.

"Your little sister was wise." Yvonne rose from the table, satisfied she'd won. But before she joined her husband for another drink, she stopped in the doorway for one last jab. "Beth realized that she's talented in other ways, but she'll never be a dancer! Clareta knew that, and even Beth, bless her heart. She tried hard but she finally had to admit that dancing isn't for her. She was just trying to walk in her big sister's shoes—although I'd say those shoes haven't been much to inspire her in recent weeks! Why, you never practice at home!"

"But—" Amy began, then realized she'd waste her breath.

Mrs. Q strictly forbid her students to practice at home. Too risky with ballet. They could injure themselves with improper technique or develop bad habits. But arguing with her mother was just as dangerous. So she nodded morosely, gathering dishes.

It was her turn to wash.

Much later, to calm and distract herself, she tried to remember her dream from the night before. Only snatches came back: snowy mountains, a cow with horns and a bell around its neck, blackened barn timbers. A cloak of gloom settled over her and hopeless, frustrated tears rolled onto her pillow.

Finally she succumbed to the mists of dark misery. As she slept, her mind traveled a well-worn energy path, rising, rising, oscillating out of her despair and up into a higher frequency than she lived on Earth. A familiar frequency.

There she found the missing pieces of her "dream."

4

Walking Lessons

ow do you describe a place where concepts of time and space are no longer limited by a third-dimensional boundary? You could say it's a *higher dimension*—but what does that mean? In some ways, Marta's present location looked a lot like Earth. And then again…

When she first arrived she went straight to sleep, lying on a crystalline pallet of radiant, cobalt-blue energy. After a long period of this rest, the same woman who met her in Switzerland and brought her to this place urged her gently awake. But when Marta tried to open her eyes, she couldn't see and she closed them again quickly. The Light was too bright. She could hear, though.

The woman was explaining to her about "the transition of consciousness known as *death* on Earth."

Marta found her familiar voice infinitely calming, like soft music.

"Each soul's transition is unique, no two alike. Some who have not prepared or who are still very young souls will reincarnate into a physical body as fast as the laws of energy and attraction allow. But you are an older soul, Marta. I was able to come to your side only because we are not strangers."

Marta tried again to open her eyes but still her vision blurred. Yet her mind awoke.

I am in a school...

She thought she could see a smile spread on the woman's face.

A school for souls...

"Yes. Do you remember more?"

Yes! The pain she'd felt when it was time to leave this place for Switzerland!

She'd known she had to go—it was the only way to learn and grow, being born again on Earth. But she had been frightened. Suddenly she found her mental voice again.

"I did it, didn't I? I made it back!" Marta opened her eyes fully and this time she could see, faintly, the woman who came to her as a Flame Being when she lay dying in Switzerland.

"Yes, dear," the woman touched fingers to Marta's hand, causing waves of pink energy to wash over her still-reclining form. "You have come back to us."

Joy flooded Marta's being and she broke down in relieved, happy tears. She gazed up with gratitude at the woman leaning near—whose countenance she now recognized as a very special friend and Teacher, one she'd known a long time.

"Coriskancsia," Marta whispered the musical name.

Coriskancsia's eyes became whirlpools of Love as she gazed back in acknowledgment.

Marta's mind filled with memories, including some she would rather not remember, such as why she feared returning to Earth. Regressing mentally during such a life and winding up in a subastral world after death would have been so easy that she feared she wouldn't make it back, and the thought of living in a subastral plane, with its endless duplication of material life, the constant, dull repetition of an earthlike existence, the lack of soulic progress...

She felt her energy body shudder.

As an older soul, she had tasted life in higher-dimensional, higher-frequency worlds such as the one in which she now lay. She knew what hell it would be to regress to a lower form of existence. Yet she'd developed a keen awareness that to evolve her mind further, to expand the Godspark within her, she needed to return to a physical body.

Now she was desperate to know: Did she succeed? Did she attain her learning objectives?

She knew that she could return to Coriskancsia's side and still have fallen behind while on Earth. If she'd lost ground, she could spend lifetimes trying to regain it! Which would mean a far longer apprenticeship before she developed sufficient mental skills to live permanently here, as Coriskancsia did, serving humanity.

Spiritual growth—on Earth it was so easy to forget! Did she remember?

A shiver passed through her energy body. Eighty-three years in Switzerland now seemed like no more than a flicker. Did she do everything she planned? Meet all opportunities? Seized by the need to know, she sat up and groped in the dimness of her mental limitations to clutch at Coriskancsia's hand. "Did I do it? Was my life a success?"

"Shhhh, shhh, please. Relax. All in good time. But first you must rest again, dear. Now breathe." Coriskancsia closed her lashes to demonstrate. "Inhale. Take in the combined energies of all your Teachers in this world, who are projecting their Love to you. Breathe, child. And we will talk later."

A golden halo of light emanated from Coriskancsia to her student. It floated in rings down over Marta's head, resonating through her energy body.

Unable to resist, Marta relaxed back onto the glowing bed as her acquired Earth habits of worry and fear dissolved. Warm radiance flickered through her, filled her with contentment, and lifted her mind into a deep psychic sleep.

When she awoke again, *much* later, Coriskancsia had vanished. Marta's vision had cleared completely and she was startled to see beside her a short, balding man with brown, wrinkly skin, a roundish face, and gleaming dark eyes. His grayed chest was bare but a long, plain-white cloth draped over one of his shoulders. He wore a matching loincloth, wrapped something like a giant diaper.

He leaned close, balancing himself with a walking stick made from a polished tree limb that extended a foot higher than the top of his gray head. He stretched out a leathery hand and chirped cheerfully, "Come with me, my dear."

She found she couldn't resist. His kind face was unfamiliar but something about him seemed safe. And *encouraging.* She grasped his fingers reluctantly. Instantly, she was on her feet.

"Oh!" she gasped, then thought, *Such a refreshing nap! I wonder how long I slept?*

The little man grinned, almost as if he heard her, but he merely said, "Now close your eyes for a moment. We have somewhere to go."

Again, Marta obeyed but opened them when she heard the soft rustling of tree branches over her head. They were standing in a lush garden. Flowers on bushes and in beds all around saturated her mind as they exhaled their rich perfumes, as if releasing deeply-held breaths into the atmosphere, one after another. Most of the flowers reflected colors she'd never seen on Earth and she had no names for them.

In a clearing before her an arching, Chinese-red footbridge curved over a stream that splashed toward a small lake she could see in the distance. As she stood absorbing the scene, a flock of white birds fluttered overhead, making its way to the far bank of the lake. Marta followed them with her eyes, stunned to see them land in perfect unison near a herd of deer feeding at the edge of the meadow that spread beyond the lake. The deer's watchful grace looked ordinary enough; what startled her were the people strolling casually among them! She'd forgotten about the fearlessness of animals here! The sight of this friendly commingling filled her with delight.

Then she remembered something else. This garden only resembled an Earth garden superficially. A second look revealed the red bridge to be as clear and fragile as if blown from hot glass by a giant. In fact, every leaf and petal glittered with spectral light as if carved from rainbow-emitting crystals. Even the benches and curved walkways that stretched away to her right looked as if they'd been dusted with shimmering white frost, but she remembered that this was pure, radiant energy.

She inhaled deeply of the summer-warm atmosphere, filled with certainty now that she had been here before.

"Oh, very good!" said the little man.

She turned to stare at him. He *was* listening to her thoughts!

"Yes, of course," he replied, and this time she noticed that his lips didn't move. "Now try the grass." He pointed with his walking stick to the glassy greenery beside the path.

She looked, hesitating. A half-memory fluttered into her mind. Quickly, she lifted one foot and plunged her bare toes into the twinkling green blades.

Oh! So soft! And exactly as she remembered! Not cold and sharp like the glass it resembled but an energy field that embraced her toes warmly. She wiggled them. A tingling boost of electricity shot up her leg and she laughed with joy!

"Why do I remember this?"

"Because, as you already know, you have been here before."

She recalled something else and looked up. She could see as far as her conception would allow, a view that to her was like looking into a kaleidoscope with ever-changing patterns of light and color.

The balding little man followed her gaze. "Other than that"—he pointed his stick upward—"you will recall that everything you see here is designed and maintained by the inhabitants of this world. We use our Minds to direct and shape energies of the Infinite Creative Intelligence to make our students feel at home. Just as on Earth, everything here is energy, a constant interplay of harmonically interacting frequencies, push and pull, positive and negative, traveling always to and fro, intermingling and building and separating, creating and dissolving and recreating. Everything—including you and me. But here you can *see* this interdimensional interplay a little more clearly."

Gazing at the crystal statues of noble men and women placed strategically throughout the garden, at the spiraling fountains spewing colored energies high into the atmosphere, at the trees reaching skyward with shimmering clarity, she couldn't help but feel a strong sense of love for everything her eyes took in.

"That is our Love that you feel," he nodded, "the Love we use to create this world."

For a moment they stood quietly, enjoying the sensation.

"This is a healing place. We designed this portion of the garden for our Earth students, although soon you will visit places where you will meet students from many other worlds. But first, we have some serious work to do." He turned to size her up, his eyes passing over her, head to toe, repeatedly. Finally he pronounced, "Yes, that is suitable for a beginning."

Wondering what he meant, she looked down at herself and gasped.

Marta's eighty-three-year-old body had vanished. She was standing in a body in its late twenties, wearing one of her favorite dresses from her early years with Hans, although spruced up considerably with what looked like sparkling threads of silver, gold, and green.

"How did that happen?"

"Your mind, dear. It created a form for you that reflects how you have always seen yourself, your true self, in your mind's eye. Quite pleasant, and it will do nicely for the task at hand. We are here to bring back certain abilities that you have forgotten.

You have already mastered telepathic communication. Now you must learn to walk again."

Marta suddenly realized that other than slipping her toes into the grass beside her, she had not yet taken a step in this world. She'd come to this garden on a wish, it seemed, or a promise. She smiled at her play on words—and felt embarrassed when the little man laughed at her simple humor.

"Indeed, I believe you have described it well! And that is a good first step. In fact, it is exactly how you will take your first step—just as you did on Earth—with a wish and a promise! A wish to get from here to there, and the promise of physics. But, of course, not the physics of a third dimension."

He gestured with his stick. "Just follow me." He took a step.

Marta stared dumbly after him.

"Try again." He took another step.

She still stood staring.

"Well?"

"Well, what should I do?" she asked, feeling a little distressed. She'd just discovered that she did not have muscles to respond to gravity, which didn't exist here anyway. Fear kept her immobile. If she moved, she was afraid she'd float away.

The man laughed heartily. "Oh, that's a good one!"

She blushed indignantly. "I don't see what's so funny about that."

He cleared his throat. "So sorry. You see, here, you cannot float away. You are held by your entire mental component. Your mind, if you will. You did not arrive here by accident, you know. You were drawn by your mental and spiritual development." He saw that he'd lost her. "Well, let us just say that you are safe— and besides, we Brothers of the Light are helping you to remain here with a mental projection of sorts. You are in a kind of protective energy bubble. All of our students are."

Brothers of the Light. It was the first time she'd heard the term since her arrival but it rang a familiar note. What about

Sisters? Wasn't Coriskancsia a woman? Was she a "Brother" of the Light, too?

"Oh, yes, we are *both* of course. *Both genders.* As are you. But my dear, you must stay focused on the lesson at hand. Your mind is wandering! Now think. Think of taking a step."

Before she could stop herself, Marta's mind responded with the thought and her foot moved all on its own.

"Oh, very good. Very good indeed," he nodded vigorously. "Now do it again!"

She did, and it worked again. Delighted, she took several steps in a row. "I'm doing it!" she exclaimed.

"Yes, my dear, you are 'doing it,' and not badly! Not bad for a beginner," he joked. "But of course, you are not a beginner and this is not the first time you have walked in a higher-dimensional world. It is no different than your sojourns on Earth. Each time, you must learn all over again how to crawl, then how to walk, eventually to run. But here we can go a little further than that. Would you like to try?"

His face was a mask of mystery, but she thought she detected an impish twinkle.

"Why not?" she answered recklessly. "Walking" had made her feel a bit giddy. "What must I do?"

"You must fly, of course." He grinned at her surprise. "Like this."

He floated up effortlessly, then landed gently on the spot where he'd begun. "Now you try. Just think the thought."

If she hadn't seen it, she wouldn't have believed it. Could she do it? What a wonder that would be! For a brief moment she puzzled over why she didn't remember anything about flying during her last visit, but with a huge exertion of mental energy, she poured her full determination into getting her body to lift from the ground.

As a result, she shot straight up into the kaleidoscopic atmosphere, terrified herself, and plummeted straight back down again when she formed a frantic thought that she needed to have both feet firmly planted on the ground. She came down so fast, she tumbled over into the grass. She wasn't hurt, of course. Except for her dignity.

But the little brown man erupted in laughter. He beat the end of his walking stick on the pathway with hilarity as his peals of delight sent streamers of Light billowing out from his heart and spinning off into the garden.

For a moment Marta was distracted from her humiliation by the sight of branches and stems leaning closer to soak up these life-giving energies.

Finally her coach took note of her embarrassment. He forced his laughter down to a grin. "No gravity, remember? So you needn't try so hard." He couldn't resist another chuckle over his prank.

"That was not very funny! I could have hurt myself!"

Why hadn't he warned her? She scowled as she scrambled back to her feet, thinking he was very careless for a so-called Teacher and forgetting that because of their schooling agreement, right now he could hear every thought.

At this he broke out in fresh laughter, but seeing her seriousness, he cleared his throat and composed his face. He looked deeply into her eyes, his own filling with so much Love that Marta's heart melted on the spot.

"You are right, my dear. I should not have taken my humor at your expense. But oh, I have wanted to play that trick on someone for so long! You see, long ago when I first arrived, a very wise woman played the same prank on me. I have never forgotten it. And I must say, I learned to fly very quickly after that!"

It suddenly struck Marta that this man—who must have been one of the Master Teachers since he seemed so at home here and he was, after all, serving in the role of teacher for her, this man who could fly, who knew all about the very creation of everything in this world—this man was *leaning on a walking stick*.

"Oh, that," he looked at it fondly. "Well, now you've caught me. I must confess, it is an artifact from one of my many lifetimes that I still hold dear—along with this unusual attire you may have noticed." He gestured to the loincloth and shoulder wrap. "It wasn't so very long ago that I wore them every day…" His voice trailed off.

Noticed? In that outfit, he stood out against the garden background as strangely as if she'd come across an elf in the dairy barn! But the smile he wore with it was so infectious, all traces of her scowl of bruised ego disappeared. She smiled back at him.

"Ah, that's better," he nodded slowly. "But you have done it again—taken us off the main subject. You will have to watch that, young one, if you want to make progress as fast as your heart tells me you do. Not only here, but when you return to an earthworld. You must learn to stay focused.

"Now, first of all, you could not possibly hurt yourself here. What would be the ultimate hurt? Is it that old Earth fear you still carry? The unconscious fear of death? The fear that lurks in disguise beneath every other fear you feel on Earth?"

She stared at him for a moment as the meaning sank in.

"Exactly. As you can well see, you have just recently died, and you are not dead at all, are you? In fact, how many times have you so-called died in your evolution thus far? A few hundred, a few thousand, a hundred thousand? So you can lose your fear now, my dear. There is no longer anything for you to fear! And one day when you return to Earth, you will carry this realization with you. On that day, you will have graduated to a new level.

"Secondly, you just leapt ahead in your flying achievements— if you will pardon my pun—many times further than you would have if I had tried first to explain to you about thoughts and gravity, do you agree? And you are one who has been recommended for the fast track when it comes to this manner of thing."

She wondered what he meant by that, but he went on quickly, using a tone so serious she forgot he'd ever laughed at her.

"So let us refine the lesson: You were using too much will, not enough mind. While it is true that the will is a type of muscular development, it is also true that many things are accomplished more effectively without force. Take doors on Earth, for example.

"If one knew nothing about doorknobs, one could expend a great deal of muscle smashing through a door and eventually accomplish the desired end, passage through the portal, though the door itself would have been destroyed and either a great deal of effort and muscle would then be applied to its repair, or a great void would remain where once there was protection.

"If one knows about doorknobs, however," he waggled a finger in the air, "one can come and go through the portal with a minimum of muscular exertion, and inflicting no damage beyond ordinary wear or entropy. And so it is with the will. My dear, you must not go smashing through doors when you know about doorknobs!"

It was probably the most helpful speech he'd made yet, but Marta had stopped paying attention. Questions suddenly crowded her mind. She suspected they'd been gathering ever since she left the energy-pallet. Lying there on that radiant bed, she focused on nothing but herself, her status, her immediate environment. But since they'd come to this garden, her awareness had been steadily expanding. Now her unanswered questions were like unscratched mosquito bites—and they were driving her mad with a need to know!

The little man stopped his speech when he saw the look on her face. "Come with me," he said gently and led her to a crystal bench. They sat. Warmth from the bench traveled up through her energy body, but this time she wasn't soothed.

Without preamble he began to answer her unvoiced questions, beginning with the most urgent.

"You have not met any Earth relatives because, in truth, the Earth conception of life after death is still misguided, despite eons of our repeated efforts to bring enlightenment to the planet. Its religions cloud the issue, unfortunately. You'll learn more about this later. For now, be at peace with this. You are not a young soul, my dear. We have become your most important and steady 'family' association for now. When you need to encounter certain individuals again, it will all happen naturally, according to an Infinite plan that you will understand a little better after your sojourn here with us."

He quickly dispensed with the next most urgent. "Coriskancsia will return to you soon."

And the next, "You do not recall flying before because you did not. Remember Coriskancsia explained that there are many levels of potential awareness after the end of a physical life? This time, your awareness here with us is more expanded than last time. That means you will be able to accomplish much more during your stay with us."

Then he went on to trickier issues. "You do not remember me? I am sorry about that. It is probably that I made a bad choice of attire for this first encounter. Yes, I am one of your Teachers— one of many. I requested to spend this time with you because, later on, you will be busy with many other types of lessons and I wanted to establish—or I should say, *re*-establish our link to one another so that when you return to Earth, I will be able to guide you from this side more easily. It is not my physical body that you will come to recognize but my frequency signature in your mind.

"You are afraid that you will fail again? And when did you last 'fail'?"

She had been sitting quietly by his side, staring off at a luminous pear tree with fruit she could see all the way through, though not really seeing it at all. She was thinking so hard and fast to absorb his meanings that her senses—even her higher senses— were fully engaged in the process. Now she turned to look at him.

He repeated his question. "When did you last 'fail'?"

Sitting here in this magnificent garden, in this no-gravity, no-time world of limitless possibility, she could not think of a single instance. For she knew that every single event of every single lifetime had led her to this moment wherein she was being asked a question by this Master Teacher. Even events so traumatic that she shuddered to recall them had led her here!

Marta stared at him in wonderment. With his single question, he opened up entire worlds of unending peace for her. She felt a great heaviness leave her being, and many answers fell into place in her mind.

"Ah," he nodded agreeably. "And now I think you are truly ready to fly," he winked at her. "So, shall we?" He stood up and offered his hand.

"Yes, let's!" she answered eagerly. She slipped her fingers delicately in his.

Before she could blink, they were spinning upward in a slow pirouette.

"Soon, you will have much better Teachers than I for this sort of thing, but I wanted to be the first to show you the view from up here." And with that, he let go of her.

Amazingly, she did not fall. She floated. And when she looked at the view he indicated, she felt as if she could float here forever. Her heart filled with so many exquisite sensations of happiness in every possible form that, without thinking, she spun off on her own in a series of gravity-free pirouettes, ending with several long-legged leaps through the energy atmosphere until she lost sight of the little man.

"Yes," he murmured, "that is our Amelia. She will be fine now."

A small tear touched the corner of his eye, but it was not a wistful tear, nor a sad or proud tear. It was a tear of gratitude to Those who had led him to lead her. "Thank you," he whispered, and disappeared.

When she finally settled back down on the crystalline grass, Marta breathed out an exhilarated sigh. But the joyful moment ended quickly when she realized the little man in the loincloth was nowhere to be seen.

"Not to worry, Marta," spoke a voice behind her.

She spun to see Coriskancsia standing beside a blooming red rosebush in a swirl of a gown that perfectly matched the cream-and-rose shades of her spun and twisted hair. She radiated warmth, friendship, and intelligence in such abundance that Marta relaxed immediately.

"You will never be alone here. The moment a question or concern arises in your mind—one that you cannot as easily answer yourself—one of us will appear to offer our assistance."

"But what about …"

"He left without saying goodbye, did he?"

Marta nodded.

"That is his style: humble, unobtrusive, except for that bizarre outfit he favors," Coriskancsia laughed.

Marta had grown fond of both him and his attire, and now she thought that perhaps Coriskancsia, with her color-coordinated hair and gown, might attract more attention than he at a gathering. But with the same thought, she realized that she loved Coriskancsia's unique display of elegance as much as she loved the little man.

Then she remembered that her thoughts might not be her own private domain anymore and she'd better keep them quiet.

"On Earth they called him *Mahatma,* Great Soul. You didn't know him then, of course. You were already here, resting. No, you knew him long before his most recent Earth incarnation. You have known him for a long, long time, in fact. Longer than you've known me!"

This explanation thoroughly confused Marta but she asked, "Will I see him again?"

"Most assuredly, although maybe not in the form you expect. And when you go back to Earth you will undoubtedly hear of the accomplishments of this 'Mahatma' and wonder why he seems so familiar."

Marta looked at her in puzzlement.

"Yes, yes, I know. You are full of questions. As well you should be. An infinite number of questions present themselves to us all. And no—not all of your thoughts are an open book to us. How to explain?" She placed a beautifully manicured nail against a dewy lip as she pondered this.

"Let me just say that, without realizing it, you 'broadcast' certain thoughts, while others are held more closely, so to speak. We do not intrude. We hear those thoughts that you have broadcast in the hopes that someone will hear them. Your concern there for a moment at being left alone, for instance. It sang out like a call from a lonely crow, if you will pardon the analogy."

Marta blushed—and blushes here were like major eruptions of rosy energy completely encompassing the head and shoulders. Which only made her blush more deeply.

"A very good example. When we are embarrassed, we usually want others to know. Even on Earth, this energy displays itself in the redness of the cheek. The least sensitive person can detect this 'blush' if they are the tiniest bit observant. But here, you will find that we are all highly sensitive—as are you, yourself. Did you not find this on Earth, that your sensitivity often put you at odds with others?"

"Definitely!" she agreed, relieved to hear a word of understanding on this issue.

Coriskancsia draped an arm around her shoulders. "Come with me. I am going to set you free in a moment, but not until I've taken you to the edge of the city. From there, you will explore on your own for a time."

Marta stiffened.

"Remember what I said? Not to worry—you will never be beyond the reach of our Minds. So if you have any need whatsoever, merely think your question aloud. That will bring a Teacher running, believe me! We live to help and to serve. Without you and your questions, our existence would be quite unbearable."

This time Marta didn't notice that they were traveling, but when she looked away from Coriskancsia's face for a moment, she discovered that they stood at the edge of something she would never describe as a "city."

5

A Family Secret

Long before she was ready, Amy's moment of trial arrived the next day. School was over, ballet class finished. The girls had leapt across the shiny wooden dance floor in their last combination, made their curtsies, and applauded their teacher. They were streaming toward the dressing room, dragging damp towels and cast-aside pink warm-up sweaters and leggings.

Mrs. Quantos stood gathering papers by the piano while Mrs. Tilden, their accompanist, hurried out the door, probably eager to get home to fix her dinner.

Amy lingered alone in the middle of the airy studio, quickly growing cold in her damp tights. She knew her mother would be waiting for her in the car when she stepped out into the frigid March night. She would demand to know if Mrs. Q had been told. What else could she do?

With a deep breath, she approached the silver-haired woman, who stood so perfectly even when relaxed. She wore her trademark long-sleeved black leotard and gray, waist-high leg warmers she'd knitted herself in the classic ballerina tradition.

Although Amy had been her student for years, no one would call their relationship warm. But they shared mutual respect—Amy, for Clareta Quantos's impressive history as a prima ballerina, and Clareta, for Amy's obvious talents.

✳ ✳

Clareta Quantos found it hard to conceal her admiration for this special student, but her policy was not to play favorites. Secretly, she hoped to see Amy progress beyond her small school and find a place in one of the country's larger companies—maybe San Francisco, and then perhaps to New York or overseas, if Amy wished it.

Of the hundreds passing through her studio over the years, Amy was one of the few who possessed that indefinable quality that separates the *prima ballerina* from the *corps de ballet*. She danced as if she were totally immune to the pull of gravity, as if her feet were actually suspended a few centimeters above the floor. Very gifted runners sometimes achieved this illusion of skimming over the earth without strain and so did the world's greatest dancers—although dancing pushed the body to even greater extremes than running.

Pumping legs alone would propel a body forward, but it took great stamina and strength to hold the body poised and balanced on the toe-tips, or to stretch the leg beyond its degree of comfort, or to move the arms into gracefully rounded shapes slightly beyond their ordinary reach. Many dancers mastered the purely physical exertions the art demanded, but few could fully create the ethereal illusion of a body unlimited by the laws that keep the rest of us bound to earth.

Amy was one of those few, Clareta believed. In young children, the phenomenon was common but as they aged, they gradually took on the weight of the world. Their footfalls grew steadily heavier until, like the adults who taught them, they no longer believed they could fly like Peter Pan.

On occasion, however, a few escaped gravity—and from among this rare group came the most brilliant dancers.

Ever since Amy appeared in her studio as a precocious four-year-old, mimicking the older dancers' poses with perfect placement when she thought Clareta wasn't looking, the former prima ballerina had kept an eye on her. She watched as Amy slowly grew into a lovely young woman, as the baby fat melted and her limbs filled in to match and surpass those of her elders. Now her straight, thick, dark hair gave her a slightly wild appearance, made more exotic by her bone-china skin, sharp blue eyes, even teeth that gleamed behind her rare smiles, and slender but strong legs.

Like most teenagers, Amy wasn't aware of her beauty. She still walked and talked shyly and awkwardly around others, and when she wasn't dancing her shoulders slumped forward. But the moment Amy struggled into her pink tights and placed her feet in first position, tuning her ear to the first strains of music, she transformed. Her back straightened, her chin lifted, an arm swept gracefully to her side, and all weight and worry left her completely.

Ah, what a talent! Clareta would sigh in envy. Never mind dancing; how sweet it must be to become so free of heaviness, so effortlessly!

Still, none of this would give Amy a career as a dancer if her heart weren't consumed by desire. Desire alone could propel dancers with far less talent to the front of the stage—desire so strong it overcame physical limitations. To live the life of a dancer would demand all of Amy's passion, focus, sensitivity, and fervent commitment. And she was still too young to be expected to know her own heart, Clareta assumed. She needed to mature and conquer more of what life would throw in her direction, especially as a teenager living under the pall that had settled over Amy's household.

So she nurtured her hopes for Amy patiently and privately,

confiding only in her husband, John, because he shared all of her dreams. Nothing would make her happier than to see her prize student fly to the top of the dance world!

Which is why Clareta's face collapsed from its usual lofty serenity when they retired to her office and Amy mumbled her intention to quit. Clareta sank into her chair as waves of cold disbelief washed over her arms and legs, the chill finally settling in her stomach. For a moment, she couldn't speak but as Amy's pronouncement settled in, her shock transformed into anger.

She knew what was behind this! In fact, she should have expected it.

Regaining her poise, Clareta straightened her shoulders beneath the loose gray cardigan she had pulled off a stand in the office corner. She pushed aside her anger, which would only sap her energy and make her words ineffective. But this time she needed to draw on deep reserves to adjust her posture into its customary upright perfection. She took a long inhale and centered herself mentally, as if for hand-to-hand combat.

"Please sit for a moment," she commanded, gesturing to a wooden chair across from her desk in the tiny but tidy office. "I know your mother is waiting for you outside but I must tell you something I should have told you a long time ago."

✳ ✳

Amy felt sick. She'd never seen Mrs. Quantos look so stunned, or so pale. And never speechless! Her dance teacher always expressed an opinion—and a firm and defiant one at that.

She reluctantly took the seat, wishing she could run instead. This hurt. She just wanted it to be over. She twisted her pink leg warmers between sweaty fingers and stared at her feet.

Mrs. Q leaned across the desk, speaking with quiet but powerful words directed to the top of Amy's head.

"You know that this decision will be final, don't you? That if you stop training now, you're going to end any hope you might have of pursuing dance as a career later?"

"A career?" Amy looked up in bewilderment. *What is she talking about?*

"You are young, I know, but your mother is forcing me to bring this up now. I hoped to wait until next winter, when I planned a surprise for you. Of course, you'll only be sixteen then, but that's the right time, I believe. Especially with your unique qualities."

Unique qualities? Was she being facetious? A veiled reference to Amy's inability to blend in with the others?

Mrs. Q didn't seem to notice the effect her words were having on Amy. She stared out the second-story window at the darkening sky, preoccupied with something that made a deep crease between her gracefully arched brows. She turned back into the room, as if she'd made up her mind.

"Amy, there's something we've all kept from you, and I believe now that it was a mistake to do so." Her gray-blue eyes narrowed a bit. "It would be far better if your mother told you herself but I have reason to believe she will never do that."

Her lips formed a hard line, an expression of disapproval Amy recognized instantly. She always held her mouth this way after repeatedly telling a student how to perform a step and the student still made a sloppy attempt, as if they hadn't heard her instruction at all.

"A long time ago, when both your mother and I were students—she was in a younger class, of course," her teacher added simply. She always made it clear that she was not ashamed of her age. And with her figure, regal carriage, and serenely beautiful features, she had nothing to apologize for, Amy agreed.

"Many years ago, we were both training as ballerinas."

Amy jerked forward in the chair.

"Wait a minute—*my* mother? Studied *ballet?* I heard she did some tap dancing for a lark. But that was before...I mean..."

She thought of her mother's bulk heaving up and down the

stairs, the sound of her gasping breath trying to supply enough oxygen to an overworked heart. "She took *ballet* with you?"

"Not with me, but in the same school. It doesn't exist anymore. Your mother was a very gifted dancer, Amy. Much more so than me—yes, it's true," she added when Amy gasped again in disbelief. "And naturally, she was offered a scholarship audition in New York. The company that invited her was so impressed with her fiery style, they planned to offer her an audition with the company itself as soon as she arrived at the school. I heard this later from our teacher, Mr. Scott."

Her mother?? A dancer? In New York? But what about—

"This was before she met your father, of course. Even we older students envied Yvonne. She was not only skilled in the technical demands of classical ballet, but blessed with the charisma that sets a world-class dancer apart from the soloist who spends her career dancing with small companies in small towns. She could have made it, Amy. She had what it takes."

Clareta hesitated for a moment. She didn't add that Yvonne also had a powerful ego, and a cruel streak toward her less-talented peers.

Unlike Amy, whose strengths lay in her lyrical grace, Yvonne seized attention as if she'd demanded it whenever she took the stage. Physically she danced with more-than-capable skill, but her appeal was sharp, not ethereal. She was a dazzler, not a floater. Her fire drew eyes and she loved to be looked at.

"But what happened?" Amy pressed, shocked into forgetting her manners.

"I'm coming to that."

Clareta decided to leave out the stories of Yvonne's temper tantrums and the mean jokes she played on other dancers. This would be hard enough for her daughter to accept, the truth had been so well hidden from her. And now it lay buried beneath layers of her mother's ample flesh.

"After the invitation to New York, your mother began rehearsing day and night with a special tutor Mr. Scott found for her at your grandparents' request. Some said later that maybe she rehearsed too much, to the point of exhaustion. Others believed it was fate…" She trailed off.

Amy felt she would burst if Mrs. Q didn't come to the point soon! But whatever happened it must not have been good, because her mother still lived here, in the same town, married, with children, and to look at her now…

"The night before Yvonne and Mr. Scott were to fly to New York for the audition, they rehearsed late in the studio. No one knows what happened exactly, but your mother fell during a *jeté*. Her feet simply went out from under her. That's not so rare; sometimes floors are slippery, rosin wears off your shoes, as you know. But how she landed made the difference. The doctors said she would heal, the fractured vertebrae would mend, but there might be some distortion in her spine, or a slight limp in her leg. Whether they were right about that or not didn't matter. The news devastated your mother. It was as if she gave up her dreams on the spot.

"She collapsed, Amy, not only physically, but mentally and spiritually, if you will. She never even tried to dance again! Your grandparents wanted her to see a therapist—a psychological therapist—but Yvonne refused.

"Admittedly, retraining would have been difficult, painful even, after months in a body cast and months more in physical therapy, but she never came back to class. Eventually she regained full movement despite the doctors' dire predictions. But by then it was too late. She'd lost her drive, her will, and apparently, her hope."

Mrs. Q sighed. "We heard that she signed up for college classes in South Bend, but then she met your father and dropped out. She lost direction, you see. The rest of the story they've told you, I'm sure: how they fell in love, got married. But they never spoke of her dancing, and when her little daughters who loved to dance begged for lessons"—for the first time in all this speech, her eyes flickered in Amy's direction, giving a hint of her affection—"she was unable to say no. What would people think? But knowing her as I do now, I would not be surprised to learn that she wanted to. When she brought you girls here, she made me promise never to breathe a word about her past. I've defied that promise, Amy, because you mean a great deal to me."

Amy was astonished to notice that her teacher's normally cool eyes brimmed with extra wetness. Mrs. Q leaned forward earnestly, every word now ringing with intensity.

"I believe she has betrayed your trust, Amy. I am probably violating a thousand moral principles, but I'm looking straight into the eye of one of them and I cannot hold my tongue. I believe she first encouraged Beth and now you to quit because she cannot stand the memories you two stir up! Everyone who knew her then and knows her today understands that she started drinking to quell those memories. And she's intimidated them all into keeping their opinions to themselves!"

The words crashed over Amy like a pile of broken vodka bottles poured from a garbage can. The sound of tinkling glass fell away in the room's sudden deadly quiet.

She thought no one knew! The subject was taboo in her family!

No one, not even Gramma Jean, dared to mention her mother's martinis or her drunken snores in front of the television (when she wasn't tossing verbal grenades). Any suggestion that this consumption might be harmful caused her mother to rise up in demonic rage and defend her right to take a drink. She was an ordinary social drinker, she insisted. Even her doctor told her so!

Yeah, Amy would think sarcastically, *that's because your doctor is a family friend who goes to the same parties, probably drinks the same martinis! Not likely he'll tell you what you're doing to your health or that you're both addicted to the stuff!*

But she didn't dare breathe a word of this aloud. She'd tried that a few times.

And then she had the excuse that Amy's father drank too. Wasn't it her right to share a drink with her husband when he got home from a hard day at work? But when her father drank, he faded. When her mother drank, she rose up as if from the depths of hell.

Amy resettled herself in the chair, trying to compose her face. She tried to speak but her throat was parched and the words wouldn't come out. She cleared it a few times. Finally she managed, "If what you say is true, what can I do about it?"

She meant about the order to stop dancing, but she might as well have meant about her mother's drinking.

"But you're right," she added. "She's the one who told me to tell you I want to quit. She said I didn't seem interested, that I never practice at home—"

"And now you know that she knows better than that!"

Her teacher's face took on a shade Amy had never seen before.

"Yes, but I'm just a kid! I have to do what she says. If she won't pay for my lessons, I have to quit. And I don't have a driver's license. How would I get here?" she added miserably. "And it's true what she said. I *have* been distracted by things at school this year..."

She felt her cheeks warm involuntarily, thinking of Jeremy.

"I know, Amy, but you're young. That's to be expected. You need to experience many things, including boyfriends and parties and other interests before you make any decisions about your future. But Amy, this decision will affect your life in a definite way. You won't be able to reverse it.

"It's unfortunate that you have to make it now. It would have been better if you'd just kept up with your lessons as always and never given it another thought until the time was right. But your mother has forced the issue. I felt you should know that she's not telling you everything—and that—" She hesitated. "That she may not have your best interests at heart.

"That's a terrible thing to say, I know. But you must realize what a devastating disappointment she suffered and how bitter it made her. I don't know how well I would cope if I were in her shoes—but still, we cannot let her ruin your opportunities! You should be free to pursue all the avenues that your own talent, your own gifts, and your own sweet self have provided for you!"

Amy felt a glow of love coming her way and she was unfathomably grateful for this unexpected sensation. Mrs. Quantos truly cared about her!

More than that—Amy finally heard what she said about her abilities. A future as a dancer! Imagine! She never considered it possible.

What a dream that would be!

"Amy, you know you are my best student. And although I've tried to keep this a secret from you and the others—I don't believe teachers should favor one student over another—you need to know, surely you must know of the hopes I've kept for your future. I believe you have sufficient talent and skill to go forward as a dancer. Whether or not you choose it as a career, and whether or not you are successful, will be up to you. It will all depend on where your heart lies. As your teacher, I'm telling you that if you add desire and passion to your skills, you may go far indeed. I would love to see that happen. And if you don't make it all the way to the top, believe me when I say that you will be glad you tried. Your life will be richer and happier for the experiences you'll have!

"There's no failure, Amy, except the one who never even tries to reach for her dreams!"

"But if my mother insists that I quit now, how can it happen?"

"If you do as she wishes, it cannot. Now you understand why I've spoken up—some would say, way beyond the proper limits! But let them say it.

"Here's what I'm going to propose: You go away and think

about everything I've said. I know it's a shock. You'll need time for all this to sink in. I suggest you don't say anything to your mother right now, except that you've given me your notice. But if you decide you want to continue your studies, you call me. I will find a way," she said earnestly, pulling out a card with a pink ballerina on the front and scribbling her home number on the back, which she handed to Amy.

Amy reached for it mechanically, still shaken. "You'd do that for me?"

"Yes, dear, I would. But I want you to think about it carefully before you decide. A few weeks away from class probably won't do too much damage. But the longer you wait, the harder it will be to regain what you've lost. Remember what they say: Miss one class, you can tell. Miss two classes, your fellow dancers can tell. Miss three—the audience can tell."

Amy knew the saying. Every student heard it a thousand times, particularly when they first began and weren't very serious. So every dancer tried it and found that it wasn't an old ballet-master's ploy. Taking class after you missed one was excruciating; after two, you thought you'd die before it ended. She had never missed three in a row.

She stood up, hesitating, trying not to cry.

The older woman came to her side and put an arm over her shoulders, walking her toward the door. "Yes, I know." She sounded as if she too were holding back tears. "There's one more thing, Amy. I mentioned that I had a surprise for you next winter. I never planned to tell you so soon; I didn't want it to cause jealousy among the others—and I didn't want you thinking about this too far in advance."

She stopped and turned to rest her hands lightly on Amy's shoulders. She gazed at her for a moment, as if trying to gauge what effect her words would have. Then she took a deep breath.

"I have a friend, Pierre Rennault, whom I first met many years ago when we danced together in Belgium, and later in Israel.

He's a dear friend, and some time ago he expressed to me his desire to try his hand at choreography.

"For years now, he's been working with the San Francisco Ballet as a teacher. But he is hoping for a quieter venue to stage his first choreographed piece, somewhere out of the glare of publicity he'd get in San Francisco. I was thrilled to offer him an opportunity to work here, with my students. It will be a small piece, and he's not certain yet if it will be classical or contemporary. But I've promised him that I have a dancer here who will inspire his best work."

She beamed at Amy, who felt confused.

"Yes, I'm talking about you, dear. He'll be here in February next year to stay for a few weeks. He's expecting to set a piece with you as his prima ballerina. If all goes well, he'll take the work elsewhere, of course—but it will be a marvelous opportunity for all of my girls, and especially for you. Besides, there's someone else I'd like you to meet—"

Amy couldn't help it—she threw her arms around Mrs. Q in gratitude.

"No one has ever been so kind to me before," she said, her wet face muffled against her teacher's sweater.

Mrs. Q didn't say a word. Couldn't. She nodded and patted Amy's back.

Finally she gently broke the embrace and held Amy apart to look her in the eye. "Now you understand why this decision you must make is so very important. Whatever you have believed about yourself, whatever your mother has told you—I want you to forget it. You must begin to believe in your abilities. Do you trust me?"

Amy nodded weakly.

"Then if nothing else, believe what I say! You are a lovely girl—and your talent deserves a chance to blossom! But this decision must come from your heart, Amy, and yours alone."

She clasped Amy to her in a quick hug—then shooed her out

the door with a final admonition to call when she'd made up her mind.

✳ ✳

As her student disappeared, Clareta walked slowly back to her chair, the strength suddenly leaving her arms until they were trembling as if she'd been drained of life-energy.

She knew all about Yvonne's violent temper. And she knew how angry Yvonne would be if her daughter defied her wishes. Had she interfered where she shouldn't?

No, dammit! What kind of teacher, what kind of human being would I be if I allowed that girl's abilities to be trampled by a vicious, jealous, bitter woman who happens to hold the reins of power over the poor girl? I can't allow that to happen!

And yet if Amy's decision was what Clareta hoped most, she had no idea how they would sidestep her mother's authority. The girl was only fifteen.

I'll just know, she thought hopefully. *Something will come to me.*

✳ ✳

Dancing for Amy had always been like dreaming.

Sometimes, when she learned a step so well that she didn't need to think it through muscle by muscle, she felt as if her body no longer weighed her down. Her heart took flight along with her limbs and the room around her melted away. She practically flew across the floor.

Only Mrs. Q's sharp voice—"Watch your arms, girls!"— could bring her back, but that didn't last. Soon, she'd fall into the rhythm of another familiar step and she'd be off again—like a butterfly...

To think that she might do this for a living!

It was more than Amy could bear to believe, and her heart broke with a resounding crack when she realized that before she had time to contemplate this joyful possibility, it had already been taken from her.

Tears blinded her as she groped for the car door where her mother waited, fuming because Amy emerged from the studio so long after the other girls.

But Amy never heard a word of her tirade. She was lost in a swirl of pain so deep she felt she would never emerge again.

6

Jeremy

"*Jeremy! Wait!*" *Amy ran* down the hallway, dropping her books on the floor as she sped around a corner and crashed into the lockers that stretched endlessly down a pitch-black corridor. But in the distance she could see light pouring through a set of double doors.

"Wait!"

She ran as fast as she could but Jeremy's navy-blue jacket disappeared through the doors. He never even turned around.

Suddenly she was floating in a pond filled with water lilies, giant satin-green pads with huge white flowers. A cobalt-blue butterfly swooped down among them, dipping in for a sip from the water beads suspended on the shiny leaf pads.

Amy couldn't feel herself anymore. She wasn't in the water. She wasn't wet or cold. She wasn't even there—except that she was watching the scene very closely and nothing escaped her notice.

The butterfly settled finally on a water lily with spots of pink dappling its pearly green petals. Long, iridescent wings beat up, then down, then rested upright like praying hands. They remained still for a moment, then separated so she could see their brilliant colors. Opalescent blues and greens and pinks and golds swirled over the surface of the delicate wings, which seemed so fragile that Amy feared the slightest breath of wind would cause them to break apart like a soap bubble, or shatter like a dropped crystal goblet. The wings rose again above the glittering body, hiding their full glory.

That's when she recognized the coach-body of the butterfly carriage. Reflected light bounced off the spun crystal, filling her senses as the butterfly grew to enormous proportions. Within moments, the hollowed body perched high above her on thin crystal legs. Towering over Amy's head, the neatly folded, now massive and magnificent wings glittered with inner light while the coach-body oscillated from one pale, pearly pastel to another, changing hues so swiftly that the colors almost didn't register on Amy's vision.

That must be why I thought the body was clear the first time I saw it. As she stared in wonder, a cloud of white energy gathered thickly around the double oval doors in the side of the coach. They swung open.

Out stepped a woman with golden hair that fell down over her shoulders. Her eyes shone like blue topaz, and her mouth graced her softly radiant face in a balance so delicate that it surely had never known a frown. She wore pink rosebuds clustered behind one ear and a close-fitting white gown that twinkled with flashes of gold. As a crystal ramp unfurled at her feet, she stepped gracefully forward, then stopped and turned to smile at the man emerging from the coach behind her.

The man returned her loving gaze, adding more light to the blinding spectacle as he extended a muscular arm to escort her down the ramp. He, too, wore his dark hair long, just grazing wide shoulders. Strong, masculine lines carved his face—no one would think to question such a man—but his deep eyes brimmed with gentleness, and the plum-colored robe he wore perfectly complemented the pink roses in his companion's hair.

Before they made their descent, the woman caught Amy's eyes with her own—two searchlight beams piercing through the cloud of billowing white energy.

Amy stopped breathing for a moment as the shimmer from those eyes touched deep into her soul, igniting something that lay dormant there. Was it recognition? Longing? Love?

Then the couple floated effortlessly down the crystal ramp, which led them to a garden path strewn with blossoms.

Overwhelmed, Amy strained for a closer look as they turned their backs to follow the path but at that instant, suffused in the fragrance of roses, Amy's eyes popped open.

Rats! She turned over in a tangle of sheets and blankets and buried her face back in the pillows, squeezing her eyes shut.

No luck. The dream wouldn't come back. All she saw were new images, most of them with Jeremy in the scene. But the radiant couple from the butterfly carriage had vanished.

Who were they? A couple she'd seen in a movie? A fairy tale? A ballet? They seemed so real…but after all, it was only a dream, she told herself.

She sighed and, with a great exertion of will, dragged her reluctant body from the soft bed. Today was Saturday. If she didn't hurry she might miss Jeremy.

Yesterday after English class, he'd finally spoken to her.

"Hi," he ventured.

"Hi," she answered.

And then they simply stared. For a minute. An entire minute, in front of everyone. She was so embarrassed!

If Maureen were there—Maureen who loved to taunt her—a scene like this would really fuel her sarcasm. And if she knew the whole story…

Thankfully Maureen wasn't there, and eventually the last of Jeremy's baseball buddies filed out of the room and left them alone.

"You going to the library Saturday to work on your paper?" he asked.

The afternoon light glinting through the deserted classroom's windows set fire to short strands of red all over his fair head, which made the freckles on his broad, bony face seem darker by contrast. He was one of the few in her class who stood taller than Amy, taller than most of his companions who hadn't finished their growth spurts. Even in late winter, lean muscles filled out his upper arms, still tanned and freckled after long hours on the baseball diamond last summer.

He trained his pewter eyes down at her expectantly, peering straight at her but with a strange aloofness, as if those flat-gray binoculars didn't quite reach her to make a connection.

She hesitated. She knew this was his way of asking her to meet him on neutral territory. His buddies weren't likely to be there. She remembered the Other Voice saying that she'd never feel right if they didn't talk about what happened.

"Um, yeah, maybe." Nervous, she flicked a dark strand from her face.

"Great," he nodded and exhaled a sigh of relief. Then he ducked out the door and left her standing there.

The week before, when she told her friends Jeremy asked her to the dance, they were shocked silent. Then they started up with the "helpful" advice:

"Be careful, Amy," Becky warned.

"He's too stuck-up," Louise pronounced.

"Maybe he likes you and maybe he doesn't," offered Theresa.

"Maybe he just wants to see what he can get from you!" Pam raised her eyebrows.

Maureen, as usual, criticized everything about him and ended with, "Did you hear about what he did to Susan Sanders last fall?"

Amy ignored them. At least she could thank her mother for teaching her how to endure verbal attacks. While her friends debated what the most popular freshman at Deerhorn Creek, the captain of the freshman baseball team, the one girls threw themselves at, *really* wanted from "kooky Amy," she kept silent. As far as they knew, no one from the jock crowd had ever spoken to her. So why would their leader suddenly ask her to the dance? They couldn't figure it. No, more like they refused to believe it. She was grateful when Pam finally stood up for her.

"I think Amy's the prettiest, smartest girl in the class; why shouldn't he ask her?"

Of course that was a lie. Her best friend trying to be loyal. But it made her feel better anyway.

"Thanks," she mumbled and busied herself with the lock on her locker while the others kept chattering.

They didn't know anything at all about her relationship with Jeremy and she wasn't inclined to inform them. In the first of many secrets she would soon need to juggle, she didn't even share with Pam what had developed between them during English class. Or what she imagined they developed.

They were stuck together for a collaboration assignment. Secretly she figured that's why he asked her out, because like her, maybe he had fun talking and joshing around? She liked his witty comebacks, which made him more interesting to her than simply an athletic body, nice face, and quick grin (which is what got all the other girls riled up). They had a blast writing bad poetry together, silly stuff their teacher made them do. To her, his invitation seemed like a natural next step.

The night of the dance, Amy spent two hours putting on clothes and taking them off again. Downstairs her mother snored away on the sofa while her father watched TV and sipped his Manhattan. Beth had gone to stay overnight with a girlfriend and Tom was mercifully absent, as usual.

Nothing looked right. Her arms were too skinny, her hair was too straight, and the cologne she borrowed from Beth smelled like Froot Loops but it wouldn't wash off.

Finally her dad dropped her off at the gym entrance, near

a high mound of dirty snow from the parking lot that looked like it wouldn't disappear until June. Just inside the doors, she slipped out of her floor-length, black woolen cloak and hefted it over a table to a coat-check volunteer, while she traded her snow boots for the shoes she'd carried in.

"Good grief," the girl complained as she struggled to drag the heavy cloak to the rack. She had trouble getting it on a hanger. "Where'd you find this thing?"

The moment Amy saw it on a store rack in South Bend, she fell in love with the thick, monkish cape with its wide woolen hood. She begged and pleaded with her mother to buy it for her instead of another of the insipid brown button-up coats she always picked out for her daughter. Oddly enough Amy won the argument that day, and to her delight, never saw another like it.

The long, heavy wool weighed her down, true, and she had to slip her mittened hands inside to make up for the lack of sleeves, but she loved the way it swept across the snow in dramatic rhythms, always a few seconds behind her stride. To move in it was like dancing with it, the push-pull of a tango.

When she was allowed to choose (so rarely!) Amy never followed fashion. Sometimes she anticipated it by years, which meant she rarely looked like her cookie-cutter girlfriends. She didn't care. In fact, she liked the distinction, although that wasn't her motivation. Some things simply called to her.

The gang appeared from nowhere and swirled around her, sizing up the outfit she'd finally selected, picking at her already wavering confidence.

Especially Maureen, who quipped, "Well, it's a good thing you didn't wear that skirt any longer. Even Miss Ballet might trip on that thing!" Maureen loved to poke fun at Amy's dancing.

The others laughed while Amy blushed. Her skirt fell only to mid-calf, but it wasn't one of the short, tight, synthetic plaid miniskirts her mother sewed for her, like all the other girls wore that year. She picked a full, navy-blue skirt with South American designs embroidered in white around the hem. One of her mother's friends gave it to her after a trip to Peru. She said she didn't know why she bought it—it never fit her right—but the women were selling their hand-made creations in the street and she couldn't resist, so perhaps Amy, with her tiny waist, might fit into it? And would she also like the thick matching strand of hand-strung navy blue seed beads, with the white-beaded tassels?

Amy loved them both, and the long tasseled necklace now swung over her buttoned up white cardigan. She didn't care how she looked; she drew sustenance from gazing at the patterns on the skirt and the designs in the necklace. When she did that, she could feel the heart of the artisans who had toiled over them. It made her feel good, and that night she needed all the feel-good energy she could find.

When Jeremy finally cruised over, coolly separating himself from a crowd of his buddies and admirers with a dismissive wave of his hand, Amy actually felt relief. Only one thing about the night gave her confidence: she could dance.

But she soon discovered that Jeremy had no intention of hanging around indoors.

"C'mon," he grabbed her hand immediately. "It's too crowded in here." He pulled her past the chaperones at the gymnasium door, who were too busy chatting among themselves to notice, and dragged her to the coat check in the hallway.

Once outside, he headed straight for a parked car she didn't recognize. It wasn't his; like Amy, he didn't have a license yet.

"Where are we going?" she asked uneasily, clapping her mittened hands for warmth.

"Someplace to talk, that's all. My buddy Joe gave me his keys. I don't like hanging around with all those people inside. Besides, the music is too loud."

Amy missed the music—and the others. She hardly knew Jeremy, and now her heart was pounding.

Her friends' dire warnings about his "fast hands" rolled around her mind like water in the bottom of a sloshing, sinking boat as Jeremy opened the door of the rusting Ford. Amy got in, wishing she hadn't.

He turned on the engine and opened his window a crack so they wouldn't suffocate with the heater running full blast. After a few minutes the car felt too hot, so Amy slipped the satin-lined cape off her shoulders—which were protected by her cardigan, she reasoned.

He didn't pounce on her. They talked. Small talk. Frivolous things. He made jokes. She laughed. They talked about things that happened at school, gossiped about other people. Jeremy loved to gossip. And he asked a lot of questions about what her friends thought of him.

While he was talking, she gradually became aware of little pinpoints of light that flashed in the atmosphere around them— tiny gold and white firefly lights that appeared to hang in midair for a split second and then disappear.

She'd first seen them one night while writing in her diary. They flickered on the page and gave her a sense of comfort, of not being alone. Oddly enough, she hadn't given them much consideration beyond that. But now they seemed to demand her attention.

What were they? And why were they here? Intuitively, she knew Jeremy couldn't see them. She wouldn't dream of mentioning it—he'd think she was nuts!

She suddenly felt uneasy again, as if the lights were trying to warn her about something.

Jeremy slipped a hand over to hers and leaned closer, his face inches from hers. He seemed to like her and that made her forget everything else. She wanted him to like her. As much as she didn't like herself, that's how good it felt to think this popular guy actually found her attractive.

So when he started to kiss her, it was a little too soon for her but she didn't protest. She didn't want to seem too shy or juvenile.

Where and when Amy lived, girls walked a fine line between being labeled "good" or "bad." So far, she hadn't needed to tread that line. She didn't hang out with a fast crowd and she'd never had a steady boyfriend. All those hours in dance class kept her out of the trouble kids with more time on their hands got into. That was fine with Amy. She didn't have to make difficult choices.

But Jeremy's hands began to wander and she grew more uncomfortable by the second. Finally, she couldn't stand it any longer and she pushed his hand away. He was moving too fast!

He backed off for a second and looked at her. Amy's attention was captured for an instant by a blue light the size of a tennis ball that glowed at the edge of her vision for a long moment before it vanished. When Jeremy spoke, she forgot she'd seen it.

"What's the matter? Don't you like that?"

"No, it's just that, uh..." She hesitated. She didn't want to be a prude.

The blue light reappeared and she felt an uneasy quivering in her stomach. She should leave, she realized. *Get out of the car right now!*

Before she could, Jeremy kissed her again. He forced himself against her with more pressure this time, put his hands on her. His left hand went up inside her skirt...

NO! I don't like it!

But his mouth covered hers, his tongue jabbed into her throat, and she couldn't speak. Her resistance met with equal force from his strong arms and she couldn't wriggle out from under him. She couldn't scream either.

In a wave of desperation and dislike and frustration, tears streamed from her eyes and she started to choke.

Jeremy sat up immediately and stared at her. By then she was sobbing hysterically.

He looked stunned, the color rapidly draining from his face. "Hey, what's the matter? I thought you liked it."

She tried to gulp down the tears but the sobbing wouldn't stop.

"Geezus—what's wrong with you?" His tone was jeering but he looked scared and very pale. "I didn't mean anything by it."

He seemed clearly unnerved by her crying but she couldn't stop. Humiliation spread a deep purplish color over her face.

What a baby she was! But she could still feel his hand forcing its way up her leg and she hated it. Her stomach churned in torment. Now he'd tell all his friends, and hers would hear it—

"Hey, look, stop crying, will you?" Jeremy fidgeted nervously, glancing around outside the car.

She cried harder, upset that he was so upset.

"Okay, that's it—I'm outta here." He turned off the ignition, pulled out the keys, and jerked himself awkwardly out of the car, leaving her cold and alone in her misery.

That was her date with Jeremy.

Now, a week later, she sat alone in the library trying not to look like she was waiting for him to show up, trying to quell the jumble of emotions and thoughts stirred up by her meeting with Mrs. Q last night, trying to forget the angry complaints from her mother all the way home, and the stares Amy stole at her, unable to imagine her mother's heavy frame balanced on pointe…

On the table in front of her sat an open encyclopedia and a sheaf of blank notebook paper. Across the room in the children's section of the one-room library, the Fontaine twins were nagging their mother to read to them while the librarian glared from her desk at Mrs. Fontaine, who was having no luck keeping the rambunctious boys quiet. Other patrons kept glancing pointedly at the trio but that didn't help either.

They certainly didn't bother Amy. If she were in a silent monastery, she wouldn't have been able to concentrate on her English paper. She staged the encyclopedia only for effect, so she wouldn't look too eager.

When she told Pam she couldn't come over that afternoon, thankfully she didn't ask why. Amy kept so many secrets now—about quitting ballet, about Jeremy, about the conversation with

Mrs. Q, and most emphatically, about the butterfly carriage and the lights she'd been seeing and the Other Voice in her diary. She'd been avoiding Pam, in fact. With all this on her mind, she feared something would slip out and she didn't want to deal with either Pam's jealousy or her religious superstitions.

Since the first day of kindergarten, Pam and Amy had considered themselves best friends. They were both terrified that day. When their mothers greeted each other as acquaintances and they learned that they lived only walking distance apart, the two girls instantly clung to one another. Their friendship was born of fear and the need for security in this strange new world of public school, with all its indignities and humiliations. But as they grew older, their differences grew as well.

Pam's family was Catholic; Amy's was informally agnostic. When they were about twelve, Amy agreed to sample Pam's church, a stained-glass wonder on the edge of town. Amy loved the elaborate, sun-warmed colors playing over the ornate interior, and the exotic mystery of Latin words she couldn't understand, and, of course, the angelic choir echoing out from the high balcony behind them, not to mention the complex dance of *sit, stand, kneel* that only the initiated could anticipate. She even loved the white lace mantilla she had to borrow from Pam's mother to cover her head, an item of clothing she'd never seen before. She found it all so appealing that for a time (much to Pam's delight) she planned to convert to Catholicism from lapsed Presbyterian (as her parents described themselves).

Then she saw a group of nuns for the first time, a rarity in the small town. Their black skirts had been shortened to keep up with "modern" trends, but something about the faces behind the stiff cowls frightened Amy. She knew they were supposed to be the most pious examples of Catholic womanhood, practically saints. But they looked hard to her, and cold, and even cruel. Amy avoided passing near them, fearful they'd notice and speak to her.

Then Pam told her about what she learned in Catechism, which Amy would have to take if she wanted to join the Church. Amy's resolve began to crumble the moment she heard she would have to study with the nuns. But when she discovered what those Latin-speaking priests actually said, her interest rapidly declined.

Ultimately she decided that the Catholic teachings about Heaven and Hell and Purgatory were bizarre fantasies, concocted to scare ignorant people into submission. She could never understand Pam's reverence toward some distant Pope, whose ring was sacred just because he wore it and it must be kissed by people. (She thought the splashing on of water at the Church door was strange but kissing rings seemed like a custom that belonged to the Dark Ages of devil worship to Amy's way of thinking.) Wasn't he just a man voted in by other men?

And somehow she finally absorbed the fact that this Church had burned people alive (although she never quite realized there were millions of them), and that "heretic" only meant they disagreed with Church doctrine, not that they necessarily cavorted with demons. Even if they had, burning human beings seemed pretty brutal for a supposedly holy organization. Who was more demonic?

Worst of all was the hypocrisy this Church displayed in creating her favorite saint, Joan of Arc, who was burned because she heard angelic voices and followed their inspiration! Wasn't she simply carrying out the ultimate example of religious faith?

Not long after that, Amy found a book by Mark Twain about Joan of Arc and his vivid storytelling explained it all. Joan's fate had much to do with exposing the vulgar weaknesses of men whose egos had established dominance over the public imagination. That is, until this upstart young girl showed up, put them all to shame, and threatened their power among the common people. So they found a gruesome way to put her out of their miserable lives—and create a saint for future worship, thus securing their positions as arbiters of this "faith" for centuries to come.

As if that weren't enough, Pam tried to explain the bizarre business of "confession," where the priest would "prescribe" a certain number of repeated prayers and this would absolve her of sins such as lying or cheating or stealing or worse. Amy was astounded. How could such a thing possibly be true? It defied all logic. It simply felt wrong. But what a great thing if you could believe in it, which is why so many people were willing to stake their eternities on it, Amy supposed. In a brief streak of clear insight, she decided that this kind of insanity was so common on the planet that no one took notice of it—except perhaps her new friend, Mark Twain/Samuel Clemens.

The bottom line was that, not only could Amy not join this treacherous organization in good conscience, she could no longer talk to Pam about religion or any other belief system. A wedge formed between them by the time they reached thirteen.

They also encountered creative differences. Pam was much more interested in outdoor sports than Amy but as "best friends" often do, Pam tried ballet when they were both seven. After the first year, it was clear this wasn't Pam's cup of tea and she quietly abandoned all dancing aspirations and talked instead about veterinary school. They lost another common interest.

Then, as Amy's mother fell deeper into alcoholism, Amy knew Pam noticed. When Pam spent the night, her mother's drunken inconsistencies inevitably appeared. One minute she'd coo over Pam, claiming she was "like a third daughter to me." The next minute she was surly and mean. To her credit, Pam never mentioned this, or the slurred speech or drunken snores. Amy longed to talk about it but not even her best friend would admit that Mrs. Longwood was an alcoholic. (No one did, until Mrs. Quantos shattered the taboo!)

Now, because of Pam's religious training, Amy's "kooky ideas" frightened her. So Amy never told her about Gramma Delphine and she knew she'd never understand why Amy was now giving thanks *to* the food she was eating instead of *for* it. And if Pam couldn't see the beauty in the broken mirror spirals on Amy's wall, then she'd really think Amy had gone off the deep end if she heard about the butterfly carriage, or the Other Voice, or the twinkling light-visitors. It had reached the point where Amy was keeping more secrets from Pam than sharing them with her.

After the dance, the rift widened into a grand canyon.

That night, when Amy made her way back to the gym, she sidestepped Pam's questions. That made Pam angry. But—typically—she didn't confront Amy. Instead she lifted her nose a notch which was supposed to mean, "I'm hurt but couldn't care less." Which irked Amy in turn, who wished Pam would speak her mind instead of pretending things were fine to "preserve their friendship." What kind of friendship was based on lies of omission and half-truths and posturing, anyway?

They'd barely spoken since. She suspected the get-together she begged off was probably Pam's attempt to patch things up.

As for the others, Amy figured their speculations about her after Saturday were pretty wild. Jeremy returned to the dance a few minutes before she did, and for the rest of the evening they stayed on opposite sides of the big room. Amy danced with Bruce and Kevin, although neither of them possessed a sense of rhythm and Kevin was at least a half foot shorter than her. As usual, she fell for the out-of-town band's lead singer, who was probably seventeen or eighteen, with curly black hair down to his shoulders and a thick resonant voice that vibrated her stomach. She, of course, was no more than a kid to him and he never noticed her, although she made sure she danced near the stage. She was too shy to put herself in the crowd of girls who closed around him during the break.

Meanwhile, Jeremy stayed in a crowd of his jock friends, making loud jokes and enjoying their admiration. She could feel the whispers all over the room. She still sensed it as she passed people in the halls on Monday. She wondered if, in anger, Pam started any of the rumors.

No way, Amy thought. No matter how much they fought, Pam was never vicious. Probably Maureen. Maureen always created that kind of trouble.

Well, let them speculate. If I say nothing, then it's all just rumor. And rumors they dream up can't be nearly as bad as what's actually happening to me.

Distracted by her thoughts, Amy randomly flipped pages of the encyclopedia as she stared at the library entrance. *Where is he? He's late.* She glanced over at the Fontaine twins, who were hitting each other with Golden Books while their mother's back was turned.

And what is *happening to me?*

Visions, voices, lights that communicate, Mrs. Q's sudden unveiling of her mother's past and Amy's potential—and then all of it snatched away by her mother's decision to make her quit ballet. Amy's mind whirled but she could tell no one about the strange things now pouring through it.

Was her worst fear coming to pass? Was she truly going mad?

Ironically, her only comfort came from the Other Voice. This week in her diary it kept repeating the same theme: *You did the right thing in that car, expressing your feelings....You are not a "crybaby."...You did the right thing...You are not alone. We are with you.*

"Who is 'we,'" she had scribbled desperately on the diary page but no answer came. "And what about those firefly lights? Why did it feel like they warned me that night—and other times like they're comforting me?"

With a loud squawk, the heavy library door swung open and Jeremy loped through, running a hand through his stiff red hair as he pulled off his stocking cap. Amy quickly looked down, pretending to be engrossed in the encyclopedia.

This is stupid, she decided after a minute. *He knows I'm faking it. What's taking him so long?*

She didn't dare look up and yet she couldn't keep up the phony scowl much longer as she supposedly pored over an entry on—what was it, anyway? She read a few of the words on the page she'd been staring at, something about an ancient, lost library in Alexandria, Egypt.

With a swiftness that defied time, a new vision floated before her eyes: A golden book. Not solid gold, and not the kind the twins were hitting each other with, either. Golden light gleamed from between the pages of a gigantic book resting on a tall, crystal-clear pedestal. Someone was turning the lighted pages now, delicately lifting one after another, showing her what was written on the translucent leaves. But the golden light was so bright she couldn't actually see...

"Hi." Jeremy's voice pierced in from above her, where he stood looking down. "Amy? Ames?"

She didn't move. Her eyes were fixed on a space in midair.

"You okay?"

"Huh? Oh. Yeah."

Jeremy shifted around awkwardly, looking over his shoulder at the people around them. "Can I sit down?"

"What? Oh, yeah. Sure." She stared as if she'd never seen him before. "I just had the weirdest experience."

Once again, an intense homesickness had overwhelmed her as the vision played out in her inner sight. She knew that book, and those gentle hands turning the pages! She felt pangs of loneliness far worse than the pain of giving up ballet.

Jeremy, maybe a little nervous himself, pulled the blond oak chair out so fast it tipped over. A deafening crash of wood against linoleum echoed through the small library. Amy was yanked back into her physical awareness so violently she jumped at the shock and hit her knee beneath the table. Heads turned all around the room.

A wash of red crept up from Jeremy's jacket collar. He tried to cover by making a show of shushing everyone around him.

"Shhhh," he said in a loud stage whisper. "Don't you people

know this is a library?!"

Amy giggled despite the pain in her knee. The physical shock had completely erased the vision from her mind. And she suddenly realized that Jeremy was here, at last sitting across from her. Now what?

"So," he said, when everyone had gone back to their books, "how have you been?"

Oh great. He's going to pretend nothing happened. We're not going to talk about it. But I have to talk about it!

She'd had enough pretending.

"Fine," she said, "except for my whole life being miserable."

He looked surprised for a moment by her admission, as if he believed her problems all centered around him. Then he mumbled, "Yeah. Me, too."

"Look, Jeremy…I'm so embarrassed," she began.

"Hey, don't be," he gestured broadly. "It wasn't all your fault. I mean, I was there, too, you know."

"SHHHH!" The librarian glared fiercely at Jeremy.

He looked up, smiled, and waved. "You don't really have to work on your paper right now, do you?" he whispered. "Come on, let's get out of here, okay?"

"Where have I heard this before?" she said wryly.

"Oh, come on," he blushed, knowing full well what she meant. "Let's go before Mrs. Cardiac has an arrest right here between Donald Duck and William Shakespeare!"

Amy laughed. She liked his cleverness with words.

As soon as Amy bundled into her cloak and they burst through the library doors into the cold but sunny afternoon, they both started to talk at once, then broke off in nervous laughter.

"Ladies first," Jeremy gestured extravagantly.

"Um, okay. Now I forgot what I was saying. " She flushed. But this was her chance to set things straight. She took a breath, noticing that the sun had warmed the air enough that her breath no longer created clouds of steam. "I guess I should apologize for making such a scene. I mean, I could have just stopped you and—you know—just said 'no.' I didn't have to get all weird. But lately, well, a lot's been happening in my life." She dearly longed to tell him about all of it.

But he only heard the part that concerned him. "Yeah, well, I understand. You're still young. You're not used to it. I probably shouldn't have run off and left you there. Makes me kind of a jerk, doesn't it?"

She just looked at him.

"Okay, I deserve that." He stared at her a minute. Then the famous grin creased his face. "I like you, Amy. You're different from other girls."

"Gee, thanks." To avoid the effects of that grin, she gazed down at a pile of melting snow in a cement planter that would hold flowers in a few weeks. She realized she always felt different from other people.

"No, I meant that as a compliment! I mean, the guys teased me about asking you out but I ignored them."

"That was big of you," she said sarcastically. "But why go to all that trouble?"

"Well, you know. We had fun in English class, goofing around. The guys all wanted to bet me about…well, you know. But I told them to back off. I just thought we could have some fun," he shrugged.

"That wasn't my idea of fun!"

Now the color that rose up Amy's neck wasn't shyness or embarrassment.

This entire conversation is an insult! He seems to think he's done me a great favor here, going against his buddies' pressure to maul my body! He calls that resistance?? Who does he think I am, anyway? We hardly know each other!

But she inhaled the chill air deeply before she breathed out, "Look, I thought you understood! Do I have to spell it out? It is NOT fun to have someone mash you into the side of a car door, jam his tongue down your throat, suffocate you and crush you"—she sputtered off into silence as the feeling of entrapment engulfed her all over again.

At first she didn't notice the stricken look on Jeremy's face, where genuine shock was turning him alternately white and flaming red. She'd just punctured the male ego that thought his tactics were suave and sophisticated.

Finally he sputtered, "Geez, give me a chance, will you? Most girls like that sort of thing. I mean, you crying and all that—that was pretty weird. What was I supposed to do?"

"Is that what your friend Joe told you, that most girls like having tongues rammed down their throats?"

"Maybe—hey, let's just forget it, okay?"

She'd thrown another jab at him, insinuating that he wasn't as worldly or practiced with girls as he pretended to be.

"I don't know, Jeremy. It was pretty awful. Of course I was upset! You would be, too, if someone did something like that to you! When you were little, didn't anyone ever hold you down and tickle you till you screamed, or overpower you and hold you upside down over a toilet?" She looked him over indignantly. "No, probably not," she reconsidered. "You don't have older brothers."

Her memories of Tom holding her down and tickling her until she cried hysterically were all too vivid. And dangling her upside down, a phobia that always left her screaming. Great fun for a big brother. And no matter how hard she fought, he was always stronger.

But Jeremy finally looked at her as if she'd made sense. His eyes grew distant and more than a little troubled.

"No, I don't have brothers. But I do have an older sister." He paused to consider. "Yeah, I kind of know what you mean... geez, Amy, I'm sorry. I didn't mean it to be like that, you know?"

He was totally flustered now, and looked sincerely miserable about his mistake.

"Hey, seriously, let's forget it ever happened. What do you say? We'll forget it—and we'll never mention it to anyone else, either. Okay?"

Despite her anger, Amy felt a wave of relief. He wasn't going to tell anyone. But her heart burned with disappointment. Jeremy alone turned out to be much less than Jeremy in a crowd. He wasn't even the threat her girlfriends believed! He was just a boy, scared, young, inexperienced, and terrified of what his friends would think.

Maybe she should make him suffer a little longer.

"What if I already talked about it?" she ventured, watching his face.

"No! You didn't! Who'd you tell?" He looked thunderstruck all over again.

"I'm not saying."

"Shit."

Amy hated the ugly sound of that word.

Enough of this—because as much as she enjoyed witty exchange, she also hated lying. And this kind of teasing was almost as bad as tickling. She got no pleasure from torturing others; why was she doing this to him?

As she often did with Beth, she quickly relented. "No, I didn't tell anyone. Why would I do that?" She looked up at him sincerely. "It's my reputation, too, you know—only I'm worried about it for reasons different from yours."

"What the hell does that mean?"

"It means I don't have anything to prove to *my* friends." She smiled sweetly.

"Hey, what do you think I am?"

"Typical," she shrugged.

He simply looked at her, at a loss to respond. She was too quick for him.

"Okay, Jeremy," she relented again. *He's so easy to tease; I have to stop.* "I won't tell a soul and you won't either, agreed?"

"Yeah, agreed," he sighed gratefully. "I don't know, Amy, you are pretty strange sometimes." He shook his head. "Maybe it's all that ballet stuff you do. I've heard about those dancer types."

Now it was her turn to bristle. What did he mean by that?

"You know, all the queers and stuff. Must be a pretty weird place to hang out, that dance studio."

"No weirder than your baseball field! What about all those guys patting each other's behinds?" she flashed at him.

"That's football," he said hotly. "And it's just guy stuff. No big deal. But you're all—I don't know—all *sensitive* about things."

"Well, dancing is—oh, never mind. It doesn't matter."

Maybe he was right. Maybe she was unusually sensitive. Another way she didn't fit in with everyone else. A dancer— maybe that's really who she was—and being a dancer made her strange to the rest of the world. Had it also made her crazy? She'd gotten the impression from school that artistic types all hovered on the brink of insanity, all those writers who committed suicide, or artists who wound up in mental institutions or became drunks like her mother. If she chose dancing, would she doom herself to a bizarre life, living on the verge of poverty? Death? Insanity?

But what if *not* dancing drove her insane?

The thought never occurred to her before. No one had ever suggested that people who crave an artistic life *need* to live it or they might drive themselves mad! Conventional wisdom was that they already *were* a little nuts and that's why they were creative.

What if it's the other way around?

Amy shuddered. It was as if the Other Voice had begun talking reason in her head even though she wasn't holding a pen over her diary.

Her memory ranged over years of experiences in the dance studio, then fixed on Mrs. Q's talk about a choreographer coming to Wilton to stage a dance Amy would star in. How "crazy" would she feel if she missed that opportunity? How long before her broken heart healed? Would that self-denial drive her mad? Or drive her to drink like her mother? Or would opposing her mother to keep dancing create such a strain she'd snap like a frozen branch in winter?

Amy stared at Jeremy. What if this silly conversation, this meaningless "trouble" they were having was all a diversion she'd created, exactly the way her mother created trouble in the family to give herself an excuse to drink? Maybe this little scene with Jeremy was diverting her mind from the terrible decision she faced.

Actually, escape wasn't possible. For all their talk, she'd been led right back to it: Should she defy her mother in order to keep dancing and reap her fury? Or should she give in to her mother and lose the dream of dancing as a prima ballerina, if only for one night? If she gave up the opportunity, would she also give up sanity? Would her heart break as irrevocably as her mother's had?

Jeremy cut into her thoughts. "Hey, look, I didn't mean anything bad by that. I just mean, well, all I can say is, you're different," he shrugged. "But let's call a truce, okay?" He smiled one of his drop-dead grins. "I'm willing to give you another chance."

Amy's eyes widened in amazement. "What?! *You'll* give *me* another chance?"

He missed her sarcasm. "Yeah. I'm just big-hearted, I guess."

She looked him over skeptically. He did make her laugh and she could use some laughter right now. "You sure this isn't a bet or something, with your buddies?"

"Yeah, I'm sure. C'mon, let's go get something to eat. It's too cold out here. You hungry?"

Maybe he'd outgrow his insecurity and chauvinism. Maybe she'd be a good influence on him. Besides, this was the first time she'd ever spent time with the guy alone, with none of the gang around. Instinctively she felt safer around him now than a week ago. And, like it or not, now they shared a secret.

She sighed involuntarily. Another secret.

At least she could talk to someone about this one. That meant something. Maybe one day she'd tell him her other secrets…then he'd really think her strange, wouldn't he?

When she didn't answer his question, Jeremy took the initiative. "Come on," he grabbed her hand and pulled on her arm, taking a few steps backwards.

"Not to another parked car, I hope?" she looked up at him, holding back.

"Very funny. Let's walk down to the Burger Bin. I'm starving."

"Will all your friends be there?" She moved a few steps, still resisting.

"Probably."

She wondered if he really wanted her company or just to show off but she let herself be persuaded. After all, which was worse? More time with Jeremy, every girl's fantasy date, or going home to an empty room to anguish over a decision she couldn't make? This choice was easy.

And the golden book was entirely forgotten.

7

Hans

A long shadow spread across the green carpet of wild grasses beneath Marta's rustically shod feet. Not Marta's shadow—hers billowed roundly as the evening wind cast her skirts in a dance around her plump legs. She looked up from the milk pails to see a tall, bony young man smiling shyly down at her.

"Good evening, Marta," he said politely. "Can I give you a hand with those pails?"

She hesitated a moment. It was not in Marta's nature to give over a task to another simply because she was a young woman. Anything a man could do, she felt determined to match as well as she could, despite the relative frailty of her feminine limbs and muscles.

She was quite strong, in fact—not too surprising after growing up in the healthy winds and climate of southern Switzerland, where fresh air, hearty rye ground at the village mill, and raw milk, butter, and cheese (goat in winter, cow in summer) made children grow as sturdy as the trees sprinkled so sparingly through the mountainous terrain. It was almost as if the land were made to grow healthy lads and lasses instead of tall timbers.

But Marta recognized young Hans Lauber from the farm down by the meadow creek. She had seen him often in the little village, driving his father's wooden wagon. Like her own, the Lauber family worked hard as dairy farmers, with a pride that stretched the length of the valley.

Hans had a pleasant smile but his face was unremarkable, neither handsome nor homely, with a pure innocence that spread from his brows to his chin. The girls would never fight over him, Marta thought, but he was pleasing enough to look upon. And always polite.

Perhaps it might be all right to let him help, just this once, she decided. She didn't stop to think why she was giving in to his request. If he'd been one of her four brothers, she would refuse in an instant. But something in her softened when she saw him standing there in the golden, slanting light.

"Nice of you. Thank you," she responded demurely and handed the heavy but empty milk pails over to him.

He fell in beside her and the two of them strolled quietly for a moment across the grasses to the barn, where her father stood waiting. Marta's stomach fluttered a bit at the sight of her father. *What will he say about this?*

✳ ✳

She needn't have worried. Marta's father knew well the young Hans' feelings about his eldest daughter. Derrin Milthwarten was a quiet man; some thought him too severe. But he knew people. He had a sixth sense about them, an instant perception about their best and worst natures. He was rarely mistaken. The moment he caught one of Hans' glances toward young Marta in the village, he knew. Soon enough, he thought, he'll make his way to the farm to ask for her hand. Soon enough. And that made him glad.

Many long nights after the children drifted off to sleep, he and his wife worried together over Marta's future. She was nearing twenty-three and that, in their parental concern, was too close to an age when a young woman passed the marrying time and entered spinsterhood. In their culture, a girl might marry as young as sixteen. A few had been known to find a suitor even up to the age of twenty-eight or twenty-nine, but thirty was considered much too old to be a proper bride for an aspiring young man.

Ilda, the schoolteacher, was thirty-two now and her family knew she would never marry—as did Ilda, who poured herself instead into the shaping of young minds, filling them up with knowledge as she was unable to fill herself up with love. Her sadness could be felt the moment one set foot in her classroom; that is, if the visitor were as sensitive to such things as Derrin Milthwarten. Most people thought the schoolteacher too aloof, even arrogant, and sometimes capable of cruel jokes at others' expense. But Derrin knew the truth.

"Good evening, Mr. Milthwarten," the young man nodded as the two approached the barn.

"Evening, Hans. Kind of you to be helping my daughter," he replied, with the hint of a smile playing around his sternly stretched lips.

"No trouble, sir, none at all."

"Will you be staying for dinner, then?" the father inquired, as was expected of him.

"I'd be most pleased to, sir, if your wife won't mind."

"Marta, tell your mother to set an extra place," the old man said to his daughter, concealing his pleasure under a rough but kind tone of voice.

"Yes, Father," she answered, and hurried off to the small, cozy kitchen where she might take comfort in the familiar surroundings and smells.

Marta's cheeks flamed red as the apples that filled a wooden bowl on the table when she explained to her mother why they would need an extra plate for dinner.

The older woman didn't say a word. She merely looked deeply into Marta's eyes and patted her hand absently, her own hazel eyes filling up with moisture.

The gesture gave Marta a chill. It wasn't as comforting as it was disturbing. She saw dark shadows cross her mother's eyes, some deep, troubled thought that she would never give voice to. Marta had seen it many times before, of course. But at this moment, she couldn't help but feel that her mother's concerns were connected to Marta's own future. Was it fear she saw? Or pity? Why would her mother not be happy for her? Wasn't this what her parents had long wanted for her, to the point of totally aggravating Marta with their inquiries?

The dinner went according to tradition, with Marta making polite and quiet replies to any conversation directed her way and Hans bravely enduring the scrutiny of her father, her mother, and all seven brothers and sisters. The younger ones giggled through the entire meal, kicking each other under the table and spilling their milk all over the floor in their excited exchanges of whispers and winks.

When they finished the meal—finally!—Marta sighed with relief. The women cleaned up, while Hans spoke in low tones to her father. Marta knew what he was asking. She wished, deep inside, that the first request might have been put to her own ears but such was not the way in their village. Before he could venture to speak more than a few words to her in private, Hans must have her father's preliminary approval.

The dishes cleaned and the crumbs wiped up, Marta slipped out the side door to gaze up at the stars, and to be by herself for a moment, freed of the pressures of so much social decorum.

If only we could live as simply as they do, she marveled. She imagined, as she often did, that the stars live lives of their own—beautiful, pure lives in which their sole task was to bring pleasure and twinkling light to all who gaze up at them on a summer night.

"Very beautiful, aren't they?"

The sound of his voice made her catch her breath, Hans had moved so silently out the door and to her side.

Then it is settled, she thought. *My father has given his approval for Hans to pursue my affection, or he would never take the liberty to approach me like this! But what of my own heart? Shouldn't I have some say in all this?*

Suddenly the whole situation disturbed Marta. She longed for the kind of romance she often dreamed about: a private agreement between two people who fall in love, with no one else to interfere, or be consulted, or have the power of approval or disapproval over something so vital to her life!

Perhaps that was why tradition required that women marry when they were young girls. They'd still be pliant to their father's wishes, not nearly so apt to question and rebel against time-honored ways of carrying on the natural progression from birth to marriage to child-bearing to death.

Marta knew of her parents' concern. But she felt no hurry to be married. She was waiting for something...no, for *someone.* The right someone. She had no idea who he might be but her heart told her he existed. He must exist. She could almost feel his presence. Hans? She wasn't sure. Was he the one?

His daughter had spent the long years between her late teens and early twenties reading as many books as she could get her hands on, which was difficult in the small village. Her mind was full of questions and contrariness, Derrin knew, so he was anxious to complete his share of responsibility to her before she became the problem that he could foresee in the not-too-distant future: a woman with an independent mind!

Hans, he believed, was the perfect match for her. The young man was not handsome, not accustomed to having things come to him easily. He possessed a strong inner fiber that would make him wise to the ways of an independent woman. *He will stand up to her, keep her in her place,* the old man thought. Yes, young Hans, should he win her heart, might be the only man in this village strong enough to keep Marta in line!

Fate be kind, he wished as he watched Hans slip out the door that night to meet his future bride.

❋ ❋

The tumbling sound of liquid in motion brought Marta's heart to a standstill. Who's there? She wanted to speak the words but her throat closed off.

Hands shaking, she slowly, stealthily pushed herself up off the cool ground where she'd been enjoying the summer sun, lying on the grass beside a boulder, high above the valley where the cows grazed peacefully on the rocky slope. Although the sun blazed in mid-sky, the ground retained the cold of winter. Here in the higher elevations, summer caused fresh blooms and rich grasses to spread over the landscape but the full warmth never took hold. Snow and ice were what these mountains had been created to display and they were never distant from the memory or the senses.

Again, Marta heard the sudden splash of liquid. It came from somewhere above her on the hillside. There was no stream nearby, nothing to explain the sound. Her heart pounded with sudden fear.

A stifled giggle penetrated the thin air. Marta stood up quickly, catching a glimpse of tan and blue frock as it disappeared behind a large rocky outcropping, about ten yards above her. Another muffled laugh, this one deeper in pitch, clearly masculine. From where she stood, hidden by rocks and tall grasses, Marta realized the mysterious couple couldn't see that they weren't alone. She thought of clearing her throat—loudly—but something made her hesitate.

She'd left the house shortly after clearing away lunch, stealing some time for herself before Hans and the three boys returned for their supper. She often slipped away to sit and stare and wonder about things. After her marriage to Hans she had far too little time for herself, but now that the boys were grown enough, she found she could squeeze in an hour here and there for the quiet time she had loved as a girl. Today she had been lying on her back gazing up at the clouds, lost in thought, her still form concealed to anyone on the slope above her.

A sudden flurry of activity from the lovers behind the rock sent a large earthenware mug rolling down the mountain slope. Marta stood directly in its path. Quickly, she crouched back out of sight.

A fair-haired woman appeared. "Oh no! Wait!" she squealed, laughter edging her words. "You naughty cup! Come back here!"

Her hair fell around her face in a loose tangle. Her dress slid off one shoulder as she ran toward Marta's rocky hiding place in a hopeless race to catch the errant mug before it shattered against the stones.

"Ilda! Come back!" the male voice called after her.

Marta gasped in shock as he stood up, his face revealed in the sunlight. *Hans!*

She wanted to die and crawl under the earth like a worm. She wanted to shrivel into nothingness like a fallen blossom at the end of a chill autumn rain. If she'd had a knife in that instant, she would have cut her own heart out in anger! She dared not think what she would do to the offending pair.

Too late. Ilda spied Marta just as the tumbling mug smashed with a terrible clatter into the rocky outcropping above Marta's head, showering a thousand pieces of shattered clay over her hair.

Hans, who hadn't noticed how suddenly Ilda halted her careening chase down the steep hill, came running down after her, his cheeks flushed.

"What happened, my darling?" he said to Ilda in mock

sympathy. Then he noticed her horrified stare. "What's wrong? It was only an old cup—we have another!"

Slowly, Ilda raised an arm and pointed at Marta, who could not move from the spot, her body trembled so violently with shock and anger. Hans followed the gesture.

"Oh, my god," he whispered. "My god…"

Marta and Ilda never spoke after that. They often saw one another in the small village. But each looked away in shame, filled with her own kind of pain. Hans was never able to say anything at all to Marta about the incident. That day he had merely turned away from the two women, bowed his head for a moment, and then strode forcefully back up the mountain to return to his work.

When he reappeared at suppertime, a deadly pall filled the room. The three boys knew enough to keep quiet when their parents looked so grim. That night as she tucked herself into bed, Marta turned her body away from Hans. Not one word had passed her lips since that afternoon horror—not even as she stood, finally, and stared into the eyes of her enemy. She vowed to herself that she would not become a haranguing wife, a jealous shrew, but the hurt deep inside lasted for a very, very long time.

For many months Hans looked miserable, overpowered by guilt. His simple flirtation with the schoolteacher had gotten out of hand. He never intended to do anything to cause Marta pain or break their marriage vows. But one thing led to another and before he knew what he was doing, he and Ilda were sharing a mug of beer on the sunny mountainside. Maybe it was the alcohol, or the rare warmth, or the sight of Ilda's shining hair as she unloosed a braid and let it fall softly to her shoulders. Next thing he knew, he was catching hold of her small waist and pulling her with him to the ground, and then, in their passionate embrace, his foot had kicked the brown mug free of its resting place and it went rolling…rolling his life with it, a fast descent into hell.

Oh, he was grateful on one hand for Marta's silence. But in

another way, it was murdering him. Every time he saw her, bent to her washing or cleaning or cooking, his heart filled with anguish. She had never done anything to harm or offend or hurt him. And he had destroyed her life. Brought shame to their household.

None of the three would dream of allowing the incident to fall upon the ears of their neighbors, but it wasn't necessary for anyone to tell the tale. Gossips have a way of noticing the slightest change in a family, the subtlest shift in glances, the quietest rumble of unrest. Ilda's reputation was destroyed forever, as those who'd taken note of her flirtations with Hans put together a story that circulated among young and old. There had been no adultery, in truth, but that was not how the gossips perceived it. They mistook Marta's silence for that of a woman who had been permanently, irrefutably shamed by her husband. And everyone knew that Ilda was the kind of woman wicked enough to play with the affections of another woman's husband. Yes, yes, they all said, it was just like Ilda to do such a thing.

But for Marta, the heartbreak of knowing how quickly her husband's attention was diverted to another woman creased her face with new lines. An older woman at that! The pain did not lessen for knowing that the actual act did not occur, nor for the deep secret buried within Marta's own bosom: that she had never loved Hans with the consuming, fairy-tale love she had long dreamed of. They had lived a good life, even a happy and fulfilling life, until now. But her heart had always secretly longed for something that did not exist in their relationship.

Neither was her hatred for Ilda lessened by these facts. Marta told herself many times in the long sleepless hours that she must let it go. She must forget, forgive, and get on with her life and her duties as mother and housekeeper. But the sight of Ilda laughing in the cruel sunshine, her dress displaced by the clutching of Marta's own husband—it haunted her. She could not forget.

Eventually, Hans and Marta repaired the broken threads between them. Many years together mended their bond, and in the subtle ways that a husband and wife have of restoring their faith in one another, they rebuilt the affection they'd known before. Occasionally some reminder would cause one or the other to stumble for a moment over a painful outcropping of memory, but for the most part the remainder of their years was smoothed by the wearing of time and togetherness.

There did come a day when Hans was finally able to say, "I'm sorry," and when he did, Marta thought surely his heart would stop, so fiercely did his whole body shake with sobs. She held him gently to her, and soothed back his hair. "It's all right," she whispered, as her own heart softened. "It was a long time ago. It's all ended now."

Only a year passed after that before the frightened cow threw Hans into the side of the lean-to the family tore down after they laid poor Hans to rest. Marta often felt grateful that they reached that moment of forgiveness before his time came. How terrible to carry such pains full into the grave!

But Marta's forgiveness stopped at her own doorstep. She stopped thinking about Ilda, but she never forgave. She simply buried her anger under decades of daily thoughts and deeds, none of which had anything to do with Ilda. In later years, even the sight of the graying schoolteacher as she passed through the village on the way to her lonely home on the outskirts did not ruffle Marta's determination to keep that afternoon out of her mind. When the anger started to rise in her breast, Marta stifled it with sheer strength of will. She would not allow herself to be bested by another, not even in her mind. And not by Ilda, of all people.

8

Maureen

Amy sighed in bitter frustration as she dragged herself out of bed. She knew the new skirt her mother had insisted on making for her—and promised to have finished by today—still lay in pieces draped over the sewing machine downstairs. She wanted to yell, "Why do you always do this to me? Why don't you just be honest and say you hate sewing and I should do it myself?" But she realized the ensuing fight wouldn't be worth it and besides, the real question was, *Why do I always fall into this trap?*

It happened over and over again: A dress would be promised for the big day. Her sober mother would be all happy and excited about the wonderful pattern she'd found, the perfect fabric, how much fun she'd have making it. Amy would catch her enthusiasm and believe that this time would be different and the dress really would be perfect for her important event. But as the day drew closer, there would be no progress on the dress. If Amy inquired nervously about it, her mother would either moan that she'd been too tired that day, or launch straight into an angry tirade hissed out between clenched teeth: "Listen, young lady, you have no idea how much I have to do…" The ensuing argument always ended with her mother downing a martini (or three), lighting a cigarette, and falling into boozy sleep on the couch before seven.

Amy didn't know if she was more angry at her mother for setting up this pattern, or at herself for believing the promises she should have known to be false. Was the Other Voice right? Did her mother create situations that kept the family in an emotional uproar to give herself an excuse to drink?

The Other Voice said alcoholism produced a physical craving but the mind needed rationalizations for drinking, because the mind understood the self-destructive result of pouring this addictive substance into the body, day after day, breaking down cells and organs. So if no rationalization existed, that mind would create one. Or several. Whether an argument, a physical illness, or any kind of emotional disruption in the family, that was enough for her mother to convince herself that she "needed" a drink to settle down or cope with the chaos—chaos she had instigated.

That seemed accurate. If she wasn't angry with Amy, she was frustrated with Beth or shouting at Tom. Only their father escaped her mother's vocal wrath, most of the time. She saved her most subtle psychological torments for him—but always managed to draw back just before he exploded in his slow-to-anger, frightening way. When she misjudged her timing and he finally erupted, they *all* cowered.

He didn't yell much or get physical but he lost his temper so rarely, it simply terrified them. One look could make everyone snap-to, completely obedient to his wishes—including their finally-subdued mother. On those occasions, Amy observed that her mother may have felt an ounce of regret for provoking him, but that never stopped her from needling him again another day, persistently, carefully, whenever she found an opportunity.

How he stood for this treatment, Amy could never fathom.

She watched him steel himself against the constant prodding and poking with stoic determination. She knew this was how he expected them to respond to their mother—and he often told them so when they complained to him in private. But as Amy grew older, she noticed that he was adding more measures of vodka to his nightly survival formula.

Amy's deepest fear, worse than landing in a mental institution, was that she would become like her mother as she grew older. She tormented herself with this idea even more after Mrs. Q described how her mother refused to dance again after her accident, how she threw hope away and exchanged her dreams for—what? A bottle of booze? Children she seemed unhappy to have? What kind of dark, mental twist caused her to fall into such a deep hole, warping any positive attributes into misery, out of which she only seemed to rise when she could spread it around to others?

What terrified Amy most was the thought that she might have inherited this mental weakness. Why else would she instinctively fear the loss of her own sanity?

If I stop dancing, will I end up like her?

Amy reached for a different skirt as she reached for more compassion for her mother's problems.

Amy had already missed four ballet classes and she could feel her legs growing weaker by the day. She had no money of her own to pay for the classes and even if she did, she had no way to get to them. She didn't know why, but she couldn't talk to her father about this. So she let herself fall into a dull routine: get up, go to school, talk to Jeremy, avoid Pam, doze through boring classes. Then go home to navigate through her mother's tantrums: first the screaming, then the threats to pack her bags and leave because no one appreciated her, then Amy's father looking grim, her brother escaping out the back door, and Beth curling up on Amy's bed, sticking as close as her big sister would allow.

Every day as her muscles weakened, Amy could feel her

opportunity to dance for Pierre Rennault slip away. She tried stretching on her bedroom carpet. It wasn't the same as a real class with room to leap across the studio floor.

Jeremy provided distraction but only for brief interludes. Never to dance again…the thought tortured her with a pain beyond physical sensation. It sank into her soul and ripped into her mind. She couldn't bear it. Yet she couldn't cry or feel anger. She felt only numb and weak. Dead from her brain to her toes.

Last night she spent forty minutes scrawling this torment into her diary, but no wisdom came. Not from the Other Voice and none of her own.

"See?" she wrote bitterly, "Not even the Other Voice can solve an impossible situation like mine. Perhaps I was born only to succumb to my fears; perhaps I will go mad! Maybe it's turning out like it's supposed to. I'll be one of those mad artists who dies in an asylum. They'll all shake their heads and sigh, 'Ah, it's such a shame; she had such great potential. If only she hadn't lost her mind…Such a pity…'

"Or maybe Mrs. Q is wrong about my dancing. After all, I'm her student; she's prejudiced. Of course she thinks I'm good…"

And so on.

Day and night beneath the mundane trickle of tasks and routines, this anguish raged through Amy's mind, underscored by the echo of Clareta Quantos's promise: *"If you decide you want to continue your studies, you call me. I will find a way."* But what way could there possibly be? Mrs. Q was only trying to console her, Amy reasoned. Nothing she could do would release the trap Amy felt closing around her. Calling her would only put her on the spot and Amy didn't think she could handle the further disappointment of Mrs. Q's failure to "find a way."

Nevertheless, she kept Mrs. Q's card with her at all times, stuffed in her purse or pocket. Sometimes she took it out to stare at the wrinkled ballerina whose tutu was beginning to flake off around the edges.

Amy sighed bitterly as she zipped on one of the short plaid skirts she hated. A large, cobalt-blue light flashed in midair near her hand. She stopped to watch as the light quickly faded, its brilliant blue halo lingering in her memory like a flashbulb.

By now she'd grown accustomed to the pinpoint flashes of white or gold that danced over her diary while she wrote. But the luminous blue flares made her stop what she was doing. Once before she'd seen one this big, about the size of a tennis ball.

Unconsciously, she'd been reacting to the lights as if they were visiting counselors. She never questioned who or why or how. They folded naturally into her inner dialogue, as if responding to her thoughts. Sometimes the flash or twinkle felt like agreement with what she was thinking and she moved smoothly along to the next issue, as if seeing lights that communicated messages were the most natural thing in the world. Other times the lights felt as if they were trying to get her attention, to remind her or alert her to something. Like now.

Amy's anger over the unfinished skirt had lifted slightly when she remembered what the Other Voice said about her mother creating emotional traumas as an excuse to drink. She certainly felt better than during her furious scribbling last night! So as she zipped the replacement skirt, her thoughts began to tread new ground, higher ground, and that's when the blue light appeared, bringing a wave of reassurance that rippled through her.

The skirt only mattered to her because today was the first day of school after spring break. Jeremy was pushing her to make their relationship more official. She still wasn't sure about his motives but they'd spent a lot of time together during the break and she expected flak from her girlfriends.

She couldn't be late this morning; they'd all be staring, trying to read her face, asking where she'd been, why she hadn't called. They knew why, of course. But they were going to give her grief about it. She dreaded seeing Pam and Maureen especially, but the blue light helped her feel better. What business was it of theirs, anyway?

For a few minutes, she felt strong. Maybe Mrs. Q *could* find a way to keep her dancing…

Then she turned to take a last glance in the mirror before descending into the kitchen. *Am I getting fat already?* Disgusted, she pulled a swatch of hair behind her ear and fastened it with a barrette. Not much better. Despair swirled back into her being and she sighed, grabbed her books, and hurried down to face the terrors of the Longwood's morning kitchen. Her stomach already churned with anxiety.

❋ ❋

Maureen spotted her first as Amy came through the double doors. "Hey, Amelia, where you been? Wrapped in the arms of your true love?"

The cluster of girls around the lockers snickered. Pam wasn't among them.

Maureen wore her light brown hair long and parted in the middle. She stood shorter than Amy but carried herself with a forceful self-confidence that others found appealing, even if her attitudes were often distasteful. All the girls copied her style, growing their hair out as fast as they could. In fact, whatever Maureen did, they followed. Which was strange, because Maureen had transferred to their school only last year when her family moved to Deerhorn Creek from Wilton.

Amy's dark hair had always been long and she still parted it on the side. She glared a "knock it off" look at Maureen and headed quietly for her locker.

"Don't mind her, Amy," Becky laughed. "She's just jealous."

"Ugh!" Maureen spat, wrinkling up her nose. "Of Jeremy O'Neill? You've got to be kidding! We all know what he really wants with our Amy and it's not something he's ever going to get from *me!*"

The others widened their eyes at this insinuation and turned to see how Amy would take it.

She wished she had a clever comeback but she didn't. She could only think of those hours or days later, when they were useless to preserve her dignity. So she slammed her locker shut and turned away, fixated on her destination: Mr. Barnes's biology class, five short feet down the hall, to the left, in the door, into her seat.

When she finally looked up again her cheeks had cooled but anger simmered through her for the second time that morning. This time no lights, voices, or visions came to offer solace.

Usually new students remained outsiders for years, unless they were sports stars or somehow landed a spot on the cheerleading squad—which wasn't likely to happen because no one would vote for them. But the other girls in Amy's crowd fell almost immediately under the strange, charismatic spell Maureen wove. They started taking their cues from her. If Maureen was loud (and she usually was), they got loud. If she teased someone, they joined in.

Amy suddenly realized how brave Pam was to stand up for her when Jeremy asked her to the dance and Maureen teased her mercilessly. None of Amy's other friends would dare to speak a word of disagreement in Maureen's presence! She made a mental note to thank Pam again. Maybe her friendship was more solid than Amy realized.

But the others disgusted her. Sheep! Not an original thought to call their own! They mimicked Maureen's hair, clothes, and attitude. If one tried something different, Maureen ridiculed them until they fell back into submission. All except Amy, that is.

She long ago decided she was a misfit, so why bother? She not only still parted her hair on the side, she often wore it swept up in a bun, ballerina style, and if she could get her hands on them, she wore bright colors that fell far outside Maureen's acceptable palette. Maureen told everyone these were Amy's "ballerina pretensions," but Amy ignored her and refused to conform. Which is probably why Maureen was now using the Jeremy issue to get her goat—and that really made Amy steam.

In fact, Amy realized as she flipped through her biology book looking for her homework paper, none of the guys her friends liked ever rated high enough in Maureen's eyes. She made snide remarks about them all! When Pam admitted to a crush on Eric, Maureen egged her on. But when Pam actually talked to him, and more so, when Eric let it be known that he really liked Pam, Maureen sneered loud enough for Pam to hear, "What a dolt! He wears white socks with his black shoes! I thought she had taste."

As Mr. Barnes set up the film projector and intoned something about cardiovascular systems, Amy suddenly realized that Maureen—the same Maureen the gang idolized—was actually *the most insecure person she had ever met.* Anything that threatened her power over others became a target for her ridicule! And Amy threatened that influence simply because she couldn't be bullied into playing follow the leader.

As far as she knew, Maureen herself didn't like any boys in Deerhorn Creek. Any who ventured close got knocked flat by Maureen's wit and sped away with his tail between his legs.

So maybe Becky's right. Maybe she's just jealous. But that's no excuse to treat people like she does, Amy fumed, surprised by the strength of her anger. She couldn't stop it—a righteous fury quickly set in. *All this time she's ridiculed us and she's the one with the problem! I can't believe I let her get to me. I'm going to straighten her out once and for all!*

Still, Amy felt a tremor of fear that afternoon when the bell rang for a fifth-period assembly. The whole school would be there and Amy wasn't used to doing the thing she planned all afternoon: a full-out confrontation. Her hands shook as she spilled out the classroom door with the others.

She caught sight of Jeremy eyeing her from across the crowded hallway. He plowed his way over and clutched her hand before the wave of bodies carried them off toward the gym. Relief poured through her fingers and up her arm. Now that Jeremy was pulling her by the hand through the crowd, she'd have to delay her confrontation with Maureen.

But when they passed Amy's friends, she gritted her teeth anyway and steeled herself for one of Maureen's ripping remarks.

Go ahead, she thought, refusing to look where she knew Maureen would be standing. *I'm ready for you.*

Amazingly, not a single word emerged from the steady roar of chattering voices. She looked over at the cluster of girls, all dressed in the same three colors. Maureen wasn't there.

"Amy!" Pam rushed forward and pulled on her right arm as Jeremy plowed ahead, still holding her left hand. "Did you hear about Maureen?" she said breathlessly.

"No—what?" She was trying to keep from being pulled in half by Pam's grip and Jeremy's forward momentum. The hall was so crowded, he didn't see Pam grab her.

Amy heard only snatches as Pam finally let go of her arm and the crowd pulled them apart: "Her father... accident...died this morning."

A chill ran over her skin, then settled in the pit of her stomach. Guilt spread slowly through her whole being.

She wanted to erase the angry thoughts she'd nourished for the last four hours! But it was too late.

When the assembly let out, Amy hurried to find the others. They were gathered by the lockers, faces full of fear and shock and confusion.

"What happened?" Amy asked with a caution that surprised her. She really didn't want to hear the answer. She didn't want to know about death. Death was not something she wanted to think about. It was easier to ignore the fact that life did not last forever (or so she thought at that moment, in the small confines of "Amelia's" conscious awareness).

"Maureen's dad was killed this morning," Jennifer repeated solemnly, with a certain pride at being the bearer of important news. "They called her out of gym class. Louise heard what happened from Susan, who was in the office when they told Maureen. I guess she really fell apart."

"Yeah, I don't blame her. I don't know what I'd do if—" Louise stopped before her thought took full shape.

"How—?" Amy asked in spite of herself.

"He was driving on the highway outside of town and some drunk guy from South Bend came zooming over into his lane. Totaled the car. Maureen's mom is so hysterical, they sent a neighbor to get Maureen out of school."

Amy didn't know what to say. She could only picture Maureen's taunting face, her haughty attitude. Her father's death was an unthinkable tragedy, of course, but deep in a part of herself that Amy didn't know very well, she thought for an instant that maybe Maureen deserved to have something terrible happen to her. Maybe she'd learn to be a little nicer to people. Maybe—

Amy was horrified! Did she actually hate Maureen that much? Was it possible for her to hate anyone so much? Worse yet, despite this terrible tragedy—a tragedy so mind-numbing that Amy couldn't bring herself to fully conceive how she might feel in Maureen's shoes—anger still gnawed at her and threatened to take full control.

Amy spent a hellish afternoon. She couldn't feel anything but the anger that burned through her thoughts and the ensuing guilt that sank into her heart. She truly must be the terrible person she always feared herself to be, the one her mother had been telling her she was, as long as Amy could remember. Her mother must be right!

How can I feel so cruel at a time like this? I don't deserve to live, she moaned.

But her self-recriminations made no difference whatsoever. A sliver of righteousness within her still insisted that Maureen deserved her suffering. By the time Jeremy called after dinner, Amy's voice had sunk to a self-humiliated mumble.

"What's wrong?" he asked, concern filling his voice. "What happened to you after school? You were talking to your friends and then you just disappeared! I was going to walk you home but you vanished."

Her voice rose barely above whisper-level. "Didn't you hear? Maureen's dad was killed in an accident this morning."

Amy couldn't help but fear that her terrible secret, her wicked, selfish thoughts, would be obvious to anyone who heard her voice. Especially Jeremy.

He should hang up right now! Never speak to me again. I'll ruin his life!

"Oh. Geez. That's awful," Jeremy whispered back, as if speaking softly might protect him from the dreaded subject. "What did she do, I mean, how did she take it?"

"I don't know. Listen, I don't really feel like talking right now, okay?"

He said he understood. He probably didn't want to think or talk about someone dying any more than Amy did. He sounded glad when the conversation ended quickly.

But for Amy, nothing else could enter her mind.

Death.

Maureen's dad was still young! He should have lived until Maureen grew old herself!

Amy groaned and sank back onto her bed, closing her eyes and rubbing her knuckles over her forehead. How could her heart be so cold?

The moment her eyes closed, a glimpse of a face passed through her inner vision. It looked like Maureen's face, filled with triumph after delivering one of her critical barbs. But it wasn't exactly Maureen's face. Matter of fact, she looked older. Her hair was faded blond, almost gray.

Amy's eyes flew open.

Where did that come from?

9

Close Calls

Coriskancsia led Marta to the edge of a wood that surrounded the city she had promised to show her. They stood quietly while Marta tried to make sense of what she could perceive.

Vast, shimmering shapes flickered into her awareness for a moment, seeming solid in their immensity, towering hundreds of stories above her head. But like a spider web fluttering in a soft stirring breeze, they pulsed gently in and out of view, moving and swaying slightly with each pulse, until she wasn't certain if she imagined them or if these structures truly existed.

"Yes, they do," Coriskancsia replied before Marta asked. "Just give yourself a moment to adjust. Your preconceived ideas confuse you. You expected something like an Earth city and this energy-creation serves only to give our students a vague hint of familiarity. We create these buildings, each for a specific purpose. As such, we need them to remain fluid and flexible.

"We all see them a little differently, in any case, so do not be too concerned with your present perception. As you grow more accustomed to this form of vision, and as your senses heighten while you study here with us, you'll perceive them in new ways."

As Coriskancsia's explanation unfolded Marta relaxed and, to her surprise, some of the buildings became vividly clear to her. One in particular loomed up out of the misty swirls of pastel as a great circular shape—now soft coral, now fluttering opal—but the shape took form and remained fixed in her mind.

It bore a domed roof, something like a museum or government building on earth but without the typical, rectangular side wings. Instead, the circular building moved slowly in a counter-clockwise motion, revealing with each shift in position a new color, a new entrance, and a different reaction deep in Marta's inner core. Some of the huge, arching entrances attracted her immensely. Others aroused her curiosity, while still others gave her a vague sense of foreboding—openings she could never pass through unless urged along by Coriskancsia or the Mahatma or someone similar who made her feel safe and confident.

As she stared at the slowly rotating structure, she lost awareness of the hundreds of surrounding buildings, in colors and shapes so foreign she could barely see them, until only this one magnificently chiseled and colonnaded creation held her full attention. Before she realized what she'd done, she found herself standing at the entrance that most intrigued her.

High overhead, carved bas-relief figures of men and women draped in robes like angels swooped down to support the edges of an archway large enough to allow entire planetary populations to enter all at once, if such a thing could happen. And in this place, Marta believed it probably could! She didn't have time to contemplate the arches themselves, formed of crystalline pillars both transparent and "alive" with motion and color. She now stood several yards inside the building, which was so vast she could not see walls or ceilings. Shelves of books engulfed her, extending miles in all directions and stacked up well above and beyond her ability to "see."

Then she looked down.

Beneath her feet gleamed a shiny, solid "floor." But when she gazed at it for a moment, three-dimensional, embedded mosaics slowly appeared in deep relief, depicting familiar scenes of life on Earth. Right beside her spread a sun-washed alpine meadow, so familiar and inviting that she must've stared at it for an hour—that is, if any time had existed here to measure her degree of infatuation with this view of her former home!

Some time later, she roused herself to look up again at the books on the shelf before her. They glittered with luminosity, beckoning her to reach up and take one down. She hesitated. Was it allowed? The place seemed so much like a library.

"Why am I here?" she whispered without realizing, and then was startled when the sound did not echo in the vastness of the apparently deserted "building."

Instantly a man in a long, black frock coat and wide, soft bow tie swooped from behind a bookshelf and presented himself with a slight bow.

"May I help you?" he asked formally. He was tall and lanky, his dark, longish, slightly curling hair parted rather strangely on one side. He had a brooding face, one that on Earth would have been filled with deep hollows and dark shadows, but here it took on a subtle glow and some hint of color around the cheeks. Most striking were his eyes, deep, rich green and filled with warmth and kindness. They did not seem to fit the rest of him.

"Um, yes, please." She'd never get used to this. Trying, she stuttered, "I—I was standing at the edge of the city, you see, talking to Coriskancsia"—she suddenly realized her guide had vanished.

"Ah, yes," he smiled knowingly. "You must have asked a very complex question. Do you recall what it was?"

Question? She'd asked so many! But at that moment standing with Coriskancsia, she was simply staring at this building, wondering about its creation and its creators.

It dawned that she *had* been mulling something over, ever since she heard the Mahatma refer to them as "Brothers of the

Light." He'd brushed her off her with a quick explanation that they were *both* genders, and after that she was too shy to ask for more information since he was so gracious about even her silliest questions. She hadn't asked Coriskancsia yet, who would probably offer such a quick answer that Marta would feel she should have known. Besides, wasn't Coriskancsia herself a woman? So didn't that answer it?

She blushed, filling her aura with warm rose, which charmed the man completely. He could see that she was a fairly recent arrival and made note to take extra care in his assistance so as not to startle or overwhelm her. That would explain why the volumes she needed hadn't done as they ordinarily would—simply manifesting themselves in her hands and opening to the pages she required.

"I think I understand your confusion," he nodded. "You see," he gestured at the miles of books stretching into the distance, "you are standing amidst one of the smaller collections of the works of the Universal Brotherhood, as they have been performed on the earth planets. Of course, not all of them left actual *books* behind—but the knowledge they carried with them to the earth planes is collected here in this form for ease of reference. Is there one individual in particular whom you would care to know more about? Or was it the entire Brotherhood that interested you?"

Marta stared blankly at him. "You mean I would recognize their names? Some of them actually lived on Earth? Were they all famous?"

"Oh, no! Quite the contrary!" the Librarian laughed. He decided not to mention that even he was a member of this Brotherhood, as were all her Teachers in this place. "But I will say that those who did come to prominence on your Earth were not always treated kindly. I should think it easier if you named an individual who is familiar to you from your lifetimes there, and I will help you find their contributions here."

Marta couldn't think of a single name. She stared helplessly at the man.

"Perhaps I might suggest a few to begin with, then," he offered helpfully. "Shall we start with a scientist? You have heard of Leonardo da Vinci?"

They'd begun moving—gliding, rather—down the aisle. Faster and faster, the books beside her blurred into a streak of light. The sensation was not disturbing. In fact, it felt rather pleasant and she had to fight off the urge to turn a tiny pirouette just for fun.

The man slowed eventually and pulled a clear, glowing red volume from a shelf, pointing to a row that extended out of sight.

"Now these represent merely his scientific sketches and postulations, carefully pared down into something Earth citizens of the time period might begin to understand. As you can imagine, that was an immense accomplishment for such a Mind as his, shrinking infinite wisdom down like that. You know, he is in his true identity one of the very Hierarchy supporting, not only this higher world, but countless others."

He glanced down at her, noted that her eyes began to glaze in confusion again.

"Well, we won't get into that—do forgive me. I have gone too far. What I meant to say was that you will have to visit the galleries and museums here to find Leonardo da Vinci's artistic expressions, and the Halls of Philosophy for his less tangible contributions to the development of humanity on Earth—and then of course, there are his other lifetimes—as the scientist/inventor Nikola Tesla, for instance, but you wouldn't know about that one since you were here with us."

Marta's mind blurred like the books had as they sped by.

"Imagine," the Librarian continued as he warmed to the subject, not looking at her again but pulling book after book off the shelf and piling them in her arms as he spoke. Thankfully they weighed less than nothing. "In both of those lifetimes, he polarized so much higher-dimensional science into that lower, dense atmosphere of your backward planet that it has taken the citizens there hundreds of years to pick up those vibrations and barely *begin* to develop his ideas! Why, with Tesla, even now only the smallest fraction of his inventions"—he stopped suddenly on an instinct and turned just in time to see Marta slipping toward the floor.

At some point his words merged into a dull noise and her vision went askew. First her feet went out from under her and she floated horizontally for a time before she sank slowly to the crystalline floor. The energy volumes fell silently out of her grasp as she slid into a deep sleep—or so it would appear to an Earth mind.

The Librarian knew exactly what had happened.

"Tch, I should have known better," he chided himself as he stooped to retrieve the volumes she'd dropped. That took only the flick of a finger, since they weighed less than Earth air and knew their places on the shelf.

He wasn't alarmed. He'd gone so far overboard that the frequency he projected was too high for her. He'd lost her, all right—all that business about Hierarchical Minds! And since her lack of mental training still limited her control, she'd left this level of consciousness involuntarily. Now she lay "dreaming" in a higher place.

"I should have started with someone a little less evolved, perhaps. Maybe someone of the feminine gender? Joan of Arc? No, no—another Hierarchical Mind! She wouldn't do. Perhaps René Descartes, a controversial figure—or maybe someone political—Mahatma Gandhi—yes, that's it. I understand she knows him well, although she missed that particular incarnation of his by a few decades, since she was here, sleeping—just like she is now. Oh!"

The man stopped "shelving" books and talking to himself for a moment and stood, uncharacteristically silent, as if listening to the atmosphere around him.

"That's what I thought," he nodded finally. "You knew her

before you incarnated in India. No wonder she didn't recognize you earlier! Does she realize how long she slept here? No? And she's to return soon, is it? I see." He gazed down at her lovingly. "Then I have really done her a disservice, haven't I? I should have directed her to the section on spiritual guidance and angelic assistance!

"Yes, yes, I understand; the error was not mine but a faulty question on her part. Well, that needn't be a problem. I will help to deliver her to just the right place," and he stooped over Marta's reclining form, scooping her up in his arms as easily as he whipped the energy books back into place.

"Yes, my dear," he mumbled to her unconscious form, "you just enjoy that classroom you've slipped off to. You see, there are no bad results from our 'mistakes' here—merely unexpected ones!"

✳ ✳

Marta awoke to find herself sitting on a glowing crystal bench that cushioned her as gently as if made from goose down. Others surrounded her but she wasn't frightened by them even though some looked very unusual to her eyes. Students, she imagined, because Coriskancsia had warned her about classrooms she might soon visit, where she would be among hundreds of individuals, some of whom were merely sleeping on their home planets and visiting this auditorium mentally—"not all from Earth," Coriskancsia cautioned.

In front of them stood a man with jet-black hair and a black goatee. He wore voluminous yellow silk robes and, although he addressed the auditorium as a teacher might, his lips weren't moving. He was using the telepathy most preferred here. She decided he looked Chinese.

He absorbed her attention so fully, Marta failed to notice the woman next to her disappear and a new one take her place. All around the vast room, in fact, energy bodies in many sizes and shapes would fade in for a time, then vanish to be replaced by others. This was no ordinary university.

"Do not worry, my friends," the Teacher was explaining, "you will *feel* the understanding of universal brotherhood one day. Be happy that now you are a part of it in your awareness here with us. Later, you will remember this sensation of brotherhood, of compassion, of Oneness with Infinite Creative Intelligence—even if your home planet does not find these concepts fashionable."

With a startling swiftness, a hologram appeared beside him, depicting a planet circling on its orbit in space.

Marta stared in amazement as the Teacher's thoughts changed their viewing perspective. Now they sped down toward the planet's surface as if on a starship. Involuntarily, she braced herself for impact but instead found herself looking down on what appeared to be a main thoroughfare of a major city. How she recognized it as one, she had no idea. Certainly this was not Earth!

Nor was it the place Coriskancsia had shown her. Some of the trees, if that's what they were, curled in spirals like inverted snails, and they displayed colors from a rainbow not seen on Earth. Something like buildings lined the avenue, but whatever they were constructed from was not wood, steel, cement, or even crystal. The people she saw moving about were definitely not Earth dwellers, but neither were they so strange as to be nauseating or shocking to her vision. They were simply different, like a new race but with a slightly familiar, almost Asian aspect, if she were pressed to draw a parallel.

A loud gasp came from a man seated too far from Marta for her to catch a glimpse of him. All eyes turned toward the sound and the Teacher bowed to him slightly in an Oriental gesture of respect.

"Yes, Glissmanna, this is your home world."

To the rest of the group, he added, "Because you are all 'trainees' for our Brotherhood, since you have all demonstrated your capacity for selflessness and a desire for personal growth and improvement—among other qualities that will prove merit-worthy in your future—you have been our students for many thousands of cycles. Through this association with us, we are able to reach you in subtle ways while you live through your learning cycles on a third-dimensional world. That is our agreement. As you strive to overcome past errors, to learn new principles of energy, and to rectify certain nonproductive relationships, we have pledged to aid you, as long as your own efforts warrant our assistance."

He stepped back, and the scene changed.

A man stood alone, and he must have been inside one of those strange structures, Marta decided, because an eerie blue light fell upon his features, as if the walls were made of thin paper and the sun in this solar system threw off blue rays that penetrated the filmy dwelling place. Marta knew intuitively that this was the student Glissmanna and the building was his home.

"It is each soul's prerogative to live and make mistakes, and to learn at his or her own pace," the man in yellow silk continued. "We would never interfere in this spiritual birthright. Yet there are moments of need—and when cycles conjunct, we can help *if we have been asked.*"

Now they could "see" Glissmanna's thoughts—another trick of the instructor's mental expertise, Marta realized. They glowed in soft green spirals, but streamers of multicolored light kept streaking through them at sporadic intervals.

"I have made visible your own thoughts as the pure energy that they are, and now you can also see our mental projections to you, Glissmanna. We stepped down these energy projections from our much-higher frequency through the mechanism of the higher self your studies have helped you to develop. Your efforts to learn have fostered this ability to receive and discern our thought projections more clearly than a less developed soul might."

The students around Marta stared in awe. Had this ever happened to them?

"All humans have this receptive ability, but not all recognize the information," the Teacher went on. "Do you recall this moment, Glissmanna?"

Marta couldn't see him—he sat several rows in front of her—so she tried to focus on him telepathically. It was the only way they could understand one another here; no language barriers! And she'd recently remembered from previous visits to this dimension that if she focused her thoughts on him well enough, there would be no visual distance barriers, either.

As she successfully dialed him in to her mental screen, he appeared younger than the man in the hologram. He nodded slowly and she understood his reply: "I was having a terrible time, a relationship with another that twisted my heart and mind beyond endurance! I asked for help, reaching inside for any scrap of wisdom I might find to guide me. Things seemed so hopeless but I knew there must be some way, some help. It came to me in a flash. A single image. At first, I didn't believe..."

He trailed off, his thoughts too jumbled for Marta to decipher. Then she heard loud and clear, "Finally I realized the image was from another life I'd spent with this soul. It explained so much!"

Glissmanna broke down then, his chest heaving in great sobs.

Marta, so closely attuned, felt his emotions: a mixture of relief, love, gratitude, remorse, and understanding so powerful, it released something he'd kept pent up inside himself. She felt no grief in his tears, frightful as they seemed. They expressed strange joy over the recognition that he had never been alone; that he had help from Lighted Ones so advanced, he felt undeserving. But they had been with him all through his trials and despair. That knowing, that Love, shattered him. The energies that carried his old feelings of isolation poured out through his sobs and dissipated into the atmosphere.

The man with the goatee bowed again, smiling. "And now

your recognition of our mental help and your gratitude extend your healing. This new energy release signifies a deeper change in you. You have gained another measure of humility. When you are reborn on your home planet, you will find ways to confirm and re-express this healing experience. Until then, your healing will not be complete, but now you have furthered your wisdom."

He drew the class's attention away from Glissmanna, as if to allow him some privacy. "Healing, dear students, is your ultimate proof of inspiration, whether it is your own, or the healing others experience through your inspired expressions in the outer world. Spirit—Infinite, Creative Intelligence—moves through us all. As Light Workers, we have only developed an ability to *shape* and *direct* this healing Intelligence, as Glissmanna experienced it, not to *create* it. We humbly offer our service to humanity in this fashion, as a brotherhood working in harmony with one another to multiply our effectiveness. You are now training to join our ranks.

"To help a soul living in a physical body, often we merely need to remind them of teachings they have forgotten. It is up to them to trust, to believe, to accept, and to act on the information. Such choices will always be yours alone. But if you choose wisely, you may, like Glissmanna, use our help to resolve a problem that has hampered you for many lifetimes!"

He stepped back and raised his arms and the holographic image disappeared.

"Now I will show you another way you have all been helped from time to time."

A new image filled the space before them—and a sharp pang shot through Marta's heart.

Before them spread the high country of her former home in Switzerland and there she appeared: three-dimensionally cloaked in a teenaged body that was just at that moment tumbling down a steep mountain slope, her skirts tangling about her as she slid down the green, slippery grasses. Her body jerked over massive rocks scattered here and there and they could see by her limpness that she'd clearly lost consciousness.

They could hear a voice screaming from above—"Marta!"—and they all "knew" it was her oldest brother who first came running and stumbling frantically after her down the rocky mountain face, trailed by others.

It was midsummer and the men of the village had led their herds to the high meadows with all the customary celebration and procession. Marta and her family, like the others, had moved to their summer home, a simple wooden structure high in the Alps. They would live here throughout the season, surrounded by spectacular peaks and distant valleys while the cows grazed on rare, nutritious grasses that turned their butter a rich, luminous gold. This special spring butter was prized by all for its powerful nutritional properties, and reserved particularly for men and women who wished to bear healthy children.

She remembered that she had been helping her brothers search for a lost cow. Every quart of milk meant survival for the Milthwarten family and the prospect of losing one cow engaged even the youngest in the search. When they found the poor creature, she'd lodged herself between two boulders on a narrow ledge. Apparently she spotted a juicy patch of weeds hiding there and got stuck trying to get at them. Marta and the two oldest boys hurried to the ledge to push and pull the old cow out of her captivity.

The boys pushed the massive brown animal from behind as Marta tugged at her neck, taking care to avoid her stubby brown horns. But the milk cow, not accustomed to such rough handling, bleated and bellowed. Suddenly, she swung her big head around in anger, throwing Marta off-balance. The girl's foot slipped on the stony ledge and down she tumbled, striking her head as she fell.

Just as it seemed Marta's lifeless form would plunge thousands of feet to the valley below, she suddenly flipped around and lodged against a large outcropping of stone. Her oldest brother reached her side first and breathlessly scooped her up in his arms—tears of guilt streaming down his face, soon to be replaced by joy at the sight of her opening eyes.

"What happened?" she mumbled.

As the brothers clustered around her burst into relieved laughter, the hologram faded.

The Teacher's incredibly loving eyes fixed upon her, among the hundreds in the auditorium. But she felt no sense of fear or self-consciousness, only his compassion.

"Marta, do you know why you did not continue your plummet into the valley, to certain death?"

She did now, of course. As the sequence played out before them, they could clearly see that no earthly laws of physics would account for that last flip of her careening body. No stone or limb appeared to cause her change in trajectory.

"But why does this not happen to everyone who falls, or has some other kind of accident?" she wanted to know. "Why do some die and others receive this help?"

"I think I know," projected a man who had lived on a planet he called Idonus, which Marta "knew" the moment she tuned her thoughts to him. "Before she incarnated in this mountainous country, she made the agreement. Those who saved her from this fall were her Teachers who sent a powerful projection of energy from the Inner Worlds."

Marta assumed he meant by "inner worlds" places like where they were now, and she supposed that would make sense if you were living in a physical body. Your access point to your memory of this place would be within your mind, so you might think of it as an "inner" rather than an outer world.

"True," the Chinese Brother nodded slowly, the corners of his mouth turning up good-naturedly. "But it might have been that the fall itself and the resulting transition called 'death' were the lessons she needed at that moment in her evolution. In such a case, we would not intervene."

He turned again to Marta. "However, you were always open to our inner help. You constantly searched for answers to the big questions about the life you were living. And you had some very important encounters that you had planned to live out in your later years. So it served your soulic education to remain on Earth. We were able to help you do so—not only on that particular day, but many other times when your physical life was threatened."

He made a gesture that drew them all in. "You have each experienced similar aid at various times in your many lives. You are not young souls. You have enough negative experiences lodged in your psychic anatomies to cause countless fatal mishaps when they reinstate themselves in your subsequent lives. Without some assistance, you would not live for long on an earth world. And now you understand—there is no such thing as an 'accident,'" he twinkled. "But understand this: we did not stop Marta's fall. We merely extended a little buffer to soften the results. If we had stopped it altogether, we would have interfered in her life's lessons. Now I believe you have had sufficient excitement for today. Let us adjourn."

As the bowing figure faded slowly from view, Marta's eyes opened again and she saw the Librarian standing over her.

"There you are, my dear!" he exclaimed pleasantly. "I do hope you have had a most enlightening nap?"

She blinked up at him. She was lying down again, this time on a soft chaise surrounded by blue and white cushions.

"Well, you see, it was my fault for not understanding your question more completely. I should have asked you for more information, but I was so happy to be helping you to know more about the Brotherhood's incarnations on Earth—it is such a rare opportunity here, there are so few Earth dwellers, relatively speaking, who make it this far—at least, it has been that way for a few thousand Earth years—anyway, do forgive me, won't you?"

She was amazed at how many words he could string together without breaking up his thoughts by pauses and flusters, like most people did. Her head started to reel again…

"Oh, no! No, please! I will slow down! I promise!" He took an audible breath. "There. Now. As I said, I am so unaccustomed to the Earth mentality. Oh yes, I lived there myself in previous incarnations, but I have been here for quite some time, acting Librarian in the Earth section, and it has been very lonely. Not enough company, indeed." Which would explain his propensity for talking aloud to himself. He glanced at her nervously and she could feel him willing himself to pause for her benefit. "Do you forgive me?"

"Of course!" she managed to reply before he went on.

"I am so glad! Now your friend Mr., er, well, your friend— you remember the little man in the loin cloth?"

Her eyes brightened at his mention. "Oh yes! Is he here?"

"Oh, no, my dear, he rarely comes this way anymore; he has gone much beyond us. Well," he took another breath, realizing he was about to betray a confidence. "He has assured me that you are nigh into your last few stages here with us, and soon you will be returning to Earth."

"What?!" she sat up abruptly. "Already?? But I just got here! I'm not ready! I don't even know one fraction of what I need to know!"

"Don't you worry, my dear," he patted her hand. "We are going to take good care of all of that."

Marta felt pangs of sadness and loneliness she hadn't felt since she was on Earth, those inexplicable longings she'd never understood in herself. Now she knew what they were: homesickness. And *this* was her home! Her true home. All she needed to do was earn her right to live here permanently.

How do I do that? she wondered desperately. *I can't leave yet. It's too soon!*

10

A New Challenge

The Librarian wasn't kidding. Marta started learning at a pace so fast she could barely keep up with her own thoughts. And every time she hit a stumbling block, someone new appeared to answer her questions.

She met philosophers in all sorts of garb from a variety of Earth lives they favored. Some expressed as musicians, others as poets or artists or teachers or even politicians, but a lot of them had lived as ordinary people in ordinary jobs. A very rare few of the philosophers she met had served as clergy members, but they either came from obscure sects or were destroyed by officials of their chosen faith one way or another—for thinking beyond the boundaries.

Then something new began to happen. Instead of a Teacher appearing to answer her questions, she would think a thought and find herself at an event.

For instance, she wondered about the human voice, having not used hers for so long. Why was it necessary at all? Sure, she could rationalize that on Earth things were still so primitive, in terms of understanding the mind's capacities, that people needed this crutch to share ideas. But why a voice? Why not something else?

Immediately she found herself sitting in the fourth row from the stage in a most incredible opera "theater." When a particular singer captured her interest, Marta suddenly zoomed in to her, almost nose to nose! Yet the overpowering volume an opera singer can emit did not bring pain to her ears, as such proximity would have done on Earth. Ear-splitting, it would have been, for the voice of such a singer is powerful, indeed.

And that's what Marta learned.

Because in that close-up experience, she *felt* rather than *heard* the power of the singer's voice. That power resonated throughout her energy body in a thrilling, magnificent sensation so exquisite that it brought tears to her eyes. The singer's voice somehow projected a tingling reminder of everything Marta was experiencing in this higher-frequency world.

"So you see, dear," said a far softer voice on her right—Marta looked to spot Coriskancsia lounging luxuriously in the seat beside her, wearing reams of sheer, sparkling apricot beneath her now-golden, neatly coifed hair, which was dabbed with diamond jewelry —"when this singer reincarnates on Earth again, after all this special training she's gaining here, her audiences will be quite literally *transported* by the sound she is able to make with her voice. And that tenor over there," she pointed undaintily, "he will have some very difficult physical challenges to overcome, but I guarantee you, the world will stand up and take notice when he opens his mouth to sing!"

She smiled radiantly at Marta. "No matter how they try to reason it out, no one will be able to explain the effect these voices have on them. Of course, not everyone will be sensitive enough to truly experience them—but millions will. They will practically leave their bodies behind in those theater seats, or sitting in their living rooms in front of their fancy new sound systems. On one level, they will be here, right where you are, listening from a higher perspective of themselves. Not consciously, of course, but some part of them will *remember*, if only for a few moments, or an hour or two. Just one more little way we have for defeating ignorance on your world," she winked.

That was the opera.

Then Marta experienced the museums.

She finally got to see Leonardo's section in the art museum, or at least the several miles she was able to take in before she collapsed in overload again. Apparently Earth is not the only place to possess some of his artwork! Then she was whisked off by her inner promptings to find herself in a lecture demonstration about "The Psychokinetic Properties of Visual Works of Art As Recreated on Earth Planets for the Upliftment of the Masses of Lesser Mental Development."

And the palaces of history! Such vivid, nerve-shattering re-creations of actual events, portrayed in full living color! She merely wondered for an instant about those who fought in battles, who died "for a good cause." Was there such a thing as a good reason for killing and/or being killed? No sooner had she formed the question than she found herself standing amidst shouting, cursing horse soldiers fully engaged in battle!

They buffeted her this way and that as she struggled in ankle-deep mud and tried to dodge flying hoofs and swords and blood. Her heart region pounded in remembered terror, and if she'd had a fleshy body, then the sensation of adrenaline electrifying her system could have been considered real.

Just as she started to wonder what it would feel like to be "killed" in a world where she was already "dead," she felt a strong yank on her skirts. When she glanced to see what had taken hold of her, she followed the grasping hand back to the face of a young boy, crouched behind her and seemingly unfazed by the cyclone of hate swirling around them.

"I always loved playing with my toy soldiers," he said wistfully as he tugged her out of harm's way. "That was before I became too sick to do so, you see. So I often come here. I can see them best from this angle."

He looked up at her sheepishly, as if to apologize for appearing as a child. "I am now very glad that I never grew up to join them. I'm afraid I might have, they seemed so noble from a distance. But as you can see from here, there is nothing but madness in it."

Marta shuddered in agreement as he led her out of the fray.

"You...saved...me," she huffed between ragged breaths.

"Oh, no," he demurred. "You were perfectly safe. They are like holograms, really. Not as real as they look. But a powerful teaching tool. You must have had some experience with them in your past."

Marta looked at him in surprise.

"You hadn't thought of that yet, had you? Well, just as well. It will all come to you in time."

"Yes, I'm sure it will," she mumbled, as lightning bursts of recognition exploded in her mind. She'd simply never thought of it. Until now, she'd been so busy taking in all the wonders, glorying in the beauty here, cramming her mind full of knowledge. Had she been storing up positive experiences to prepare her for this?

"Look here," the young boy-who-really-wasn't said to her. "You'd better step back a bit and take a seat. Over there," he pointed, "some benches for spectators. I'm afraid you were so intent on whatever it was you wanted to know that you chose a very prime location for your first experience of the war theater!" He grinned. "Now that you've had your taste, I'm sure your Teachers won't mind if you take a longer view."

She looked closely at him, his face so full of compassion and wisdom. Wasn't he her Teacher?

"Who, me?" he responded. "Well, perhaps." He blushed. "You've blown my cover! That's why I like to come here. To hide out for a bit. You know, being a Teacher isn't all fun and games. We have our own karmic residue to wrestle with. I will also be going back soon—although not too soon. I believe you will be returning long before me."

"I will? Do you know when?"

"*When* is such a relative concept!" he laughed. "It's better to ask yourself, what do I still need to learn to help me in my next lifetime? That's what you'll be wishing you'd asked once you get there, believe me. That much I remember quite clearly!"

She thought about that for a moment and agreed that he must be right. "Yes, thank you—I will do that," she managed to utter before he vanished from sight. Or rather, before she vanished from his and reappeared in yet another location.

She was sitting in a room facing a blank, wall-sized white screen. Compared to the spacious opera house and art museums and libraries, even the history theaters, this little room felt terribly like a room in an Earth house, cramped and claustrophobic with white walls and ceiling pressing close around her—meaning the ceiling was only twenty feet above her and actually looked "solid" instead of filled with kaleidoscopic mists, and the walls that formed the twenty-by-thirty-foot room appeared impenetrable.

But the seating was extremely comfortable, as Marta discovered when she leaned back against a soft head pillow. As she let herself relax, the reclining seat molded perfectly to her energy body and soothed her with tiny electrical impulses. She closed her eyes but could still feel the warm, colored energies playing over her from an exquisite lens configuration overhead. It looked like an Earth chandelier, only here the purpose of the inverted crystal pyramid was known.

A gentle voice spoke words into her mind. "Relax, Marta," Coriskancsia urged. "You can't see me but I am with you—much as I will be while you're on Earth."

This was so different from everything she'd experienced thus far! So formal! Even Coriskancsia sounded serious and perhaps a little dismal. Or was that Marta's imagination? She knew what this place was—she'd been told. And she was afraid.

"It's perfectly understandable," Coriskancsia said. "But not knowing should frighten you more."

She'd never considered that.

"The courage you show now will make a huge difference in your life to come. Would you prefer ignorance of your past lives, to repeat errors you might otherwise master before they get out of hand? You can't avoid the replay of your past, but you can enter in with knowledge. You don't want to repeat lessons you should have learned, do you? That will only delay your soulic development."

For an instant Marta wasn't so sure. Then she reconsidered.

Going back—repeating life experiences that she'd already lived. It sounded far more stifling and restrictive than sitting in this little room with the blank screen! She only had to remember the opera, and the paintings, and even the young boy at the war theater who was himself already a Teacher of great wisdom. Or to think of all the books in the cosmic library that she would love to be able to open! To think what it must be like to live here permanently—to have mastered all her earth lessons and developed her mind to such a fine point that it was capable of sustaining her in this beautiful world or another one like it *full time*—never to be reborn again in a shell of physical atoms, so dull and heavy and prone to breakdowns.

And to be able to serve others, to give of herself as Coriskancsia was giving, to dip into her overflowing heart and share widely the unutterable joy she'd been tasting here ...

As these reasons to go on passed rapidly through her mind, Marta realized Coriskancsia was projecting many of them to her, enhancing her own ideas to strengthen her conviction and bolster her courage.

"All right, all right! Enough!" Marta exclaimed. "You're right. I know."

"Yes, dear," Coriskancsia said softly.

"Okay then." Marta drew in a deep breath—an old Earth habit for centering herself. "Let's get on with it. What's first?"

"First, we take a trip back to Switzerland."

Before Marta could feel a moment's uneasiness, she was standing in the kitchen of her old home where her youngest son, Carl, sat at the table and his wife Bettina rinsed dishes at the sink. The warm, familiar sensations of home filled her senses, pushing out the realization that the screen in the little room hadn't really been necessary—it was only a prop. Because here she was in her old house, feeling as alive as ever. No flat screen could do that! But clearly things had changed.

Coriskancsia didn't need to narrate. Marta just *knew* things. For instance, she knew suddenly that Hans was a younger soul than she.

"More physically-biased," Coriskancsia agreed.

And that because he still had much earth-learning to achieve, he would benefit from reincarnating very quickly after his accidental death, which he had done. Maybe that explained why he hadn't met her when she "crossed over," as so many people believed would happen?

"Very true, Marta. The fact that you didn't look for him or ask about him or expect him only proves this difference between you. In your higher self, you knew, didn't you? You were not really compatible, spiritually speaking. But you did care for one another."

Marta had to agree. She'd been so busy, she hadn't even thought of poor Hans, killed by a farm accident at such a young age. Now she blushed at the omission. It seemed ungrateful somehow.

Her eyes were drawn irresistibly to the old crib, abandoned in the kitchen's corner. It had been handed down for generations on Hans's side of the family and it reminded her of the red-faced, squirmy little creature born just before her own passage from the physical body, Carl and Bettina's firstborn—

"*No! Truly? Hans?!*"

"Exactly," Coriskancsia said.

"But why didn't I know this?"

"Be patient. There is much you don't know; that is why we are here."

Marta ignored the affront to her ego. She was much too distracted by the influx of memories about the way Carl and his wife hadn't wanted to expose the baby to his grandmother's sickness; how they worried that the baby's fussing would disturb the elderly woman's rest. But Marta had insisted on seeing him, and while she drew breath, she was still in charge. They had finally given in.

"The moment I laid eyes on him, that little baby lifted my heart!" she told Coriskancsia now. "No wonder! Poor Hans. He was such a strong man; how he must hate being trapped in that tiny body!" She laughed. And the more she imagined how confined he must feel, the clearer the newborn Dario appeared in her consciousness.

Had he looked at all like Hans? No more than a grandson looks like his grandfather, she decided. The family resemblance was there. *I wonder if he acts like his grandfather, his former self? If he has any mannerisms that might give him away?*

As her curiosity rose, Marta forgot all about Coriskancsia and the little room with the screen. All she knew was the kitchen in which she stood, looking around for Dario in the rustic house, which Carl and Bettina had moved into after Marta was gone. And then she knew: Carl was the youngest, but his older brothers respected his need for a larger winter home for his new family. They agreed that he should move into their mother's house in the valley with his bride and new son. Soon after, they converted the little building Carl and Bettina lived in when they were first married to a real barn for the livestock, replacing the old lean-to. Marta discovered this when she looked out the window.

She could see how Carl had worked the farm, and when she looked at his face, she was shocked at how old and lined it had grown.

"My poor, dear son! Has life been so hard for you?" she exclaimed, reaching her hands out to him, then wringing them with concern. Instinctively, she knew she could not touch him and that he could not hear her, but the full awareness of her discarnate status evaporated in the immediacy of her feelings for Carl.

She turned to see Bettina leaning over the sink, wiping a fallen strand of hair from her damp forehead with a soapy hand. She, too, looked tired, and older. Vanished was the fresh bloom of youth that had so enlivened the couple during Marta's lifetime.

And then she saw him—Dario running across the field, his books swinging wildly out behind him as he swung the strap carelessly, leaping over a hedge that divided yard from pasture. She caught her breath. "Hans? Oh, Hans!" Tears streamed down her face.

Dario looked to be almost ten years old and he so closely resembled his grandfather Hans, she suddenly knew that the family often remarked about it. "You'll take over one day and run the farm," they used to tell him when he was three, and by the time he was five, Dario was telling them.

"I'm going to be master of the farm!" he proudly informed any stranger who listened. "Then you see how much milk my cows will give!"

When he was a baby and Carl bounced him on his knee, the young father often found himself rubbing a tear away, the boy so touched his heart and made him think of days spent with his own father. He often wished Hans were alive to see his grandson. But at least Carl's mother had lived just long enough to smile over the newest addition to the family.

All this Marta *knew* as the boy burst through the wooden door. But it was his expression that made her throat catch. How many times had she seen Hans come in from his early milking, his cheeks flushed in just that way? His eyes lighted as if by the sun that was still the merest sliver touching the highest peaks.

Something in those early mornings always seemed to ignite the spirit in Hans, and more often than not, he swept her into his arms and planted a joyful kiss on her cheek—a quick peck because of the children, of course, but filled with love. This was in their early years together, before the incident that cast a dark shadow over their lives...

Marta couldn't help herself. She reached out her arms to the young boy careening through the door toward her, expecting to scoop him up into a warm hug—but he passed right through her! It was a shock for which she was totally unprepared.

She'd forgotten that she was no longer living among these people! Forgotten that she was much more than one short lifetime...

Panic seized her. How had she gotten here? How would she get back? She spun now—sideways, upside down—a terrible sensation, out of control, plummeting through clouds of black energy. She tried to fight back the terror and remember...

It came back in a rush.

"Coriskancsia!" she screamed.

"Yes, dear, I am here."

The voice was so calm, Marta felt as if she'd skidded to a halt. She opened her eyes, panting, and there stood Coriskancsia in a blue gown, her eyes like jewels of pure Love.

"You are here, Marta, where you belong. You never left."

"But—"

"Only your thoughts traveled, dear. That is how powerful thoughts can be."

"But it was so real! I could smell the apples on the wooden table!"

"Yes, dear. It was real—but, well, not in the sense that you will believe things to be 'real' when you are reincarnated in a physical body."

Marta thought that over, and decided she couldn't understand it yet. "But why did I need to go there? What did I need to see? I thought you brought me here to look at past lives!"

"In a sense, you just did. You are not Marta anymore, are you?"

Quite honestly, she had never thought about the fact that it was an old name now—a used-up name. So who was she now?

"We will get to that later. But first you must realize that many Earth cycles have passed since you left that planet. You traveled back in time and into space to see individuals you will meet again in your next Earth life. You may not recognize them immediately, or perhaps not at all. But we are trying to make certain that when and if you do, you will be able to take full advantage of the opportunity. Working here, now, we can give you some advantage over the dull insensitivity your new physical body will impose." Coriskancsia patted her hand. "So if you are ready, let us continue."

Marta wasn't sure she was ready, but she nodded anyway. She wanted to get this over with as soon as possible.

11

Relationships

$\mathcal{A}$s *she opened her* mind to receive the information, Marta knew instantly that she was in a place of danger—not like the war theater where the horsemen were merely holograms. The blood spraying toward her was too real, and the shouts and screams and stench and deadly clashes of metal that pierced her eardrums were too familiar.

Men in dark shreds of slashed and torn homespun fell to the ground all around her or staggered from wounds not yet fatal, clutching stomachs or groping for missing limbs. She gave in to instincts to crouch, and swing, and heave, and dip, until finally her instinct for survival overpowered all else and she turned to flee from this field of senseless slaughter.

As she spun around in desperation, forgetting that she was here in consciousness only and not truly the hulk of a man she believed herself to be, she thudded into a figure lying at her feet. His still-open eyes were glazing over in death as pain wrenched him slowly from his physical body.

She froze to the spot. *My hand felled him.*

The recognition struck her more fiercely than any broadsword, cleaved her mind with remorse. That last blow she had heaved—blindly, madly—she felt it strike solid, stop for an instant, then give way as the blade sank home.

And now she stood dumb with horror, staring down at the victim she hadn't truly seen. *He's only a boy—a mere boy!*

The sound that erupted from her bearded throat was not human, could not be, for she felt like a beast who deserved to die. She turned wildly from this horrible evidence of her inhumanity with a death-wish that plunged her huge body back into the fighting with but one purpose fixed in her mind: to reap the fate she had so carelessly, with a single blow, convicted herself to suffer.

Without hesitation, her enemies swiftly carried out her self-sentence and she slumped to the ground in a pool of her own blood, fleeing painfully from her body. She did not travel to a higher world of enlightenment, but into a hell of her own making.

Wild, grotesque forms careened toward her. Menacing faces laughing maniacally. Bony fingers from bloody fields grasped toward her. They laced into her hair and yanked her head from side to side. Pain pierced every part of her body as she flailed her arms and legs to find some kind of solid ground on which to balance herself and mount a defense, but to no avail. She twisted and spun in dark space but she was not alone. All around she heard and smelled and felt the anguish of the dead and dying, victims of violence—her own and others'. The pain she felt in every region of her body was more than physical; it shredded into her soul.

"Marta," Coriskancsia steadily repeated the name her charge might recognize. "Marta, wake up. You are here with me; you have never left. You are a Being of Light, Marta, a student of the Infinite. Come back to me."

As she spoke, colored beams of healing Light played over Marta's still form from the crystal lenses above. The power of

Coriskancsia's thoughts added another measure of Love to this projection. Marta's confusion of identity held her trapped in a subastral dimension.

But that hellish nightmare world into which she'd thrust herself so long ago in her moments of suicidal despair no longer resonated with "Marta's" psychic anatomy. Long, long ago the Brotherhood had sent specially-trained emissaries to rescue her (and others like her). They were motivated by her own expressed desires to change her circumstances (they would not have interfered otherwise) and powered, in part, by the love of family members who cried out on her behalf, who supplied an earthly energy-force the Brothers could redirect to aid her in their rescue work, where they must reach into this lower-frequency world of thought-forms without succumbing themselves.

Before her fall that day on the battlefield, lifetimes and eons before, she had been a soul of some training and development. This also supplied a beacon of harmonic connection to help the Brothers locate her, lost as she was in self-created torment. Only a highly skilled, elite team of Lighted Ones attempted such rescues, and their success depended completely on the state of mind of the one they reached. By the time they found her, she was ready to go with them.

Since then, she had undergone so much rehabilitation that a mere glance back was not likely to consign her permanently to a lower frequency. But until now, she had not gained full awareness of all the implications and circumstances surrounding this incident.

Coriskancsia understood the risks of showing her more. Her student could relive the trauma and fall back again, as she had just done. But her Teachers felt she was strong enough this time to pull herself back out. And the lesson needed to be mastered before she could progress further on her spiritual journey.

Coriskancsia called her name again. "Marta. Come back to us."

This time Marta's eyes reopened to meet her Teacher's brilliant gaze.

"What happened?" she mumbled. "Where am I?"

Coriskancsia touched her hand and a ring of gold rippled up Marta's arm.

"Ohhhhhhh," she groaned, jerking up from the reclining seat as the tears exploded.

She felt as devastated as if she were still in the body of the grizzled fighting man. Convulsing sobs of remorse tortured her energy body and she rocked it like a baby, holding her midsection, feeling as if her stomach would turn inside out. She struggled to speak, gulping in habit for air that didn't exist, which would have been useless to her energy-lungs anyway.

She had to know.

"Who? Who was he?" she managed in spurts. "The boy—"

"You know the answer already, don't you?" Coriskancsia replied gently.

Marta nodded with a renewed bout of choking remorse.

"And that is why you agreed to marry him in Switzerland, even though you knew he was not the one for whom you had waited and hoped."

"Then I'm glad I did!" she spat out, rubbing at the wetness on her cheeks. "Because I owed him a life—I owed him *my* life! I took his when he was only a boy! What was he doing on that field of death? Tell me, Coriskancsia, what were *any* of us doing there? Can you tell me that?" Her eyes filled with pleading confusion, guilt, remorse, and despair.

Coriskancsia merely smiled with compassion, letting her face reply to questions Marta knew the answers to. She knew them deep in her soul, for she had spent lifetimes searching them out, experiencing them, hammering them out of the hard steel of painful circumstance, beating them out of her own flesh, and wringing them out in tears.

But Coriskancsia added one thing that Marta had not yet

realized.

"He was one of your teachers."

She looked up at her Teacher in surprise. "But I thought you said—"

"A younger soul, yes, I did."

"Then how could he be? I don't understand."

"Our teachers in life come in many forms. That boy, younger soul that he is, taught you that you do not want to serve as a soldier. That there is no honor or glory in hacking apart the bodies of others who are, in Infinite Truth, your brothers and sisters in the Circle of Life. That boy is one of the reasons you are here now! Because from that day forward, you strove mightily to become a better human being than what you felt you were on that battlefield—or countless other fields of conflict before it. And my dear, on this point you have succeeded!"

She had trouble accepting this.

"It is very important that you believe me. And now, after your lives together in Switzerland, you have repaid your 'Hans' with the many lessons you taught him—more than you will ever know, which is as it should be. We do not need to take credit for our good works. They are the products of Infinite Intelligence coursing through us, as naturally as rivers seek the sea on your planet. Your striving will always draw many others along in your wake, including those you may never meet.

"Yet that battlefield was not the first time you and your Hans had met. There are other lives, older lives and experiences that remain between you. But you will have opportunities in your next encounter."

"Is he here, then?" Light broke across her face. "Are we to prepare together?" *Maybe his life as Dario helped him catch up to me,* she thought wildly, still suffused with guilt.

"No, my dear. He is, as we have already said, a younger soul— as were many of those you knew in Switzerland—so he is preparing himself in a different way, at a different level. When the time is right, you will meet again and that will be your opportunity to test your new convictions in the fires of life experience."

Coriskancsia draped a slender arm over her shoulders and helped her to her feet.

"Now that you know the screen was only an aid to help you become accustomed to viewing your past, let us find a more comfortable setting for our discussion!" She filled the little room with her smile and a wink. "I know just the thing to raise your spirits."

❋ ❋

Coriskancsia took her to the crystal woods at the edge of the city. They passed through the glistening trees, where birds sang and squirrels scampered tamely beside them, to emerge at the edge of a forested cliff. A shimmering, green-blanketed plain stretched below and beyond as far as her inner eye could see.

How limited her perception of this world had been! The endless meadow with its peacefully waving grasses of pure, gleaming crystal and its patches of fuschia and purple flowers stretched up low-lying slopes and down into little valleys. But she was awestruck by what lay beyond the meadow.

A steep mountain of rainbow-reflecting crystal rose abruptly from the plain. Perched on its highest reaches gleamed a crystal castle—or maybe a temple, or a school? Because here, Marta now understood, a gracefully arranged and elaborately domed and spired structure did not automatically mean "church" or "castle" as it might on Earth (although on Earth such magnificence existed only in faint echoes by comparison). She'd seen dazzling buildings here already, but this—she could not imagine the purpose for such a grand and imposing structure.

"Is that also a product of the Minds who inhabit this world?" she whispered in awe. It frustrated her that she could not think of a more intelligent way to express the emotions that welled at the sight of it.

Coriskancsia nodded silently.

So many questions tumbled through her mind at once that even if she'd been able to ask them, she wouldn't be able to focus her mind on any answers Coriskancsia might provide.

She didn't yet realize that she need not rush her learning in this timeless dimension. Even if she had to wait until after she returned to Earth, she could return here in a moment's thought and pick up with Coriskancsia right where she left off. No limitations.

So they stood quietly for a long time, watching a spotted fawn munch green crystals at the base of the cliff while his mother stood guard, her ears flicking back and forward, sensing every sound and movement for miles in the distance. No danger existed here for the pair, of course, but like Marta, the doe practiced skills she would need later, when she, too, returned to Earth.

From the open plain, a flock of bright-colored birds with tremendous wingspans lifted off and swooped toward where they stood on the cliff. On any earthworld, these birds would terrify simply because of their enormous size. Should they take cover? She glanced at her teacher. Coriskancsia raised a hand skyward. Marta dearly hoped this was some form of friendly greeting.

But then she saw the scintillating energies stream upward from Coriskancsia's fingertips. As the birds flew near, they dipped down to scoop the golden sparkles into their beaks, as if skimming a drink from a pond.

"What is that?" Marta asked with some relief as they flew back into the distance, streaking the sky with brilliant rose and gold and blue.

"A snack to keep them flying brightly," Coriskancsia winked.

And Marta reminded herself that every single living element of this world depended on the energy of Infinite Intelligence for sustenance—including her. That thought kept her preoccupied for another long silence.

Love-food, she decided. *That's what keeps them all going! Me, too! And we are also the products of our own minds—in my case, one not capable of existing here without a lot of help from my Elders.*

She looked again at Coriskancsia, took in her luscious waves of now-silvery hair which contrasted so strikingly with the deep purple scarves draped over her shoulders. They fell to the ground, accents for a gown that glimmered with tiny faceted crystals. When she moved, the crystals sparked pastel rainbows into the atmosphere.

I want to be like her. She epitomizes feminine beauty! I can't imagine anyone more beautiful, or intelligent. She knows every-thing about everything! How far must I go, how long will it take me to achieve her state of brilliance?

Coriskancsia laughed gently and little oscillations of lavender light emanated from her as she did.

"My dear child! I am so far from achieving my own goals! You have placed me on a pedestal from which I shall surely fall in the next instant, or the one after that," she laughed. "But I do remember having similar feelings about my own Teachers. I still do. In your very near future you may meet others who will change your mind about me. For now, though, let me just say that you are not so far as you believe from achieving a more infi-nite state of mind—nor are you as close as you might imagine!"

Her laughter rang out in happy peals—not derisive or sarcas-tic in any way, but the happiest sound Marta had ever heard. She couldn't help but join in.

As their laughter faded, Coriskancsia added, "That is why we are so fortunate, my dear. We have so many wonderful develop-ments to witness in ourselves as our souls awaken to new and higher realities of life! For this path we've chosen is never-end-ing—oh, but I sound like one of those books they have on your world these days, full of trite platitudes," she added with a grin and a cluck of her tongue.

"You see? I am not so perfect. I am told that my language leans toward the over-expressive at times, as does my choice of dress!" She laughed again. "But of course, no one chastises me for this. They merely shake their heads and smile. I know they're glad that I finally dropped that drab, black nun's habit I was so fond of in previous lifetimes. Now they wish I would drop some of her old ideas—and so do I! But we can only progress at our own pace—tch! There I go again, spouting silly clichés! You see what I mean? That's why they call it a nun's *habit!*"

And she laughed so hard she lifted into a wild dance that spun her onto her back in midair. She threw back her head and sent gales of laughing energy reverberating through the crystal woods, until all the glassy leaves tinkled in soft reply.

A nun? Coriskancsia? Not possible! Marta could not imagine this woman spouting a nun's doctrine, nor the dogma of any religion for that matter. She found it hard to grasp that her Teachers had lessons of their own to learn.

"Oh, yes! Of course!" Coriskancsia put herself upright again, softly setting her feet back on the grass. "And I should not laugh. My lives in religions truly set me back in my course—nasty to overcome, those misconcepts. But I will never stop my efforts to do so, because it is the only way.

"So you see, I am not only helping you. You, my dear, are helping me learn what it means to be a full-fledged member of the Universal Brotherhood. We learn together." She slipped a slender hand in Marta's. "That temple in the distance?"

"So that's what it is!" Waves of warmth flowed into her palm from Coriskancsia's touch, and into her mind as it filled with recognition of the temple. It had felt distantly familiar, as if she'd dreamed it, but now...

"It is of a higher frequency than where we stand, you see. We are only viewing it mentally, and remember, our minds are capable of stretching into much higher frequencies than those we presently inhabit. In fact, that is a good thing for you to remember when you reincarnate. This is excellent practice for you!" Coriskancsia patted her hand.

Marta stared at the crystal spires, which radiated first one color and then another, giving the whole a blinding, mother-of-pearl luminescence. Her mind must be stretching to its utmost capacity to perceive the temple at all, she realized.

"Coriskancsia," she said. "My next lifetime—will it be hard?"

"That will be up to you, my dear. Totally up to you. But what you're doing now will definitely make it easier. Everything will be easier if you can take in as much as possible while you're here with us. And after you reincarnate, you'll not only have me looking over your shoulder but others as well."

"Others? How many others?"

"Countless numbers. Now let's get back to work. There are a few more things we want you to know before you begin your training."

"Training?"

"Isn't there something you love more than anything in the universe? Something that makes even a dull and heavy physical form into an instrument of creative expression?"

Marta looked at her blankly.

"Hm. Well, perhaps you'll remember it soon enough. I understand you're going to a very special performance later on that should help to remind you. It's true that you did not use this ability in your most recent lifetime."

She looked into the distance, as if seeing Marta's past. Then she clapped her hands as if to change the mood and said, "So let us find a nice, comfy spot..."

She glanced around the clearing where they stood at the cliff's edge. "Yes, this will do." She indicated a towering, crystal pine. Sprinkled beneath it, among the feather-crystal grasses, glowed tiny white and yellow and pink blossoms, which made the area look as if it were covered by a fluffy comforter with a delicate floral design.

Coriskancsia's narrow gown and trailing purple scarves transformed as she settled in beneath the tree. They flowed around her like mist to create a soft blanket for Marta, which she patted invitingly. "Why don't you lie down?" she suggested. "I think you'll feel more at peace."

Instantly, Marta drifted down on the cushiony layer and lost consciousness again, although a better description would be *changed* consciousness.

Her mind freed itself from the illusion of physical form she'd been maintaining. Her thoughts began to drift in timeless, space-less consciousness. But with Coriskancsia and others guiding, Marta's mind soon zoomed back through Earth centuries to her life as a woman in a barely civilized setting. Distinctly, Marta heard Coriskancsia's familiar voice direct her gently, gently, gently into a scene that was anything but gentle.

The screams that suddenly pierced her hearing were her own. Sweat poured off her brow as she thrashed about on a sodden mat of bedclothes over straw, shouting what must have been pro-fanities, judging from the way she spit them out through gnash-ing teeth. She didn't recognize the language at first. Then, after a moment, everything became clear. Too clear.

She was in the throes of labor, but she knew with perfect clar-ity that the baby was too early—at least two months early. More shocking were the emotions that coursed through her mind in pulses that kept time with the contractions: anger, pain, terror, despair, and overpowering hatred. She twisted and contorted, threw off the ministrations of what must have been two mid-wives—rustic-looking women who tried to pat her brow with damp cloths between ducking her blows and flinching at her foul expressions.

"I will *not* have this baby!" she chanted through clenched teeth. "I will not, will not, will NOT," she screamed in escalat-ing volume. "I never wanted this brat and I—"

A stabbing pain wrenched through her, cutting off breath and words.

"Breathe with me," Coriskancsia cooed in Marta's mind. "Let

go of that body; it is not you, only a memory," her spiritual mentor coached—and to her, Marta listened.

With great effort she drew a mental breath—inhaled long and deeply, taking in a spiritual Essence she knew to be with her this time. In a flash she separated from the form writhing on the straw mat.

Now she looked down at it with disgust. The desired effect had been accomplished: Marta felt the thoughts in that woman's mind—her own mind—and they were vile. Surely such anger and hatred killed that innocent babe struggling toward life? So foul were these emotions—did they not kill her own soul?

"No dear, not your soul, but your body, yes, in a few hours. Both you and the unfortunate child died from this self-inflicted trauma. Wake up now, here with me, beneath the trees of the crystal forest, and I will explain."

Marta opened her eyes painfully, as if the Light from Coriskancsia's face hurt them. She wanted to cry but she could not. She thought she should be feeling tremendous remorse, but she did not. She felt cold and clammy. She felt nothing. Least of all for the child who did not survive her body's rejection of it.

"I killed that baby, didn't I?" she asked quietly. "With my own hatred."

Her eyes widened as she realized all the implications of the re-experienced emotions.

"They are so powerful…I had no idea…I didn't realize that's what I was doing, but it was true what that woman screamed. What *I* screamed. I did not want that baby! I felt as if it were an alien force invading my temple, my body, my life. What could I do but defend myself? I would have done anything to be free of it—in fact, I tried, didn't I? But they stopped me somehow. Still, they could not stop my thoughts …and neither could I," she trailed off in stunned recognition.

Coriskancsia remained silent.

"Why?" She felt weak, as if she had once again lost too much blood and were barely holding on to life. She could not die this time, though. She was already "dead."

"Ask yourself," Coriskancsia encouraged. "This skill of self-searching will serve you well in the future. The answer lies within your own psychic anatomy, your true energy Self, embedded there for all eternity—unless and until you do something to change its imprint."

The light broke into Marta's traumatized mind and her eyes flickered up at Coriskancsia. "This soul who tried to enter the world through my womb…was no stranger? No innocent babe?"

"Exactly."

"Was it a boy or a girl? Oh, but that wouldn't matter, would it? Why did I hate this soul so thoroughly? No—not hate. It felt like hate. But it was really blind fear, wasn't it?"

"That is a story that you will discover, for you will meet this individual again. And in your new lifetime, you will find more opportunities to learn the answers. And more opportunities to improve your relationship.

"Your experience is not so rare, unfortunately. Many miscarriages and stillbirths are the result of destructive pasts shared by mother and child, or even father and child. But a mother's body becomes so intertwined with her infant's that this is a most dangerous and important time, a soul's entrance into an earth world.

"Sometimes, the working out of past-life imbalances occurs during this interaction, and the child's life does not need to continue, for the two souls have 'mysteriously' resolved their past differences and their higher purpose is fulfilled. It may be the outpouring of a mother's unconditional love that heals their past— or the infant's for its mother—a love they never felt toward one another when they were rivals or enemies over some trivial issue of physical life."

Coriskancsia sighed. "Each circumstance is so unique, dear. I cannot tell you how every encounter between souls will unfold. But the energy principles of soulic responsibility always apply:

What you do remains with you; what you do to others is multiplied in its impact on your own self. And if you share destructive thoughts and deeds with another, you will meet again, drawn together by this bond. Depending on the souls involved, you may try to change this negative bond in subsequent lives. And therein lies progress, albeit in the slow, methodical way of many lives over a long period. You, my dear, have stepped on a faster beam now."

"But I failed, didn't I?" Marta couldn't forget the scene of her thrashing, angry body, suffering and hating all at once. "I fought this incoming soul with all my might, as if we were swinging swords at one another!"

"And well you might have been, for the result was similar. The sensation you felt during your pregnancy, of having the life sucked from you, was not your imagination. Neither is your present belief that your thoughts killed this unborn child. You fought one another like the devils you'd become, for it only takes a thought to change a saint to a devil, if we can cautiously borrow some terminology from Earth's religions. One single thought can change your mental bias from constructive to destructive. Imagine what a barrage of thoughts can do! The child you conceived entered your aura with vengeance in mind, and you, recognizing an enemy, fought for your life! But you both lost this battle."

"Was it—"

"No, this was not your Hans. Do you recognize the difference in your feelings?"

Now that she mentioned it, Marta didn't feel the same overwhelming grief and remorse she had felt on the real battlefield. This time she felt nothing.

"With 'Hans,' you felt remorse while still in your body—and began to grieve even then. With this individual, you died fighting, still angry and full of fear and hatred. In your present state of elevated consciousness, such emotions are foreign. They leave you feeling empty, yes?"

Marta nodded.

"Your history with this second individual is quite difficult," Coriskancsia added with uncharacteristic bluntness.

That answered Marta's question about why, of all her thousands of past-life experiences, this comparative nanosecond of her existence had been presented to her.

"We are choosing information that will help you prepare, dear. Your karma with this individual remains unresolved. You will meet again."

Marta felt a thud in the pit of her stomach. "Will I recognize this soul?" she managed to ask.

"I do not know. That will depend on you."

"And what will I do if I do recognize them? He or she will be full of hatred, surely, after what I did! After all, despite what you say, I was the adult. I was supposed to be the mother! Mothers who kill their children..." She couldn't complete the thought.

"Shhhh," her teacher soothed. "We all learn about love through the most difficult situations. You are still learning, I am still learning. We must not condemn ourselves, but only strive to improve. And now I sense that you have seen enough for the time being. Come. Let us change our frequency."

She added knowingly as they stood up, "Do not be concerned over your lack of compassion for that soul. Healing in a situation like this takes time, often many lifetimes. Right now, you are still in a form of psychic shock. But one day, you will bring together all the threads of your learning, your understanding, your compassion, and your spiritual growth, and the full and total healing will seem to occur in an instant."

Marta heard her encouragements but they tumbled through her mind without connecting as she followed Coriskancsia numbly back to the city.

Much later, after she returned to the place that was her own on this world, her energy body reclined in a restful state that mimicked Earth sleep. The Teachers encouraged this for those more familiar with earthly life than with the non-physical existence. It gave the soul time to process new information, much like dreaming on Earth.

As Marta lay comfortably on her glowing blue energy bed, her mind filled with scenes of other experiences she had lived with the individual who tried to become her child. Her Teachers drew the information from her psychic anatomy's memory banks and highlighted it for her as she drowsed. None of it was pleasant.

When the time was right for her while living on Earth, this preconditioning might help her be more receptive to the pertinent facts as her Teachers presented them mentally, details to help her survive and conquer the challenges she would experience from this relationship. It would not be easy for her. But such challenges are the fires in which a strong soul is forged. There is no other way. And no guarantees.

If she survived her birth, the length and quality of her ensuing life would depend on how much she had learned, and how well she could apply it. She'd have help—but only in a measure to match her own inner strength and desire.

12

The Helping Hand

Was that really Maureen? The gray-haired woman in her vision right before she fell asleep? The thought did nothing to quell Amy's guilt about her anger at the grieving girl.

If she could come up with a good excuse, she would skip school for the rest of the week. She feared her friends would sense the fury that simmered through her when she should feel only sympathy for Maureen. But she couldn't think clearly anymore at all, and no Lights appeared to guide her way.

She needn't have worried. When she arrived at school that morning, her friends barely noticed her. It was Maureen's father who died, not their own, but the proximity of death frightened them all into silence. When they ate lunch together as always, no one laughed. Even the ever-optimistic Pam could find nothing upbeat to say. She sulked into her sandwich, uncharacteristically mute.

Still, Amy knew none of them felt like she did. Try as she did, she could not appease her anger toward Maureen. The girl had behaved hatefully from the first and Amy could not forgive her, bereaved or not. She sighed as she added this new dark element to her growing storehouse of secrets.

Far back in her mind, a glimmer of a thought suggested that perhaps her anger was out of proportion to Maureen's faults, but Amy couldn't hear this faint echo of the Other Voice very well. She was too mad.

Maybe Maureen's mother will move them back to Wilton, she nursed a wild hope, *and I'll never come face to face with her again!*

But a week after the funeral Maureen came back to school. The skin on the back of Amy's neck prickled alternately with disgust, then guilt, every time she saw her. All day she managed to avoid any direct encounters. Then classes let out.

Amy, intent also on avoiding Jeremy as she'd been doing all week, took a detour out the front door instead of her usual back-door exit and ran smack into Maureen.

Well, not exactly. She ran into the sight of her standing alone, leaning against the big beech tree on the front lawn near the sidewalk. Gloomy gray clouds scuttled across the April sky, pushed by a chill wind, as if trying to decide whether to drop late snow or break to let the weak sunshine through.

She must be waiting for a ride home. Amy gathered the collar of a beige trench coat around her neck (color chosen by her mother, of course).

Quickly she shifted behind a cluster of chattering sophomores so that Maureen wouldn't see her, so she wouldn't have to try to think of something to say. *Like what? "I'm sorry your dad died—but really if you want to know the truth, I don't care because I hate you"?*

If only she'd joined Pam's church when she had the chance! She could go to Confession and get this terrible burden off her mind. Maybe a few Hail Marys would remove the sting of her own conscience.

But she knew they wouldn't.

As she turned to sneak back inside, Amy glimpsed another flash of the fair-haired woman. This time her face looked sad, not arrogant. And something about Amy's feelings toward her: it was strange, but they connected somehow to the sight of Maureen standing alone under that tree with grief permeating the air around her.

On an impulse that took Amy completely by surprise, she suddenly changed her course. Before she could stop herself, she was walking toward Maureen saying, "Hi," and slipping in beside the forlorn figure to lean against the beech trunk, which was wide enough for two backs.

Maureen looked over at her, eyes glazed in disinterest. "Oh. Hi Amy."

What am I doing? Have I finally flipped out? Just gone right over the edge?! her mind screamed. But her mouth disobeyed: "I was wondering if you'd like to come over this weekend, you know, spend some time together Saturday. Maybe we can go to a movie?" *What am I saying?*

"Yeah? Um, I dunno…"

"It'll be fun. You've never been to my house, have you?" *Who is this chatty idiot operating my mouth?*

"No, I don't think so…" Maureen hesitated.

"Come on," urged some part of Amy she didn't recognize. Except for Pam, she rarely invited friends over. She let them invite her instead. Easier to avoid explanations about her mother. *So why am I doing this?*

A bright gold light flashed in the air above Maureen's head.

No, Amy thought, *I don't want to think about you right now. Go away!*

It flashed a second time, proving that at this moment, like it or not, her wiser self was in charge—the eternal, interdimensional "Amy" who knew a lot more than life as a teenager in the twentieth century.

Maureen looked at her for a moment. "Well, maybe—I guess

it would be okay," she shrugged without enthusiasm.

"Great!" Amy cried. She propelled herself off the tree as if shoved by an unseen hand. "Gotta run now—see you later!"

Consciously—meaning in her mundane, earthbound consciousness, the part of her that didn't remember who she really was—Amy had no idea what power had taken over her mind and body like that but, oddly, she felt relieved by what she'd done.

In fact, she felt like living again!

As she strode away with a ballet-straight back, layers of guilt she'd built up over the past week melted with each step she took. She didn't know if she still hated Maureen, but she had to admit she felt a thousand percent better than she had for days. She'd found a solution! She would be as good as she'd been evil!

Never mind missed ballet classes. Dancing didn't matter now! She'd been so depressed she hadn't thought of it for days anyway. Her new mission was clear: to cheer up Maureen. Doing a good deed meant being selfless, didn't it? So she would give up any thoughts about her own problems and focus on Maureen's. Having to force aside her anger to do it made her feel even more righteous about her new mission. Being a kind and generous person felt a lot better than hating, didn't it?

Although some vague part of her that she wouldn't acknowledge secretly dreaded the weekend, she let herself feel insatiably curious about what crazy thing she might say next, when the two of them were together for so many hours.

In a rush of manic enthusiasm, she called Jeremy the minute she got home. He didn't know anything about the tortured thoughts that had squirmed around in her mind all week, but he sounded glad to hear the lift in Amy's voice. He'd been upset like the others. Cheer from any source was welcome.

"So you won't mind if we don't see each other on Saturday," she pronounced as she explained her spontaneous invitation and made lame excuses for her week of avoidance.

"Nah," he offered generously. "I've got ball practice anyway."

He seemed to adjust very quickly but Amy was too busy chattering to give it much thought.

"I mean, we can be together all day Sunday if you want. But I think this will be good for Maureen, to be around friends again, get away from all that dreary mourning going on at her house. I'm going to talk her into seeing *Midnight Cowboy* in Wilton. They say it's a good movie and I like Dustin Hoffman."

"Yeah, I'm sure you're right. It's a good thing you're doing, Amy. Go ahead and have fun—but not too much fun without me," he teased, although he didn't really sound jealous.

She was preoccupied with thinking that he probably didn't realize how much this all meant to her, being able to do something kind. If you're helping someone, how can you hate them? It was so easy—why hadn't she thought of this before?

In the days leading up to the weekend, she felt as if some unseen force had taken over her life. Not an evil power. Quite the contrary! A force that was guiding her to take action. It was the only explanation she could think of for that sudden impulse to invite Maureen over. First the visions, then the Other Voice weaving in and out of her diary entries (although not lately), and the Lights (she'd stopped seeing them after that day under the beech tree, though)—and now this. If she wasn't so busy cleaning her room, and even picking up in the living room when her mother wasn't looking, she might have worried about her sanity again.

But it was her mother she worried about instead.

She'd already convinced Tom to drive them to Wilton and sit somewhere else with his friends in the movie theater so she and Maureen could be "alone." He always hated having to take his little sister places, but when Amy played the grieving friend card, how could he say no? She knew that even Tom got chills when he thought about Maureen losing her father.

And Beth—Amy encouraged her to stay overnight with her little friend Marcia on Saturday; she volunteered to put the question to their mother herself. Last thing they needed was Beth blurting out some embarrassing question about Maureen's father! She knew her own father would act his usual aloof but gracious self around her guest. But what about her mother? Would she get drunk as usual and make a scene?

When Maureen finally rang the bell on Saturday, Amy's palms were sweating.

Tom dropped them off an hour early for the three o'clock matinee, telling her he decided to skip it and would be at his friend Mike's house. He ordered them to wait on the sidewalk in front of the theater as soon as the movie let out. He'd be back for them. (He knew better than to lose his little sister in Wilton; he'd never get to borrow the station wagon again. Which was why asking him for forbidden rides to ballet class was out of the question. Amy knew his driving privileges meant more to him than sibling loyalty.)

To fill the hour, they decided to tour the steep main street of Wilton, down one side toward the river, up the other and back again to the movie theater.

Amy felt a little quiver in her stomach when they passed Mrs. Q's on the way down the hill and Mrs. Tildon's piano-playing drifted down to the sidewalk from the upstairs windows. She straightened her shoulders unconsciously, but this time it was her selfless chore at hand that stimulated her pride. Missing ballet, like pushing aside her anger, made her feel like she was really doing something in this good-deed attempt to lift Maureen's spirits. The more painful her own losses, the greater her sacrifice, the better she could allow herself to feel about her selfless deed.

Any sadness either of them felt vanished entirely when they got to Wilton Dry Goods, halfway up the other side of the street. They ignored the emaciated, gray-bunned clerk who glared at them as they tried on men's hats and performed loud imitations of people they knew as they set fedoras and dumb-looking fishing hats and sleek driving berets on their heads in sequence. They left the rack in a terrible mess. When the stern-faced clerk finally asked them to leave, they whined in mock innocence, "But we were only trying on hats!"

Once outside the double glass doors, they looked at each other for a minute and broke out in hysterical laughter.

"Did you see the look on her face?" Maureen gasped.

"Perfect!" Amy agreed.

Her pride deepened. Mission accomplished! Maureen was laughing and grinning and back to her old trouble-making self.

Maureen could be a lot of fun when she wasn't with a group of people, Amy decided. So why had she always avoided being alone with her? Amy didn't know, but had to stop wondering about it when a chill of last week's indignation over Maureen's teasing threatened to ruin everything.

She experienced another close call during the movie, which turned out to be horribly depressing. All her good intentions to "cheer up Maureen" seemed thwarted. Dustin Hoffman wasn't anything like the actor she remembered from *The Graduate*. He was nauseating to watch as he limped across the screen in this dark and twisted movie. Why on earth did people like it?

Amy watched helplessly out the corner of her eye as Maureen's mood crumbled and she sank visibly into her red-velvet seat in the stuffy theater, as one dreary New York sidewalk after another smeared across the movie screen. If this movie had a plot, neither of them got it. And the ending! It couldn't be worse! All her plans foiled by this terrible movie.

Amy's heart sank into its own red-velvet cocoon. She couldn't wait to get outside and breathe fresh air again. Of all the things she might have chosen, she felt stupid for bringing Maureen to see this particular movie. Being a compassionate do-gooder wasn't as easy as she'd thought.

By the time Tom skidded to a halt in front of the sidewalk (if his father knew how he drove that car, they'd be walking home now), Maureen had lapsed into complete silence. Amy's own mood wasn't much better.

When they got back to Deerhorn Creek, Amy's mother met them at the door and *she was sober*. Amy couldn't believe it; it was nearly six-thirty!

Her mother treated Maureen like an honored guest—had even fixed herself up a bit, wore blush and lipstick, with a supper of lasagna waiting for them. Her lasagna was famous on the local potluck circuit when Amy was little, but lately it lived up to its reputation only if her mother stayed sober until she put it safely in the oven. This time it was thick with two kinds of cheese and extra meat and spicy homemade red sauce, gooey and delicious.

Amy wondered if her mother took extra pains because of what Maureen might say when she got home. "What will the neighbors think?" was always a big concern for Yvonne Longwood.

Or was she trying to cheer Maureen too? Maybe Amy's new mission helped her mother as well, Amy mused in her diary that night, after they drove Maureen home. Doing good for others—that was the ticket! She'd convinced herself of that now, even though her first attempt fell flat. All through dinner, Maureen hardly said a word and everyone shifted around uncomfortably, trying to think of safe topics.

But Amy knew she could do better. She would try again!

This time the Other Voice didn't chime in, and no Lights danced over the page.

✳ ✳

Amy, determined to fulfill her new do-good aspirations, invited herself to spend the next Saturday with Maureen again. Pam wasn't happy to hear it because they'd made plans together for that day but Amy explained to her that Maureen actually smiled and laughed the previous Saturday, something no one else had seen her do since the funeral. (She omitted telling Pam about the depressing movie or the glum state in which she left Maureen that night.)

"You can come too, if you want," Amy offered, but Pam graciously declined.

"No, Ames, you go ahead. Maybe she'd clam up if the whole gang was there, you know? You say you didn't talk about her dad at all?"

"Not once."

"That's creepy. I mean, what if she needs to talk about it? I heard that people who're grieving need to talk about their deceased loved ones." Pam loved pop psychology. She planned to major in psychology when she got to college but said she didn't like traditional methods. She wanted to counsel people, not give them drugs or lock them up. Amy heartily agreed with this plan.

"I don't know, Pam," she said now. "She seemed pretty happy not to bring it up. I'm sure she's talked enough about it at home."

"Well, just keep it in mind. In case you get the opportunity, I mean."

This time Jeremy was even more supportive. He eagerly agreed that he could make do without her again. Vaguely Amy wondered why he wasn't worried about his friends for once. Wouldn't they tease him for being without his girl? Ridicule him the way guys do, and ask awkward questions? But she was too busy making plans to give it much thought.

So it was that a week later Maureen and Amy were rummaging through a sale table at Berkman's in Wilton, while Maureen's mother bought herself some new stockings.

Mrs. Widdington looked relieved that her daughter was doing something besides moping, and before she left the girls alone while she visited her mother (Maureen's "Gram" who lived in Wilton), she drew Amy aside and whispered, "I'm so glad you two girls are having fun! Thank you for taking care of my Maureen." She turned away quickly as her eyes filled up.

A few minutes later Mrs. Widdington was waving with manufactured cheer from the Buick window, "I'll pick you girls up in front of Massino's Books in two hours!"

Maureen brought up the subject of death all on her own.

"Amy—do you believe in reincarnation?"

They'd gone back inside by then to check out more sale tables. The question zoomed at Amy from nowhere so fast that she dropped a shoe she'd been holding while looking for its mate. Maureen was crouched down near the floor, digging through piles of carefully folded scarves waiting to be put up on the table. She looked up almost shyly at Amy from beneath her carefully parted hair, waiting for her response.

Once again the image of the fair-haired woman flashed through Amy's mind. She looked troubled.

"I don't know," she answered slowly. "I never thought about it before." *Why not?* she wondered now. The idea intrigued her.

"Me neither," Maureen quickly agreed, as if trying to cover herself in case Amy thought she was crazy. She stuffed the scarves back and stood up quickly. "But I've been thinking about it lately."

Of course she would be! Amy realized. *Death in her family...no one wants to think that's the end: You live here for a little while, you've got all this stuff inside your head, you do all these things, and then poof! You're gone. It's over. Nothing left of you but your offspring—and even they aren't really "yours."*

That scenario made about as much sense to Amy as God being some kind of Santa Claus/Angry Avenger on a big throne somewhere. No, that wasn't right.

But the notion of living again, over and over again—something in that rang a deep chord in Amy's mind. And it shook her. Hard. Before she knew what was happening, her body was quaking from head to toe, a powerful trembling that welled up from deep inside her and said in no uncertain terms, "Yes. This is truth."

She stared at Maureen in shock for a moment, while Maureen started to speak, to quickly brush away the subject with a casual, "Oh, never mind, I was just—"

"No, Maureen. Wait." Amy's eyes burned with blue intensity. "Something's going on here. You're right. I *do* believe in reincarnation." And she not only believed; in that moment, she knew that she had lived before. Simple truth.

"You believe in it?" Maureen's face lit up. "I wonder if it's true?"

"Maureen—I know it's true!" Amy proclaimed, surprised by the strength of her conviction. "I've seen it!"

"What?!"

"I've seen things that I couldn't explain any other way!"

"Things like what?" Maureen's hands shook a little as she set down the scarf she'd been clutching. Her green eyes fixed on Amy's with the desperation of a starving child led into a bakery.

"Come on, let's get out of here and I'll tell you."

13

Clues

They found a bench in a city park beside the river, donated by the Wilton Beautification Committee, according to a small brass plaque. Warm glimmers of sunshine flickered through the lightly-leafed trees and sparkled over the bench, while a nearby cluster of yellow daffodils bounced in the breeze that played through the neatly-kept gardens.

It was early May and the chill had gone. The air smelled fresh and damp as the tall, strappy leaves of unopened tulips promised brilliant color in a few days. Where the wide river passed beneath the bridge that led into Wilton, its usual roar was mellowed into a steady lapping.

Maureen barely waited until they were settled on the green bench before she turned to Amy, perched her elbow on the back, and pulled one blue-jeaned knee eagerly up onto the wooden slats. "Have you read books about this or something?"

"No." Amy was staring out across the rippling dark water, as if it held answers.

"Then how do you know it's true?" Maureen persisted.

Her keenness surprised Amy. Where was the Maureen always ready to put down a new idea?

But right now her own thoughts didn't give her much time to consider Maureen's motives. Her mind swirled like the eddy pools gathered around the bridge supports. The same shivers of recognition she'd felt in Berkman's ran up and down her spine as certain mental threads linked up.

The butterfly carriage, the radiant couple and the emotions she felt when she saw them, her longing and familiarity, the Other Voice, the golden book's turning pages (which she'd suddenly remembered), the flashing Lights she'd been seeing for weeks, the ghostly image of the fair-haired woman, and oddly, a dream she'd had about mountains and cows—it all started to weave into one picture when Maureen said the word "reincarnation." But the tapestry refused to complete itself! How could she explain any of this to Maureen when she herself didn't understand how these things connected? Yet she knew that somehow they did.

What about the fair-haired woman? What if she really was Maureen—but in a *previous life?* Amy remembered how angry she'd been at Maureen that day and how that face had come into her mind on a wave of fury.

"There was this thing that happened to me..." she began, keeping her eyes on the moving water.

Maureen sat up sharply. "Tell me! What?"

"It happened the day your father, um, died." She glanced over to see if she'd gone too far but Maureen didn't blink, so she went on, "I was really furious with you that day—something you'd said to me. I spent all morning in class thinking about how I was going to get even, how I was going to get back at you for it."

How long ago that seemed! All this week, she'd been developing a completely new picture of Maureen. She wasn't as haughty as Amy had believed—or as confident.

"When we got the news about your father, I felt horrible about what I'd been thinking." She turned to Maureen now, who still stared at her with unblinking intensity. "I'm sorry, Maureen, it was really awful. I was hating you for things you'd said and done, and feeling like the scum of the earth for thinking it at a time like that. But that night, just before I went to sleep, I saw this flash of a face in my mind—I was thinking about you, see, and then there was this image of a woman, an older woman with grayish blond hair. She didn't look like you, but it was you I was thinking about—"

Maureen interrupted impatiently. "So you think she was me in another life?"

"Well..." Amy hesitated.

"What makes you think so? And if she was me, I mean, if I was her, why didn't I see her? Why you?"

"I don't know. I don't have all the answers, Maureen. I just have feelings."

Maureen sighed in disappointment. "Come on, then," she jumped up. "Let's get out of here." And their conversation about reincarnation was going to be over, just like that.

But now it was Amy who couldn't let it go. She stayed on the bench. "What if that's why I was angry at you that day? What if it was something that happened to us before?"

Maureen looked at her. "Yeah? What if?"

"Well, that would explain why my feeling was so strong, wouldn't it?"

"Look, Amy, you've rubbed me the wrong way lots of times, too, but I don't think that proves reincarnation, does it?"

"I suppose not, but—"

"Then come on. My mother will be at Massino's soon and there's a book I want to show you." She hesitated. "It's something I found at home." She flushed a deep ruddy color when she said it, but Amy was so relieved by Maureen's change of attitude, she missed that cue.

As they walked back up the hill, Amy stopped talking about past lives but her mind kept picking up those threads, tying them together with knots, making them fit into a neat and tidy picture. By now she was certain that Maureen had been the fair-haired old woman and that she had hated that woman with the greatest intensity. She just didn't understand why. And strangely, right now she felt no resentment toward Maureen at all. In fact, she felt closer to her than anyone else she knew! Because at last she'd been able to share some of her deepest thoughts—not to mention getting that terrible guilt off her chest about the day Maureen's father died.

When they got to the bookstore, Maureen searched and searched, even asked a clerk, but she couldn't find the book. She wouldn't tell Amy anything about it; said it was something she needed to see for herself. So they rode back to Maureen's house talking about meaningless aspects of the day—the warmer weather, the flower beds by the river, the sunshine, avoiding any mention of their antics in Berkman's, and definitely not bringing up the subject of reincarnation.

Maureen's mother also seemed subdued. By the time they pulled into her driveway, they'd all lapsed into complete, uncomfortable silence.

The two girls disappeared into Maureen's blue bedroom, with its perfectly matched curtains and bedspread. Maureen's room was as neat and sparse as Amy's was cluttered. But she reached under her bed and dragged out a cardboard box crammed with old books, some with ragged covers half missing, others with torn paper jackets. From it she lifted a slim, sky-blue book with no pictures on the hard cover, only fading gold letters spelling out the title, *The Voice of Venus*, and the author's name, Ernest L. Norman.

"I found these in a closet when we were clearing out my dad's things." She stopped for a minute, working the lump out of her throat. "Look at these books, Amy—they're all about strange things, and reincarnation seems to be a big theme! This one, *The Voice of Venus*—it starts out with some guy from another planet introducing himself as 'Mal Var.' Then it talks about universes—*plural, Amy*—and soap bubbles and a lot of stuff I can't understand, but it has pictures. Look at this—"

She handed Amy the musty-smelling book.

Amy flipped the yellowing pages until she came to a dim, black-and-white illustration. The sketch depicted four robed figures with halos around their heads who looked like they were tending to a long line of—Amy couldn't tell what they were, but they looked like little tables or baskets on legs with a dark blob lying in the middle. Above each table, a circular fixture of some kind beamed down a stream of something into the blob; sparks drawn into the sketch indicated that it was light.

The illustration was primitive, but it triggered something in Amy that seized hold of her stomach. "What is this supposed to be?"

Maureen pointed to a paragraph on the facing page and read aloud over Amy's shoulder, "*'Shortly before the time approaches for the actual moment of conception, she will be taken to the earth-plane and placed in contact with the aura of her future mother, which supplies her energy until she enters the womb.'* Amy—it's about reincarnation! Those are supposed to be bassinets filled with the energy bodies of people who are getting ready to reincarnate! Only it says these babies were suicides, so that little blob there is all that's left of them, and those women are helping them, and the lights overhead are somehow repairing them so they'll be strong enough to enter a new body."

Amy shuddered violently and handed back the book. The tremor rippled through the bed on which they perched.

"Are you okay?"

Amy nodded but couldn't speak. She shivered uncontrollably.

"Here," Maureen tossed her a knitted afghan from the foot of the bed. "Amy—do you think this is real?"

She reached numbly to take the book out of Maureen's hands again, turning the pages reverently until she found another faded, black-and-white illustration. It looked like a futuristic city sitting on top of a cliff in the distance. A path led up to it from a flat valley below, and in the foreground, several pine trees and another cliff. Two small figures stood on that observation point, looking toward the city in the distance. The taller one, the one with a large halo around their head, had raised a hand to point toward the city.

Amy dropped the book to her lap and Maureen grabbed it before it fell to the blue shag rug beneath their feet.

"What?" Maureen demanded. "What is it?"

"I've been there," she breathed. "Maureen, I think I've been there!"

"You what?!"

"This is too crazy," Amy shook her head, jumping up from the bed. "Were these your father's books?"

"I guess so," Maureen shrugged. "I didn't know he was into this kind of thing. No one did. You should have seen my mother's face when we found this box in the back of the closet in his den. When she saw what the books were about, she didn't want anything to do with them. I snuck them out of the pile of stuff to be thrown out and hid them in here. I've been reading them ever since.

"But this book—I thought we'd find it in the bookstore. I wanted to show you the pictures. I wonder where he got it? Here—look." She opened the inside front cover and pointed to the only four-color image in the book, a painting of the author and his wife, white hair and deeply lined faces the artist had intensified rather than softened.

Amy had been moving unconsciously toward the door and now she stared down at the picture from several feet away. The couple from the butterfly carriage? Not hardly. These two people looked to be in their sixties at least, and he wore a suit and tie. But she bore a large corsage pinned to her blue dress. Something in their eyes, though, even all the way across the room...

A brilliant streak of blue flashed on the page.

I have to get out of here. This is too much. I can't tell Maureen about the visions! She'll think I'm crazy! What does she want me to say, anyway? I have to change the subject.

"So are you going to read the whole book?"

"I dunno," Maureen drew it back close to her, cradling it as if it were her father. "Maybe." She kicked the cardboard box. "But look at all these!" She read off the titles of hard covers and cheap paperbacks, "*Many Mansions, Heaven and Hell*—that one looks religious, written by some guy named Swedenborg. And these—*Autobiography of a Yogi, Cave of the Ancients, The Infinite Concept of Cosmic Creation*—look how huge that one is! I could never read all that. It has pictures, too, but they're just diagrams and spirals and that sort of thing. Way over my head. I can't believe my dad was into all this stuff and never talked about it!"

Amy could believe it. After all, wasn't she hiding worse things than a pile of books? She wasn't reading about these things—she was experiencing them! And she couldn't speak a word about it.

She had decided she liked Maureen but she wasn't ready to bare her soul to her. The pangs of her recent rage hadn't healed yet. She didn't fully trust Maureen, even though she'd just invited Amy into one of her own deep secrets: the fact that her father might have been totally crazy himself!

But Amy could see the idea of reincarnation gave Maureen something to cling to. If it were true...then her father wasn't really dead. He might come back some day. But would she meet up with him?

She knew Maureen wanted someone to answer those questions for her. It wasn't going to be Amy. Not today.

"You know what—look at the time! I said I'd be back before dinner. I gotta go now," she said breathlessly, trying to adopt a light tone. "Let me know what you find in that book, okay?"

Maureen came out of a reverie and looked up at Amy with a

worried frown. "You're not going to tell the others are you?"

"Why would I do that?" She tried to smile, feeling guilty all over again for keeping her own secrets.

"Because I would have done it to you a few weeks ago."

Her honesty surprised Amy.

"But seriously, don't tell anyone, okay? Please?"

"I won't tell a soul." Amy raised a hand in teasing allegiance. But she meant it. Bringing up a subject like this was the last thing she wanted to do. "Look, I should go now. We'll talk more later."

"And see if you can find out anything about that gray-haired woman you saw, okay? I wasn't making fun of you about it, I was just impatient. But really I'm curious. Was she me? Do you think? Is that possible?" Maureen looked more confused than convinced.

"I don't know, but she gives me the creeps. I'm not sure I want to see her again."

Maureen walked Amy to the front door and they waved good-bye absent-mindedly when Amy reached the sidewalk.

Her house wasn't too far and the day was still warm, which was good because she could walk slowly. She was struggling in a tangle of speculations. She needed time and space to sort out the intensity of their revelations that afternoon.

If that were even possible.

14

Without Gravity

Coriskancsia drew back the curtain that separated Marta from her future, revealing a place filled with Light. Nothing but brilliance, piercing into her mind like a chill wind "pierces the bones" on Earth—except that the Light gave her a pleasant feeling.

She'd become so accustomed to encountering strange new energy sensations, she would have been disappointed if she didn't encounter something new here.

Coriskancsia laughed at her. "That only means it's nearly time for your return, dear."

Marta didn't laugh. Reincarnating on Earth still gave her a sense of foreboding.

"Does anyone ever refuse to go?"

Coriskancsia laughed again, more heartily. "Nearly all of us at one time or another, or *every* time. Not to worry, dear. You just wait and see. Right now, however, there are matters you must attend to, for we each have our own evolution to look after. No one can do for us what we must do for ourselves. Can you see a little better now?"

When she tried again, Marta saw dim figures emerge from within the Light. First one, then two, then five or six—finally a whole roomful, although this "room" was so expansive you could pasture a dairy herd in it. But as before, when Marta focused her thoughts on the tiny silhouettes, they appeared to move closer.

Actually, it was she who moved closer to a young woman wearing a short tunic of briskly flowing energy of an indefinable color—because every time Marta tried to define it, the color changed. One moment it was electric pink, the next, shocking orange, then streaks of resonating silver, then flaming red, and so on. For a second or two, it transformed into a vibrant blue that gave her eyes a rest, the same way a lyrical phrase in music refreshes the mind. Then the tunic went back to its rhythmic ripples of fiery hues.

Unstartled by Marta's sudden appearance, the woman—who wasn't as young as Marta first assumed from her strong, lean, dark arms and legs—merely turned to her and nodded while sizing her up: "Ahhhh, yes. Greetings, child. We have been expecting you."

Me?

Marta looked around to ask Coriskancsia what this place was but she'd gone. And now she noticed that a fog of Light floated and oscillated around her ankles. She couldn't see her own feet, so dazzling was this radiation, yet it didn't hurt her eyes like her initial view of this limitless space. As far as she could see, the Light-fog shimmered low to the floor—or was it ground? Marta wasn't sure because no trees or vegetation grew up from it, but she couldn't see that any walls confined the space. The door through which she'd passed—or thought she had—had disappeared.

The woman at her side wore her ebony hair shaped closely around the curves of her gracefully molded head, and her dark eyes burned with fire as they took Marta's measure. At first she spoke aloud, as if she feared Marta might not comprehend telepathy, but she shaped her words with a rich, rolling, tropical-island rhythm so thick that Marta had to rush to replay and translate in her head. The woman lifted and dropped each vowel as if it were a song to savor with her resonant voice, and struck each consonant with her tongue to add percussion, all with precise enunciation.

"My name is Madame Piiottssiiz, but you may call me Teacher, if you prefer. I know that's not a name easy for an Earth-accustomed ear or tongue. Have they not told you why you are here, child?"

Marta looked guilty, as if she should have known.

"Oh, I see-ee. They often forget that Earth students are not so good at reading thoughts and subtle nuances. I am to be your dance teacher for now. You will meet many others later on."

Marta's eyes widened. Dance? She was to learn dancing? Excitement tremored in the pit of her stomach and moved up into her heart. Unaccountably, her limbs began to tremble.

"Ahhh, very good! Very good! You are already vibrating with the special energy of this room. Let me explain: On Earth, you must battle with gravity, and as you have learned in your movements here, gravity is not an issue. So what benefit would it be to you if you learned how to pirouette here—as I am told you have already done—and then fell to Earth and landed on your backside? Not pleasant, child, no, not pleasant at all!

"So here, in this spectacular room," she swept a slender hand in a wide-ranging gesture that sent orange sparks from her manicured fingertips, "we have created a very unique atmosphere. Here, we combine the benefits of both planes—of both the physical and the astral, or the fourth-dimensional as your Teachers have taught you to comprehend it. Let me show you, child."

With that, her body twirled away from Marta while her feet danced out a mad flurry of small steps, staying close to the oscillating Light-fog at her ankles. Marta could only see her feet because they glowed with golden intensity that broke right through the foggy radiance. A halo of gold enveloped Madame Piiottssiiz's gleaming dark skin as the muscles beneath it rippled in rapid, perfectly controlled spins.

"Now watch me closely," her rich tones rolled back to Marta.

She stopped suddenly in an arabesque—perfect position—and very slowly and gracefully lifted her right arm up from its extension in front of her nose into a new pose, a graceful arc rising above her head. In concert with this movement, her entire body rose gently up from the fog, until she paused, suspended about three feet above it, the tunic fluttering into a steady pulse of orange-red. Her golden toes pointed perfectly down, displaying an exquisitely arched foot.

She hadn't bounced abruptly to a halt as she would have if suspended by wires, an Earth trick used to create this illusion on a stage because so many artists have fond memories of their sojourns in higher worlds. They try to recreate this liberation from time, space, and gravity, and Earth audiences gladly join in, suspending their disbelief to revel in their own transcendent memories of realms without gravity.

Oh! I'm receiving her thoughts!

"That is correct, child," Madame Piiottssiiz replied aloud as she soared higher and slowly unfolded her body, stretching it into unimaginable feats of elegant athleticism. "You are learning in two ways: through your psychic eyes, and through your psychic attunement. When you go back to an Earth body, you can still learn this way if you choose. You can come to us here in your mind."

She spun suddenly back to Marta's side and settled softly on one golden toe. "It is a matter of desire, my child, a deep, abiding passion to express yourself!"

Her eyes blazed as she looked off into the bright room, where now Marta could see hundreds of dancers and acrobats spinning and leaping and slowly moving their bodies into fascinating shapes, all radiating an intensity that twirled powerful energies out into the atmosphere.

She saw lyrical ballerinas in short tutus, statuesque couples in tuxedos and flowing gowns sweeping by in a spinning Viennese waltz, dark tango dancers clinging and tangling their legs into impossible puzzles, springy circus performers flipping mid-air with no net to catch them, bodies spinning on their backs on the floor, then leaping up and turning their limbs to rubber, natives from all regions and time periods shaking brilliant feathers and beads and rings as they pranced out their tribal rhythms, Irish steppers holding themselves stiff and upright as their feet seemed to dance without them, laughing folk dancers winding their circles and lines, whirling dervishes spinning like tops, German polkas and Latin sambas and French minuets and Hindu poses and Russian squat-kicks and Island sways…dances beyond anything she'd ever seen before…and one solitary figure who stood quietly, intently moving her stomach in steady ripples as her fingers beat out a seductive rhythm on tiny, ringing cymbals.

Marta felt a strange sensation in her own midsection as she watched the belly dancer. Matter of fact, as each dancer came into her view, she felt something flutter in her energy anatomy. Some gave her a sense of dull dread; others filled her with elation and she wanted to scamper off and join them. Others were so foreign, she didn't know what to feel about them.

"It is your history you sense mostly, although some of these dances haven't yet been 'invented' on Earth," Madame Piiottssiiz intoned solemnly. "The ones that make you feel something— they remind you of dances you have danced, lives you have lived. Some were happy lives; others were not. But dancing—it weaves through your history like a gleaming circlet of Love!"

"Why didn't I dance in my last lifetime, then?"

"But you did, my child! At every opportunity, even if they were few."

Marta remembered the holidays, how they'd had to drag her

away when the festivities were over, how as a very young child she spun and twirled until she fell exhausted into her mother's lap and still she couldn't keep her fingers and toes from moving to the music.

She gazed around the vast, foggy space again. This time her eyes landed on a cluster of women in brightly-colored layers of rough skirting they lifted slightly to show their footwork. Their heavy hooped earrings jangled as they threw back their heads and flung out their arms, almost in defiance of anyone who might tell them to stop. Marta felt a cold knife run through her energy system.

Suddenly she saw a man, short, with dark-hooded eyes and greasy jet-black hair. He advanced toward her menacingly, then threw up his arms in a *paso doble* pose and stamped his heels commandingly. He was inviting her to dance! She could feel herself respond involuntarily, throwing herself wildly into the rhythm, laughing, pulsing, sweating, clapping, twirling. The flamenco rhythms from a nearby guitar drove her body on as the man came close, veered away, then swooped back and clasped her waist tightly to him, then spun and spun until she lost all awareness of anything but his hot breath and strong arms...

But just as quickly, she felt the center of her being fall away and all motion ceased. She was standing in a grimy wooden wagon, lit by firelight from outside and filled with the clutter of nomadic life. Although she stood perfectly still, her heart throbbed in fear—or was it anger? The man approaching her this time was taller, less bulky, but far more terrifying. His eyes were those of a man driven by rage into absolute madness and before she could move to defend herself he caught her neck in a long scarf, squeezing, squeezing as the wagon and the man faded from her view, as her heart broke with the unfairness of his accusations—yet she could no longer speak! He had been lied to and she could not defend herself! She loved this man— and no other—but he could not hear her, had not been able to hear her for hours, had only heard the vicious lies uttered by an angry, spurned, and bitter rival with greasy, jet-black hair...too late...too late...too late for either of them...

Madame Piiottssiiz' voice brought her back but the shock of this past-life flashback made Marta unable to scream or cry or utter a sound or even collapse to the floor. She stood rigid.

"He suffered terrible remorse for that deed performed in a jealous rage. He was your true love, your only love in that hard wandering life, traveling from town to town, dancing for spare change and hot meals, ridiculed and harassed by those who did not understand your ways or your poverty. The other man, a dancer in your troupe, was deflated by your constant rejection of his advances. In bitterness, he told your musician lover a tale of lies sufficient to boil the blood of any ordinary soul. But your man was not an ordinary soul. His inconsolable grief over your death killed him soon enough. Before he died, his love for you brought him to realize the deception, the evil he'd succumbed to, and he sought revenge. Or perhaps a quick death. He got his wish."

After long, quiet moments in which Madame Piiottssiiz said nothing but gazed off as if hearing from a higher plane, she said to Marta, "You will need to grow stronger, my child. Not in body but in mind." She tapped Marta's forehead with firm fingers. "In the past, you have been weak in your self-identity. You have not known who you really are while trapped in an Earth body. But of course, that is why you take on that body—to grow, not only a physical anatomy, but knowledge of your most beautiful Self!

"Art, creative expression of any form, is the way we take up when we are beginning to sense something beyond ourselves. We become vessels in which a great, inner welling-up begins to build a presence. And then the pressure increases, and increases, until we feel we will burst if we do not find some outlet to express this Power, this universal Love into the world we inhabit at that moment!"

She looked deeply into Marta's eyes. "Have you ever felt such a welling-up, child? An overpowering sense of Love that beats into your veins and flows out your pores? Not physical love like you felt for your traveling man—but cosmic, spiritual Love?"

"Oh yes," Marta answered without thinking.

Madame Piiottssiiz's melodious voice had been filling up the gaping hole her flashback left. She led Marta back from the tragedy of unwarranted accusation and death at the hands of her beloved, back from the dingy wagon and hungry life, back to the abundance of this realm of limitless beauty and opportunity. Life Force rushed back into her energy meridians and filled her up again with infinite possibilities.

"I feel it now!"

"And well you should!" The woman laughed, a rich, throaty sound of happiness. Then she grew intent again. "No, child. I mean do you remember a time when you felt this feeling *while living in one of your Earth bodies?*"

Marta needed only a moment to recall the alpine meadows of her most recent life, the immensity of the mountains among which she'd lived. She nodded.

"Then you know what I mean. Here," she tapped Marta's chest, "and here," she patted her stomach, "and here," she laid a palm over Marta's head. "You have *felt* the Pulse of Creation! Infinite Creative Intelligence is a pulse-beat of Love, you know. It has a rhythm and an oscillation, this infinite Godforce." She indicated the Light fog at their feet. "You can see the oscillation in the change of colors, but you can also sense that Infinite rhythm within yourself when you know of this principle and seek the welling-up inside. That is what happens when you desire to dance—you are feeling the pulse beat of Infinity!"

In a sudden gesture, she reached her palms up above her head, stretching her lean arms up, up, until they formed a cup to capture the Infinite Wellspring into her being. She tilted her head back and inhaled this Power.

"Breathe, child!" she commanded. "Breathe *life* here, where we do not need air! Let it fill your being until it spills over into your dancing and into your words and into your own small life!"

Marta copied her movement and tried to feel the energy flowing into her. She reached as far as she could with her mind to receive and reached deeply within herself to see if she could feel the Pulse.

At first, she felt only tremors of nervousness.

This was not like other encounters she'd experienced here. At any moment she feared she'd be expected to do something—and after watching her Teacher's astonishing dance, she knew that she could not possibly do what was expected! With a surge of painful memory, she remembered her inelegant attempts as the little man in the loincloth tried to help her relearn how to walk in this gravity-less dimension. She vowed to ask for help this time *before* she humiliated herself.

But this reaching to Infinity...it wasn't so hard. In fact she began to feel something, a deep pool that formed in the center of her being. Warm, radiating, loving, intense. Why was she reaching, anyway? Wasn't Infinity right within her being? Wasn't she herself—

"Well, child, that is all for now." Her new Teacher dropped her arms and extended one toward Marta as if to shake her hand.

Marta drew her own arms back down self-consciously. She reached to touch Madame Piiottssiiz's smooth fingers.

"I will see you next time." Madame Piiottssiiz smiled, paused to look through Marta again, then winked and swirled off into a group of dancers who disappeared in a flurry of energy that rose so high, Marta felt as if she were looking up at an ordinary Earth cloud. And then they were completely out of sight.

She stood exactly where Coriskancsia had left her.

"But..." she sputtered as her heart sank with disappointment. *What kind of dance lesson was that? I haven't even moved my feet!*

Much later, as she lay on her blue Light-bed, she thought back and realized something she didn't notice when it happened.

When she had turned to leave the dancing place (couldn't really call it a room), she at last tried to lift her feet. They felt different than at any other time since her arrival in this timeless place. Each time she moved a foot, she felt a suctioning resistance. She hadn't paid much attention, though, because she was so frustrated that Madame Piiottssiiz left her alone the minute she recovered from her traumatic flashback and started to feel comfortable in these strange surroundings.

But now she remembered how much effort it took to walk out of the dance space, an effort she hadn't needed since Switzerland! She had walked all the way to the arched doors—which reappeared—without noticing how good and natural it felt to move that way. But it had felt good, hadn't it?

I want to visit that room again.

That was one of the few problems she encountered here. If you wanted to go back to a place, you had to think your way to it. And if Coriskancsia had led her to it originally, she usually failed. When Marta complained, Coriskancsia merely said, "It means that you've completed the lessons associated with that location. Remember, no time or space here. It's all about interlocking cycles. And when you've completed the cycle of one learning experience, you are no longer relative to it and you move automatically into a new cycle of learning." Marta looked blank and Coriskancsia had sighed, "I cannot explain it with words. You'll understand after you've had enough experience."

But I can't possibly have "completed my cycle" with dancing, she reasoned now, *because I never danced a step!*

She felt a little indignant about that. She'd been dismissed without being given a chance! (By now, she'd completely forgotten her fear of being put on the spot.) She only wanted an opportunity to try that floor again, or Light-sponge, or whatever it was.

No sooner did she stubbornly settle on that objective than she found herself back in the place with the foggy Light floor. As her inner sight adjusted to the brightness, she saw that she was completely alone. Feeling safe in her solitude, she tentatively lifted a foot. Then another. Sure enough, she could almost hear a suctioning sound!

She closed her eyes and thought over which kind of dancing she wanted to try. She rejected all the folk dances she learned in Switzerland. *I've done those. And no Romani dances!* Her energies swooped uncomfortably at the thought of it. She considered the pirouettes she taught herself in the garden, but they wouldn't do. She was tired of them already. Too easy.

Then she remembered the magnificent sight of Madame Piiottssiiz rising in a perfect arabesque, moving like an Angel— like you imagine figures in a Renaissance painting might move if given real wings. Or a room like this!

Marta laughed aloud and shot up an arm in exuberant expectation. Nothing happened.

She tried it again, this time putting more *ooomph* behind it. She didn't move.

Frustrated, she tried lifting a leg. It rose as you would expect— in an Earth classroom. Nothing magical about it at all.

"Hey!" she called. "Why isn't this working?"

A voice behind her replied quietly, "It's your ego, child."

She spun to see Madame Piiottssiiz watching her, one lean finger tapping thoughtfully on her chin.

This time she wore a long, sheer, neon-lime tunic of spinning patterns over a neck-to-foot, skintight, dark leotard with long sleeves and legs. She reminded Marta of a lean black panther concealed by jungle foliage, waiting to leap into action.

"What is your motivation?"

Marta flushed. "My motivation? What do you mean?"

"Why did you come back? To dance? Or to prove something to me?"

"Why, to dance, of course! I...I just wanted to see if what I remembered about this floor or whatever you call it is true."

"Is that so? Then why are you not dancing?"

"That's exactly what I want to know! I mean—" Marta stopped suddenly. Why wasn't she dancing? After all, every other thing she desired here immediately came to pass. That must mean...

"That you did not really desire to dance. And so you have now proven to your own satisfaction the lesson we had yesterday. Excellent, my child! You understand the first principle!" Madame Piiottssiiz moved toward her. "To dance, all you will ever require is a strong, unshakable desire to do so. Without it, your feet will never leave the ground properly."

Marta was admittedly rooted to the spot.

But didn't I come here to dance? Wasn't that my desire? she asked herself over and over again. She couldn't get an answer, and right now she didn't trust herself to be honest anyway.

"Better to ask yourself what you have achieved thus far," Madame Piiottssiiz hinted as if reading her thoughts. "That will give you a clue to your real motivation."

What *had* she achieved? Beyond complete humiliation, that is. She tried to think clearly. *Well, I did manage to lift my feet and prove that the floor has some kind of suction. I guess that was one of my objectives, to prove to myself that I wasn't imagining it, that I wasn't crazy.*

"Ahhh," Madame Piiottssiiz interrupted, "that one I think you will spend much time in your future trying to prove: that you are not crazy!" Lush laughter spilled out of her throat. "One day, you will understand that *crazy* to one person is *brilliant* or *enlightened* to another. It is a matter of spiritual development, of course. And what else did you hope to achieve?"

"I, um, I wanted to prove that I deserved dance lessons." She looked down in embarrassment for a long moment. Then up again with a sudden laugh, "I certainly proved that, didn't I? I've just demonstrated that I do not have the first clue about how to do what *you* can do!"

Madame Piiottssiiz chuckled warmly and laid a hand on her shoulder. "You are going to be a wonderful student, child. You have an ego, it is true. But you also have the capacity for humility. That is good, very good. Without ego, you will not try, but without humbleness, your desire will not lead where you truly want to go. Remember this lesson, my child. It will carry you far and far indeed!"

Marta heard the chill warning about ego as an unpleasant resonance that shuddered through her.

But Madame Piiottssiiz had taken her by the hand. Instantly her mind filled with the happy realization that she was about to learn from a Master Teacher! Her chill vanished as warmth swirled up into the soles of her feet, traveled to her head, and burst from her crown in fountains of Light-energy. Just as predicted, her feet suddenly lifted and she found herself floating effortlessly, trailing one graceful arm in imitation of something she'd seen Madame Piiottssiiz do.

As they soared together, her Teacher explained, "This room in which we fly was created for learning. You choose: You can rehearse with the same gravity you must fight on Earth, or you can practice your ability to replicate the weightless freedom of the higher worlds. With a thought, you can eliminate our artificial gravity, as I have done for us. With another, gravity returns, but your mind still soars without limitation—and your body seems to follow!

"Either way, you are preparing yourself for your future. You will be like a memory, dancing on the chords of remembrance your audience carries to the theater. From the sight of you, they will resonate with the flights into higher realms that they too have taken between lifetimes. Your dancing will lift them above their fears, worries, and anger, so that the Brotherhood's emanations of Love may enter, as their hearts open to us once again."

They floated back down and Madame Piiottssiiz laid a soft hand on Marta's shoulder, her words rolling deep into Marta's soul, "Your dancing will be a service to humanity—and when you take the stage, many Light Beings will join you to add their Love to your movements. Never forget this, child! You will not be alone. But you must also dance your own Love into that sorry, sorry world of Earth. You will be water to its parched and dying soil."

15

Remedial Reincarnation 101

"Dear Diary," Amy wrote, "I'm so confused! First I hate Maureen and want to strangle her, even when I should feel sorry for her. But instead I invite her to a movie and find out she's not so bad when she's not in a crowd. Then she brings up the subject of past lives and I start shaking all over! I don't know what to think about any of it."

Amy's pen paused over the paper, then scratched furiously, "Who is the gray-haired woman? Why do I keep seeing her? Was she Maureen? Why did I hate her?"

She stopped writing.

I have no real reason to hate Maureen, she reasoned. *All she did was tease me—okay, and a few other reasons. But I was so angry! Maybe it was really the gray-haired woman I hated and Maureen reminded me of her. But if she was Maureen, how will we know?*

She wrote the last question in her diary. Then a thought struck her and she scribbled, "So what did I do to her in a past life?"

No, no—she'd wanted to write "what did *she* do to *me* in the past" but it came out backwards.

"That's right, Amy," she kept writing, as if giving herself a lecture, "what you do comes back to you. Remember the Golden Rule? Why would it be any different from life to life?"

The Other Voice! It was back! The wise one.

"So what *did* I do?" she scratched across the page as her eyelids began to droop.

"Sleep, Amy. It's late."

She agreed, as she could barely hold the pen now. It kept streaking off the page, making straight lines to the edge as her eyes shut involuntarily. She put her head down on the pillow to rest for a minute and sank instantly into a deep sleep.

Marta wondered if she'd made a mistake. After her experience in the crystal woods, she told Coriskancsia she wanted to know more about the scientific aspects of reincarnation—and now she was stuck in a lecture hall.

She glanced around the room as others appeared. Some walked, some simply manifested like she did. If it weren't for the fact that the lectern far below the tiered seats gleamed like clear red crystal, or that the atmosphere radiated with a rosy haze of energy that gave her a tingling sensation of alertness, she would have been filled with dread. She hated dull lectures.

And why red? she wondered.

A voice behind her shoulder spoke aloud in distinct reply to her question, "It's a scientific frequency. Haven't you noticed the different colors wherever you go, depending on the subject you're studying?"

She wasn't sure which was more shocking, the sound or the mental intrusion! No one should be able to read her thoughts like that unless she wanted them to! Unless they were a very advanced Teacher…and if that were true, wouldn't they be down at the lectern, addressing the students now filling the seats?

She turned to protest the intrusion but the words died when she saw the young man standing in the row behind her, grinning down at her. She flushed inexplicably and the pinkish glow merged with the radiant atmosphere. Not a Teacher. Definitely not. But who was he? And how did he gain entrance to her thoughts?

His appearance wasn't particularly familiar. He towered over her: lean, muscular, with ordinary-looking light brown hair. But his eyes flashed and glittered with dancing light, flecked green and blue and amber. She couldn't tell which color they actually were because she found herself looking beneath their surface, returning a look that went right through her, as if these eyes knew everything about her and she knew everything about them. But of course, she didn't know a thing that words could describe.

The man who owned these extraordinary eyes went on as if nothing unusual were passing between them. He kept using words instead of telepathy.

"Didn't they tell you? The colors here all mean something; they signify a particular frequency. Entire planets are devoted to science, which is the rosy-red frequency we're sitting in. Or healing—that's blue. Or teaching, yellow."

He clambered over the seats to the one beside her, settling himself in comfortably without missing a beat.

"Or the arts—that's my favorite. It's a delicate shade of pinkish-coral. Then lavender or purple for devotional practices. Green—philosophy. Let's see, did I leave anything out?" He counted on his fingers. "Oh, yes, orange. Leadership." He grinned at her again. "I always try to leave that one out. Scares me, you know?"

She was totally befuddled. Not a word formed in mind or on lips. She could only stare at him with the same dumbstruck expression she must have had on her face from the moment she realized he was able to hear her thoughts.

"I'm sorry," he apologized. "I should have introduced myself properly, shouldn't I? I forgot. You can call me Kriss. It's an old name but it will do for now." He held out his hand.

Relieved by the formalities, Marta reached hers to his in an automatic response—and nearly jerked it back again when she felt the energies tingling into her fingers and palm from his.

But he gazed into her eyes warmly and held her hand firmly for a few long seconds. Then dropped it—again, as if nothing out of the ordinary had happened. "And your name is?"

"Oh—sorry—Marta," and the moment she said it she knew it was wrong. That was not her name. But she had no idea what her true name should be.

"Yes, I know how you feel," Kriss nodded. "Mine's not exactly right, either. But we'll soon have new ones, won't we? You don't mind if I sit here, do you?"

Mind? She would have been upset if he'd sat anywhere else, but she had the presence of mind to say simply, "No, not at all." Or she would have, if the Teacher hadn't appeared at that moment.

The students now filling the hall all looked so *Earthean* to Marta. Clothes from both ancient and recent eras, hair colors ordinary to her sensibilities, the usual number of appendages and placements—not that she'd seen any grotesque or horrific beings from other worlds, but there were *differences* she'd noticed that she couldn't really put her finger on. Like the man who experienced the healing in that class about intervention, Glissmanna. And she'd received a few second glances herself from individuals she knew were from different planets. She didn't know how she knew that but now, glancing around the room, she noticed how distinct the Earth people were. An overall commonness, for lack of a better word. Nothing spectacular in dress or aura. Nowhere near the impact that someone like Coriskancsia carried. She decided it was a matter of mental development more than planetary affiliation.

We simply aren't evolved enough to cast out a large, luminous radiance, she thought.

Then she snuck a glance at Kriss. On the other hand, some

of us do carry a certain *something*. Or did he only seem that way to her? As she began to wonder about her own radiations of personality and Spirit, the Teacher, a slender woman with silvery hair, began the lecture.

She wore Earth clothes, a white lab coat over a dark blue suit. Only her shoes, shooting out sparks of red and blue light, gave a hint of the higher-frequency labs in which she normally conducted her work. Marta got the impression she had dressed to make them feel at home. And at first she spoke without using telepathy, then gradually shifted into it as the students in the room grew more comfortable.

"Welcome to this remedial class in reincarnation science, which has been designed for Earth dwellers only, since your world is so backwards in this subject. You'll be well ahead of most people on your planet if you do well in this course."

She explained that she was a past-life scientist, "a breed soon to be born on your world, though perhaps not during your next lifetimes. You will have psychics, and readers, and hypnotists, and theorists, but as far as I understand, you'll have only a handful of scientists who fully comprehend and teach the science you are going to learn in this class."

Then she launched into a much-simplified explanation of the interdimensional physics that governs the expression of life, beginning with the principle of cause-and-effect.

Marta struggled to will her thoughts away from Kriss, whose presence was mightily distracting, so she could absorb every word. She knew this information would make a huge difference in her next Earth life. Mostly she lost the battle, though. But her attention flew back to the Teacher when she heard these words:

"Now, this physical anatomy you will soon inhabit will be a very precise electronic instrument. You might think of it as an undersea navigating and information-gathering device, an outward extension of your energy body that you'll use for a time and then discard. The data you collect through your experiences in life—or you might call them your 'experiments in truth,' as did our Brother, Mahatma Gandhi—this data will become a permanent part of your psychic anatomy, which is the *you* that you carry from life to life.

"Your psychic anatomy, your true Mind, is an energy body that contains all the electronically-impinged information of everything you've ever done or thought or experienced. Nothing is lost, which is why the principle of cause-and-effect becomes so important. When living in a physical body, you will re-experience the *effects* of many past-life *causes* you've encountered or created by your previous actions, and especially, by your emotions," the Teacher explained.

"Most of this replay will occur unnoticed by you. This is evolutionary information that keeps your body functioning, and makes your awareness relative to the planet you will be inhabiting.

"But some psychic impingements, stemming from more significant incidents, will reappear with dramatic consequences. A negative impingement may cause an after-effect that could appear in your future lifetimes as illness or deformity, violent emotion, or intense repulsions and attractions to people, places, and things.

"Before I go on, does anyone have a question?"

Now that she'd seen some of her past lives, Marta wanted desperately to understand how and why one affected her so strongly while another left her feeling cold. She wished the Teacher would give examples but she was too shy to ask. She forgot to block this thought.

When no one else moved to ask a question, the Teacher's eyes flickered over Marta but she continued, "All is energy, including every so-called 'atom' on Earth. Solidity is an illusion, a fact that has led the Earth people astray on so many levels, despite the hard efforts of those who have incarnated periodically to teach them otherwise. As you can readily see around you now, the 'self' that we so treasure as young souls—our 'beingness' as they say on Earth—both your physical and mental bodies are entirely composed of energy.

"So, as I said before, your psychic anatomy becomes the repository of the electronic impingements of all that you have lived, thought, and believed. Every single experience. It is the blueprint from which your physical bodies are created; and it is also the receptor of input from the Infinite Creative Intelligence, the Wellspring of life. It contains your past, present, and future. The complete workings of this psychic anatomy are a complexity that you will endeavor to understand for hundreds of thousands of lifetimes, long after you have ceased to require physical incarnations on physical planets for your trial-and-error learning."

A silence filled the hall as the students tried to imagine the scope of this statement.

Kriss looked over at Marta and made a face, as if to say, "Yeah, right, and I really understood that."

She made an answering face, and a little tingle of shared knowing shivered through her. Her happiness at finding a friend here soared beyond words. Oddly, she felt as if Kriss shared her thought. He winked at her, but the Teacher went on:

"The psychic anatomy exists at a higher frequency. It is, you might say, fourth-dimensional and therefore invisible to most people on Earth. You see, past-life information is stored in a portion of the psychic anatomy not readily accessible to the physical, 'conscious mind' state in which you live most of your life while on Earth. On other planets, some of the instruments you see around you"—she pointed to glass display cases lining the room—"are used to make the psychic anatomy visible. They are used primarily to aid in the process of past-life healing."

"So how do we get to live on one of *those* planets?" Kriss asked, startling Marta with his boldness. A titter of laughter rippled through the rosy atmosphere.

The Teacher smiled. "Evolution, friends. Mental and spiritual growth. Right now, your psychic anatomies—your mental capacities—are developed to a level compatible with planet Earth. Until you do something to change and grow, to rectify the destructive energies oscillating from your past learning experiences into your present, that is where you will be drawn in future lifetimes."

A collective groan replaced the laughter.

"No, it's not what we like to hear. But it is the truth. Personal development has to be your choice. No one can do this for you. But you have all come here precisely because you have already made that choice. You are now well on your way! So during your next incarnation, you will want to use what you're learning here to speed up your rectification of past-life negative energies residing in your psychic anatomy."

That sounded good to Marta, and wonderful, and she knew it was vitally important that she keep listening carefully but her eyelids began to droop. She caught herself and tried to sit up straighter.

Not now, she chided herself. *I can't lose consciousness now! I must learn this…*

When her eyes reopened, the Teacher was saying, "So as you have seen, ripples of thought-energy reach far beyond any boundaries you can imagine, deep into the subastral, or high up into the highest spiritual realms. And never forget that once expressed, thoughts remain a permanent part of your psychic anatomy. The lower-frequency thoughts make up what we might term your 'lower self,' while your positive thoughts and deeds will build the foundation of your 'higher self' or Superconsciousness. One day, that Superconsciousness will be developed sufficiently by your own hard efforts to fully support your life in a realm such as this one. So caring for your thoughts is absolutely the first step in self-mastery!"

Marta glanced around the lecture hall self-consciously. Had she slept? How long? She looked at Kriss, but he was focused intently on the Teacher and didn't notice her gaze.

"The second step is healing the aberrant information you stored up in ignorance, before you learned a better way. This is *how* you learn—by making mistakes. But the so-called 'permanent' energy impingements in your psychic anatomy can be changed—by you. You must 'revisit the scene of the crime'—that is, reincarnate to the world and dimension where you originated this karmic incurrence in order to accomplish your healing, using the principles I have just demonstrated for you with the holographic projection. By so doing, you will not only improve your own life, but the lives of others with whom you've involved yourself.

"Next session, I will show you how."

Next session! thought Marta in a panic. *What principles? What demonstration? What hologram? Kriss!* She turned to him but he was standing up with the others who had already begun filing or popping out of the hall.

No, wait! Marta's mind bubbled over in anxiety. *I missed it! This can't be! I'm done for!*

Kriss suddenly looked at her, as if coming back from a long sleep himself and remembering that she was there. "Did you say something?" he asked sleepily.

"What happened?" she grabbed his arm without thinking and he jumped as if the touch gave him a jolt of electricity. In fact it had. She let go but her words spilled out audibly, "You've got to tell me—I missed it, didn't I? I fell asleep again and I missed the whole lecture and now I'm going to be stuck on Earth forever and I won't know what to do and I've got to know what she said! Can you help me?"

She said that last with a bit more restraint, suddenly feeling uneasy about her outburst. After all, he hardly knew her. What was he going to think now?

But Kriss turned those magnificent eyes on her and his face slowly broke into a grin. "Fell asleep, did you? Tch, shame on you," he chided with a big smile. "Well, I guess you'll just be falling behind the rest of us, won't you?"

Was he teasing her? Or really that cold and cruel? But his eyes said he couldn't possibly be that cruel, not to her...and why not?

That was a mystery that started to pull her attention away from her panic about the class.

He finally took pity on her.

"Don't worry, Marta—oh! You're so right! That name doesn't fit you, does it? I won't call you that again. Sorry. Didn't anyone tell you anything? All of these classes—they don't take place in time and space like on Earth, remember? They're all available for you, any time you wish."

She'd never thought of that. Completely overlooked it. But he must be right. No time and space. Just like the library, she supposed. She could probably access this class by a strong desire, could repeat the entire lecture as many times as she liked.

"That's right. And you can even do it from your body on Earth when you get there, if your desire and knowledge are strong enough. Happens in your sleep, I understand. Matter of fact, didn't any of this seem familiar? Oh, right. I forgot. You slept through it."

He laughed.

"Well, that's okay. You missed some horrible images of sub-astral entities obsessing some poor bloke on some dark planet because he was angry—and then he decided not to be and he got hooked up like we are now, with Supercelestial Beings who filled his psychic anatomy with a lot of Light. Quite beautiful, actually. You did miss something there…"

She wanted to punch him for some reason—which was a very unnatural thing to think in a dimension like this. Not an angry punch but a playful, familiar one. Then it hit her: he'd made her feel completely calm again. How did he do that? She'd lost every bit of fear and anxiety.

Now he looked at her with a twinkle. "C'mon," he urged, "I know something you haven't seen yet and I think you're going to like it."

"But shouldn't we rest before the next class session?"

He grinned at her. "Didn't you just have a nice rest?"

This time she really did punch him. But he grabbed her hand gently and spun her around toward the exit.

"I suppose we don't get physically tired here, anyway," she conceded. "Just transcended right into a higher dimension." She finally laughed at herself.

"That's right," Kriss smiled at her and sent shivers into her stomach. "It's all mental. And if we'd known that while we lived on Earth, you can bet I would have climbed more mountains before that last one got the best of me!" He laughed good-naturedly. "I always said I'd rather die on a mountainside than behind some clerk's desk. But not that mountain, and not so soon." He looked as if he wanted to say more but stopped himself.

"What mountain?" she asked as they left the hall and strolled out into a brilliantly lit portico. Beyond it a green lawn beckoned invitingly.

"The one that killed me."

She stopped walking and stared at him. Why did this seem familiar? As if she'd heard him say that before?

He stopped and turned back. "What?"

"What you said—it's as if you said it before."

"Déjà vu? Here??" He laughed again. "Well, I suppose this is the original source for déjà vu experiences, wouldn't you say?"

On a whim she implored, "Kriss, tell me about it. How you died, I mean. This last time."

He shrugged. "It might be boring."

"Oh, no. It won't be. I'm sure of that."

She indicated a soft-looking patch on the lawn. "Let's go sit and you tell me everything. Then we can go do whatever it was you had in mind."

As she said it, she realized she was finding ways to extend their time together. She had no idea where he was planning to take her but it was so wonderful to have a friend suddenly. Someone at her own level. Someone who seemed to understand her without asking questions.

He hesitated a moment, then sighed. "Well, why not. It's probably good for me to go over it again. Even if it is the most humiliating experience I can think of right now."

"Why?" she asked as they settled on the crystalline grasses, which moved to conform to their individual energy bodies. She could stay here for hours, she thought as he began the tale.

He had been an adventurer—an alpinist, he called it—and much to her surprise, he'd actually planned a trip that would have taken him close to her home village in Switzerland at the same time she lived there. She didn't interrupt his story to ask for specifics, but in this place of expanded knowing she suspected it might have coincided with her early twenties from the clues he gave about the time period.

A little pang crossed her brow as she looked at him now. Was he still wearing physical features from that lifetime, as she was? Right now they seemed to be about the same age—maybe mid-twenties. *What if I'd met him then, in Switzerland? Does he know that was my country?*

If he knew, or if he even heard her mental question, he didn't let on. He told her he was diverted from his plans by a friend's suggestion that they explore instead the Theodul Pass, a nearly eleven-thousand-foot mountain pass between Switzerland and Italy that featured a breathtaking view of the still-unconquered Monte Cervino.

"That's what the Italians called it. You might know it as the Matterhorn," he added.

Such adventures always exerted a strong pull on him and he quickly agreed. "But I regretted it from the first moment we set out. From the beginning, everything went wrong. I cursed myself a thousand times for not following that subtle inner prompting to tour the region on the other side of the range, further north. I'd become infatuated with my friend's promise of great adventure."

Again, he gave her that look as if he wanted to say more, but he went on with the story.

"Secretly, I think he'd already planned to make some assault on that unconquered peak, but we did not have any of the sorts of equipment they use now for such things. The moment we arrived in view of that sharp-edged monster, he insisted that we attempt to climb some portion of the lower ridges, just to touch its majesty. All were forbidding enough, and I should have known better. Plus, it was very early spring and we really weren't outfitted properly."

They never dreamed of trying for the summit, of course. No one had ever reached it, not during Kriss's time on Earth. But nevertheless, they spent endless, miserable hours struggling and fighting their way up icy rocks.

"It was a land never meant to be conquered by man or beast," he told her now. "Such mountains are meant only to soar above humanity as a symbol of all that we have not yet achieved, especially on Earth! But our foolish egos led us on, as they always do."

Adding to his mental torment, knowing he was in the wrong place at the wrong time, they attempted their climb in a driving, white-out snowstorm and deadly cold. Their spontaneous "adventure" was pure folly. The storm moved in on them faster than they could descend to safety. Long before his friend lost his footing in the blinding storm and dragged all three roped-together members of the party down a sheer rock face to their deaths, Kriss had understood that his own mistakes would be fatal.

Worse, he crossed over knowing that he missed some important facet of that lifetime, all because of his youthful arrogance and inflated ego. He knew without being told that no "angels" stepped in to rescue him that day because he needed the deflation his death provided, a lesson in humility never to forget.

He shuddered then, and slipped into silence.

Without thinking, Marta reached over and stroked his hand. Lights sparked and danced at the gesture. "You're being too hard on yourself," she consoled, not noticing the light show.

If Kriss noticed he said only, "And what about you? Don't

you have regrets about choices you made in your last lifetime?"

She blushed. How did he know? She often wondered, if she had it to do again would she marry Hans? Had she chosen too hastily?

"That's what I thought," he said. "Come on. Let's stop feeling sorry for ourselves. It's too late now! And besides, I've got something to show you, remember?"

He stood up. "Just take my hand." He reached down to her and she lifted her hand to fall into his.

Immediately, she felt a warm tingle rush all the way up her arm to her shoulder, and all the way down to her solar plexus. Before she could gasp at the sensation, they were standing on a quaint country lane. Masses of red climbing roses tumbled over rock walls on either side of the deserted road. Only the quiet glitter of the blossoms' crystalline energy structure let Marta know they were still in a higher-frequency world. Otherwise, they might have been on Earth.

Kriss led her a few steps down the lane. She felt as if they should tiptoe in reverence on the pounded dirt, it was so pristine and perfect here. Birds filled the air around them with happy song and it might have been a summer day, if there had been any sun such as the one they'd known on Earth. The smell of flowers filled her nostrils—nothing she'd smelled in Switzerland; they reminded her of dense fragrances from other lives, in other places, happy lifetimes of peace and contentment.

"Do you recognize it yet?" Kriss whispered.

He must feel as I do, she thought, *as if talking here would destroy the comfortable atmosphere. I feel like an intruder! But yes, something about this country lane is familiar.* "Why is that?" she asked him.

"Shhh…we probably shouldn't really be here, but I couldn't resist. I first found it shortly after one of my Teachers described some of the more accomplished couples on Earth, those who were true polarities. They often choose to live together in the higher worlds for a time, to develop their unity in an atmosphere that will further their future work for the benefit of humanity. You know, 'where two or more are gathered.' Did you learn yet about the principle of polarity, where the energies between the two opposing poles, positive and negative, are stepped up to a higher level by the back-and-forth oscillation? How they can be of greater service with the positive Force they regenerate?"

She hadn't exactly studied the principle he was talking about, but she knew it. Instinctively, it seemed. Or perhaps she'd learned it during her previous visits to the higher planes?

"I wondered a great deal about those couples and their work," he said as he led her around a bend in the lane. "And then one day, I found myself here. If I directed us correctly, right over the next little rise should be a cottage. Yes! There! Can you see it?"

Marta saw only a flickering of rainbows where he pointed, something like the shimmer that rises in the heat above a desert floor.

"Try, if you can. I can't see all of it, either, but if you focus hard, you should be able to see as much as I can," he urged.

She struggled for a moment to quell the many questions that rose—not a few of them about Kriss himself—and finally she could see within the hazy rainbows the barest outline of a country cottage, surrounded by blooming gardens. The walls and roof would flicker into focus for a moment, then vanish.

"Why can't we see it?" she asked.

"Because it isn't finished yet."

"Why not?"

"Because the couple who will live in it are still building it together."

"You mean, they're building it with their minds, right? Because that's how all buildings are constructed here? We *are* still in the same dimension, aren't we? The higher world?"

"Um, well, sort of. It does reside at a higher frequency than Earth, one of many such places. But I think we'd better go back now," he glanced around nervously. "I'm not sure we're supposed to see this just yet—I mean, it might be too soon. I mean, well, you know how I've gotten myself in trouble in the past, all that adventuring and exploring." He flashed her a brilliant grin. "I don't want to get you into trouble, too."

"Kriss, what aren't you telling me?"

He stopped smiling for a moment as he gazed into her eyes, giving her that feeling she'd had before, of him looking, not at, but *into* her being. She shivered more than a little.

"Only things that you already know as well as I do—you've just forgotten for now. You will remember them when the time is right. But we'd better move on, seriously. Help me focus."

He reached for her hand.

"Let's go back to the classroom. Before we have to take our rest, I think we can sneak a look at some of those display cases the Teacher was explaining. Oh, right—you probably slept through that."

He smiled again and clasped her outstretched hand, which Marta found to be infinitely reassuring. With one last, fond glance over his shoulder at the rainbow cottage mirage, he turned back to face Marta and closed his eyes. She followed his lead and next she knew, they stood exactly where he predicted, in the life science lecture hall, in front of the display cases.

Well, he definitely didn't 'die' on that mountain because of poor navigational skills!

She hurried to keep up with him as he moved rapidly among the display cases, expounding on the instruments they contained.

"After our next class, I'll show you the museum and the library—have you seen the libraries here? You won't believe it!"

She smiled but didn't say a word. Instead, she let herself feel an eager glow of anticipation. She wouldn't be going alone this time. Maybe together they'd be able to peek inside one of those books without passing out—or rather, *up* a few levels!

She gazed at him again. *I wonder if he likes to dance?*

For a flash she felt her midsection drop away and her body began to spin. A tall man with a beat-up guitar, swirling skirts, wagons, and a grimy, dingy neck scarf...Kriss advancing toward her...Kriss wracked with grief and remorse...thick blood flowing from a knife wound...

She blacked out.

16

Twin Flames

Marta," *Coriskancsia crooned over* her resting form, "it's time for you to make a journey on your own."

Marta sat up in alarm, as it all came back to her.

When she blacked out in front of the glass display cases, Kriss caught her and laid her gently on the floor. She awoke to feel his wet tears pressed against her face.

"You remembered," he whispered as he clung tightly to her energy body, pressing her to his own.

"Yes," she murmured, stroking his hair, her tears mingling with his.

They lay together on the soft floor of the deserted classroom for a long time. Neither uttered a word, for words could not convey what their hearts, minds, and souls experienced in those long moments of joined despair, love, grief, joy, remorse, regret, and finally, healing.

When they separated their energy bodies much later, they were renewed. Their love had grown, not diminished, by their mistakes.

Now Marta understood why the rainbow cottage was

incomplete. They must return to Earth to finish their healing and to build a greater knowledge of Infinite Love before their mental abilities would be sufficient to maintain life in such a place. On Earth, they would practice loving:

They would care for and respect and treasure each moment together—in whatever relationship they found themselves, whether parent/child, brother/sister, friends, even designated "enemies." They would strengthen the love-polarity they'd been building together for so many lives.

Together and separately, they would learn how to conquer the dark swirls of energy that had engulfed them in the wanderers' wagon, obscuring their vision and lashing out to destroy them.

Many times before, they both now knew, their bonds were cut in physical lives by their own ignorance, ego, fear, or anger, and many times they met again in higher worlds to examine their errors and make new plans to return to a physical world to try again. And again.

They did not meet in every lifetime. They each had other lessons to pursue, other individuals to face, other traumas to overcome. But each time they found one another, they learned more about Love. And each time as it grew stronger between them, they learned a little more about how to blow on that ember and protect it from strong winds, even when the threat came from within themselves.

Kriss and Marta stood a little taller now, aged a bit in their energy expression. They grew quieter and perhaps a little less frivolous. And they became inseparable, parting only when Marta went off to her dance lessons and Kriss pursued his own crucial studies, which they knew they must undertake separately. But at every opportunity, they gleefully toured all the special places Kriss had promised to show her, while their hearts made silent plans.

She never wanted to leave this place—or Kriss! So despite all of her preparation and training, Coriskancsia's words about making a journey alone made Marta's stomach seize up.

"What do you mean?"

Coriskancsia smiled. "Nothing to be frightened of, dear. Far from that!"

"Then what is it? Why must I go alone?"

Coriskancsia would not say. She held out delicate, bejeweled fingers that dripped with glittering stones set in swirling metals, which captured glints of the soft light that filled Marta's resting space. "Take my hand," she commanded gently.

Marta complied, trying to remind herself that there was no such thing as alone *anywhere in the universe*. She was never alone. If she learned nothing else here, that should be engraved in her psychic anatomy by now.

Yet fear tends to erase all but the deepest grooves, at least temporarily. She exercised some of her new mental skills to push it back and met Coriskancsia's hand with equal grace—newly learned from Madame Piiottssiiz.

"Very good," Coriskancsia smiled. "Now close your eyes for just a moment. Remember what I told you about the temple on the crystal mountain? Can you picture it?"

Marta envisioned the wooded cliff they'd visited, where the birds had dipped down to snatch a bit of energy from Coriskancsia's fingertips. She saw the sparkling plain that spread beyond, and in the distance, a shimmering mountain. Near the peak, she could make out the many spires and pillars of a magnificent structure. Coruscating light beams emanated steadily from the crystalline temple, shooting up into the atmosphere and disappearing out of sight.

"Now open your eyes, Marta," she heard her Teacher whisper.

She obeyed. Coriskancsia had vanished.

Marta was no longer in her resting space. Long grasses of delicate-soft crystal cushioned her feet, tinkling in the caress of a light breeze. She stood on the edge of the high crystal plateau, faced away from the green plain that stretched off behind her, and in the far distance on its other side, the cliff she'd once stood upon with Coriskancsia. Now she gazed up at the forest that ringed the lower levels of the mysterious crystal mountain she first saw from that distant cliff.

The clearly sparkling trees loomed taller than any others she'd seen, with a quality of beauty unsurpassed. They shimmered in lavender, indigo, sapphire, emerald, gold, peach, and rose, glittering in perfect rainbow order, pastels and deeper tones blending harmonically in a soothing pattern of light and color. All trees in this world were magnificent, but these seemed to call to her.

"Come," they said. "Join us!"

Her heart welled up and she quickly gave in to desire. She scampered toward them with her arms outstretched, trailing her fingers through soft, low-hanging foliage. From every smooth leaf she touched, tiny light-rays exploded, permeated her energy body, and left a trail of color to waft behind her as she danced through the wood. Exhilarated, she let the trees caress her as she leapt through the dappled glades beneath their soaring height, touching, sensing, inhaling their life energy into her own.

Beneath her bare feet the clear grasses and fallen crystal leaves crunched each time she landed but did not stab. Nary a root nor twig nor rock offered painful resistance. Like the trees themselves, the ground welcomed her feet with embracing encouragement and sprang her back into the air. As she neared the top of a small hill that led up to a meadow clearing, she glanced back at the crystal forest. From this height, she could see a path of opalescent radiation where she had run through the grove. Everywhere she'd touched them, the trees seemed to glitter in happy contentment.

She reached the top of the rise with ease, not expecting to see anything more beautiful than the woods she'd just danced through. Yet there it was on the other side of the hill, a formal garden that must have been designed by Lighted Minds!

As far as she could see, blossoms twinkled in every color she knew and a few new ones. For miles, they formed glimmering spirals, circles, diamonds, and squares. Here and there, a flowering plum or peach or twinkling hedge rose from the flower beds to add artistic balance—surely, the work of a Master gardener! Reflecting pools and streams with gentle falls added their music as they trickled over crystal stones and passed under delicately curved bridges. As she stared in awe, they pulsed rainbows of refracted light straight into her mind.

And the fragrance!

It wafted up the hill on which Marta now struggled to stay conscious, so overpowering were the sights, sounds, and smells of what many on Earth would call *Heaven* if they glimpsed it in a dream.

Slowly, she followed her instincts down into the flower beds, inhaling the heavenly essence with every step. At the first massive bloom she reached, she stopped and reached out to cup a pearly rose that one minute glistened deep carmine, then vermilion, cinnabar, then pale rosy shades of pink and peach. In an instant it oscillated a thousand variations. When she leaned over to breathe in the fragrance, the flower's huge petals enveloped her entire face. She nearly keeled over from the pulse of Love that filled her being.

Happily, she began to dance again, moving lightly from bloom to bloom, practicing her new steps as she experimented with touch and smell and vision, learning all about each flower's unique qualities. One made her feel *happy*, another blissfully *warm* and *comforted*. She danced the feeling. Others filled her up with *Love*, or *energetic ambition*, and overall, she consumed great amounts of *confidence* and *joy* and *contentment*. She danced it all. She felt that she could soar as easily as in the anti-gravity room, so filled was she with the *possibility* of all things. No limitations!

Curious to test the feeling, she imagined herself cloaked in a gown of sheer, pale yellow littered with diamonds—and immediately she was!

In exultation, she swept her arms and body into a tight spin,

then sprang like a gazelle around in a circle, her long legs flashing out with ease as her delicate toes pointed the way. She spun
and stretched, then moved her arms lazily overhead in a flowing
expression of her feelings, then turned and leaped again, flying
high over the flowers with her legs in a perfect arch of fluid grace.
Laughing in delight, she landed on a grassy plot near the clear-
running brook whose music had accompanied her spontaneous
dance. Her sudden arrival scared up a trilling flock of tiny birds
that took her place in the sky as she took theirs on the ground.

But where are the bees? she mused. *Such a garden must have
bees!*

On cue, a fist-sized, yellow-and-black buzzy insect landed on
an orange-pink zinnia nearby, a blossom big enough to hold the
bee's considerable weight. Marta wasn't frightened at all. Not
here. Her excursions with Kriss and others had shown her that
even in deepest wilderness in this world, the animal life inter-
acted with the human inhabitants without fear or aggression.

Many times, as they instinctively stepped around a snake or
jumped back from a tiger's face in the brush, their Teachers had
to remind them that none needed to fight for survival in this
Mind-created world. Abundance was the rule; lack unknown.
Sustenance flowed in through the consciousness, not the hungry mouth. So humans and animals (and fish and reptiles and
insects and plants and birds) came to know one another on new
terms in such a place, as offspring of the same Infinite Creator.

On earthworlds, they gave and took of one another's energy
by eating and being eaten. Here, the eating ceased but the energy
exchange continued. And here they all knew from whence that
Infinite Energy sprang. Humans learned of their essential need
for one another and all life expressions in order to connect with
and to extend the Infinite through their unique imprint of self.
This was true of both human and animal. Earth words could not
encompass the knowing and sensing and Love they absorbed,
regenerated, then passed from one to another.

People who spent time here could not ignore the lesson: Whether in physical or astral world, Infinite Intelligence suffuses every living thing, right down to the tiny atoms of seemingly solid rock formations on Earth, which are as alive and intelligent as any human being. Just because they oscillate at a slower frequency, doesn't mean they don't carry the same capacities for change and adaptation and growth, guided by an inner Pulse of information stemming down from higher dimensions.

Marta and Kriss were taught that if you looked closely on an earth planet, you could see it happening. What were rubies and diamonds and sapphires and citrines and watermelon tourmalines, if not evolutions of rock into crystalline structures that gleamed with Infinite Intelligence?

To communicate with other species and inanimate objects is purely a matter of spiritual knowledge, their Remedial Reincarnation Teacher told them. "All you must do is learn the universal language of energy."

Well, this is certainly a great way to study, Marta marveled now, as she let her fingers trail over another blossom. The flower's deep blue penetrated her fingertips, and the place she touched gleamed with a bright new shade of yellow.

Eventually, she realized that her adventure in this exquisite garden must be more than visually dazzling. She could feel her energy body absorb new healing rays, which she recognized as additions that might help her in future lifetimes. She wished Kriss were here to share the experience...

To shake off her sudden pang of loneliness, she took off at a run toward a mound of giant purple-and-blue anemones, sent herself airborne at the last moment in a perfectly arched *jeté*, then let herself tumble down among the energy petals with a peal of laughter. A snowstorm of purple and blue petals flew up around her but as expected, the springy blossoms broke her fall. She rolled in their soft embrace as she inhaled their unusually sweet fragrance. When she turned over on her back to gaze in full bliss at the light-beams that streaked through the sky, she was not surprised to see a gauzy-winged butterfly flutter closer.

Long and lacy, the wings swooped overhead with soundless grace, lifting up on an invisible wind, then settling on a nearby bloom. Marta quietly scrambled to her knees for a closer look.

To her astonishment, the butterfly began to grow.

As she quickly slid out of the way it stretched to four feet, then ten, then fifty, and so on, forcing Marta to retreat all the way across a conveniently placed bridge to reach the far side of the brook!

The garden itself had to move aside as the butterfly grew on newly emerging ground. Its legs extended around the blossoms, so not a single petal was crushed nor tree trunk battered as it grew until it was as large as a small jetliner on Earth.

This was not a butterfly at all, she realized, but a magnificent construction of filigreed crystal shaped to look like one. Light sparked from the multicolored wings, now folded upright, which sent harmless fireworks through the trees and flowers and waterways. One of these beams struck Marta with such gentle force that she stumbled backward into a thornless rose. Unhurt, she regained her balance and stood again, stunned and speechless.

The temple she hadn't noticed before suddenly drew her attention. Through the trees on the far side of the butterfly carriage, it shimmered like countless chandeliers fused into one massive creation of diamond intensity. So crisp and pure and alive was its beauty that Marta felt it like a sharpness in her chest, almost painful to view.

From her current proximity, it appeared so delicately carved and ornamented that the slightest breeze would surely shatter its fragile walls. She could not tear her eyes away from it—until a swirl of motion from the giant butterfly drew her attention back to the new clearing.

Attendants dressed in silvery blue appeared at either side of two oval, carved-crystal doors at the top of a ramp that extended down to a flower-strewn path. Slowly they drew open the doors and a great Light burst out, obscuring Marta's vision.

As her sight cleared, she could discern two Flame Beings whose intermingled auras created the dazzling brilliance.

She'd been told of such Beings. While they sometimes took on human form to serve as Teachers among less-evolved humanity, they were far advanced from the need for physical worlds, much beyond the spiritual development of Marta's Teachers in this dimension. Coriskancsia told Marta that she would only see such Beings in their true form on rare and special occasions, and always for some great, significant purpose.

Was I invited here? she wondered frantically. *Or am I trespassing?*

She quickly slipped behind a tall cluster of swaying sunflowers on the brook's far bank where she hoped her yellow gown would serve as camouflage. Through the platter-sized blooms she could still make out the two forms.

As their Flames diminished slightly, she could see that they were man and woman. When their faces gradually emerged, she realized with sudden terror that they were looking straight at and into her, as if the sunflowers didn't exist!

And they smiled at her in unison.

A thrill of Love passed through her, so unimaginably sweet that once again she lost consciousness and tumbled for the last time onto the twinkling grasses.

When she opened her eyes again, she no longer sprawled beside the brook. Her energy body reclined on a soft-pillowed lounge beside a small indoor lake. Alabaster statues of robed men and women graced the water's edge, while far overhead vines of purple wisteria and red climbing roses entwined a crystal lattice to form a roof for this airy pavilion.

She could feel the cooling effect of the surrounding greenery caress her face with its whisper of moving air, but when she turned to look she saw, not ferns, but a swan as large as herself gliding smoothly over the sparkling water. Fearlessly, it swam close for a moment to investigate her presence, ruffling feathers so pure in their whiteness that they reflected the rainbow of colored energies that swirled through the atmosphere.

"Welcome to our home," said a voice beside her.

She turned to see the woman from the butterfly carriage.

She beamed Marta with a blinding smile. "You might know me as Uriel, but I have many other names, on many worlds." She followed Marta's gaze to the man who stood behind her. "You may know my beloved as Michiel. Some call us Archangels but we do not care for the limitations of such titles and designations. Or the implied suggestion that we are in any way different from you." She winked, "Except perhaps that we have traveled a few paces beyond your present development."

Tears welled in Marta's eyes. Her heart feasted like a starveling on the sight of the woman's long, golden curls, on the eyes that seemed a link to Infinite realities she could sense but not define. So familiar, this hair, this face, these eyes! Marta could not look away from them.

The woman's answering gaze turned to silver fire, penetrating deep into Marta's being. The lake, the swan, Michiel, the flowers—everything around them disappeared for several long moments and all Marta knew was the depth and breadth of those eyes, those whirlpools of Intelligence. What passed into her in that exchange needed no words. Love never does.

"Beloved daughter, child of the Infinite, do you know why you are here?"

Weakly, Marta shook her head. Her heart chakra whirled feverishly.

The smile that enveloped her warmed the surroundings by several degrees. "You are one of my long-time students. Did you not recognize me?"

Yes, but how could that be? Marta thought wildly.

By now, she knew she was in the presence of two highly advanced Beings, Twin Flames. *Only the more evolved souls study with such individuals! How could I have been her student?*

"That is a question you will strive to answer for yourself for many lifetimes to come. We have been together before, you and I. We have incarnated side by side on physical worlds, when you had reached a level of development in which you were capable of lending a positive hand to the work that we have chosen to perform among the earth peoples. Our cause is enlightenment—spiritual liberation, if you will. But like many others, you lost your direction once you incarnated in a low-frequency world such as your most recent home, planet Earth.

"It is difficult to maintain one's interdimensional awareness when living within the restrictions of a physical anatomy. You strove mightily but failed, dear one."

Her words hit Marta with resonant ferocity, freezing her soul in terror. She remembered. Tears rushed again from her eyes, only this time they were not mild reflections of happy sentiment but the spontaneous release of a sudden and searing psychic pain. If she'd had a pumping heart, it would have torn free from her arteries at that moment; her stomach would have turned inside out. And if she hadn't already been "dead," she would have died from the sharp fragments of memory rushing into her mind.

Uriel continued as if Marta's response was the one most hoped-for. No recrimination filled her voice—and no sympathy. She gave sound to infinite compassion. She knew what images played in Marta's mind for she said, "Yes, that is true. Atlantis was the downfall of many of our Light Workers.

"But others maintained their higher level of attunement. They were able to serve humanity by retaining some measure of our teachings as brought to the Atlanteans. These few traveled to Egypt, as you have been told, and to other locations around the world of Earth. There, they reinstituted some degree of the scientific, spiritual concepts that were taught among the Atlanteans, but they were never able to fully achieve or re-establish the great accomplishments of Atlantis."

Marta's bones—if she'd had any—would have been trilling with the resonance of her past. She knew the Being by her side could speak nothing but Truth, could emanate nothing but Love. Her tears flowed unabated as memories of her personal fall from a higher consciousness flooded her mind.

Uriel extended an exquisitely formed hand to touch Marta's own. "Now is not the time for despair, dear, for now you have returned to me in an open-minded state of being! This time we share together will prove most valuable to you in your future incarnations.

"I am here to remind you of your spiritual birthright and of the steady climb that you have been attempting, to regain your status in the infinite, creative scheme of life! You are meant to be a Light Worker once again, as you restore your lost knowledge. You turned your back on the Light of Infinite Wisdom in exchange for promised gains and power of a material nature. But now you have turned your face to the Light once again! So I have been informed," she grinned and winked.

Angelic humor, thought Marta. No one needed to *tell* her anything. Such Beings mentally attune to whatever they need to know. A confusion of joy and remorse, ecstasy and apprehension tumbled through her at that moment, but she managed a shaky smile.

"I have been informed by my Brothers and Sisters, your Teachers, that you have made steady and courageous progress in your studies, and that you have been willing to expose your lower self in an effort to heal, but also to help others. That is an admirable trait, dear one, and it shows that some of the fire that once burned within you has been rekindled! I must take some small credit for that achievement," she beamed, "for I have worked with you in many lifetimes—several in which you did not recognize me as your spiritual teacher, and even some in which you fought against my efforts, not only those made for you, but for all of humanity. But those instances fall behind us now, into the distant past, as we let them slide from us and focus our attention on your future."

The future? Marta could barely consume the present.

But Uriel persisted, pushing Marta's thoughts out of their despair, forcing her to think ahead.

"You will be one of many who sets a new standard for the Earth people, both in the way you live and the words you speak—and the expressions you make. Yes, we enjoyed your dance in our garden of Light—perhaps as much as you enjoyed our garden!"

Marta glowed pink.

"No need to be embarrassed! Yours was precisely the reaction we hoped for when we created our healing garden. You have delighted Michiel and me beyond measure!"

Michiel...she'd forgotten all about him. He still stood quietly behind Uriel, towering above them. With his golden-reddish aura extending out for hundreds of feet, mingling with Uriel's and filling the immense pavilion, how could she have missed him?

Marta's stomach turned over again with a new wave of guilt and fear. She'd let him down as well in the past, the very distant past...

But he smiled at her with such beneficence that her fear subsided. She sat up in the lounge, startled when it moved with her to support her back.

Again Uriel touched her hand. "We realize this is all very astonishing to you. I suppose even our butterfly carriage was something of a surprise!" She glanced up to grin at her psychic twin—her biune, polarity, soul mate.

Marta knew the terms but had not remembered the Power two highly-developed souls could regenerate between them. They oscillate like magnetic poles, positive to negative, back and forth in a continuous energy exchange. Now she understood more fully why such polarity relationships were coveted developments among the spiritual-minded.

A flicker of thought flashed through about Kriss, but it was quickly dispersed by another wave of Intelligence directed to her as Uriel went on, laughingly, "Michiel warned me that it might not be the best way for us to introduce you to our home, which you have called a temple. I suppose it is that, for we invite many here to continue their work for humanity, although certainly not in any religious order. But I do so love my butterfly carriage, which he designed for me! I couldn't resist giving you a glimpse of it. Someday perhaps, we will take you for a turn through the garden?"

Uriel's sounds of delight drew another swan to the water's edge, and a flock of white doves settled on the crystal paving stones near her feet. She lifted a palm and a hummingbird swooped from the overhead vines to land on it for a moment, preening its feathers. She petted it absentmindedly.

"Shrunk down to the butterfly's perspective is the best way to view the flowers, I think. Still, I believe you have shown us yet another way to enjoy them. Michiel, we shall have to dance through the garden next time!"

He joined her laughter, executing a slight bow, "My pleasure, of course!"

The doves gathered at his feet, expecting food. He dipped into his robe and scattered what looked like diamonds among them, which they greedily devoured. As he turned his attention to Marta she saw that, like Uriel's, his eyes bore no solidity. And something more serious lurked within them.

"We have pushed your awareness to the limits of comprehension—and perhaps beyond," he told her. "But our time together is short, and we needed to make this special contact with you so that during your incarnation on Earth you would recognize our frequency when it presented itself to you."

Marta looked a question at the two Golden Beings. *Recognize their frequency? On Earth?*

"It is true; we will be on Earth, in a manner of speaking, while you are also there," Michiel explained.

Uriel agreed. "At this moment my physical counterpart, what you would consider an 'incarnation,' is busily preparing a teaching curriculum for future generations of Earth people, working together with our quadrocentric polarity known as Raphiel, while his own biune—twin flame, you would say, or polarity, Muriel, remains here with us in full Consciousness. Just as Michiel remained behind to help me while I lived many of my lives on Earth." She smiled up at him. "And I, of course, did the same for him each time he made the journey to your world. This is how we strengthen one another's efforts."

Michiel continued, "You see—and this may be somewhat complicated for your conception at this time—but we never fully leave these higher realms once we have developed a Consciousness that makes our residence here a natural part of our lives. We can extend a physical body into the earth worlds through the normal means of conception and birth, but a part of our awareness remains in higher realms where we truly reside. Our earth counterpart may not be at all times fully conscious of our larger identity or Presence. However, that is unnecessary. Just as you will function on Earth, naturally drawing from your higher intelligence, our earth selves also draw from that Superconsciousness or the full expression of our Selves."

If she'd been feeling more at ease, Marta might have laughed. As he well knew, her Superconsciousness had minuscule capability in comparison with the highly developed, unimaginable mental resources such Beings as these two must by now encompass! They were millions, perhaps billions of years ahead of her on the path of personal progression, if such a thing could be measured in earth-time. Still, she'd been studying. She knew that the principle of attunement through frequency and harmonics would hold as true for her as for any Advanced Intellect.

Uriel took up where he left off, "Even now, as you perceive us in some recognizable form, you are not viewing the full totality of our enjoined Consciousness. Such a vision would be beyond your sensing capability, completely incomprehensible and perhaps damaging to your psychic senses. We have demodulated these forms for you and others, much as we demodulate physical selves at any time that we choose to incarnate on an earth planet for the purpose of furthering our mission.

"We realize this is a complicated explanation. But perhaps in future times it will return to you and help to unravel certain mysteries you may encounter. The information you absorb here and the experience you are enjoying will remain a permanent part of you, as you surely must realize."

Marta nodded, glad at last that she was able to demonstrate some form of mental perception.

"The most important thing for you to remember, dear Sister of the Light, is that we will be with you constantly, in Consciousness. All you need do is direct a thought to us! It is possible that you will encounter some of our teaching curriculum on Earth, but *even if you do not*, you will have moments when you recall this meeting—and many others like it.

"You may even see my Brothers and Sisters of Light flash near you as tiny pinpoints of white or blue or gold, or colors you haven't seen before. When you do, you will have an inner sense of well-being, knowing that you are not alone, and that your Guardians and Teachers are looking out for your welfare and furthering your positive ambitions in any way they can assist—without interfering, of course. These Light displays will remind you of our lighted worlds and homes. And perhaps if you allow me the opportunity I, too, may dip into your consciousness from time to time with a word or two of advice."

Marta couldn't tell if she meant this literally or whether she was teasing, since the twinkle in Uriel's eyes indicated that it could be either way and that she, Marta, would experience many unexpected boons during her life to come.

"Yes, dear, that is true, but we would not wish to spoil all the surprises that await you! Just be open-minded, and *feel* our Love, which we give to you to pass on to all our Earth brothers and sisters as you encounter them. But Michiel has one surprise that he would like to unveil for you now."

Uriel unfolded her light-body from its crystal bench so that Michiel could assume her place at Marta's side.

"Dearest Marta," he began, then stopped. "Or perhaps we should call you by another name, for Marta is now a thing of the past, is she not?"

"Yes," Marta replied shyly. His face epitomized masculine strength but as he leaned closer she also saw in it a gentle compassion.

"I have been told that it is allowable to show you some small representation of your future." He turned slightly and gestured toward a gleaming pedestal behind him, upon which suddenly appeared a coruscating sphere of golden light. Its needle-fine radiations extended in all directions before dissolving into the energy atmosphere of the pavilion.

"Look more closely," Michiel suggested.

She glanced at him.

"No, you do not need to move closer but focus your full attention on the object resting atop the pillar."

She gathered every mental tactic she'd learned and put it to the task. Gradually, the glow subsided. She could make out a rectangular form within it, about three feet by five feet in Earth dimensions.

"Very good," he nodded. "This has been called the *Book of Life* by many on your world. In this symbolic form, it was given to the people of Atlantis as a reminder of the teachings originally brought to them by the Founders of their once-great civilization."

In one smooth motion, he rose and lifted a page of the book.

The light released was so intense it blinded Marta again. She focused hard until she could see shining designs on the page.

"You have 'read' this book before, Marta," he continued. "The Atlanteans lived by it. The foundations of their spiritual technology are written here. But you must realize, this book is only a symbol of true and complete knowledge of interdimensional life. No single volume can contain that never-ending stream of universal knowledge, but much can be held within your eternal mind, just as much vanished from your people's collective awareness. Some few elements remain, scattered in fragments across the face of the Earth. Some of this information has been distorted and perverted by selfish individuals into warped and even destructive teachings. Elsewhere, more useful elements of this Truth can be found on your world.

"But now the time has come for many souls to rectify their karmic involvement in the destruction of this *Book of Life*. Soon on your planet, people will rebuild a civilization that surpasses what they destroyed in the last days of Atlantis." His eyes met hers. "You will be among them, for you had much involvement in the destruction of these teachings at various times in history."

This time the words didn't shock. She'd seen the visions; she knew something of the roles she'd played. But Michiel was offering a way out of guilt and she leaned forward to absorb every word.

She'd heard of the *Book of Life* before, but only now did she realize that it was not some giant book where all the deeds of all the souls were written out, as if by some Godly hand! Or if it was that, then it was not as an Earth mind imagined. As Michiel pressed his Mind closer to hers, she knew it contained the missing explanations people of Earth had sought for all time: the design of the unity of life, the interdimensional energy principles that, if she could begin to understand them, would explain why souls travel from dimension to dimension, from lower world to higher world and back again, learning, absorbing, rectifying, building an Infinite Consciousness. For a brief shining instant, she glimpsed realities she had yet to achieve in her limited mental development. And then the window closed. But she'd gained a tiny new edge of knowledge.

"During your next lifetime, you will have opportunities to rectify many of these past mistakes as you help in our effort to restore knowledge on your planet. This restoration of the inter-dimensional understanding of science is ongoing with many planets in your physical universe. Your role will be but a tiny fraction of all that is involved in this re-awakening of the earth peoples. Still, to you, it will be the utmost and ultimate achievement of all your lifetimes to date. It will mean a great deal to you, and therefore to us, your Teachers, who hold in our hearts and beings absolute, magnanimous wishes for your success!"

Uriel moved forward to slip a hand in his. Her lighted countenance displayed her agreement as clearly as if she'd spoken.

Marta felt herself rise up inside, swelling with new confidence that she could achieve anything at all.

No limitations!

She managed to utter an expression of gratitude, but quickly realized that words, as she'd known them on Earth, could only attempt to reduce these infinite thoughts into measurable quantities. They failed miserably. So much more had passed between Teachers and student during this brief visit than words could encompass.

"That is true, dear," Uriel agreed, "and the fact that you've sensed this proves that you are ready for your next mission on Earth—your personal mission!" She looked up at Michiel.

He added, "The dance you did in our garden—remember it well. It is one of your special expressions, your way of carrying our Love to Earth. All who look upon you will feel that Love coursing through your veins, into your muscles, and out into the world through your graceful movements. As you have learned here, teaching does not require words. Some things are better felt than heard, better seen than spoken. It is our high, healing frequency that your audiences will sense, passing through you to them."

"In truth," Uriel added, "you do not need to dance to serve as our Light Bearer. But it certainly is a lovely way to capture and draw attention to the flow of Infinite, Creative Intelligence, is it not?"

This time Marta joined in the sparkling laughter that flowed from the Two who were One, sending trails of silver light throughout the crystal pavilion. Her heart lifted to meet theirs for a moment, soaking up the magnificence of this magical place. She longed to stay forever.

Was it true? Would she carry such Power to Earth? Open her mind and heart and allow it to flow through her?

If so, then that Power would heal, would awaken, would touch and ignite the Flame of Life in souls who were otherwise dead to their infinite potential. She would become a link in the chain of Infinity—not an impediment of clay feet wedded to a dense, material, flesh body, interested only in eating, sleeping, procreating, and otherwise amusing itself.

One of her Teachers had said that many Earth people were little more than an alimentary canal with teeth, eating their way through life and excreting their offal on the planet's surface. But a soul with a slightly higher development, one who had struggled and failed and tried again and finally made some spiritual headway in understanding the infinite inevitabilities of interdimensional science, such an individual, in the very smallest ways, could serve. Could change life for untold numbers. With the smallest of actions.

Uriel said softly, "We shall leave you now, dear Sister, though, of course, we will never leave you completely."

And before Marta could protest, the Twin Flames melded into One great blaze of cobalt blue, then silver, then brilliant white, leaving behind a lingering golden radiation as they vanished from the pavilion.

Marta's energy body soon followed, only instead of translating to a higher-frequency world as they did, her frequency fell to a level more familiar to her experience.

That it had been possible at all to rise to such a state of mind as to meet the Twin Flames of Uriel and Michiel was one of the most vital pieces of knowledge she acquired during her sojourn between lives. She would never forget, she vowed. *No limitations.* She did not need permission or priesthoods to commune with the highest levels of mental expression in the universe! She only needed a harmonic link, some connection built through her own lifetimes of hard-earned experience until she recognized that the link had been there all along, silently feeding her energy body until she activated its higher functions.

At first, she did not realize how far she had fallen from that dazzling encounter with the Twin Flames. The echo of Uriel's voice in her mind distracted her: "Remember, you can visit our garden any time you please. All it takes is a thought! Our doors are always open to you, beloved Sister of the Light."

I love you! Marta responded mentally, wishing she'd found the expression sooner.

"That's *our* Love that you feel, dear. Share it with all you meet! Dance our Love out into that needy world you will soon inhabit, *Amelia Longwood!*"

That was her first clue that this had been her graduation ceremony. Not at all what she expected! But then, neither was her sudden return to Earth.

17

Terror & Kindness

I know just what would happen if we got you a piano, Beth. You'd practice it for a few weeks and then you'd lose interest. Like your father and me. Our parents made us take piano lessons and we hated it! You'd have to practice scales for hours. Trust me; you wouldn't like it."

"But Mo-om, I do like it! I want to play the piano! No one is making me! I want to! Please?"

"I'm doing you a favor, Beth…"

From outside the front door, Amy could hear the rising voices coming from the kitchen, a conversation she'd heard a hundred sickening times: Beth pleading, her mother trying to convince her that she'd hate the piano. But for as long as Amy could remember, Beth had gravitated toward any keyboard she could find—a deserted church organ, her grandmother's ancient, out-of-tune upright. Amy purposely let the door slam. Hard.

"Amy! How many times have I told you NOT to slam that door!" her mother shrilled from the kitchen.

Amy sighed. Well, at least she'd put an end to Beth's misery.

"And where have you been? It's nearly four o'clock!"

Her mother came striding from the kitchen. Her hazel eyes were already bloodshot but she still wore her "dress-up" clothes: an olive green sheath large enough to cover her increased bulk with a goldenrod scarf angled artfully around her neck. Her greasy skin was beginning to gleam unflatteringly beneath the slippery makeup, which didn't conceal her heavy jowls or the puffiness beneath her eyes. Her copper-dyed hair was neater than usual but still hung unevenly around her thick neck where she insisted on cutting it herself.

By now Amy barely noticed her involuntary cringe at the sight of her mother. Long gone, the movie-star smile and full-flowing hair from the WWII-era wedding photographs. Everyone said her mother had been the most beautiful girl in school but they all kept the full truth from Amy: that she was also a dancer! That still astonished her, but what disturbed her more was how thoroughly the alcohol had destroyed her mother's looks, and how rapidly over the course of a day it transformed her personality, from a college-educated participant in local society in the morning (her public image) to a raspy-voiced hulk who threatened and taunted with hurtful words in the evening (her family's reality).

"I was walking," Amy mumbled, trying to keep all inflections out of her voice.

"Don't you talk to me in that tone, young lady! I've had just about enough of you," her mother spat with sudden vehemence. "Now you get up there and clean your room. I've told you a dozen times already this week!"

"Can I get something to eat first?" Amy ventured, hoping the change of subject might distract her mother from the outburst.

Anger often consumed Yvonne like a sudden avalanche, but sometimes, if Amy stayed calm, she could divert it. At least for a little while. It all depended on how much of the first martini her mother had consumed. A few sips and Amy could sometimes get her laughing instead of yelling. But from the sound of things, they would wait a long time for dinner tonight.

"Oh!" Her mother glanced back at the kitchen. "I think I left my cigarette burning…" She lumbered off to fetch it.

Amy followed her into the smoky room, where a few burn holes in the synthetic carpet tiles reminded her how often her mother left cigarettes burning. Beth had already escaped.

"Now don't spoil your dinner," her mother chided as she inhaled deeply and picked up her drink, seating herself behind the ashtray on the breakfast bar. She gestured sloppily, "I've thawed thome pork chops."

Her anger had vanished but her slurred speech kept Amy on guard. The raw meat sitting next to the sink might see a frying pan before nine or ten, but it wasn't likely because, as Amy finally remembered, this was bowling night. Her father wasn't coming home for dinner so her mother didn't need to wait to share the first drink of the evening.

Amy hated bowling night. When her father was home, her mother rarely treated them badly. But when he wasn't home they were on their own. Things could go from bad to worse very quickly. Even when he was there, dinner might never get cooked. And if it did, it might be inedible because by that time, her mother would be sloshing her martinis over the counter and burning the pork chops for which they'd been told for hours that they must wait. And no one dared enter her domain to try to cook them for her! She would rise up in a fury of indignation at the implication that she might be incapable. After all, when sober she'd built up a well-earned reputation for her culinary skills. They ate marvelously well when their mother stayed sober. But alcohol destroyed everything, stealing away any kind thoughts, creative impulses— and most significantly—self-esteem.

So whenever possible they snuck food from the cupboard. On rare, happy occasions, Amy or Tom might be allowed to make an early dinner for themselves and Beth while her parents "enjoyed their drinks in peace."

Where is Tom? Probably hanging out with his weird friends.

She couldn't really blame him. Watching her mother pick up the drink in one hand and draw on the cigarette with the other, a sick sensation boiled in the pit of Amy's stomach. She knew she shouldn't, that she'd never be heard, but sometimes her own frustration and resentment were more than she could control—much more—and the words escaped from her mouth in a rush of emotion.

"Do you have to drink that?"

"Now you listen here, young lady." Her mother's red-rimmed eyes narrowed fiercely as her voice rose and her finger wagged at Amy's face. "How dare you question me! You have no idea what my day has been like! I had to take your little sister to the dentist—I didn't even have time to wash my hair! And then I had to pick up the dry cleaning and do the shopping and pick up after you kids! No one ever helps me around here! Then I have to listen to you and your sister complain. Spoiled brats! So by golly, I have a right to enjoy this martini! It's my only pleasure in life! And no one's going to tell me otherwise!

"And don't you start in about my smoking, either," she rasped after an inhale. "This is the first cigarette I've had all day."

Yeah, right, Amy thought bitterly, *as if you would have washed your hair. And now you're going to smoke half a pack, now that you've started drinking martinis. You won't remember how many of either you've had.*

Her mother always rationalized that her drinking and smoking weren't problems because she never touched them until late in the day. Social drinkers drink in the evening, she'd say, while alcoholics—Yvonne never hesitated to speak with disgust about the few "genuine alcoholics" among her acquaintances—*they* drank in the mornings.

Amy knew this was a terrible self-deception and frankly, it didn't matter when her mother drank. She couldn't seem to live her life without booze and for Amy, it turned life into hell with the first sip.

She grabbed some graham crackers and moved to escape to her room as fast as she could, before her own temper brought the walls down.

But not before her mother managed a sharper dig with, "I suppose you were out walking with that *Jeremy*."

She shaped the name with a certain twist.

"I don't know what you see in him. He's just got that dopey look on his face all the time. Kind of hang-dog, like"—and here she drooped her lower lip disgustingly, pulled down her cheek jowls to look something like a bulldog, and stuck out her tongue with a vocal imitation. "Ploogh," she tried. Then tried again to get it right, "Poohhg." Not disgusting enough. She tried again. "Blooghy."

She was working hard not to grin during all this. From the stricken look on Amy's face, she knew she'd hit pay dirt. She seemed to delight in this kind of torture; she would find a sensitive, emotional spot and she wouldn't stop jabbing it until Amy (or whoever) broke down or fought back.

This time Amy chose anger.

"He does not!" she blurted, then realized she'd been had and fled to her room in tears of frustration and self-pity, as Beth had done half an hour ago. All the way up the stairs she could hear her mother making "hang-dog" noises, then laughing hysterically.

Amy ripped off her school clothes and wrapped herself in the Navy-surplus work shirt she'd stolen from Tom's closet. The faded denim hung to her knees. If he caught her stealing it, he always demanded it back and then it would hang unworn in his closet—until she stole it again. Back and forth the shirt would go, neither realizing that it comforted her to wear it simply because it belonged to him, and if it never hung in his closet, it would have lost its appeal.

She pulled the shirt snugly around her body and threw herself on the bed. Would she ever learn to keep her mouth shut?

You can't argue with a drunk, she told herself over and over again. But she could never control herself. *I've inherited her temper!* she wailed silently. (That's what she'd been told.)

But she couldn't form her most terrible fear into words: that she would turn out to be as fat and mean as her mother when she reached middle age. Since childhood this dread had haunted her and she knew it already tortured Beth.

Beth! Poor thing.

Amy got up and crept to her sister's door, calling softly, "Beth? Beth are you in there?" *Silly question, Amy. Where else would she be?*

"Go away!" came a muffled voice.

"Beth, it's me." She tried but the door was locked. "Open the door, Beth."

"No! I don't feel like talking! Go away!"

"You sure?"

Silence.

The door opened a crack and Amy could see her little sister's tear-stained cheeks. "What do you want?"

"Nothing. Just wondered if you're okay."

Beth opened the door a little wider, stepping out of the way. That was Amy's invitation.

She took it, pushing her way into the room. "Hey, what's this?" She picked up a drawing Beth had left lying on the desk. It was a colored pencil sketch of an otter.

"Did you do this?"

"Yeah," Beth mumbled shyly.

"It's really good!" Amy's admiration was genuine. Her sister possessed a special talent for drawing animals. "You should do more of these," she encouraged.

"Really?"

"Yeah, really. Do you have plans for this one?" Amy indicated the otter.

"No."

"Can I have it?"

"Sure." Beth couldn't hide her pleasure over this.

The two of them spent the next half hour looking through Beth's drawings, discussing which one Amy liked best and where in her room she should hang the one she picked. They forgot all about their mother—until they heard her thump heavily up the stairs, stopping halfway to pant from exhaustion.

"Shhh," Amy whispered. "Stay here."

"Wait!" Beth pleaded but Amy quieted her with a gesture as she got up and tip-toed to the door. Her mother hadn't reached the landing yet.

Amy slipped silently out of Beth's door and headed for her room. She never made it.

"I see you there," her mother hissed.

She'd slipped out of her stockings and shoes and into some old slippers but she still wore the olive green dress. The scarf was gone.

"I came to check if you've cleaned your room like I told you to." She hurled herself through Amy's doorway, spying the clothes she'd thrown off after school lying on the floor. "Just what I thought!" Yvonne exploded. "Well, that's the last time! I'm not putting up with this any more! You'll be sorry now, sister! And what's this?"

Amy stood frozen in the hallway. Yvonne had spotted the white diary lying open on her pillow and seized it up in her swollen fingers. "I'll bet it's all about Jeremy, isn't it?" she mocked, thumbing through the pages.

Amy charged into the room, reaching for it. "Give it back!"

Her mother turned easily to evade her, enjoying her torment.

"You can't read my diary! It's not fair!"

"Oh? And you think my life is fair? I'll tell you about fair!" But her eyes landed on something that made her pull the diary close to her face. "What's this? *'The Other Voice.'*" She dramatized the words to sound ridiculous. "What's that? You're hearing voices now, too?" She smirked.

"Stop it! You're drunk! Leave it alone!"

"Oh, drunk, am I? So now you're calling your mother a drunk?" Her voice rose a level, suddenly dead serious.

"Yes I am—because it's true!" Amy shouted back at her, not caring for any consequences. Her mother had invaded her private sanctuary, her one place of uninterrupted solace. It was an unforgivable act and Amy was beside herself with grief. She yelled the most hateful, stinging words she could think of.

"You're a drunken alcoholic! And I hate you!"

The forbidden words hit their mark. Her mother's face grew dark. She flung the book back toward the bed. It hit the side and rolled to the floor, crumpling pages beneath it. She stuck a finger in Amy's tear-streaked face as Amy backed away, bumping into her desk chair. Behind her, the mirror fragments reflected her mother's twisted facial expressions.

"You're spoiled, you're lazy, you're hearing voices, and now you're calling me an alcoholic? I'll tell you something, young lady. Your father is going to hear about this! That's no way to talk to your mother! And it's high time you learned some respect," she hissed hoarsely, but instead of slapping her as Amy expected, she lumbered toward the door instead, then stopped to fling one more arrow. "And this time we're going to take you to that shrink, you hear? Hearing voices! Huh! And you think *I've* got a problem. You're the one with the problem, kiddo! Now clean this mess up before I get back!" Then she headed for the stairs, muttering, "I know what you need. I'll show you some respect!"

Amy heard her clump down the stairs and hurried to slam her bedroom door. She chanted reassurances to herself: *She'll forget when she's sober. She's just drunk. She'll forget. She always does. She didn't mean it about the shrink.*

She carefully retrieved the diary from the floor, smoothing its wrinkled pages with shaky hands. One page was torn, the one where the Other Voice spoke about her mother creating chaos as an excuse to drink. She closed it quickly and hid it at the bottom of Gramma Jean's old straw trunk. She flumped down on the edge of the bed, emotionally exhausted.

Downstairs she heard a door slam. It sounded like the back door.

Where is she going now?

A few minutes later she heard rapid, heavy steps coming up the stairs. Before she could react, her door burst open and a blur of fury streaked toward her, wielding a long, thin willow switch apparently cut from the tree in the back yard.

"Come here, you little brat!" her mother spat in hoarse slurs, swishing the whip through the air, knocking things over but missing Amy, who leaped up in terror and shock. She darted from one corner to another, dodging blows and screaming as much from fear and surprise as anything.

Her mother had never struck them with objects before—only slaps with the flat of her hand. Her weapons of choice were verbal spears of wicked intent, cruel jabs like the one she'd taken at Jeremy a while ago. This unexpected violence terrified Amy.

As her mother landed a sharp, stinging blow across her legs, she yelped in pain and lunged for the door, frightened and now furious.

Her mother followed. By now Yvonne's face was distorted into a demonic mass of reddened flesh. Spit trailed out of her mouth as she hissed, "Come back here, you spoiled brat! I'll give you something to think about! I'm sick and tired of you making my life miserable! And now you're hearing voices! I've always known something was wrong with you! You're not right, young lady. You're just not right! You're a *bad seed!* I should have had that abortion!" she hollered as Amy plunged for the stairs

Another streaking blow singed into her bare legs, stinging like the fires of hell and Amy screamed again, sobbing hysterically as she ran for the front door.

The abortion—her mother's second favorite weapon. On a

calmer day, Yvonne would tell how she risked her life to have Amy when the doctors thought she should have an abortion instead. But because she "couldn't do that to her unborn child," she suffered all the pains of Amy's birth by Cesarean section. This plea for sympathy and guilt usually worked on Amy as well as tonight's version: shouts about what a terrible mistake she'd made by not having that abortion.

Amy fled down the street in complete despair. Tom's shirt flapped around her legs as her bare feet pounded down sidewalks still slightly warm from the fading mid-May sun. She had no idea where she was running to, only that she was running away from the madwoman behind her.

Her world at last reached its breaking point, and she felt all reason and sanity shatter. Everything she did now came from deep survival instincts. She ran and sobbed, catching her breath in great gulps of air. Finally she sank to her knees on a neighbor's grassy lawn and doubled over in hysterical anguish. She heaved out sobs of torment, her guts turning inside out.

She wasn't in physical pain. Her anguish came from the psychic shock of her mother's attack. Her own mother—had she really tried to beat her? Like a bad movie come to life? It seemed both unreal and too real all at once. If they took her to a shrink, what would happen? Could this madwoman really have Amy locked up? If anyone needed a shrink, it was her mother! But who would believe her? To them, she was just a kid. A troublesome teenager.

Amy wasn't aware that most of her life had been rimmed with the violence of psychological destruction, a subtle, undermining force that had infiltrated her mind since birth. Her mother's words, example, and beliefs had embedded themselves into Amy's thought processes. Deep down, she'd begun to believe it was true, that she was a bad person, a "bad seed" who should have been aborted because she was "cruel," "selfish," and "unkind" to the mother who loved her! Who suffered for her! In fact, they *all* treated her mother cruelly—Beth, Tom, and Amy. "Ungrateful brats" who made their mother suffer for all her kindnesses to them!

That's what they'd been told, over and over and over again. Their mother rarely swore and only occasionally slapped—until today. But every day, every week, she accused one or another of ruining her life, and she found her revenge in undermining their self-confidence with hurled invectives.

And now she'd found "proof" that Amy was crazy, hearing voices, seeing visions. She would never let it go, Amy feared. She wouldn't forget. Now she had new ammunition and she just might carry out her threats.

Is it true? Am I really insane? What is wrong with me? What if she's right? What if I'm the one who's crazy, not her? I'm the one having visions and hearing voices. She's just a drunk, but what if I'm losing my mind?

Oddly, between Yvonne's fits of anger, on "good" days she suffocated them with fearful clutching and worry—even Amy's father. She saw terrible harms that would come to them, scenes that plagued both her waking and sleeping nightmares. She grew hysterical if Amy's father ventured forth on any vaguely risky endeavor, such as taking a hunting trip with friends or driving in a snowstorm or operating any kind of power tool that might sever a hand or render him blind. Yvonne saw it all in her mind and she related it in gory detail despite their protests. Her powers of description were so vivid her family often suggested she write books, but perhaps they only hoped that would persuade her to stop including them in her nightmare visions. Apparently this frightened, emotional clinging was her best attempt to express love, which maybe she believed she should feel for them?

How could anyone be so self-destructive, so self-hating, and still love others, Amy wondered. That would defy the order of the universe. No love could reach her mother and so she had none to give. Yvonne's life was hell, as she always told them, not aware she made it so. She insisted that her only solace was her martini hours, "my only pleasure in life!"

That is so wrong.

Suddenly the tears stopped in Amy's throat. She sat up, remembering the diary entry.

What if the Other Voice is right? That we're not really the cause but only the excuse for her drinking?

Beth! She'd left Beth alone in that house!

Amy scrambled desperately to her feet. But she couldn't go back. She'd have to go forward. Frantically, she turned and ran toward the only place she could think of: the town's single phone booth. Twelve blocks away…

Panting, disheveled, she yanked open the door. But she had no money. Through the glass she spotted Tim Withers and his friends, lounging on the stone wall outside the post office across the street. She dashed barefoot across the deserted pavement.

"Tim, loan me a dime, okay?"

The high school sophomore looked up at her, taking in the bare legs and loose shirt. "Uh, didn't you forget something?" he joked, nudging Bob Young with his elbow.

Bob and George Ward, who sat beside him, guffawed as if someone had told a dirty joke.

But Amy just stared fiercely and said again, quietly, "Tim, loan me a dime, will you please?"

Something in her look shut them up for a minute and Tim reached into his pocket. Then a thought apparently surfaced in his half-formed teenage brain.

"What do I get for it?" he smirked, holding it aloft so she'd have to reach up for it. He still wanted to make something out of this solitary event of interest in a long, boring afternoon.

The others sniggered and laughed, imagining the view they'd have as Amy reached for the dime and her brother's shirt rode up her bare legs.

She started to reach, but realized the trap before it was too late. She pulled her arm back down as cascades of anger, humiliation, fear, and frustration broke loose within her. Fierce physical energy welled up with her temper, filling her arms and dancer's legs with tremendous power. She lunged for Tim's throat.

The others saw her look and scrambled to their feet, scattering. But she caught Tim by the shirt with both hands.

"You stupid son of a bitch!" she screamed, tugging and shaking him back and forth, her face inches from his. "It's for my sister, you idiot! You don't know anything! You stupid, slimy bastard!"

Blind fury, weeks, *years* of bottled-up anger coursed through her, unleashed now in mad strength that flooded down her arms. She could have snapped his neck like a twig but Tim dived and ducked and managed to pull free of her powerful grip, twisting and turning as she tore a section from his shirt.

"You're crazy!" he gasped indignantly as he stumbled and ripped himself out of her violent grasp.

He was shaking visibly, pale as the dime he threw at her. It bounced off her shirt and rolled into the nearby gutter.

"Take the fucking dime and get away from me! They call you Kooky Amy but you're not kooky, you're insane! You keep away from me!"

He backed up the hill to where his buddies waited at a safe distance, staring in frightened amazement.

Amy grabbed up the dime and ran back to the phone booth, sobbing now as the adrenaline subsided and left her an emotional and physical wreck. She'd terrified herself far more than she'd hurt Tim.

Now she knew she was going mad. What had come over her? She could have killed him! Her hands shook so hard she couldn't get the dime in the slot.

The boys kept moving away up the hill toward the wealthy section of town, looking back at her and shaking their heads, their stupid-white-boy jokes and pseudo-macho innuendos replaced by the genuine fear the suspected "insane" inspire among the ignorant.

Maybe she was crazy but she had to get help for Beth. She'd memorized the number—just in case—if only she could get the stupid dime in the stupid slot!

At last it slipped in and she spun the dial with trembling fingers. As soon as she heard it ring at the other end, Amy's mad outburst left her. She forgot it completely. Her only thought was about the scene she'd left at home and her little sister's safety.

Answer, please, please answer.

Involuntary tears welled up again and her throat closed off.

What if she's not at home?

**

Amy was crying so hard and talking so fast, Clareta couldn't understand a word at first. She only heard her student gulping hard, reaching for breath.

Finally some words made sense: "Beth! You've got to help Beth!"

"Where is she? Is she hurt?" Clareta motioned to John, who was sitting with a book in his armchair across the room.

"No, I don't think so." Amy sniffed loudly. "I mean...not yet. It's..."

Her conditioning must be clogging the words in her mouth, Clareta realized. *She can't say this. Not about her mother.* The family never talked about their mother to outsiders. They thought no one knew. But Clareta—and half the town—knew.

"My mother" was all she managed.

"Ah. I see." And indeed she did. "Where is your father?"

"Bowling."

"And your brother?"

"I don't know, with his friends somewhere. But what about Beth? I can't leave her there! I have to go back but—"

Clareta heard her choke back tears, apparently concerned

that her mother might physically hurt her little sister for some reason. She sensed that Amy hovered on the brink of complete collapse and broke in with soothing authority, "You stay right there. You're at the phone booth on Main Street? John will be there in fifteen minutes."

He nodded at Clareta's gesture, taking in the fragments he heard and the expression on his wife's face. He grabbed his coat. In seconds he was gone.

Half an hour later, Clareta heard the crunch of car wheels and hurried to the door. When she saw her husband help Amy out of their car, tear-streaked and half dressed, stepping gingerly over the gravel in her bare feet, Clareta had to calm her own emotions. Her prized student looked cold, humiliated—and terrified.

She met the girl at the door and drew her indoors with an embrace, stroking her long dark hair. "Shhh, shhh," she soothed for long moments, as much to calm her own reaction as Amy's.

John, still standing outside the open door, caught his wife's eye and Clareta followed his look down. The back of Amy's bare leg bore an ugly red streak. She nodded and gently drew Amy deeper into the foyer.

"Tell us what happened."

✳ ✳

Amy pulled away and stared at her teacher, full of fear and horror at the possibilities running through her mind. They hadn't gone back for Beth!

She had tried to tell him but the words were tangled and Mr. Quantos insisted on driving her immediately to their house as soon as he laid eyes on her. He didn't pester her with questions but he gave her his coat to drape over her legs in the car. Amy's anguish over the whole ordeal emptied her brain and she couldn't think of another word to say, so they drove the entire distance in painful silence.

But now she had to convince them! They must rescue her little sister from that house!

"She thinks I should check on Beth. What do you think?"

Mrs. Q studied Amy's face for a moment, as if to gauge the danger to her little sister.

"I think I can go back and take a look without intruding," Mr. Q suggested, "while the two of you talk. I can call you from the pay phone. Without an invitation, I can't go inside, and Amy tells me her brother and father aren't home. We could call the authorities."

"Not yet, John," Mrs. Q said, to Amy's great relief. "I want to hear Amelia's story first."

The couple exchanged a look and he was off again.

Mrs. Q led her into a tiny but warm and immaculate living room, filled with books and plants and art. An overstuffed blue armchair still had a half cup of cooling tea beside it. Amy had heard that her teacher's handsome husband made some money writing adventure novels, but they weren't wealthy. Their house was smaller than the Longwoods. Still, Amy marveled at the richness of the room.

"Let's sit here." Her teacher lowered her long body onto the deep cushions of an ivory couch, which was draped with a lavender chenille throw. She patted the spot next to her. "We'll help Beth, don't you worry. But please tell me what happened."

Amy sank into the couch, glancing at the maplewood piano nearby. She knew Mrs. Q had traveled during her dance career and the evidence of her global adventures decorated the room: a brass table from the Middle East, a glittering pink-and-gold cloth from India draped over the piano bench, small alabaster statues of Grecian figures on shelves and the fireplace mantel. But her attention was drawn to the steady trickle of water she heard from the skylighted atrium that opened off the living room.

In one corner of the leafy enclosure sat a cut-open rock as big as Amy's upper torso. Inside the hollow interior glistened hundreds of purple crystals, growing at odd angles to one another. Water streamed over these faceted gems, twinkled in the beam of a miniature spotlight, then splashed down into a fountain pool filled with clear quartz and surrounded by deep green potted plants.

"It's beautiful!" she breathed as a sense of peace settled over her.

"It's a Brazilian amethyst geode," Mrs. Q replied as she wrapped the soft chenille around Amy's legs and feet. "I picked it up when I danced in São Paulo. What a time I had shipping that thing home," she chuckled.

A sudden movement above drew Amy's attention from the shimmering fountain. A bright canary darted, chirping loudly, across a long cage fastened high up, just beneath the atrium's skylight. He clung to the bars and scolded down at them.

"That's Sherbet," her teacher smiled. "He's our opera singer—when he's not frightened by the commotions we stir up. He loves to fly around the atrium during the day but he should settle down for the night now. Go to sleep, Sherbet." She got up. "I'd better cover him."

From a bookcase shelf she extracted a dark blue cloth. She spoke soothingly to the bright yellow-orange bird, who looked at her skeptically and let out a few more irritated chirps. She slowly closed and latched the door of his cage and covered it with the drape. "This blocks the light so he can sleep in peace."

To Amy's disappointment, she also switched off the little spotlight that made the amethyst sparkle.

"This is our scrap of paradise here in Wilton." She sighed and settled back on the couch. "Now please tell me what happened."

Amy turned reluctantly from the atrium but couldn't meet her dance teacher's clear eyes. Her heart had stopped pounding and the blood in her veins no longer screamed to get out. The beauty of the little garden had somehow calmed her. Especially the sparkling purple crystals. But how could she tell this horrible story, which was even now beginning to fade, making her doubt her own experience?

That's how she survived her life. By forgetting the bad scenes, pretending they never happened. Tomorrow morning her mother would deny it all, tell her she imagined it. And she had learned to believe this. Each time. Her own mother wouldn't be so cruel, would she? She *must* have imagined it. And soon she'd forget— until the next time.

But Beth—she had to explain something! Now that her fear was fading, and her anger, she didn't think her mother would really hurt Beth. She wasn't that kind of drunk. Not usually, anyway. But Beth must be terrified! She must have heard the screaming and shouting.

"Well..." She didn't know where to start.

"Has your mother been drinking? Is that what happened?"

"Yes, but..." Amy was grateful for the help to get past that part. "Tonight was different. She..." A lump caught in her throat. Another word and she'd lose it again.

Mrs. Q moved closer and wrapped an arm around her shoulders. "Shhh, you don't have to say. John will find Beth and Tom. Where was Beth when you last saw her?"

"In her room," Amy whispered, nestling gratefully closer to Mrs. Q, who had never seemed so subtle or delicate as she did right now. Like a feather of kindness that might blow away in the slightest wind. Waves of comfort passed through her and unaccountably brought on a new flood of tears. She felt embarrassed again as the water washed over her cheeks. This time she had no reason for it!

Mrs. Q handed her a tissue. "You go right ahead and cry, Amy. Let it all out! It's just the two of us here. Sometimes we don't really cry until the worst is over, and then I think they're tears of gratitude as much as anything. Gratitude that we're alive, that no worse harm has come to us."

"Gratitude for you and your husband," Amy blurted, surprising herself and bringing on more emotion. "You're so kind to me! How can I ever thank you?"

"No need," her teacher blushed.

✳ ✳

"No need, Amy," Clareta whispered again, touched by the maternal feelings the girl brought out in her. She smoothed the hair out of Amy's face.

She didn't have children of her own; she had many children, students all, and that's just the way she and John wanted it. The world had too many already, they felt, and they longed to do things that would make that world a more beautiful place for future children to grow up. One day, maybe there'd be fewer who suffered as Amy was now.

It had always been Clareta's dream to expand her school into a place for all the arts, where talented young people could come and stay, find encouragement, and fulfill their heart's creative desires without the warping influence of a jealous society.

Clareta knew that jealousy from her own first-hand experience. It could cripple the strongest soul, if that soul didn't find a helping hand here and there. But she believed passionately that creative expression, if nurtured and encouraged properly, could heal the world, one person at a time.

"Amy?" she asked softly. "Do you remember what we talked about?"

Amy nodded, dabbed at her eyes with the tissue. Her tears were gone now as she stared at the glitter of the amethyst, which caught light from a living room lamp.

"We've missed you at the school."

Amy was silent.

"Have you thought about my offer?"

"Every day! But it's a dream! Impossible! How can I sneak off to a dance class without my mother knowing? And if she finds out, she'll kill me."

She looked genuinely frightened, completely convinced that Yvonne could stoop to such a thing. It broke Clareta's heart. Her own mother.

"And if my mother doesn't approve, my father won't go against that."

Before Clareta could answer, a phone ring pierced the room's quiet. "That must be John."

She jumped up to reach the wall phone in the kitchen. She'd been worried since he left, although she didn't let on. As everyone knows, domestic violence poses a serious danger to outsiders who interfere.

"It's okay," John reassured her immediately. "I simply went up and knocked on the door. Yvonne didn't answer, so I rang the bell. Still no answer, but I saw a willow branch lying by the front door." Clareta could hear him suck in a breath, trying to calm his anger at this.

"Which told me she probably didn't go after Beth with it. That's when Tom showed up and let me in. We found Yvonne passed out on the couch, drooling on herself and snoring. My god, Clareta, I didn't realize how far she's fallen. Have you seen her lately?"

"Yes, yes, go on," Clareta urged, "what about Beth?" Through the open archway she could see Amy perched on the edge of the couch, holding her breath.

"Beth is fine, although pretty shaken. When she heard the commotion with Amy, she dragged her dresser in front of her door and hid in her closet. Yvonne never made it back up the stairs, though. Beth says she heard her shouting and grumbling downstairs. Looks like she didn't follow Amy past the front door."

Clareta put her hand over the phone to call out, "She's okay. Beth is fine!"

"Where is she?"

"Guess she didn't want the neighbors to see her," John was saying about Yvonne. "You know, keep up appearances and all that. She's still passed out, even with us traipsing through."

"John," Clareta interrupted, "I want Amy and Beth to stay with us tonight. Tom's old enough to take care of himself. Besides, I doubt she'll wake until morning—or at least until Donald gets home. Tom can explain it to his father. Will you please go back and ask Beth to gather some of her own and Amy's things and come with you? I don't want either one of the girls sleeping in that house tonight!"

She glanced over at Amy, who looked grateful despite the words of protest that sprang to her lips. Clareta raised a finger, as if to say *no argument now*, and for a moment she let her stern teacher's demeanor return—just enough to brook no arguments.

Amy sank back into the couch, a little smile of relief and maybe gratitude playing around her lips. The sight was a balm to Clareta's nerves and she, too, breathed a sigh. The worst was over now.

❋ ❋

By morning, when the danger seemed faint and distant, Amy's humiliation crept in again. At breakfast in the Quantos' sunny kitchen, a terrible shame came over her.

Beth was easy. She had thoroughly enjoyed herself, irritating the canary with her piano plunking last night, and when Mr. Q offered to teach her a simple tune, her world was made perfect.

But Amy felt deeply confused. She barely remembered her attack on Tim Withers, and now she wondered if she had done the right thing, running to Mrs. Q, getting so many people involved.

Her teacher seemed like she was trying to put Amy at ease as she served the girls French crepes with sautéed bananas, which they devoured hungrily. (In the hubbub, no one had thought to ask if they had dinner the night before.)

When Beth jumped up after breakfast to play with the piano and Mr. Q politely excused himself to see if he could guide his new pupil into making more palatable sounds, Mrs. Q said quietly to Amy, "As far as I'm concerned, and this goes for everyone in this household—including the canary," she smiled, as they could hear him trilling exuberantly in the atrium, trying to show Beth how it should be done—"we'll never speak of last night again."

Amy looked up, grateful to hear it.

"No one else knows, except your father. Right now, we're not sure what Tom told him but I suspect it wasn't the whole story. Amy, for your sake, I am going to speak to your father privately."

She started to protest and once again, Mrs. Q held up a hand for silence.

"But I will not let your mother know I've done so, and not another soul will ever hear of it. Not unless your mother herself tells them, and I think that's highly unlikely! Or if you or Beth say something. You might want to talk to your little sister about that. Would you rather I did?"

"No," she said quickly. "I'll do it. I know what to say to convince her."

"Then it's our secret. Now you'd better extract Beth from the piano bench. We need to get you both home so you can get ready for school, don't we?"

"Mrs. Quantos—" Amy began as she got up to help clear the dishes and clean up.

"No need to thank us, Amy. And I want you to remember this: You come to my door, either here or at the studio, *any time at all*. You understand? You are always welcome!"

"Thank you," she breathed despite her teacher's protest.

"And I think it would be all right if you call me Clareta now. Outside the studio, at least."

Amy had to turn away fast, busying herself with the powdered sugar. The water in her eyes made it hard to see as she tried to pour the contents of the crystal serving bowl back into the box like her mother always did.

18

The Decision

That afternoon when Amy got home from school she found her mother sitting at the breakfast bar, weepy, hung over, and apologetic.

Yvonne remembered they had a fight and that she went into the yard to cut a willow switch, but she seemed unaware that Beth and Amy slept at the Quantos' house. If Amy's father knew, he didn't tell her.

"I don't know what came over me, honey," she cooed and blubbered. The martini ingredients were still in the cupboard and she was sipping at a cold cup of coffee. "My father used to do that! He'd make us go cut a willow switch for him—"

"Well, you didn't have to hit me with it!" Amy snapped.

She couldn't help herself. The pain in her legs was gone and the welt had disappeared but her heart still ached from the psychic blow. This soggy mass of human being before her was, after all, *her mother,* and her mother had hurt her, deep down, where the scars don't heal so fast.

Yvonne's tone changed quickly. "Hit you! Why, I barely tapped you—if that," she protested windily. "I'd never do such a thing!"

"You sure did!"

Amy couldn't believe she was trying to deny this one! How could she forget? Phone messages, conversations, appointments—she could forget things like that, but that terrible scene in Amy's bedroom? Chasing her down the stairs? She was going to deny that it ever happened?

"I most certainly did not hit you, as you say," Yvonne huffed indignantly, putting an authoritarian edge on her voice.

Then she added with a cackle, "I may have swished at you a little. Just to scare you."

Amy had often observed that her mother relished the demon inside her. Maybe that's why it came so often and stayed so long. She loved to court danger—by drinking too much, by smoking too much, by not taking care of herself, and by saying words that made people livid with rage, provoking them until a full-blown fight erupted.

The only person she wouldn't taunt was Amy's father. Not usually. Occasionally she tested him to see how far she could go. Then he would erupt and she would regret it. He was the kind of man whose disapproval alone could intimidate. And if you moved him to anger...you felt miserable for days. He never raised a hand, just gave you a terrifying look of disappointment. That was enough, even for her mother.

Amy loved and respected her father to the utmost, despite his inability or unwillingness to protect them from her mother. Maybe he didn't understand how vicious she could be? Or maybe because he drank with her most evenings, falling asleep in front of the television, he simply wasn't aware. Whatever it was, Amy forgave him. His drinking only made him absent; his obvious love for them never seemed to diminish. She made all her attempts to get along with her mother out of respect for her father. He had asked her to try.

Finally she conceded, "Okay, Mom, whatever you say." That

gave her a chance to escape to her room.

Thankfully her mother didn't notice that she'd come home early because she cut her last class. Too much in her life had suddenly thrown her sideways and she couldn't concentrate. She needed to find some balance.

After the nightmare with her mother, and the wonderful care and generosity of Clareta and John Quantos, she'd gone to school in a daze. By lunchtime, she had planned to spill at least one secret to Jeremy: Mrs. Q's offer about the dance classes.

She needed to talk to someone outside her family—and not a girlfriend, either. Amy knew that her dancing made her friends uncomfortable. After Pam dropped out of ballet class, none of them understood her passion for it. Or they were jealous. She remembered well enough Maureen's teasing. So that left Jeremy. She hoped he would have some idea about how she could sneak off to ballet class and get away with it. Guys did this sort of thing all the time, didn't they?

She was so absorbed by this idea that the shock when she stepped into the cafeteria that afternoon nearly knocked her over. Across the room she spotted Maureen, flirting unmistakably with Jeremy! And Jeremy clearly enjoyed her attention!

Maureen's voice cut through the room's dull roar like an ice pick, piercing Amy's already-damaged heart. They didn't see her. They were too preoccupied. Jeremy held a paper cup high above his head while Maureen tried to grab at it, laughing and pretending to be offended. Actually, Amy saw her make sure to press her chest against Jeremy with each leaping reach for the cup—she could see that clearly from where she stood, Maureen deliberately making moves on Jeremy!

Anger crowded everything else from Amy's brain. The scene resonated with her encounter with Tim Withers and his dime, which poured more heat on her fire. She would not ignore this affront! Not this time! She would make them *eat* their actions... she would walk right up to them and say...

"Jeremy! Maureen! How nice to find you here *together!* My two *best friends!*"

Her words dripped venomous sarcasm and her intent was unmistakable.

Jeremy blushed a terrible dark ruddy color. Immediately dropped the arm that held the cup over Maureen's head.

"A-Amy!" he stuttered. He'd been caught red-handed. "Uh—hi!"

Maureen seemed oblivious to her wrongdoing.

Oh, she is a cool bitch, isn't she? All that nonsense about, "Come over to my house this weekend!" What a slut!

She was about to utter the same aloud when Maureen interrupted.

"Ames! I'm so glad you're here! Maybe you can get Jeremy to share my milkshake with you, since he's decided to claim it for his own." She glared at him.

What a good job she's doing of feigning frustration with him, Amy observed wryly. *Not a trace of guilt in her inflection!*

Meanwhile Jeremy, embarrassed well beyond clear thinking, offered, "Yeah, Amy, here—would you like a sip?"

Amy fumed. "You both know I'm allergic to it," she hissed, and spun on her heel.

What a stupid thing to say! And she hadn't planned to retreat! But she didn't know what else to do. The events of the past twenty-four hours had completely exhausted her emotional reserves.

That afternoon she felt like an empty shell. She didn't hear a word spoken in any of her classes, until finally she realized it was useless to stay. Besides, she didn't care if she got caught. She simply walked out the front doors and strode home.

She had navigated the expected scene of denial with her mother in the kitchen and now she huddled in her room with her violated diary.

Where to begin? She held her pen over the wrinkled page,

staring numbly at its whiteness. Suddenly a blue glow about the size of a nickel appeared and disappeared against the paper.

She drew the spot on the white page, a circle with radiant spears extending in all directions, labeling it *Blue Light* defiantly, as if to prove she was *not* crazy.

Then she wrote, "What was that? Who is that? What are you saying to me?"

No answer. But now the pen was moving so she kept writing, pouring out her pain and confusion and distress. Every so often, a tiny pinpoint of light twinkled near her writing. White. Then golden. A combination of silvery layers. And those lingering blues, so much bigger than the other lights. After a while, she got used to seeing them and didn't notice when they flashed at her. Her busy pen scratched her heart and soul onto the page.

Gradually she depleted her storehouse of woe and started asking questions. Really only one question mattered: "What should I do?" It covered everything, from Maureen and Jeremy's betrayal to her mother's drunken madness and her command that Amy quit ballet.

She knew she had neglected Jeremy these past weeks. Too many things distracted her. She could cope with all of it—she'd had a lifetime to practice "forgetting"—but not the trauma of giving up her ballet classes. On that point, she was desperately confused.

Should she defy her mother and try to find a way to keep dancing?

Or succumb and become the "good daughter" she never seemed to be?

Rebel?

Or give in—to what? A life of misery like her mother's?

Her belly twisted at the thought of it: Never to dance again. To miss the opportunity Mrs. Q—*Clareta*—offered, a chance to dance in a piece choreographed just for her.

So many weeks had passed since she danced at all. Was it

already too late? She glanced at her profile in a mirror fragment.

Suddenly Amy realized that the solution to the Jeremy/Maureen problem was staring her in the face! She had started out fuming with righteous indignation over the cafeteria scene—and quickly forgot all about them!

Dancing was far more important to her than Jeremy. She *needed* to dance. Nothing could interfere, and no one!

I may be "only fifteen" as Clareta says, but what does that matter? I know what's right. I know what I want. I can feel it right here, in my heart.

After all her weeks of turmoil and indecision, her love for ballet suddenly and swiftly elevated her consciousness and the anger naturally fell away. It was as if she were back in the anti-gravity room with Madame Piiottssiiz, or in the garden palace with Uriel and Michiel. She resonated again with her higher self and that put her fully in tune with her Teachers in those elevated realms. In that state, her decision instantly shone clear in her conscious mind—which was always last-to-know in the chain of her full Being.

She stared at herself in the mirror fragments, trying to look behind her eyes to see her real Self. She couldn't do it. The face was too distracting. It showed too many things that she didn't like to see. Instead, she turned back to her diary and picked up the pen.

As she did so, the scene from the cafeteria stubbornly floated back to her, but this time without emotional impact, and without that, she realized she had been all wrong about it. She replayed the scene again.

Maybe Maureen wasn't acting after all?

Amy's cheeks burned, remembering the names she wanted to call her. (Amy hated the b-word, which is what made it so powerful.) But now she saw things differently.

What if it was Jeremy who made the first move, stealing Maureen's milkshake and teasing her with it? What if he started the flirting and Maureen was only irritated by his immaturity?

She smacked the pen back down against the paper, laughing aloud for the first time in days, maybe weeks. *That's it!*

She was so quick to blame Maureen. But really, Jeremy's behavior was completely in character for him. And his guilt—she laughed harder. *Written all over his face, the slime!* And the best part of all—she felt wonderfully relieved.

In a flood, Amy knew that Jeremy's affections for her weren't as pure as he claimed. For one thing, he wanted a kind of physical relationship she wasn't ready for. And for another, he still liked to flirt with other girls. It had been so obvious all along! She just hadn't wanted to admit it. But of course! And why shouldn't he? What ever gave her the notion of exclusivity in the first place?

"And you know what?" she said aloud. "I don't care!"

She jumped up gleefully, twirling around the cramped room in a spontaneous dance—the first she'd danced in weeks. A huge weight lifted from her heart. She knew exactly what she needed to do.

But first she grabbed her pen and scribbled something in her diary. She wrote it in jest, but the thought jelled.

Could this be true?

She'd written in fun, "Maybe we were reliving another lifetime!"

But now she paused, and added, "And maybe Maureen was the other woman! The fair-haired woman? Did I catch them together and blame her, when it was really my unfaithful husband I should have blamed?"

Fascinated by the idea, she kept writing.

"Maybe I was blinded by my ego. How could I admit that my husband did not love me enough to remain faithful? It would be a lot easier to believe he was seduced by some sleazy whore! I'm sure that's what I thought of her!"

Am I making this up?

But it felt right. In that lifetime, she must have protected herself from public humiliation by convincing herself, and everyone else, that it was the other woman's fault. That her husband still loved her enough that he would never consider violating their marriage vows, unless he was tricked into it…

For a long time, Amy stared at the page. The blue light reappeared, brighter than before.

"Who are you?" she wrote again. She drew another star on the paper where the light had shone and vanished. Immediately, a sprinkling of tiny white pinpoints covered the page so rapidly, she couldn't draw fast enough to catch every one.

"You must be my guardian angels," she smiled, knowing she only half-believed in them.

A big gold light flashed in and out.

Slowly, thoughtfully, she marked the place and drew shooting beams all around it. They covered her letters and extended all the way out to the edge of the page to signify its greater brilliance.

A new warmth filled her up. She wasn't alone anymore.

And she no longer felt frightened or confused.

19

Resolve

Amy hurried back to the school, where she knew she'd find Jeremy finishing up baseball practice.

Before she had gotten so distracted by her efforts to cheer up Maureen, they met a few times after his practices at the bleachers on the edge of the field. She waited for him to change and they walked home together. Now she stood deliberately where he could see her from the baseball diamond. He scowled.

As he sauntered toward her after they finished, she noticed for the first time the long strides he took—like an old farmer crossing a field. In a flash, her dream of mountains and cows reappeared in her mind and the two scenes melded for an instant. Amy smiled slowly.

That must be him. The farmer she'd been married to. Imagine! Herself a farmer's wife! It seemed so different from anything she knew in the present, and even from her tastes and personality. And those cows! She laughed.

As an eager three-year-old at her first county fair, she had begged her parents over and over again to "go see the animals."

But as soon as they entered the cow barn and her father lifted her in his arms so she could peer over the stall railings at those huge heads and dull eyes, terror rippled through her little body. When one quickly swung its big head around to look at her, she burst into screams and tears. Her father had to carry her out of the barn and it took them a long time to calm her down. She'd been afraid of cows ever since—not to mention allergic to cow's milk.

So Amy chuckled at the notion of herself as a dairy farmer's wife. She was certain that's the kind of farm it was, somewhere in the Alps, from the looks of it.

I guess I had enough with milk in that lifetime.

"What's so funny?" Jeremy demanded as he reached her. He glanced around nervously as his friends streamed by on their way to the locker room.

"You'd never believe me."

"Try me."

"You sure?"

"Yeah—what it is? What are you laughing at?"

He was turning red now, the color creeping up into his coppery hair. He brushed nervously at the dirt clinging to the side of his leg from his last spectacular slide into home plate, which had drawn cheers from his practice mates. Jeremy lived for such accolades.

He thinks I'm laughing at him! Figures. Always concerned about what his buddies might think.

Once she would have used that weakness to tease him but today she had more important things on her mind. Although he probably deserved to suffer a little after what he put her through in the lunchroom. But she let him slide one more time.

"No, it wasn't about you—well, not exactly."

"Well, what?" He seemed really irritated now, probably because he felt guilty—an odd way of reversing the internal pressure, casting it off on her.

"Oh, never mind." She knew that wouldn't suffice, so she

fibbed a little. "I mean, I was just thinking about you being so flustered in the cafeteria that you offered me some of Maureen's milkshake. And you know I'm allergic!" She laughed sincerely at the thought and shook her head. "Of all the things for you to say to make it better, you really blew it, didn't you?"

She could feel how much he hated this. *He must have hoped he wouldn't see me until tomorrow!*

She grinned, which made him grumble, "I don't think it's so funny. Why are you here, anyway? I didn't think I'd see you again for a while…I mean…you know…"

Now she smiled up at him kindly, understanding him fully and feeling generous in her new resolve.

Everything began to feel so simple to her, as her Earth-consciousness took over and started to fit her higher-inspired ideas into familiar and workable categories and solutions. She was on the brink of making a very common error, but she didn't know it.

"Come on, I'll walk you back to the school and after you change, I'll explain everything."

"*You'll* explain?" He seemed genuinely surprised at this.

"Yes. You see, it wasn't really your fault. I mean, well, just hurry up. I'll tell you everything when you get back."

He shook his head, hurried off to the showers, and met her outside again in record time.

"So what's going on?" he demanded. "What kind of game are you playing?"

She could see he was ready to turn everything around and make her feel as if she had been causing him trouble instead of vice versa, but he couldn't ruffle her. She was now very confident that she knew the truth and she knew what she must do.

"No game, Jeremy," she said quietly, linking her fingers in his and urging him to match her long-legged stride.

"Where are we going?"

"Just for a walk while I explain some things. Jeremy, do you believe in reincarnation?"

"Do I what!?"

He stopped walking, pulled his fingers free, and stared at her as if she'd lost her mind.

"Reincarnation. Do you believe we might have lived before?"

"Amy, what the heck are you—"

She started walking again, forcing him to follow. Grasses poked up through the sidewalk seams now but a chill wind cut through the late May sunshine.

"I mean, don't you think one lifetime isn't enough to explain how you just sort of know things all the time? How you feel so strongly about some things, and how you really like some people and don't like others at all, even when you've never met them before?"

"Yeah, I guess, but…"

"Well, I believe in it. I really do. And lately, I've been having flashbacks of other lifetimes. Maureen's the one who brought it up, actually."

"Maureen!? Look, Amy, I didn't mean—" he started to apologize, looking relieved for a chance to finally explain himself.

Wow, he really feels guilty. Have there been others? Well, too bad. If he's suffering from guilt, he brought it all on himself!

But she interrupted him. "Forget about that, Jeremy. There was a reason for it, I think. In fact, I'm sure of it. Let me explain: I think you and I, and Maureen, have known each other before, in another lifetime."

She let that bombshell settle for a minute before she went on, "And I think the two of you, well, you had some kind of affair while we were married."

"Amy—"

"No! Listen to me for a minute," she cut him off. "This is true—I know it! Just now when you walked across the baseball field, I saw you. You were a dairy farmer and I was your wife and we lived in the mountains somewhere, like in the Alps. I dreamed it, Jeremy. Mountains and cows and snow. A few weeks ago. But I didn't realize I was dreaming about another life until some other things happened."

"This is crazy." He stopped walking and looked at her. "You really are nuts, you know that Amy? Total fruitcake!"

"Yes," she smiled, radiant in her new confidence. "Maybe I am, but it makes perfect sense to me. And so does this." She gazed back at him steadily, ready to spell it out. "Look, Jeremy, we're only fifteen. Okay, you're almost sixteen, but that's young. Some decisions about my life I'm ready to make, but not this one!"

He started to protest, but she stopped him. "Don't even try to say anything. I know you agree with me. Your behavior shows it! It was you who started flirting with Maureen, wasn't it?"

His ears turned red, but he didn't speak.

"Then that proves my point! We're too young to not be seeing other people! We're just not meant to be a couple, Jeremy. I think we've tried it before—and it didn't work." She thought of another tack. "You know, your behavior with Maureen was perfectly normal for a guy your age. But why do you feel so guilty? Because you *remember* feeling guilty! And why was I angry? Because I remember being angry—but not at you!" She laughed. "That's the weird thing. I blamed Maureen—and I think that's because I blamed her in the past to preserve my reputation! My husband cheating on me? I couldn't admit that."

She looked closely at Jeremy, whose face showed little comprehension of anything she'd said. She sighed. "Jeremy, you don't have to believe any of this, okay? However you want to understand it is fine with me. You don't have to believe in reincarnation or anything else. But I want to be free to know a lot of people and have fun while I'm a teenager. I'll have plenty of time for serious commitments when I'm older. So I think we should call this off for now, whatever it is that we had."

She finally stopped for breath, confident she'd explained it all neatly and that he could see the wisdom of her logic.

Jeremy exploded. "What kind of bullshit is that? 'We're too

young!' You sound like some old lady! *You're too young to know this, you're too young to know that,"* he mimicked. "You're so full of shit! You don't know what you want!"

Amy was shocked silent by his outburst. He hadn't heard her at all.

"I don't buy this 'we're too young' crap! And don't give me any bullshit about other lifetimes. What are you really trying to say?"

This was it. He'd backed her into a corner. He wasn't going to go easily, she realized. Probably too much humiliation for him to accept that she was breaking up with him. She'd tried to put it nicely, to spare his feelings. She thought if she explained it all to him, he would realize that it was the best choice, that they really weren't right for one another, that they were only attracted because of that past-life experience, because they needed to make amends for their mistakes. But he wasn't getting it.

"So?" he demanded. "What are you trying to say here?"

She looked at him with a kind of pity. Such an ego. So dense. No one had ever rejected him before. But her mind was made up, her heart sealed. She felt she had no choice. She drew her new, shining dagger of truth (or what she believed to be true) and plunged it.

"I can't see you any more."

Jeremy looked like she'd hit him square in the jaw. His mouth dropped involuntarily. For a minute she thought he was going to yell at her, but instead his eyes filled up and he spun away.

"Fucking bitch!" he yelled as he ran from her.

A deep cold chill ran down her neck and into her stomach. She fully believed she'd done the right thing. But it hurt.

The moment she got home, she hurried to the phone in the den, determined to carry out the next part of her plan before she lost courage. The scene with Jeremy shook her up but her resolve held firm.

Her father was asleep in his chair, so she half-whispered,

"Maureen, don't hang up."

"Amy?" She sounded startled.

"Yeah, it's me. And don't worry—I'm not mad anymore."

"You're not?"

"Remember the fair-haired woman?"

"Yeah..." she drawled skeptically.

"Well, I know the whole story now!"

"You do? How?"

"Never mind how, but I know what happened."

Silence.

She's probably embarrassed. "Anyway, it's okay. I broke up with Jeremy."

"Look, Amy, what happened in the lunch room, it really wasn't—"

"But it was, Maureen, don't you see? It was exactly like it happened before! Well, almost. Only this time, I'm not blaming you for it!"

"What are you talking about?"

"Right—I'd better tell you everything from the beginning. But I can't talk here. I'll be over in five minutes, okay? At least you'll believe me when I say it has to do with"—she dropped her voice even lower, stealing a glance at her snoring father— "a past lifetime."

Maureen let her in five minutes later and led her upstairs to the blue bedroom. As soon as she shut the door, Amy started in.

"Okay, the fair-haired woman—she was you, we already knew that. But I saw it, Maureen, and a few weeks ago I dreamed it. Jeremy was my husband—get this: a dairy farmer! And I was his wife, and you were the other woman. We lived up in the mountains and there was snow on the ground. I think it was somewhere like Switzerland. I caught the two of you—just like I did today—only in the past, I blamed you. I hated you. That's the feeling that I was telling you about—this is where it came from! But Maureen, I was wrong!"

"You were? Why? I mean, didn't you have a good reason to hate me? If I was fooling around with your husband..." She seemed doubtful. "I don't know, Amy. I've been reading my father's book and it talks about negative karma, where you feel guilty for things you did in other lifetimes, but this doesn't feel right to me somehow. I don't feel guilty, really. Just stupid for what happened today."

"No, Maureen, it's true! I know it! See, I blamed you instead of him because it was easier. If I admitted that my husband was interested in another woman—well, where would that leave my pride and reputation? I think I invented reasons to hate you because I wanted to escape from the truth of my marriage: that we really didn't love each other as much as we should have. Maybe it was an arranged marriage or something, I don't know. You know how they did things in the old days. And now, with Jeremy—"

"Whoa, Amy, slow down! First of all, I want you to know that I didn't start that thing with Jeremy. He came by and started teasing me, then grabbed my drink, right before you showed up. He made me really angry. I hate that kind of juvenile behavior! But then, when I saw your face—I couldn't think what to say. And then I said that stupid thing about you drinking some..."

"Maureen, I still consider you to be one of my best friends."

It was the first time she admitted that to herself or Maureen.

"You're the only one who understands what I'm talking about. I'm not angry, don't you get it? And I believe you about Jeremy. Not only that, but I think it's good that it happened. I was the stupid one, getting all jealous. I shouldn't be having that kind of relationship with a guy yet. I want to stay free and unattached for now!" She laughed.

Maureen joined in, relieved. "You mean, 'So many guys, so little time'?"

"Exactly!"

The rest of their conversation concerned unmet lovers and

future weddings, adventures they promised to have before they got old. They joked and giggled until Maureen's mother came up and reminded them how late it was.

Now Amy had only one more thing to resolve. She needed to ask Maureen a difficult favor but she decided that could wait until tomorrow.

She fell asleep that night feeling very satisfied that she had tied things up all neatly, and very soon her life would begin to sail along. Talking to her friends about reincarnation wasn't as hard as she expected, once she had it all figured out.

20

The Rose Garden

*Y*ou *have made a* mistake, Amy, but do not be alarmed. It is very common on your world; that is, among those who suspect something about the continuity of consciousness. Such mistakes happen easily when you go back to live as an Earth dweller."

Amy was sitting on the golden steps of a small, filigreed-crystal temple at the edge of a rose garden glimmering with Mind-energies. She twisted her fingers nervously.

Now that she lived on Earth again, she often visited here at night while her body slept.

Beside her in this crystal wonderland sat a beautiful, gentle woman who moved like fluid glass and looked like a dream. She said that Amy knew her once as Coriskancsia, and that she had served as Amy's femininity counselor and close advisor since before she was reborn. Often she coached Amy intuitively—mind-to-mind—on matters her Earth mother neglected.

But at this moment Coriskancsia's slender figure glowed in cobalt-blue, dark hair flowed around her delicate features, and she was trying to calm Amy's horror and dismay.

"Identifying the souls around us is not always a simple matter when we're living in a physical body. While it may have seemed to you that your friends, Jeremy and Maureen, were playing out the incident between Hans and Ilda, they only reminded you of that earlier time.

"Because of its emotional impact, your memory of that day on the mountaintop as Marta is vivid. It colored what you saw through your Earth eyes in your present life as Amy. You really aren't as objective about it as you would like to believe," she added matter-of-factly. (Truth here was never soft-peddled.)

Amy groaned with humiliation.

"But you mustn't be too hard on yourself over this mistake," Coriskancsia hurried to say. "It is a common error, this lack of objectivity—especially when we have been hurt in the past by others who were close to us. Your friends merely helped you identify certain past mistakes you needed to recognize. They served as stand-ins, you might say, to help you face the real Hans and Ilda."

Amy stared at her.

Quickly she went on, "You and Hans and Ilda—the history is long, and deep, and violent. Your souls are bonded in a much stronger way than your friendship with Jeremy and Maureen. Many deep rivers of revenge, fear, and hatred colored the events in Switzerland. We showed you some of those rivers, previous times in which Earth lives were cut short. For such karma as this, subsequent relationships are complex, troubled, and not so easily shifted into a positive give-and-take, as you were able to do with your school friends. Do you see the difference?"

Amy had to admit that she didn't.

"Let me explain further, then. Your conflicts with Maureen— didn't you transform them into friendship, with minor effort?"

They had fallen so easily into shared dreams and laughter and worries and fears in their current status as teenagers. In all honesty, she had to make a great leap of imagination to convince herself of Maureen's identity as the fair-haired woman, whose image filled Amy with violent emotions.

"Exactly. That is because your conflicts with the soul now named Maureen have existed in the past, but in a small way. You have been competitors, and you have shared some unpleasant interactions—just enough to give you both some guilt. And this you confused with having been serious enemies. In the future, you will see your friendship with Maureen expand into a very important alliance. You will understand that soon enough.

"With Jeremy, your relationship is fairly new. You have met before, but as passing acquaintances. You narrowly escaped creating new karma with him," Coriskancsia twinkled, "with a little help from your Friends, of course!"

That night in the car! So it was Coriskancsia who came to her rescue!

She dipped her head in a humble little bow. "With a few of your other good Friends, including some who tell me they have been your grandparents. But let us make sure you understand this situation on Earth."

She paused for a moment, regarding Amy with great compassion. Her eyes became pools of swirling light that gave Amy deep sensations of comfort and love, reminding her of her treasured moments with Uriel and Michiel.

"Amy, you know that you have lived darkly by the side of the one you knew as Ilda. And that with the soul who was once named Hans, a powerful attraction has drawn you together repeatedly. Do you know who these two souls are to you in your present life on Earth?"

Shock ran through Amy's astral arms and legs. Now? She knew them now, and they were not Maureen and Jeremy? But who—?

A sensation passed through her mind as if it were cleaved in two by a heavy blade.

Her mother. Ilda.

"You are correct," Coriskancsia agreed softly. "And Hans? Have you recognized him, now that you are here with me and can see more clearly?"

Amy stretched and pulled her mind, grasping to find the answer, but she could not. She looked at Coriskancsia, waiting. *Who is he?* she asked inwardly but reluctance filled her heart. This, more than Ilda's identity, frightened her for some reason and she wasn't sure why.

"That is because your relationship is so different from what you knew in your most recent past. It is frightening to you because it is unexpected, and you were so unaware. But I am told that it is time you knew. He is your father, dear, the one known as Donald Longwood."

A feeling like crawling skin on Earth passed over Amy's energy body. *My father? Hans? But—*

"No, it is not some abnormal abomination. In fact, two souls often will incarnate in a series of close family relationships if they have serious negative associations to overcome. In the closeness of a family bond—parent and child, or husband and wife—there is hope that the natural desires for harmony and love will help to overcome past intentions of harm that the two souls may have shared. You and your father have been working in this way for many lifetimes, and those efforts have already born fruit.

"Currently, he has hit a snag with his drinking habit, but your own courage and honesty as you grow older on Earth might help him. With the higher connections you have now established," she winked in self-acknowledgment, "you, 'Hans,' and 'Ilda' will have another opportunity to resolve your destructiveness toward one another."

Amy thought this over carefully. "It doesn't seem like we're doing so well."

"Do you recall your lessons on astral influences?"

Amy's entire aura tinted pink. She definitely remembered that second class in Remedial Reincarnation, although not a word of the lecture. Kriss kept drawing pictures in a notebook and turning the instructor's words into ironic poetry. He didn't seem to care that the Teacher could probably clearly see his every scribble. And she let him get away with it! Amy was powerfully distracted by his cleverness.

But she could recall one bizarre image he sketched: a masculine face with a tube attached and a slimy worm-like creature sucking the brains out of the man's head. Disgusting!

"That's close enough," Coriskancsia laughed as if she could see the picture too. "Your friend is quite an artist!

"But he also seems knowledgeable about the ways of subastral entities. They are so broken, they can no longer sustain a physical body that they might use for the pursuit of their addictions—addictions they feel keenly in their out-of-body state—for they have not risen to any further level of development than their previous earth existence. Thus, they cannot pursue a course of expanding personal development. They have trapped themselves at a disembodied, low frequency—a kind of smog-like dimension that envelops Earth. There, they look for ways to suck life-energy from unsuspecting earth dwellers, puppets they can use to satisfy their cravings for food, sex, drugs, alcohol, violence, power, and so on."

"Ewww..."

She nodded. "The lecture probably bored your friend because he already knew something of about these forces, this energy principle—no doubt from first-hand experience."

Amy shuddered, thinking of their life as Romani travelers. Maybe that explained how he was able to take the life of one he professed to love so deeply? Were his hands on her throat guided by subastral influences, her true enemies?

"An excellent question. Very likely from the moment he allowed his emotions to overpower his reason, he lost control of himself. An earth dweller is always in danger of being used by one or several of these subastral forces. Your present earth mother is a good example.

"Amy, dear, you must realize that your mother copes with, not only her own desire for alcohol, but the subtle and not-so-subtle persuasions of the leech-like entities who find her state of mind compatible to theirs. They suck the stimulants and depressants she ingests through a mental link they have established with her. This gives them some relief from cravings they could only fully satisfy if they had a physical body. Now their thought-influence intensifies her own addictive cravings."

"That's terrible! No wonder it's hard for addicts to break free."

"Indeed so. And by now, these particular astral entities have become your mother's constant companions, so their personalities may filter out through her words and actions. Any threat to their supply source, and they may influence her to express violent anger toward that threat."

"But what can I do to help her?"

"Sadly, not much. These are her own choices, the thoughts she harbors."

Amy's face fell.

"She is not alone in this, dear. Millions of people living on Earth are so entangled because the majority of its inhabitants remain ignorant of this interdimensional aspect of life. Some few know—but most haven't been taught. And the ancient teachings on the subject are largely dismissed as 'primitive.'"

Amy would have liked to stop there. The images being shown to her mentally frightened and nauseated her. She saw tangled energy bodies writhe together and function as one. And human forms completely encased in what looked like small slime-creatures. A fairly normal-looking individual appeared, until he turned and Amy could see the hideous monkey-like creature attached to his neck.

But Coriskancsia went on, "Some of these psychic leeches may eventually find a way back into a physical body from the hellish dimensions they inhabit between lives. Others have degenerated too far."

Again Amy saw the images projected to her, smears and blurs of life-substance no longer distinctly formed into any shape.

"If they have done nothing to change or seek help, degenerates who reach this stage will soon disintegrate into complete reabsorption, as raw energy material returned to the Infinite supply. They will no longer express as individualized souls. That is the only true 'death.'"

"Will this happen to my mother?"

"Right now, she only allows herself to be used by these entities; she is not one of them. She is not exactly an innocent victim, for her thoughts invited them in, but she is presently far from the non-human point of no return. Although joined by others, her individualized energy anatomy, which she has developed through many lifetimes, still remains intact.

"The choice will be hers: to go back to a progressive pathway by seeking rehabilitation, either in her present lifetime or between lives—or to follow her subastral companions after death into their dark and shadowy state, lingering close to earth and seeking to relieve her sensory cravings through vampirish attachments to living individuals."

They may have been enemies in the past but this stirred Amy's compassion beyond measure. From her current perspective in the higher-dimensional beauty of Coriskancsia's rose garden, nothing seemed worse than such a hellish state of decline and depravity.

She almost feared to ask, "Could this happen to any of us?"

"It can. Do you not remember your recent explosions of temper on Earth?"

Amy shuddered as the images came back to her—only now, she understood that nursing her anger over the course of hours opened a door in her consciousness that should have remained locked.

"And when your thoughts unlocked that door, you allowed yourself to become overwhelmed by angry astral forces. Do you remember how strong you felt when you took hold of that young man's shirt?"

She nodded meekly.

"That strength was not only your own. And that feeling of murder flowing down your arms? It was so seamlessly woven into your being that you did not identify it as foreign, yet it was. It is a dangerous thing to 'lose your temper.' So much more can be lost!"

Immediately she saw visions of insane asylums, and cold ice ran through her being.

"Yes, that too is a possibility, given the rampant ignorance on Earth. But do not fear, Amy. Living on earth, *you must remain free to feel emotion*. It is a major aspect of your learning experience! But you can learn—not to *suppress*—but to *shift* your thoughts free of lingering, destructive intentions that invite unwanted influences to join in.

"Pay careful attention to what I'm going to say: In some cases, the added strength comes from a positive source, and in other instances, from a negative one. It all depends on the actions, the thoughts, the emotions, and especially the *intentions* of the individual living on earth. A mother lifting a car off her fallen youngster? A positive influx of higher frequencies riding into her Being on the waves of her overwhelming love. An angry man seeking vengeance? A negative surcharge filling him from dark and twisted astral beings who join him in his rage and hatred.

"I know this is not an easy concept to accept or comprehend, but it will be one of the most important for you. You have always feared madness, am I correct?"

"Yes." Amy looked down at her feet. She felt so small.

"Learning these discernments are your protection from something you've experienced in the past. Feeling brief anger is not the concern—in fact, far better to feel it than to suppress it. Else how would we learn? But nursing anger, hatred, or any other destructive or selfish emotion over time leads to the disintegration of consciousness.

"Your mother is demonstrating for you the path you do not want to take. Her experience differs from the momentary flashes of interdimensional influence I've described. Those who do not allow their minds to dwell in the lower frequencies, who keep their thoughts elevated on more positive pursuits, are not susceptible in the same way as someone who perpetuates a sad heart, an angry soul, or a violent spirit.

"Your mother created these bonds along the lines of mutually agreeable thought patterns, regenerated over long periods of many lifetimes. These are old friends of hers. You cannot 'save' her from them—remember that. She and she alone can make that choice, recognize that she needs help, and ask for it. We will be at her side in less than a human heartbeat. Our specialists are expertly trained to carry out the delicate extractions required, sending the separated entities off to the healing wards."

As Coriskancsia described it, Amy saw Light Beings working over a dark mass of parts laid on a table. Using various instruments, they projected beams that separated black blobs from what sickened her to see: a human lying helpless beneath the pile. Amy watched each blob rise and transform into a mist, which was then escorted off to another level of expression, disappearing from her view.

"Until she makes a request for help, we cannot interfere. Your mother has willingly broken down her natural forms of protection from such invading forces. She cooperates with them by the thoughts she maintains."

This was suddenly too much for Amy, far too ugly. Why hadn't anyone warned her of these things? Then she remembered the lecture she'd missed and she lost all composure.

No wonder she was so easily distracted! She hadn't *wanted* to know! These were her worst fears illuminated in all their horror. Her chest began to heave in rhythmic gasps, but tears did not fall. She felt as if her own life force was being cut off...

Coriskancsia quickly slipped an arm around and drew her close in an energy embrace that kept Amy from plummeting back to her earth body.

"As you have guessed, in your long evolution, your many passages to and from earth life, you have been influenced by subastral entities from time to time. It happens to all of us. Usually, when the earth-dweller brings his or her thoughts back up to a more positive level, these brief attachments slip away, no longer compatible. It can take place in the passage of mere moments, as you recently experienced. None of us exist in a vacuum; we are always associating ourselves with one level or another."

"But I have to know—have I ever been as bad as her? Have I—" She paused. "Have I been carted off to an asylum?"

Coriskancsia gazed at her for a long moment, as if to weigh her strength.

"You are brave to ask this. Yes. Long ago. You have also formed addictive relationships with various substances, and your physical cravings were compounded by subastral vampires whom you drew into your psychic centers, exactly as your parents experience now. But from your lives of training with us, from your constant search for self-betterment, you recognized your fall in consciousness. You cried out and we came to you immediately. And look at you now! You have risen up to take your place in the shining realms of Light at the moment. If you can conquer these subastral influences, so can anyone!"

Amy felt the Love that once rescued her but thankfully she couldn't recall the experience. She knew without being told that it happened many times, and still no one judged her here except herself. She remembered the battle scene she was shown, when her suicidal state dropped her into a deep pit of subastral despair. Shining tears of gratitude for those who came to her aid, time and again, polished her glistening face.

Coriskancsia brushed them away gently.

"Now you understand that your parents still have great

potential. Your mother's disappointments and memories of the past have caused her to make regrettable choices, it is true. She's on an extremely self-destructive path and your father has now joined her addiction. But all is not lost. Not yet.

"You will serve as their positive example, and trust me, they will take note of your better choices. They may not have the strength yet to follow but you will help them find help, one way or another."

The task seemed impossible.

"Your life on Earth will be a long one, Amy. You have only begun. Don't hurry yourself or be concerned. Among the three of you this time around, no serious harms have been committed thus far. This is progress! As you each live, you learn. How far you go in this healing trio will be up to you, and you still have years to re-awaken your understanding!"

Coriskancsia smiled at her. She reached out to smooth her fingers through Amy's hair, draping it behind the gleaming shoulders of her energy body.

"I have faith in you. And besides, you have a greater awareness of our Presence with you than you have previously experienced on Earth. Remember your visit with Uriel and Michiel? You have mapped out a brilliant future for yourself! As you grow, so will your ability to help your mother and father. In ways you cannot predict or plan. You will see. But remember, you need not wait for them to make positive choices. It is your own attitude that you must focus on and heal."

She released the gentle grasp she'd kept on Amy's shoulders, apparently confident her student had re-established her mental link into this magnificent world of unlimited possibility.

"Now let us discuss something much more cheerful, shall we? We need to choose certain fabrics for—" she glanced at Amy and noticed that she still stared vacantly into other dimensional realities. "You have more questions first, don't you? All right then. This can wait."

She set aside a gleaming turquoise cloth she'd manifested, with silver laser beam patterns. "Ask me."

"If he lived as Hans, why is my father so aloof toward me now?"

"As you grew into a young lady, the closeness you shared with him as a child made him slightly uncomfortable. Even though he does not know consciously, subconsciously he still carries the memory of having been your husband.

"If the science of reincarnation were more commonly understood on your planet, many awkward feelings could be so easily dissipated," Coriskancsia sighed. "This ignorance causes much hurt and confusion, which is why we are working so hard here to change that. Too many Earth people have no guidance to cope with these out-of-place emotions! Sad situations abound: The young boy who remembers too clearly being a woman, and feels out of place in his new body. Or the father who feels guilty for warm feelings toward the daughter who was once his wife." She glanced significantly at Amy. "But far, far worse: the ignorant parent or other adult whose mind is so unbalanced that he or she follows those impulses into inappropriate, adult relationships with that child. Do you understand?"

Amy nodded, feeling ill.

"Your father has handled this strangeness by putting some distance between you. It is not a bad solution, although not ideal. Some of your new understanding will travel with you back to Earth and make things easier for both of you. If he knew clearly of your past relationship, the past-life impulses would evaporate in the light of this knowledge."

For the first time in this troubling talk, Amy felt a glimmer of hope that she might do something right on Earth. But immediately she thought of something else. Her aura burned again with embarrassment.

"Ah, yes, I understand. Do not be concerned about the error you made with your friends. They were not harmed by the misinformation. In fact, their eyes were opened to a possibility. But as they quest within themselves to weigh the truth of your statements, they will not find a resonance to convince them of those particular identities, as your Hans and Ilda. Eventually, they will recognize the reality of reincarnation, because that notion has already rung its note of familiarity with the process of their own lives. But you will never convince them that they lived with you in Switzerland! And after this visit, you may not recall our conversation in full detail but certain doubts will arise in your own mind. Eventually, you will suspect the truth.

"Still, their flirtation triggered your flashbacks, and you did some rethinking about some of your judgments in the past. You cannot overlook this healing benefit! You have done them a service by opening their minds to new ideas, and they in turn, have helped you change old thought patterns."

Coriskancsia stood up from the golden steps of the jewel-box temple where they'd been sitting. She nodded toward the lacy latticework of the glittering little enclosure. "Shall we go in for a moment?"

"Can we please?"

The temple was smaller than Amy's bedroom on Earth and looked more like a garden gazebo than a place of healing. Just inside the crystal filigreed walls, three round tiers—ruby, gold, and sapphire blue—led like steps up to a clear top tier, on which rested a sparkling white Energy Flame. Its twinkling oscillations extended up to connect with a focusing lens high above, which looked something like an inverted chandelier in a swirling "ceiling" Amy really couldn't discern.

"I've created this little temple to serve those who make their night visits. It's easy enough to slip from my roses into the Flame without a lot of travel time," Coriskancsia teased, knowing full well that such a thing did not exist in her world. No travel required, no space involved, only thoughts that led them from place to place.

Amy didn't need encouragement. She had experienced Healing Flames before. They weren't hot. They felt cool and soothing and wonderful. She was told that the Minds who create them set the frequency at a rate to cleanse and rejuvenate the psychic body, which collects energy debris through the natural processes of living. But she also knew the Flame would help her realign old energies from past lives, correct their dissonance with higher frequencies of Infinite Intelligence.

In some of the larger temples she'd visited, the Flames were separated into rose, gold, and blue, each on its own tier and each one increasing in frequency, as the colors indicated. But often, as in Coriskancsia's garden temple, the healing energies combined into one brilliant white Light. Without another word, she took the symbolic three crystal steps up the tiers—rose, gold, and blue—and strode confidently onto the clear level and into the white Flame.

She stretched out her arms to absorb the tingling energy. When she stepped back out on the other side a few seconds later, she felt renewed, refreshed, and invigorated! She practically danced down the opposite side of the tiers to return to Coriskancsia. Her energy body glowed with new brilliance. All the fears, worries, and concerns she passed through during her talk with Coriskancsia had been swept away.

As they strode back down the jeweled temple's golden steps, Coriskancsia left a wake of cobalt energy that stirred the nearby roses.

"With your new resolve, Amy, you have made a brave first move. As you act on your decision, I believe we will witness a great blossoming of your expression on Earth! But that will depend on you, dear."

She beamed a smile at Amy.

Amy swayed for a moment under its warm influence, then closed her eyes to focus on the inner radiance...

The alarm by her bed shrilled a harsh note as the last of

Coriskancsia's words echoed:
  "Be at peace, dear little sister. Your mistake did not lead you far off-course. You've only taken a small detour!"

21

To Be or Not

*A*my groaned with humiliation. She woke up filled with doubt: What if Maureen wasn't the fair-haired woman? What if she was wrong about Jeremy?

What was I thinking?

She dragged the pillow over her head, completely certain now that she was wrong.

She needn't have worried. When she got to school she discovered that Jeremy and Tim Withers were collaborating on rumors about her bouts of insanity, and Maureen confronted her at the lockers.

"Ames, I don't think it's true. About the fair-haired woman, I mean. It doesn't feel right to me."

"Me either."

She wasn't sure who felt more relieved, herself for not needing to bring it up, or Maureen for not stirring her friend's anger.

Just as Coriskancsia promised, her visit to the rose garden filtered information into her Earth life, even though she didn't consciously remember a bit of it. Her higher Self, with all its elevated connections to advanced Beings, was beginning to influence her more often. Especially (and only) when she maintained a positive attitude.

But that wasn't easy.

"Have you heard what they're saying about you?"

"No, but whatever it is doesn't surprise me. That slime ball Withers tried to look down my shirt and I let him have it, so he ran away in front of his friends. What else is he gonna say but something foul? He has to cover for himself. Can't let some girl get the best of him!"

Maureen laughed at the scene she described.

"And Jeremy! I told him I didn't want to see him any more and he freaked out. Called me an effing b-i-t-c-h. You know how conceited he is! He's afraid his friends will find out that *I* dumped *him*."

Maureen laughed again, then suddenly looked sympathetic—rare for her. "But what are you going to do today? I heard they're planning to chant 'Kooky Amy' whenever they see you."

Amy paled a bit. Chewed her lip. "What are my choices?"

"You could tell them to eff-off."

"Not my style."

"Well, you could try to avoid them."

"That used to be my style."

"So what's your style now?" Maureen grinned, which made Amy feel a little calmer.

She thought for a minute. *Who am I now?*

Not Jeremy's girlfriend, that was for sure. But not the girl she was a few weeks ago, either. She was so much more than she used to be, but only because of what had passed through her mind and heart. How to put that into words?

Suddenly it came to her, something that summed it all up, the feelings that words couldn't embrace.

I'm a dancer.

Elated by this recognition, she dropped her books on the

linoleum and lifted her arms in first and second position, placed a foot carefully behind her in preparation, and spun up into a series of rapid *chaînés* turns that traveled down the hallway.

As people scattered and stared, she grinned back at Maureen, "I'm going to dazzle them with my pirouettes and blind them with my brilliance!"

The shock left Maureen's face as she registered the implications and broke into another approving laugh.

Amy spun back to retrieve her books, completely ignoring the uproar she'd caused in the hallway.

"C'mon, before Mr. Spock shows up!"

That was the nickname they'd given the vice principal who regularly patrolled the halls.

The two girls hurried off to class, their heads held in mocking height like ballerinas ready for their curtain call. They dissolved into laughter as they slipped through the heavy wooden door.

Later that morning, a group of Tim Withers' friends did exactly as Maureen predicted. When they spotted Amy, someone shouted, "Look, it's Kooky Amy!"

That started the chant, with a variation, "Kooky Amy, Kooky Amy, she's so wild, she's smelling gamey!" Followed by sniggers and guffaws of contentment with the brilliance of their attack.

But Amy was ready for them.

I'm not crazy; I'm a dancer, she reminded herself.

She shifted her books to realign her balance and as she passed the taunting cluster on her left, she made a quick sharp turn to face them, which stunned them immobile. Slowly, she drew her right toes up her standing leg in a carefully measured *coupé,* placed her pointed foot precisely below her left knee—then quickly flung out her strong right leg in a perfect *développé,* straight into Bob Young's crotch.

She was down the hall before he knew what hit him.

Maureen, Pam, and Louise, who watched the whole thing, collapsed in gales of merriment at poor Bob's expense, while his

friends—including Tim Withers—gathered around him protec-
tively, shouting, "See? She's crazy!"

"She's a nutcase!"

"They'd better haul her off to Kalamazoo!"

By afternoon, the whole school had heard and repeated the
story. Amy expected she would soon hear from the vice principal but strangely, no faculty members approached her. It was
like a silent nod of approval.

Still, she felt a slight twinge of regret for stooping to violence
to confront her attackers. Some part of her wondered if one had
to go so low to fend off bullies. In the higher reaches of her true
Mind, she posed the question to her Advisors.

After school, Maureen suggested the girls escort Amy to the
Burger Bin in victory. They eagerly agreed, and serenaded her
along the way with, "Lovely Amy, Lovely Amy, she's so swift,
she made him lame-y!"

Amy cringed a little every time she heard it, her cheeks blazing as their gang made its way down the street.

As expected, Jeremy and his friends appeared in the doorway
of their usual after-school haunt, which they were accustomed
to ruling unchallenged. But this time Maureen and the rest of
the girls stared them down from the back of the room, where
they clustered around Amy in raucous celebration.

Amy watched Jeremy's face turn a humiliated purple and she
felt a pang of sympathy. She hadn't wanted to hurt him. She tried
to be nice, and fully intended to remain friends, but he forced her
into bluntness out by the baseball field. Now she felt his pain.

"C'mon, let's get outta here," she heard him say. "That crazy
bitch has contaminated this place."

How she hated that word! It struck a nerve in the pit of her
stomach and the anger began to take her over.

But then something amazing. From deep within her welled a
soothing sense of calm.

Not violence, it said. *Wit.*

It was as if the Other Voice had answered her earlier question about bullies. In the midst of her angry reaction, it somehow pierced through to reach her higher Self, which trickled a few drops of wisdom—a very few, but enough— down into her conscious, waking awareness (always last on the chain of knowing).

In that split second, she formed words to express the only wit she could summon. She recalled she'd once heard someone say that if you *owned* a hurtful taunt, it could never hurt you again. "Don't fear an ugly name cast at you by a bully—*own* it! Make it yours! Use it!"

She stood up.

Her friends stared at her.

"Hey Jeremy," she called from across the room.

He was so surprised he turned in the doorway to look.

"I may be crazy and I may be a *bitch*," she proclaimed loudly, "but no one has to hold my hand and tell me how to spell it!"

Maureen let out a whoop. Jeremy scowled and scuffled off. Amy's friends cheered.

Okay, that wasn't brilliant but it sure feels better than a stomach full of anger!

She allowed herself a small but smug little smile.

Later, as she walked home with Maureen, her friend admitted that it wasn't the idea of reincarnation she doubted—just the story about her and Jeremy cheating on Amy.

"I know," Amy sighed. "It doesn't fit. I felt the same thing when I woke up this morning."

"I'm so glad! I didn't want to hurt your feelings."

Amy grinned. "No one's ever going to hurt my feelings again! I'm strong! I'm invincible!" She did a few leaping *jetés* down the sidewalk, pounding her chest.

Maureen laughed and skipped to catch up. "Me too."

She linked her arm in Amy's and they hopped along like that until Amy stopped, dead serious.

"I have to ask you a really hard favor."

"Name it," Maureen said, still grinning over the day's events.

It wasn't that easy.

First, Amy had to explain about her mother and the ballet classes. She left out the parts about the willow switch, but she included the fact that Mrs. Q thought her capable of dancing the lead in a new ballet choreographed by a friend of hers from the San Francisco Ballet, and that if she didn't go back to ballet classes soon, she would lose that chance.

"So far, I've figured out that I could pretend to be visiting you on Saturdays, and that I could find a way to pay for the classes myself, but I don't know how to get to Wilton. Clareta—I mean Mrs. Q said she'd help me. But…"

"Is that the favor? You want me to ask my mother if she can drive you?"

"Oh no! I could never ask her to do that! Not every Saturday. But maybe just once? So I can talk to Mrs. Q in person? Maybe this weekend?"

"Done!" Maureen proclaimed. "That's easy. I'll ask her tonight."

"Maybe you shouldn't tell her what I'm up to."

"Don't be stupid! Of course I'm not going to tell her! 'Hey, Mom, Amy's lying to her mother and she wants you to help her do it.' She's never met your mother but if she did, I'll bet she'd—"

"What?"

Maureen looked suddenly uncomfortable. "Um…agree with you? C'mon, Ames. Everyone knows about your mother. Or at least, they think they know."

Amy felt surprisingly defensive. "Know what?"

"That she drinks too much!"

Amy's face fell.

"Don't take it so hard. It's not like it's you they're talking about."

Somehow that didn't comfort Amy. She suddenly felt as humiliated as if the drinking problem were her own.

"Amy, you're not her!"

"Yeah, I know."

"You're nothing at all like her! Come on—I've got a mirror you need to look into."

She grabbed Amy by the hand, laughing and dragging her the last few steps to her house. Amy played along, pretending to resist, but secretly she felt Maureen's words sink deep into her heart, where they left a little pool of truth.

I'm strong, she repeated to herself. *I'm invincible. And I'm not my mother. I'm not even crazy!*

A bright blue light flashed on the wall beside Maureen as she opened the front door.

"Hey, Mom!" she hollered. "Can you give us a ride to Wilton on Saturday?" She winked at Amy.

Her mother came out of the kitchen, drying her hands on a towel. "Maureen, please don't shout like that. Now what's this?"

"Can we visit Gram on Saturday and drop Amy off at Mrs. Quantos's ballet studio? Her mother can't drive her."

Amy looked at her sideways.

"You don't mind, do you? Don't you want to visit Gram?"

"Well, I suppose…"

"Great! Thanks, Mom!" Maureen planted a kiss on her cheek. "Come on, Amy. I want to show you something I read in that book I was telling you about." She winked again.

"Thank you, Mrs. Widdington," Amy said quietly, and followed Maureen up the stairs before her mother could ask any questions.

I'm not my mother. I'm strong. I'm invincible. I'm only a little bit scared.

But all in all, the day had been a triumph.

I'm not crazy. But if I'm kooky in their eyes, then so be it! That's what I am. And soon, I will be a dancer for real.

22

Reunion

A my's stomach lurched as her feet struck the pavement, and her arms felt weak and trembly as she pulled herself out of the car. What she was about to do, she never dreamed she would have the courage for, but the alternative was nothing she wanted to contemplate.

To live as her mother lived? To grow old and weak and unhappy? To become a burden to everyone around her because she believed she had nothing to be grateful for, no sense of enjoyment from hour to hour or day to day, only a drug to quiet her inner pain?

No! That was no alternative at all, to Amy's way of thinking. What she was about to do, she *must* do. And never mind that nonsense about being "too young" to decide. She was not too young to know her own heart! About that, Jeremy had actually been right. But of course she could never tell him that.

The street door to Mrs. Q's upstairs studio stood slightly ajar and Amy slipped in quietly, staring at the worn and narrow wooden stairs she had passed over a thousand times since her first visit to this place.

She heard Maureen's mother drive away as Maureen called out the window, waving, "Go Amy!" They would come back for her if she called Maureen's grandmother's house. Otherwise, she told them, she would find another ride home.

She gushed her thanks so steadily on the trip over that Maureen finally told her to shut up about it.

Her friend had helped Amy secretly stuff her ballet things in Maureen's bag so Yvonne wouldn't see them—yet she made sure her own mother noticed. That was part of the cover story Maureen cooked up: they were driving Amy to her ballet class.

"It's not an actual lie," her friend rationalized, "just a little shifted around in time and place."

Now Amy stood in the musty stairwell, which felt comfortingly familiar after her weeks away. She'd never realized how this place had served as a refuge for her all these years. She'd spent hours here, forgetting the rest of her life, immersing herself in music and dancing and the sweet atmosphere of creative art. Here, the high aspiration for beauty was all-encompassing. It pushed students to the limits of their physical and mental abilities—at least for the hour or two they spent in this quest. Amy inhaled the memory of it gratefully. She had missed this feeling!

The hour was still early, twelve-thirty. The afternoon's first students shouldn't appear until one. But the loud clunk of piano keys played in awkward patterns drifted down the stairwell, disrupting the quiet.

Beth? How did she get here?

Amy hurried up the stairs to scold her for playing with the piano, and for not being where she was supposed to be, which surely couldn't be here in the studio! She burst through the door with a word on her lips, ready to drag her little sister away from trouble before it could descend.

But it was Amy who was caught by surprise. Across the gleaming hardwood floor, where the afternoon light from the tall windows picked out patterns of rosin dust on the floor, she saw a figure she didn't recognize seated at the piano with his back to her. She took in the longish light brown hair that reached to his collar, the white T-shirt that covered his muscular arms. It wasn't John Quantos.

At the sound of her noisy entrance, the figure turned.

"Oh—you caught me! I was just trying to figure out how to play one of my guitar pieces on the piano. I always wanted to learn but I'm afraid I never had the chance."

He smiled. Gleaming white teeth highlighted a strong and friendly face with features that made Amy's heart jump.

"Hi. I'm Ed."

He got up and started to move toward where she stood, struck dumb at the opposite side of the room where she'd halted her pell-mell rush to retrieve Beth. His standing only caused her astonishment to spread to her face, where it must be unmistakably obvious.

"I guess you really don't know what to think of me now," he laughed, indicating the black tights that gripped his muscular legs beneath the long-hanging T-shirt.

Amy was grateful the shirt was long enough to give her a few moments to adjust to the idea. She'd never before seen a guy in one of Mrs. Q's classes, let alone one who looked like this Ed person.

Not a sound came from her mouth.

"Are you a student here?" he encouraged. "I haven't seen you before, and I've been coming here for a couple of months now."

He crossed the dance floor so they wouldn't have to shout their introductions across the deserted space. His closeness jolted Amy back to her senses.

She stuttered, "Um, hi, yes, well, I was, I mean…I'm Amy," she finally managed, sticking out her hand. "I thought you were my sister."

Instead of taking her hand, he hooted with laughter.

"Well, I've been given a hard time about these tights but that's really the worst I've heard so far! Thanks a lot," he grinned.

"No, no, I mean—"

She was totally flustered. She stuck her hand quickly into her jacket pocket. "I mean I thought when I heard the piano my little sister loves to play with keyboards and I thought it was her and I was coming up to tell her to stop before Mrs. Q found her and…you're a student here?"

"Certifiably," he nodded.

"You're taking ballet?"

He laughed again. "Yep. And you? Did you just come to retrieve your little sister? If so, you're early. The afternoon class doesn't start for another half hour."

"I know. I mean, I'm a student here, too, but I quit for a while."

"Uh-oh. So you changed your mind?"

"Sort of. Um, where is Clar—er, Mrs. Quantos, anyway?" Amy looked around nervously, finally noticing that they seemed to be alone in the studio.

"She went out on an errand and asked me if I'd keep an eye on things for a while. So I suppose I should ask you for some sort of ID," he teased. "Amy, is it?"

"Amelia Longwood."

His face showed genuine shock, and a flush rose in his cheeks.

"Oh! I'm sorry! I didn't recognize you in all those clothes! I mean, shit, I mean—" He pointed helplessly at the corridor behind her which led to the dressing rooms, where photographs of recitals and performances covered the walls. "You're the star! The one at the front in all the pictures!"

He seemed sincere in this praise.

Which made it Amy's turn to blush. She'd forgotten about the pictures. Since the age of six, she had performed stand-out roles in nearly every recital piece Mrs. Q choreographed for them. She was about to protest against the appellation of "star" when Clareta herself came through the door.

"Oh, Amy!" She smiled with genuine happiness, then twinkled, "I see you've met my nephew Edward. Isn't he a fine addition to my beginner's class?" She slapped his hardened arm affectionately. "I'm sure he didn't tell you what he's suffered to be here."

"No, and I'm sure she doesn't want to hear it," he hinted, clearly hoping she'd let it drop.

But Clareta seemed almost as proud of her nephew as she was of Amy and couldn't resist bragging, "He's captain of the track-and-field team over in Springwater and I happen to be an old friend of his coach's. I've been after him for years to send the boys over here, where we can really teach them how to jump, can't we, Amy?"

"We sure can," she agreed, glad the attention was back on Ed—and none too soon.

Ed looked down for a moment, embarrassed by his aunt's effusiveness. But he looked back up to gaze at her affectionately while he explained to Amy, "Yeah, and she harassed him so mercilessly that when he heard I was related to her, he decided to get even—*with me*. He sent me over as a guinea pig."

He nudged his aunt teasingly—a casual gesture none of her other students would dream of making. "I think it was that stuff you told him about ballet dancers proven stronger than football players."

Clareta beamed smugly. "Our arrangement is that if Ed's performance improves, his coach will send the whole team next semester. What he doesn't know is that Ed is also a wonderful dancer!"

"Now wait a minute," he protested. "Don't tell her that—she'll get the wrong idea. She means I'm okay with the waltz, tango, and Lindy Hop she taught me as a kid, so I must be okay with ballet. But Aunt Clareta, you know I'm terrible."

She just smiled at him, "I'm sure that will change soon enough," and turned to Amy.

"I'm sorry you two had to meet this way. I planned to introduce you more formally. But Amy," she dropped her voice conspiratorially, "did you come to talk to me about anything special?"

This was it. Time to decide the rest of her life. At least that's how it felt. She nodded shyly.

"Then come into my office. Ed? Will you please keep the little ones entertained until I get back?"

She indicated a guitar case propped in the hallway. Amy hadn't noticed it before but remembered Ed had mentioned his "guitar pieces."

"Sure. Anything to avoid the humiliation of doing *pliés* with little girls half my height, half my age, and twelve times as strong!"

Amy laughed but her stomach bunched in anxiety and her throat felt like someone had hung it out to dry.

When they were safe behind Clareta's office door, she finally let her heart burst into words.

"I want to keep dancing! I'm sure of it now. But how can I? My mother will kill me if she finds out!"

Clareta didn't hesitate. "I wouldn't be so sure of that, Amy. I've already spoken to your father."

Amy's jaw dropped. He'd never given a hint of it. She figured her teacher forgot her promise to call him.

"You told him about the dance classes?"

"I told him that you were my best student, and that you showed even more promise than your mother did when she was your age. He was very pleased to hear it—and surprised, I might add. Apparently, your mother never mentioned a word to him about your dancing. You know how he hates recitals."

Even now, the recollection caused her pain. He'd begged off every one of them.

"Apparently your mother kept silent about what her eyes could surely tell her, as well as mine told me. Your father was very apologetic about not coming to watch you dance, Amy. He said he would like to have that pleasure sometime before he dies."

Amy turned away to look out the office window, hoping

Clareta wouldn't notice the tears welling up. Seemed like she was always crying these days.

"I told him I would offer you the chance to work here in exchange for your tuition, and he thought it was an excellent idea, because if you were willing to do that, it would mean you were serious about dance. He made me promise not to tell you about our conversation. He wanted you to be the one to decide, and gave me permission to tell you only if you approached me first." She smiled broadly. "And now you have. Amy, I can't tell you how happy I am!"

She could barely believe it. "But what about my mother?"

"I wouldn't worry about her right now. I don't think she'll oppose your father's wishes. He told me he would talk it over with her and make his opinion clear. I'm so glad I didn't have to suggest to him that she might be jealous of you. He seemed to know. But neither of us spoke the words.

"Besides, I don't believe your mother will want to appear— how shall I put this? Too harsh in the public eye after she reads my announcement in the Wilton and Deerhorn Creek newspapers about your appointment as my new assistant."

Her teacher grinned with satisfaction as Amy gaped at this news, but she barely took a breath.

"How can she refuse to allow it, with the whole community watching? You see? I can be both fierce and crafty when it comes to protecting my students' artistic careers. Just like I did for Edward."

Amy blushed involuntarily at the mention of his name.

"Speaking of which, I'd better go rescue him from the girls. Would you like to take up your new position immediately?"

She'd like nothing better! She forgot to say the words out loud but Clareta responded as if she had.

"Then come with me!" She rose to her full, elegant stature and swept Amy with her into the studio.

"Girls!" she announced imperiously, "I want you to meet

Amelia Longwood. She will be your new teaching assistant. You may call her *Miss Amelia*."

Dutifully, a dozen little girls in pink tights and black leotards—and one relatively huge young man—applauded their new teacher. At a signal from Mrs. Q, Mrs. Tilden began her familiar melody. The girls scurried to their places at the *barre*.

Amy couldn't suppress a giggle as she watched Ed, who'd been so self-assured, look frantically around to find the best little set of arms and legs to mimic. Awkwardly, he placed his feet in the turned-out V of first position and stuck his left arm out at shoulder height.

"Amy, will you please show Edward the proper arm position?"

Amy obediently moved to his side. They were both embarrassed as she tried to move his arm correctly, elbow to the rear, slightly curved. The arm refused this abnormal demand, which humiliated him, while Amy marveled at its strongly defined muscles, which distracted her.

"What are you doing after this?" he whispered as she struggled with the task.

"Shhh," she replied in genuine concern that Mrs. Q might hear them. No matter how friendly her teacher became outside the studio, Amy knew it was all business here.

Ed obeyed, and did his best to imitate both Amy and the curly red-haired moppet beside him as they demonstrated the proper stance, the perfect movement, the repetitions in time to the music.

In between hurrying to help one tiny ballerina or another, Amy watched him out of the corner of her eye. Something about his face seemed so familiar (not to mention attractive). She tried to guess his age. Twice as old as the eight- and nine-year-olds, he'd said—seventeen maybe? From his aunt's description, she realized he must have driven himself over from Springwater. Captain of the track team—at least a junior? But she'd seen him somewhere before…maybe at a football game?

Too soon for Amy, the class ended. Her new job thrilled her

nearly out of her body—aside from the distraction and embarrassment of having Ed in the class. From now on, she'd be expected to help with all the younger classes, except when she took class herself, Clareta explained as she drew Amy back into her office.

"We don't want to wear you out too much. For now, why not tell your mother you're looking for a part-time job for summer? Lots of girls your age work jobs here and there. She shouldn't be too surprised by your desire, and this will give her time to get used to the idea. Then, when the news hits the papers…well, she knows the whole community knows what I know about her history. Only her children were left in the dark."

She smiled with the same softness Amy remembered from that terrible night that seemed so long ago.

"I'm sorry you have to carry out this little deception, but you won't regret it in the years to come. There's so much you'll be able to do with your dance education! It will take you so many places, open so many doors. You'll meet wonderful, fascinating people. I sincerely believe you have made the right decision.

"Which reminds me—how would you and Beth like to come over to our house for dinner occasionally? John says it's been years since he had as much fun with the piano as he did watching Beth's eyes light up when he showed her a few simple tunes. He wouldn't mind doing it again."

Amy's heart leaped. "Really? He'd do that? Beth will be so excited!"

"Good. How about next Thursday? Do you mind if I invite Edward? I'm sure my brother won't miss him too much for one evening, if we can get him away from his sports activities. He can pick you girls up on his way—he lives on a farm between Deerhorn Creek and Springwater. I'll go ask him now."

She started off, but stopped in the doorway and turned back to Amy, who was trying to conceal her happiness about this idea to salvage some composure. She fought to look complacent as Clareta added, "You know, I was thinking today that we need to challenge Edward with something more suited to his size and dignity than dancing with little girls—or we might lose him before he learns what he's come here for," she laughed. "What do you think of a partnering class?"

Amy recognized the term, a class that taught men how to lift ballerinas. *But who would be his partner?* She wondered for a confused second before she understood why Clareta was giving her such a penetrating look.

"Me? And Ed?" Her cheeks burned.

"Yes. I think it would be good experience for both of you! And it will definitely help when Pierre Rennault arrives to begin work," she winked, then turned swiftly and left Amy to weigh all the implications of her remarks.

She was shy, though she liked Ed the moment she saw him— even in those silly tights! Riding with him to dinner at the Quantos' home and taking class with him alone, standing with her back to him while he tried to lift her in an *arabesque*—it was either going to be lots of fun, or excruciating humiliation for both of them.

But then, he had a nice laugh and a good sense of humor about all this. Maybe it wouldn't be so bad, she reasoned. She might even get to hear him play his music. She loved the sound of acoustic guitars.

I wonder if he sings?

That night lying in bed, she filled up pages of her diary before she finally flipped off the light and lay wide-eyed, gazing out the window at the stars, daydreaming about her future. Would she become a famous dancer? Or would she wind up teaching little girls and—she smiled at this—maybe a few little boys? *That might not be so bad.* She loved to dance so much, she wouldn't mind doing it for the rest of her life. Whether on a stage or in a studio felt all the same to her at this happy moment.

And how would she do, practicing lifts and *pas de deux* with Ed? The prospect both terrified her and excited her imagination.

Some small part of her felt that they would be fine. When she tried to picture it, the picture took on a life of its own and they dipped and swooped and soared away together as if they'd been doing it for, well, *lifetimes.*

Eventually she drifted off to sleep but not before a dozen extra Lights flashed among the stars. As she left her body behind in a dreaming state, Amy arrived in full consciousness at a familiar place.

A voice behind her said quietly, "It's beautiful, isn't it?"

She turned slowly to face her friend, the handsome young man with light brown hair who had so amused her in their remedial class, who'd shown her wonders beyond belief, and who beamed at her now with tender love. He gestured toward the distant castle of gleaming crystal and the fields of glorious flowers separating them from Uriel and Michiel's fairytale home.

"Makes me want to sing," Kriss added. "Like these birds!"

He pointed overhead, where a small bright flock of long-tailed birds flew noisily toward the castle spires. Then he looked back at her.

"You know we're sleeping on Earth, don't you? That we aren't students here anymore?"

She looked surprised.

"Remember? They told us this would happen, that we could visit any time in our dreams. And the last time I visited, Uriel promised me that one day, you and I would go for a ride in her butterfly carriage. But not until we meet on Earth. Do you think it's happened yet?"

She looked at him with shining eyes. "I'm not certain," she admitted. "But I hope it won't be too long."

He smiled broadly and moved to take her hand. He swept it high above his head as he pulled her into an airy twirl and set her gently down on a single toe, a few feet away.

"Let's dance, shall we?"

✳ ✳ ✳ ✳

Author Q & A

This is a work of fiction but some parts of it seem very real. Are elements of your story taken from your own experience?

Perhaps the parts you'd least expect. Yes, the mother-daughter traumas resemble my own but the higher-world visions and the past-life scenarios also derive from my personal flashbacks and visions. I was fortunate to discover resources in my early twenties that have led me on a life-long spiritual awakening to the principles of universal life that my little story touches upon.

In the front of the book, it says that the illustrations are "torn from Amy's diary." But you drew them yourself, didn't you?

The quick answer is yes, but there's a story and a healing behind it.

When I was little, crayon age, someone convinced me that I could not draw. It might have been my mother, who tried to block every creative aspiration. Later, a school friend agreed that her crayon drawings were better than mine and how sad it was that I could not draw very well. I believed this "I can't draw" mantra until I was in my mid-thirties, when the spiritual school I attended offered an art class as part of our psychic training. We were supposed to learn how to open up to the influence of the Great Ones. It was a way to prove the school's motto, "No limitations."

The first drawing exercise was a still-life set up with an antique chair and a hat. I was stunned by what came through my pencil! Very soon I was completing a full-sized oil pastel of an eighteenth-century aristocrat, copied from a classical painting. I still can't believe I recreated my own version of that one!

When I first published *Cosmic Dancer,* I remained reluctant to think of myself as an artist as well as writer, so I only included a few of the sketches I'd done. For the new edition, I pushed my reluctance aside and went all out.

It proves one thing: NEVER believe the "experts" who try to limit anything you desire to do! My sketches are rough but they do express a piece of me, in a way that photography (or AI) cannot.

How typical is Amy's experience of the alcoholic mother syndrome?

More of that long-term, emotional damage syndrome—typical for children of alcoholic parents—may come out as Amy gets older. When the book opens, she is still under the complete control of an unstable parent. Although her father also drinks to excess, he is less involved in her day-to-day, hour-to-hour life, and he handles his inebriation differently.

Amy's story lives up to the social "taboo" that keeps society from talking about alcoholic mothers, a taboo that was certainly in place during the 1960s and may continue today.

I drew from my own experience as a child, and from an interview with an alcoholism counselor when I worked as a journalist. As an adult, I was still struggling with the aftermath and reality of my mother's mental problems. That counselor was the first to explain to me how and why the addicted create chaos around them to emotionally justify their physical cravings. Later, I picked up a book called *My Mama's Waltz,* which helped me understand that I wasn't alone.

The alcoholic mother is a unique, largely unaddressed problem in our society. I was shocked, years after I read that book, to learn that my own first cousin was one of the anonymous case studies included. I hadn't recognized her. That's how strong the taboo is. No matter how many family visits we shared, we never knew of the suffering behind the other family's closed doors. No one spoke of it. And the outward presentation was as if all were perfection.

Apparently the "doting mother" ideal is so iconic in our society, no one wants to discuss the reality. Which means that countless children, teens, and even adults suffer both physical and invisible emotional abuse. That was one of my motivations for writing this book. A problem not spoken of can never be resolved.

What do you want readers to take away with them?

Hope. A positive vision of their future. Many have written to me about how the story reminded them of things they'd forgotten. Some returned to spiritual practices they'd left off. Others picked up new ones. What interests me is that very few (if any) took my vision as the one and only way, but many were urged back into their own unique spiritual pursuits. I love that! That's how it should be.

When Amy dances, those who watch will be touched in that place that is uniquely theirs, that ember burning brightly within, that flame of connection to higher resources that we all share— and yet in individual, infinitely variable ways. If something I write blows on that ember, brings an evolutionary memory back to life, I am deeply humbled and grateful to have served.

Will there be a sequel?

I hope so. There's a love story yet to be explored.

Acknowledgments

So many people participated in the creation of this book, in multiple dimensions. Some live here, some live there. Such a work could not be done without many hands and Minds coordinated. If only we could see how far this web of Consciousness truly stretches! But I must thank specific actors in this particular drama:

First and foremost, my deepest thanks to the woman I knew as an earth representative of Uriel, Ruth Norman. She became my Mentor in ways few will ever understand. Without her influence and teaching, this book would not exist and I probably wouldn't either. My gratitude is boundless.

To Ernest L. Norman and his extraordinary books, from which my concepts of interdimensional life derive, my humblest gratitude. (Although please do not blame him for my personal biases or errors in thought which may have colored my story.)

To all of my interdimensional mentors and co-authors, especially those who allowed themselves to appear in this tale, thank you for all of your LOVE!

To Joseph, who has supported, encouraged, paid for, edited, cheered, inspired, and endured this book for years and lifetimes, so much to thank him for! He has stuck with me through eons of ups and downs. He took me back to dancing after a long hiatus, and he's never stopped taking me dancing, despite all obstacles, infirmities, and calamities. What a priceless gem he is.

To Donna Eden, David Feinstein, and Gary Craig, many thanks for their pioneering, inspired teaching of the Energy Medicine and Energy Psychology that keep me writing, dancing, and smiling daily. To Chelle and William, for their early encouragement, and to all the readers who wrote to share their spiritual experiences with the book. That means more than you'll ever know. Thank you, dear friends!

And very importantly, to all the teachers and dancers who have furthered my passion for dance over the years, I deeply appreciate all that you have done for me, starting with the ballet teacher at the top of the stairs in the nearby town who put me in an older girls' class and spoke up in my defense, one of my first mentors ever.

Although this work is fictional and I chose writing as my life-long passion, my forced absence from dance training at seven years old was real and heartbreaking. It lasted only until I made it to my first semester at college, on my own. Ever since, I have sought the influence of some marvelous, wonderful, committed people who deserve mention by name:

The modern dance instructor at Michigan State University; Greta Howard at the San Diego Ballet School; Greek dance teachers at San Diego's Folk Dance Cafe; jazz, modern, and ballet teachers in Berkeley and San Francisco; Gretchen from Solano Community College who put me on a musical stage; the teacher at U.C. Davis who let me assist in his pioneering ballet class for male athletes, and who taught me how to clog; Magaña Baptiste's famous San Francisco school of belly dance (and later, the inspired dancing of Dondi and Titanya); Wafic Baradei, Lucia Powers, and their disco frenzies; Ruth Norman for her opportunity to choreograph and film my Inner Dance visions; Joseph for introducing me to salsa via Mel Carrillo at Mira Costa College; Gelsey Kirkland for her early example, her painful and courageous healing, and her willingness to share it with the world in book form; Mary Pinizzotto for dreamy waltzes and fiesty guerilla dancing in the streets; the Encinitas studio of Patricia Rincon for their wild Friday salsa nights; Dave Tomko, who first made Argentine tango accessible to us, and Elena and Victor Pankey who drew us deeper into its drama; Vanessa Williams for taking some kinks out of our "smooth ballroom;" all the staff and dancers at Mary Murphy's Champion Ballroom—plus Mary herself; John Selby whose skilled personal instruction took Joseph and me up another level; Jason Rivers and Nicole Wooding who have rekindled our dancing yet again; and the thousands of dancers whose performances lift my heart and ignite my Love and Spirit!

Thank you, thank you, thank you all!

Meet the Author

Early in her professional career, Lianne Downey was covering a San Diego Arts beat for a major Southern California newspaper when her employers suspended her for speaking publicly about her experience with past-life healing. They warned her never to do it again. She quit on the spot.

She went on to become an author, book editor, and magazine contributor, while self-publishing three books on the inter-dimensional continuity of life, i.e., the *science* of reincarnation. Her viral articles about past lives proved there's a global audience eager for more about this "forbidden" subject. To meet that need, she and her husband launched Jolibro Publishing, a small press dedicated to bringing forth books for "spirit nerds, humanitarians, and nature lovers."

She holds a B.A. in Mass Communication (Theater/Film/Journalism) from the University of California, Davis. She's served as co-director of classes in Past Life Therapy at the Unarius Academy of Science, on the Steering Committee of the San Diego Professional Editors Network (SD/PEN), and as co-founder of the Visionary Writers Retreat. She loves wild rabbits and ballroom dancing with her husband Joseph. Find her on Facebook, Instagram, and at **www.liannedowney.com**

The Pulse of Creation Series

Newly Illustrated Collector's Editions

By Ernest L. Norman

Curious about past lives? How and why? Start here!

Enjoy channeled visits to the higher celestial worlds in the company of the Lighted Ones who teach there. Books 1 & 2 of the *Pulse of Creation Series* form the best introduction to Ernest L. Norman's advanced Science of Life, encompassing an interdimensional science of reincarnation.

New editions feature *exclusive,* visionary illustrations by Roslynn E. Moore, in your choice of dust-jacketed hardcover or eBook (full color illustrations), or black & white paperback. Only from **Jolibro Publishing.**

Available wherever you buy books